"—imperative! This is the Kobayashi Maru, nineteen periods out of Altair VI. We have struck a gravitic mine and have lost all power! Our hull is penetrated and we have sustained many casualties—"

Despite the layers of distortion imposed by both distance and disaster, Archer immediately recognized the English-accented voice on the other end of the channel as that of Kojiro Vance, the flamboyant master of the *S.S. Kobayashi Maru.*

"*Kobayashi Maru,* this is *Enterprise,*" Hoshi said, her fingers entering commands at a brisk pace as she tried to isolate and enhance the tenuous subspace lifeline she had just reestablished. "Please confirm your position."

"*Enterprise, our position is Gamma Hydra, section ten. Hull penetrated. Life-support systems failing. Can you assist us,* Enterprise? *Can you assist us?*"

— STAR TREK —
ENTERPRISE®

KOBAYASHI MARU

MICHAEL A. MARTIN
& ANDY MANGELS

BASED UPON *STAR TREK*®
CREATED BY GENE RODDENBERRY,
AND *STAR TREK: ENTERPRISE*
CREATED BY RICK BERMAN & BRANNON BRAGA

POCKET BOOKS
New York London Toronto Sydney

Pocket Books
A Division of Simon & Schuster, Inc.
1230 Avenue of the Americas
New York, NY 10020

First Pocket Books paperback edition September 2008

POCKET and colophon are registered trademarks of Simon & Schuster, Inc.

For information about special discounts for bulk purchases, please contact Simon & Schuster Special Sales at 1-800-456-6798 or business@simonandschuster.com.

Cover art by Doug Drexler

Manufactured in the United States of America

10 9 8 7 6 5 4 3 2

ISBN-13: 978-1-4165-5480-6
ISBN-10:   1-4165-5480-7

For Jenny, James, and William, for helping to stave off the "no-win scenario." And for my niece, Becky Estepp, for continuing to kick ass and take names among the high and the mighty in pursuit of justice for autistic children and their families everywhere.

—M.A.M.

I dedicate this volume to Chip Carter for transporting us into the *Star Trek* universe with the fastest approvals known to man, and for sending our careers into warp speed. Long Live Bo'Q!

—A.M.

I am a man whom fortune hath cruelly scratched.
—Shakespeare, *All's Well That Ends Well*, Act 5, Scene 2

For the growing good of the world is partly dependent on unhistoric acts; and that things are not so ill with you and me as they might have been, is half owing to the number who lived faithfully a hidden life, and rest in unvisited tombs.
—George Eliot (Mary Ann Evans), *Middlemarch*

The future's uncertain
and the end is always near.
—James Douglas Morrison, Robert Alan Krieger,
Raymond Daniel Manzarek, and John Paul Densmore,
"Roadhouse Blues"

HISTORIAN'S NOTE

This story is set in the middle of 2155, shortly after the founding of the Coalition of Planets (*Star Trek: Enterprise—The Good That Men Do*). The fledgling Coalition was born out of the actions of Earth's Starfleet, who brokered several treaties between the founding members, proving that Earth was ready to join the interstellar community (the fourth season of *Star Trek: Enterprise*).

PROLOGUE

The Year of Kahless 781
The Klingon-Romulan border

YA'VANG, *HoD* of the *Imperial Klingon Battle Cruiser SIm'yoH*, studied the main viewer in silence, watching with fatalistic equanimity as the winged specter of death stalked ever closer.

RomuluSngan, Ya'Vang thought, nearly overwhelmed by his feelings of contempt. *Cowards, accomplishing by sabotage and ambush what they never could through honorable combat.* Given the improbable pattern of malfunctions that had cascaded through virtually every system aboard the *SIm'yoH* over the past *kilaan*, those green-blooded *Ha'DIbaH* could only be testing some subtle new weapon of war—a weapon that appeared to leave its targets essentially whole, yet largely nonfunctional.

Ya'Vang was therefore unsurprised when the other vessel came to a sudden relative stop off the *SIm'yoH*'s starboard bow, scarcely a thousand *qelI'qam*s distant. Despite the swirling emerald-and-ocher-tinged eddies that marked the boundaries of the *SuD'eng* Nebula, Ya'Vang could see that the hostile's weapons tubes were still hot. What remained of his own crippled vessel's tactical systems could detect no sign that the other ship was attempting to establish another weapons lock.

If only as much remained of our *weapons systems*, Ya'Vang thought, his fists clenching involuntarily as the moment stretched into a seeming eternity.

"Why aren't the *RomuluSngan* finishing us off?" asked Qrad, the callow young gunnery officer who had just taken over the duties of the *SIm'yoH*'s first officer, Ra'wI' Qeq, whose corpse had recently joined the many others that still lay scattered about the smoke-filled, ozone-redolent command deck. Despite his disconcertingly smooth forehead and his lowly enlisted rank of *bekk*, Qrad had commendably risen to the occasion this day.

Using the back of his gauntleted hand to wipe away a crust of congealing blood from the crisped flesh of his chin, the *HoD* squinted into the main viewer. Though the attenuated cloud of gas and dust that marked the *SuD'eng* Nebula's ragged edge obscured portions of the hostile vessel, there could be no mistaking the dark, threatening markings that adorned her nearly flat belly. They were the shameful stigma of a lowly carrion-eater rather than the proud striations of an honor-worthy predator.

"Isn't it obvious by now, Qrad?" Ya'Vang growled. "Those *petaQ* want to take this ship."

"But they have not yet boarded us," Qrad said as he consulted the readout on a slightly charred nearby console. "Our intruder alert system still functions well enough to confirm at least *that* much."

Ya'Vang nodded, grateful that not every sensor system aboard his damaged vessel had suffered the same fate as the now-defunct autodestruct mechanism. Dealing with this treacherous adversary would have been much simpler were it still possible to blow up the *SIm'yoH* with a single command. Or even to manually trigger an abrupt explosive release of the warp drive's supplies of antimatter. Unfortunately, Chief Engineer Hojlach had jettisoned the entire supply of fuelstocks in the interests of safety after the *SIm'yoH* had been essentially crippled by the cowardly *RomuluSngan* ambush.

The overly cautious engineer's corpse was presently

tumbling through the void, following roughly the same trajectory as the precious supplies of positive *Hap* and negative *rugh* particles that he had squandered.

"Those *RomuluSngan taHqeq* need not board us in order to triumph, Qrad," Ya'Vang said. "At least, not before our life-support system fails entirely and the cold of space claims everyone aboard this ship who yet lives." He paused, peering toward the com consoles. "Are they still jamming our communications?"

"They are, sir," Qrad said, his bizarrely *Tera'ngan*-like brow wrinkling in barely contained frustration. "They must expect to simply bide their time and wait us out. They will win a coward's victory, and we can do nothing to prevent it."

An idea occurred to Ya'Vang at that moment, like a thunderbolt hurled by one of the long-ago slain gods of Qo'noS.

"Perhaps, Qrad," he said. "But we need not make it easy for them."

Even though the *SIm'yoH*'s artificial gravity had gasped its last shortly after both her main and backup life-support systems had flickered out, Ya'Vang's combat pressure suit—now home to the only thing that still breathed aboard his vessel—seemed to grow heavier and more oppressive with each passing *kilaan*. Ya'Vang struggled with mixed success to avoid thinking about his asphyxiated crew, some of whom had expired in hard vacuum, the one foe that no Klingon warrior could hope to best by the *bat'leth* alone.

Ya'Vang felt certain that he already would have joined his officers and men in death but for the dying Qrad's persuasive argument that the *SIm'yoH*'s commander had to remain behind—alive—to surprise the *RomuluSngan* when their boarding party finally came to call in person. He clung to no illusory hopes of escape or of overcoming his enemies' superior numbers. But he hoped, at least, to fall in honorable battle rather than meeting death like a spring *bregit* in some fetid, fear-redolent abattoir while his foes quietly bided their time and waited him out. Only by forcing death's hand could he hope to redeem his fallen crew members, all of whom had died as a consequence of perfidy rather than of battle wounds; they deserved seats in *Sto-Vo-Kor* at the right hand of Kahless nonetheless.

And, more important, he might yet succeed in keeping his ship out of *RomuluSngan* hands. Failing that, he could at least make their acquisition of a Klingon battle cruiser a very expensive proposition by taking as many of the fatherless *bIHnuch* with him when death finally claimed him.

As the passing *kilaan*s accumulated until they had become a full *DIS*—one complete turning of Qo'noS upon its axis—Ya'Vang occupied himself by finishing his systematic destruction of what remained of the *SIm'yoH*'s computer banks, rechecking the traps he had so laboriously set throughout the ship, and sitting quietly before a darkened starboard viewport, through which he studied the *RomuluSngan* vessel.

The enemy ship, which remained motionless with respect to the *SIm'yoH*, still showed no sign of having noticed that Ya'Vang had dispatched his ship's log buoy several *kilaan*s ago. Using only the strength of his muscles, he had pushed the buoy out an airlock on the *SIm'yoH*'s port side—which faced away from the *RomuluSngan*—and set the dark, unpowered device on a slow, tumbling trajectory into infinity, away from both the *SIm'yoH* and the *RomuluSngan* ship's immediate line of sight. He could only hope that the buoy's chances of being picked up would prove somewhat better than his own chances of survival. Otherwise, no songs would be sung of what was about to happen here this day. No statues would be raised in his honor, or ships marked with his name.

After having waited an entire *DIS* for them to make their move, Ya'Vang felt only relief when the green-blooded scavengers pounced at long last. The reverberating clangor of external grapples engaging and hull-penetrating breach pods fixing themselves to the ship's exterior demonstrated that the *taHqeq* had finally decided it was safe to come aboard. As Ya'Vang stood in the cruiser's relatively narrow boom section, roughly equidistant between the bulbous forward command deck and the wide engineering section that lay aft, he could only wonder whether or not his pressure suit's stealth functions had obscured his presence from the boarders sufficiently to allow him to surprise them, or if they had detected his stubbornly persistent lifesigns through his suit and decided that he didn't pose enough of a threat to warrant waiting any longer.

Whichever way the *RomuluSngan* had done the math, Ya'Vang was determined to teach the enemy a very painful and very sanguinary lesson about the foolishness and lethality of overconfidence.

Ya'Vang heard a muffled explosion that momentarily rang the hull like a bell, followed almost immediately by another. Fallen bits of conduit that lay in the corridor shifted in the induced breeze, which was swiftly stanched by the harsh clang of a fast-closing emergency bulkhead. Hull-breaching charges, he realized, fore and aft. He reflected contemptuously upon the exaggerated sense of caution of the boarders, who were clearly unwilling to risk transporter ingress to a vessel whose internal configuration was no doubt still largely unfamiliar to them.

It will remain *unfamiliar to them,* he thought, raising the long-barreled disruptor pistol he clutched in his vacuum-gauntleted right hand. *So long as air remains in this suit, and breath in my lungs.*

A swiftly moving shadow cast against the ship's dim emergency lighting suddenly drew his attention aft. The approaching party's booted footfalls echoed loudly through the otherwise silent vessel, the sounds seeming to originate in the direction of the engineering section, from which the most recent explosion had sounded. His training instantly taking over, Ya'Vang flattened himself against one of the narrow corridor's walls and watched as the initial shadow lengthened and resolved itself into multiple shapes, all of them vaguely humanoid. A pressure-suited figure stepped directly into view, immediately followed by at least two more.

Arm raised, Ya'Vang stepped forward abruptly and fired. The foremost of the approaching raiders doubled over the fireball that suddenly threw him backward into his fellows. The Klingon maintained a merciless fusillade, taking full advantage of the element of surprise.

He heard a footfall behind him and whirled toward it. The sudden heavy impact against his chest threw him supine to the deck an instant before he felt the fierce heat penetrate the charred front of his pressure suit.

RomuluSngan *disruptor,* he thought as he realized that his own weapon had somehow slipped from his grasp, no doubt because of the ungainly bulkiness of his gloves.

Despite the tumult of running booted feet all around him, Ya'Vang noticed that the hum of his helmet's air circulation system had ceased. That meant that his final signal had been transmitted. The dead-man switch was to engage either when his suit's life-support system failed, or the moment his lifesigns ceased to register upon the suit's internal monitors. The trap he had so laboriously set over the past *DIS* had been sprung at last.

And the motherless carrion-eaters had done it themselves.

The deck shuddered and rattled as the individual charges, adapted for their current purpose from the *SIm'yoH*'s armory, began detonating in series throughout the battle cruiser's superstructure. Within but a handful of *lup*, very little of the ship would remain intact, to say nothing of the misbegotten *mu'qaD* who had dared to try to take her.

Ya'Vang bared his teeth in a warrior's grin as several *RomuluSngan* converged upon him from both directions, their weapons raised and poised to fire once they all had gotten out of one another's line of fire.

The deck plating sheared away beneath their boots and Ya'Vang's back.

Freefall. Airless space penetrated Ya'Vang's body like countless icy blades. His last breath rasped in his chest like dry leaves, and he methodically emptied his lungs, just as his training demanded.

The Klingon captain awaited death calmly. Today, after all, was indeed a good day to die, for he had prevented a hated enemy from acquiring one of his people's mightiest battle cruisers intact. And he also may well have booked passage for himself, as well as for his entire crew, aboard the Barge of the Dead, bound for eternal *Sto-Vo-Kor*.

But even as tumbling debris and oblivion took him, he wondered what fate might befall his beloved Empire the next time a treacherous, dishonorable attack such as this one were to occur.

After all, whatever else the contemptible *RomuluSngan* might be, they were nothing if not tenacious. . . .

ONE

Thursday, May 22, 2155
Enterprise **NX-01**

"*Admit it, Jonathan. You're already at least as bored with this mission as I am.*"

Unable to deny his fellow *NX*-class starship captain's assertion, Captain Jonathan Archer smoothed his rumpled uniform and leaned back in his chair with a resigned sigh. Porthos, whom Archer had thought was fast asleep behind him at the foot of his bed, released a short but portentous bark, as if voicing agreement with the woman who looked on expectantly from the screen. Archer turned away from the lone desktop terminal in his quarters just long enough to toss a small dog treat to the beagle, who immediately became far too preoccupied with the noisy business of eating to tender any further opinions.

"My feelings really don't matter all that much, Erika," Archer said to the image on the terminal. "And frankly, neither do yours. This was Starfleet's call to make, not ours."

From across the nearly six-parsec-wide gulf of interstellar space that currently separated *Enterprise* from *Columbia*, Captain Erika Hernandez punctuated her reply with a withering frown. "*All right. Who are you, and what have you done with Jon Archer?*"

His lips curled in an inadvertent grin. "I'm just an explorer, Erika. I don't make policy. And I don't like babysitting Earth Cargo Service freighter convoys any more than you do. But you've got to admit that there *have* been enough attacks on the main civilian shipping lanes over the past few weeks to justify keeping Earth's two fastest and best-armed starships out on continuous patrol, at least for a while."

She shook her head slightly. *"Maybe. But not indefinitely. And certainly not if you're interested in treating the underlying disease instead of just the symptoms."*

Archer couldn't really disagree with that either. The past six weeks of mostly uneventful patrol duty, spent endlessly covering the same roughly twenty-light-year stretches outbound from Earth, followed by a virtually identical inbound course which intermittently brought *Enterprise* and *Columbia* together from opposite directions, put him in mind of the ancient Greek myth about a man whose misdeeds had earned him the divine punishment of rolling a huge boulder up a hill, only to have to repeat the process endlessly after reaching the summit and seeing it roll down again. Archer sometimes half-seriously considered asking Starfleet to send the new *NX*-class starship *Challenger,* still under construction in the skies above San Francisco, to relieve him—after rechristening it *Sisyphus,* of course.

But he knew better than to think that either he or Captain Hernandez could do much to change the minds of Admirals Gardner, Black, Douglas, Clark, Palmieri, or any of the rest of Starfleet Command's determined brass hats. After all, each of them had shot down essentially the same argument Erika was making today when Archer had first brought the topic before them weeks ago.

"We still don't have any hard proof that the attacks against our freighters are anything other than exactly what they appear to be," Archer said. "The work of rogue pirates and freebooters."

"That's probably only because those alleged 'rogue pirates and freebooters' have been keeping us both so busy waiting and watching, not to mention wearing a triangular groove in the space between Earth and Draylax and Deneva, that we haven't had any time to go hunt down the real *culprits."*

"The Romulans," Archer said.

She nodded, confirming that he had completed her unvoiced thought. *"Or the Klingons. Or maybe even both. The disruptor traces we found on the hull debris are consistent with either of them."*

"As nasty as the Klingons can be, my money's on the Romulans," Archer said.

Her eyes widened. *"Why? You know something I don't?"*

He nodded. "Is this line secure on your end?"

"I trust my mother and God, in that order," she said with a nod of her own. *"Everybody and everything else has to go through the most stringent of security protocols. Go ahead."*

He paused to gather his thoughts. From the edge of the bed, Porthos released a low growl that almost made Archer wonder if his own dog wasn't spying on him on behalf of Admiral Gardner.

"The attack on Coridan has overshadowed just about everything else that's been going on in a dozen sectors in every direction," Archer said at length.

"That's understandable. Over a billion people have died on Coridan Prime so far, and people are still dying there three months later thanks to all the environmental damage, not to mention the damned civil war they're fighting. Have you found some evidence linking the Romulans to the Coridan attack?"

"No," he said with a glum shake of his head. "The Romulans are way too subtle to leave any fingerprints behind."

She frowned again. *"So why bring up Coridan?"*

"Because Starfleet has been able to use it as a diversion to keep a lid on something we discovered on Andoria a little bit before the Coridan attack. The admiralty has classified my report on the subject. But in my judgment you have a legitimate need to know what they've been sitting on these past few months."

Hernandez's brow furrowed. *"You've found evidence of some sort of Romulan incursion on Andoria?"*

"Indirect evidence. But it's as close to a smoking gun as you're going to get with people as slick as the Romulans. You've been briefed about their use of telepaths to pilot remote-controlled attack ships, right?"

"Of course. I know that you and your crew destroyed a telepath-guided Romulan prototype last year."

"Right. But what you *haven't* been told is that the Romulans have recently been trying to get their hands on more telepaths for similar military applications, using the services of third parties brokered through Adigeon Prime."

A look of understanding crossed her olive features. *"The Adigeons. Gotta love those tight-lipped Swiss banker types."*

"Believe me, the Adigeons make the old Swiss bankers look like the village gossip. In spite of that, we managed to track down and rescue about three dozen Aenar-Andorian telepaths that a third party had captured on behalf of the Romulans."

Hernandez's face became a study in horror. *"Enslaving all those people. Just to launch another remote-control attack against us."*

"And they're not going to back off, either. Not when they can just lie in the weeds and wait until they're ready to try again."

The horror on Hernandez's countenance slowly solidified into an almost palpable anger, and her words carried the timbre of blood and fire. *"And you're content to let Starfleet just go on reacting instead of actually* doing *something?"*

Archer endured her not-so-subtle criticism with all the stoicism he could muster. "What makes you think I'm not doing anything?"

"Let's see. Maybe it's the fact that you're still out here patrolling the boonies, just like I am."

"Let's just say I'm working on the problem through a back channel and leave it at that."

"I know you have political pull that I don't, since you're the man who saved Earth from the Xindi. But I can't believe you've got a special back channel with Starfleet Command that I don't even know *about."*

Archer grinned. "What makes you think I was talking about Starfleet Command? Their hands are full at the moment just keeping the Coalition from collapsing into four squabbling pieces, especially since the Coridan attack."

"Unlike either of us," Hernandez said as the door chime sounded.

"Be careful what you wish for, Erika," Archer said, even though he was half hoping for news of another so-called pirate raid, if only to break up the tedium of the past several days of utterly fruitless patrolling. He held up a hand for silence, then turned toward the door.

"Come."

The door hissed open and Commander T'Pol stepped gingerly over the slightly raised threshold, then paused in the open hatchway. She wore a standard-issue, dark blue Starfleet duty uniform, a sight to which he was still only beginning to become accustomed, though she had adopted it nearly three months ago. To the Vulcan woman's credit, she appeared as comfortable and unselfconscious wearing Earth's service attire as she had in the somewhat more formfitting uniform of the Vulcan military from which she had retired over a year earlier. Despite the lateness of the hour, her clothing looked fresh and neatly pressed.

"I apologize for disturbing you, Captain, but I have received some news that you will wish to hear immediately," she said, still hesitating in the open hatchway. She glanced toward the image of Captain Hernandez, which was clearly visible from her vantage point. "Am I interrupting anything?"

Archer smiled gently at his second-in-command. Long before their respective careers had conspired to draw them literally light-years apart, there had once been a time when anyone "walking in" on him and Erika Hernandez might indeed have interrupted something rather intimate. Had Hernandez, who had never been sanguine about making love in Porthos's presence—and was allergic to pet dander to boot—not issued a fateful *it's-me-or-the-beagle* ultimatum, the lives and careers of both captains might have taken radically different trajectories. Only very rarely, such as that time his canine companion had become fragrantly flatulent after snarfing up an entire wheel of Chef's fancy Gruyère cheese, did the captain have cause to regret his decision. Regardless, fair was fair, and since he'd known Porthos longer than he'd known Hernandez, the dog had ultimately won the contest.

Remaining in his chair, Archer fanned the fingers of his left hand toward himself in a "come in" gesture. "Not at all, Commander. I'm sure you know Captain Hernandez."

T'Pol finished crossing the threshold and allowed the hatch to hiss closed behind her just as Porthos jumped off the bed and approached her, his tail wagging. "Captain Hernandez," she said, nodding toward the screen and apparently ignoring the dog.

"Good to see you again, Commander," said Hernandez. *"T'Pol and I met on Earth a couple of months ago, Jon. While you were busy panicking about your speech at the Coalition Compact signing ceremony."*

Archer nodded, recalling the extremely jangled state of his nerves on that recent red-letter day. Facing the adoring crowds, the legions of media cams, and the all-seeing eye of history that day had made him more anxious than the prospect of fighting off whole phalanxes of Klingons or Xindi. Hell, he might have welcomed a firing squad as a dignified alternative. He scarcely remembered what he'd said, and later had to refer to the recordings of his words to reassure himself that he'd not made a complete ass of himself. So it came as no surprise to him that there were small gaps in his memory regarding matters peripheral to the speech itself.

He tried not to think about what the two women might have said about him behind his back while he'd been fumbling through his speech; he preferred to believe that the Vulcan's standoffish sense of propriety would have brought a certain decorum to the conversation. But given the uncharacteristically casual manner in which T'Pol now bent down to scratch the insistently expectant Porthos's head—there had been a time when her acute Vulcan sense of smell would have driven her very quickly from the beagle's presence—he couldn't assume his first officer would always hew to the Vulcan cultural stereotypes.

"What do you have for me, T'Pol?" Archer said, deciding that getting right to business was the best possible diversion. "Any new piracy incidents to report?"

T'Pol straightened and Porthos quickly withdrew with a muted whine, his tail drooping in evident disappointment at the commander's failure to toss him a snack. "Not to my knowledge, Captain."

Archer felt both relieved and disappointed. "Then I suppose it's too much to hope that Starfleet has finally seen the light about the futility of this wild goose chase we're on?"

"If you mean to ask whether Starfleet Command has finally acceded to your request to permit *Enterprise* to conduct an independent investigation of the recent attacks on Earth Cargo Service vessels, I'm afraid the answer remains 'no.'"

Still seated, Archer felt his shoulders slump in resignation. "So we keep rolling the damned rock up the hill and back down again."

"Sir?" T'Pol said, her right eyebrow raised inquisitively.

"Never mind," Archer said, waving his hand as though wiping his words off an imaginary blackboard. "Let's hear your report."

"Do you want me to close off the channel, Jonathan?" said Hernandez, reminding him that she could hear whatever his first officer was about to tell him.

He glanced in Hernandez's direction momentarily before fixing his gaze back upon T'Pol. "Not unless there's some security concern I'm not aware of. T'Pol?"

T'Pol approached the desk and addressed Hernandez. "Unless I'm mistaken, Captain Hernandez, you have the same security clearance as Captain Archer. And the same need to know, since this may well impact upon your duties as well."

Hernandez grinned. *"Well, don't keep us in suspense, Commander."*

T'Pol nodded. "Minister T'Pau has just sent us a response to your request for assistance with our . . . predicament out here in Earth's shipping lanes."

Archer felt his spirits buoying, however cautiously. "How many Vulcan ships can she send to reinforce us?"

T'Pol shook her head almost sadly. "None at the moment, unfortunately. Vulcan's military resources are still stretched somewhat thin because of the Coridan relief efforts, and that situation is unlikely to change soon. However, Minister T'Pau has made an urgent request of her own."

Archer's brow furrowed. "Of us?"

"Of the United Earth government, the United Earth Space Probe Agency, and the Coalition of Planets Security Council," T'Pol said, sounding almost pleased. "Minister T'Pau is well aware of Starfleet's insistence that Earth's fastest ships be kept on continuous patrol along the shipping convoy routes. She agrees, however, that Starfleet's time and resources would be put to better use trying to reach the true root of our current piracy problem. As, incidentally, do I."

Archer grinned. "Your support is anything *but* incidental to me, T'Pol. Especially *now*." With his old friend Trip Tucker still officially listed as killed in the line of duty—and therefore unavailable as a sounding board for the foreseeable future—Archer had come to depend on his first officer's input more than he ever had before.

"Well, it's nice that somebody *on high agrees with the three of us,"* Hernandez said. *"It's just too bad that Minister T'Pau really can't do a lot of effective arm-twisting inside Starfleet, or in Earth's government."*

Archer shrugged. "Granted. But I'm betting that won't matter as much as her influence over the Coalition Council."

"Indeed," said T'Pol, nodding. "While she cannot order anyone outside the Vulcan government to do anything, Minister T'Pau's sway with the other Coalition Security Council members is considerable."

"Do you think she'll come to Earth to address the Council—and make our case for us?" Hernandez wanted to know.

T'Pol shook her head. "Minster T'Pau's present duties overseeing the rebuilding of the Vulcan government and the Coridan relief efforts will keep her away from Earth for at least another few weeks."

"A lot can happen out on the Romulan front in another few weeks," Archer said, his earlier rising arc of hope now sliding inexorably into a downward parabola of despair.

"True," T'Pol said. "However, under the Coalition's parliamentary rules, the authorities of every member world must consent to meet with any surrogate that Minister T'Pau appoints to speak before the Security Council—so long as whomever she nominates is willing to do so. The minister's only question is whether or not *you* are willing to serve as that surrogate, Captain Archer."

Archer allowed a smile to begin spreading very slowly across his lips before he answered. "And not even Admiral Gardner himself can stop me."

"Not unless he wishes to commit a direct violation of the Coalition Compact," T'Pol said. "What should I tell the minister?"

Archer did a few quick back-of-the-envelope calculations in his head. *Enterprise* was on the inbound leg of this latest iteration of her Sisyphean journey, three to four days out from Earth at maximum warp, as near as he could figure.

"Tell her I'll be on Earth just as soon as *Enterprise* can get us there," he said. "And with bells on."

One of T'Pol's eyebrows launched itself skyward again. "Respectfully, Captain, I would recommend a more dignified choice of apparel. However, I will advise

Minister T'Pau of your decision. And I shall instruct Ensign Mayweather to make best speed for Earth." With that, she turned back toward the door and exited, leaving Archer alone with the subspace-transmitted image of his fellow starship captain.

"*Vulcan, Jon? That's one hell of a back channel. Not exactly part of the officer's manual.*"

His smile widened into a broad, triumphant grin. "When have you ever known me to stand on ceremony, Erika?"

She beamed at him. "*Now that's the Jon Archer I know. By the way, I hope you'll accept my apology for implying that you might have been replaced by some sort of overly complacent shape-shifting alien monster.*"

"No offense taken," he said, returning her grin at a comparable wattage. "It was just your frustration talking anyway."

Hernandez's smile abruptly turned mischievous. "*Would you like me to tell Gardner about this, or do you want to break the news to him yourself?*"

Archer felt his own smile begin to sputter out, like an old-style propeller-driven aircraft running out of fuel.

"*And there's yet another unpleasant reality to consider here, Jon,*" she continued, sounding grave.

"What's that?" Archer asked.

"*You have to get busy preparing another big speech.*"

Though Hernandez's grin returned, what little remained of Archer's own smile immediately stalled, crashed, and burned.

TWO

Monday, May 26, 2155
San Francisco, Earth

"THE PRIME MINISTER'S MOTION amounts to nothing less than a blatant attempt by the human species to dominate this alliance!" Gora bim Gral of Tellar shouted from behind the negotiating table. He punctuated his words by pounding his hirsute fist against the curved wooden table before him, then paused briefly to point an accusing finger toward the rostrum at the front of the room. "My people, for one, will not stand for it!"

From his position at the central lectern that faced the semicircular array of conference tables that filled most of the main council chamber, Prime Minister Nathan Samuels thought that the murmur of reaction passing through the assembled Coalition of Planets delegates sounded uncomfortably like general agreement. Other than his nearby negotiating partner, Interior Minister Haroun al-Rashid, Samuels suspected that no living human besides himself understood as clearly as he did how truly rare it was for the Tellarites, the Andorians, and the Vulcans to achieve such a complete consensus regarding *any* issue.

"Our advocacy for Alpha Centauri's admission as the fifth member of the Coalition of Planets is hardly a bid for galactic domination," Samuels said with a mild smile, meeting the hostile glare of Gral's dark, beady eyes without flinching. "Frankly, Earth's Coalition delegation finds it surprising that the government of Tellar has chosen to make such an issue of it. Unless, of course, Tellar would prefer to make its own deals for access to Alpha Centauri's abundant ship-building resources rather than allow them to benefit the entire Coalition."

But Gral clearly wasn't buying that line of argument today. Brushing off Samuels's question, he said, "Do you deny that the world you call Centauri III would be empty of sapient life but for the presence of a handful of cities built and inhabited by Earth humans and their descendants?"

"Of course not, Ambassador Gral," Samuels said. "The history of Earth's first extrasolar settlement is common knowledge."

Gral fairly snarled his response, pounding the table again for good measure. "Just as it is common knowledge that the admission of Centauri III to this body will give humans *two* votes, rather than the one each to which Tellar, Andoria, and Vulcan are entitled, in both the general Coalition Council and Security Council. Why should the other members of the Coalition stand idly by while the human species effectively doubles its influence over every future decision taken by this alliance?"

Haroun al-Rashid, the interior minister of the United Earth government, folded his hands atop the table nearest to Samuels's lectern. Still seated like the other Coalition delegates, he began speaking, his smooth voice carrying an equanimity that Samuels couldn't help but envy.

"And why should any of the other members of this body assume that the human species is a monolithic entity that always achieves unanimity on every issue?" al-Rashid said. "I think we humans would be making a grievous error were we to harbor the same presumption about *your* species, Ambassador Gral."

The Tellarite's only vocalized response was a guttural,

harrumphing growl, which may or may not have been a Tellarite curse that the room's universal translator system had mercifully failed to recognize. *Ouch,* Samuels thought, suppressing a triumphant grin.

"The interior minister makes an important point, Ambassador Gral," he said aloud. "Moving in lockstep is not something that comes naturally, even to us humans. I'm sure I needn't remind anyone here that it has been only five years since the last of our world's great independent nation-states finally agreed to join the global government of the United Earth."

As he watched the grave nods that passed among the Vulcans and Andorians, the latter group displaying a potent mix of emotions via their writhing antennae, Samuels thought, *I can't believe I'm trying to mollify these people by pointing out how bad humanity's résumé looks when it comes to playing well with others.*

Ambassador Jie Cong Li of Centauri III rose from her seat, the slightness of her form doing nothing to negate the quiet dignity of her bearing. The room's assemblage of scowling Andorians, grumbling Tellarites, and stonily impassive Vulcans made no move to interrupt as the prime minister nodded to yield the floor to the Centauri representative.

"I do not wish to risk appearing overly agreeable with the ministers of the United Earth government," the Centauri woman said, filling the room with the round, resonant vowels that characterized her people's dominant accent. "But I must point out that New Samarkand, Alpha Centauri's capital, is a good deal more remote from the center of Terran power than was Australia, the last of this planet's nonaligned nation-states to allow itself to be enfolded into the UE government. I therefore implore all of our friends and allies from here to 61 Sygni and Procyon and 40 Eridani A to mark this occasion well. It may be the last time in the careers of everyone assembled here that the Earth and Centauri governments agree on *anything*." Her grim smile provided the only clue that her words weren't entirely serious.

Great, Samuels thought, his guts churning as the Centauri delegate quietly reseated herself. *If Li and I keep this up much longer, these people are going to start wondering why the hell they signed the Coalition Compact in the first place.*

The moment of discomfiture passed, however, dispelled by a wave of politely indulgent laughter, apparently started either by Ambassador Avaranthi sh'Rothress or the newly promoted Andorian Foreign Minister Anlenthoris ch'Vhendreni. The encouraging sound rippled quietly across the rest of the usually taciturn Andorian delegation. Vulcan's contingent—the recently promoted Minister Soval, flanked by Ambassadors L'Nel and Solkar—reacted as one with gently surprised expressions that probably would have been polite laughter had the Vulcans belonged to just about any other humanoid race with which Samuels was familiar.

In the VIP observation area located behind the semicircular array of diplomatic tables, Admirals Samuel Gardner and Gregory Black, along with Captain Eric Stillwell, the man in charge of Earth's new warp-seven stardrive development program, and General George Casey, the iron-haired commandant of Earth's Military Assault Command Operations, all looked like still-life studies with their medal-bedecked coats, folded arms, and grave attentiveness. From the press area positioned behind the Starfleet and MACO officers, several members of the media—including, Samuels noticed, that entirely too persistent female reporter Gannet Brooks—used the holocams that rested on their shoulders or in their heads to soak up every word and gesture. Grethe Zhor, the observer from Draylax, sat behind the press corps, taking in the entire tableau with an unreadable expression.

Samuels clung to the hope that Zhor would prove to be the key to working through the Coalition's current difficulties, the keen blade that would slice through the tangled dual Gordian knot of galactic one-upmanship and cutthroat domestic politics.

A flash of motion in the observation gallery momentarily caught Samuels's eye. When he recognized the small group of people moving quietly toward the balcony railing, he felt simultaneously relieved and disappointed that the newcomers weren't yet another group of xenophobic former Terra Primers out to assassinate him in the name of God, Earth, and the late John Frederick Paxton's obsession with human racial purity. Instead, Samuels found his eyes drawn to the one person he knew besides Grethe Zhor who might help bring the current unsettled situation to a satisfactory resolution: Captain Jonathan Archer, a man whom he'd once heard Minister al-Rashid describe as "a crisis that walks like a man," perhaps because wherever he went both peril and opportunity seemed inevitably to follow. Samuels could only wonder which of those two aspects Archer's presence here today augured.

"The Centauri representative is as clever a talker as the Terran prime minister," Gral continued, apparently as unmoved by the words of Ambassador Li and Earth's ministers as by the Andorians' uncharacteristic good humor. "And I do not doubt the truth behind anyone's claims of human contentiousness, which no doubt fuels the obstinacy of both Earth and Alpha Centauri on the issue of the admission of Centauri III." With that, the senior Tellarite diplomat sat, leaning back from the table with his arms folded truculently before him.

Anlenthoris ch'Vhendreni of Andoria, known to most of the other diplomats present simply as Thoris, rose and began to speak before either of Earth's ministers had time either to formally give him the floor or to interject any response of their own.

"Indeed," Thoris said, his antennae flattening aggressively backward along his well-groomed, white-maned skull. "Could this stubbornness be born of the fear that whatever remains of the outlawed Terra Prime movement might pressure the United Earth government to withdraw from the Coalition absent some guarantee of a human parliamentary advantage over the other members of this alliance? Centauri III's admission would appear to represent just such a guarantee."

"That's both ridiculous and unfair!" al-Rashid said, startling Samuels, who wasn't used to seeing his colleague react with such vehemence. Samuels saw his usually phlegmatic colleague's overstressed outburst as an ominous sign. It was also a tacit admission that the Tellarite's assertion was anything *but* ridiculous. After all, no one who monitored Earth's popular media, its independent editorial journals, or its talknets could plausibly deny that humanity's small minority of committed xenophobes still maintained a formidable presence in the planet's collective hindbrain, if only on a rhetorical, propagandistic basis.

Nevertheless, this was a point on which anyone representing Earth's interests could ill afford to give ground. Playing up *Homo sapiens*'s lack of unanimity for the purpose of defusing the other Coalition members' fears of human hegemony was one thing; making Earth's population appear ungovernable, or portraying its leaders as dysfunctional without the advantage of a potentially unfair plurality, were other things entirely.

At the Vulcans' table, Minister Soval rose, his hands

clasped before his conservatively adorned Vulcan diplomatic robes as he addressed Samuels's lectern. "Ridiculous or not, it is abundantly apparent that we will not
resolve this matter soon or simply."

"At least *that* much is certain," Gral muttered, evidently just within the universal translator system's hearing threshold.

Depressing as the realization was, Samuels had to
admit that he was inclined to agree.

"No wonder nobody's been listening to my warnings
about the Romulans," Archer said quietly to Doctor
Phlox, who sat to his left, his uncannily blue Denobulan
eyes riveted to the diplomatic tableau unfolding beyond
the railings that separated the balcony from the council
chamber below. "These guys have their hands full just
keeping the alliance from unraveling."

"I pledge never again to complain about the difficulties inherent in practicing medicine," Phlox said with a
somber nod.

"Indeed," said T'Pol, who was seated at Archer's other
side.

Lieutenant Malcolm Reed leaned forward against the
railing between T'Pol and the seats that Ensigns Hoshi
Sato and Travis Mayweather had taken. "Makes *my* job
look dead easy," Reed whispered, to silent nods of agreement from Hoshi and Travis.

Archer watched as Soval addressed Minister Samuels, who stood at the central lectern. "I recommend we
table the issue of Alpha Centauri's admission pending a
special meeting of this body dedicated to that purpose.
We must move on to other essential business, most no-
tably our collective security."

"Agreed, Minister Soval," Samuels said, nodding. He
then turned toward the observation gallery and did his

best to make his voice project to the back of the room. "I call Captain Jonathan Archer of Starfleet to address the Coalition Council on these matters."

Phlox offered an encouraging smile as Archer rose from his seat. "Good luck, sir," Hoshi said as he passed her chair and began making his way toward the nearby staircase that wound down toward the center of the council chamber.

As he stepped onto the central dais to stand beside Minister Samuels, Archer did his best to ignore the sheer terror that always gripped him whenever he was called upon to address the crowned heads and eminences of the Coalition of Planets. *Is it too late to order Malcolm to shoot me?* he thought. He could take some comfort, at least, in the fact that his slightly late arrival seemed to have come just in time to preempt a filibuster that might have lasted for days.

Samuels shook his hand warmly, gestured toward the lectern, and took a seat, yielding the floor to Archer. The delegates of four worlds, all of them once again seated behind a semicircular array of curved tables, watched him quietly, jangling his nerves further. Archer looked up and past them toward the gallery, where his senior officers sat watching him expectantly. Not far from them, Admiral Black, Admiral Gardner, and General Casey uniformly glowered at him over folded arms, like a trio of gargoyles. The light babble of applause that usually accompanied a guest's ascension to the lectern was conspicuously absent, creating a lacuna of uncomfortable silence that Archer's imagination filled with the stridulations of crickets and the low, warp core–like thrumming of his own anxious heartbeat.

Wishing he hadn't neglected to bring along the padd upon which he had organized his thoughts during the voyage to Earth, Archer cleared his throat and searched his mind for a way to get at what he had intended to say.

Before Archer had uttered a single word, Gral suddenly rose to his feet and shouted, "I object!" Absurdly, Archer felt only gratitude for the interruption.

"I presume that surprises no one," Soval said, one eyebrow raised in what might have signaled droll Vulcan humor.

"Captain Archer has addressed this body more times than has any other military officer from any Coalition world," Gral continued, ignoring Soval's verbal jab. "This is yet another sign of creeping human hegemony."

"Again, I must agree with my Tellarite colleague," Thoris said, though he remained seated. "While I certainly respect the captain's accomplishments on behalf of my world and other Coalition members, it is not appropriate for humans to so thoroughly dominate these proceedings."

Archer fumed quietly. *So it's all right to have me around* only *when you need somebody to keep Andoria, Vulcan, and Tellar from blowing each other's fleets out of the sky.*

"Gral is correct," Thoris said. "Under the Coalition's parliamentary rules, a member world cannot unilaterally call one of its own people to address the Council if that person is not a duly recognized planetary delegate."

"That is true, Minister Thoris," Soval said. "However, the United Earth government did not call Captain Archer here to speak. In fact, I have little doubt that the captain's military superiors would prefer that he be elsewhere today."

Archer stole another glance at the admirals and the general, all of whose scowls seemed to deepen and intensify, confirming Soval's contention, if only inadvertently. *Boy, Soval, you don't know the half of it,* he thought, then allowed his gaze to drift back to the Vulcan minister to make certain that Admiral Gardner's basilisk stare hadn't just turned him to solid stone.

"If Earth's delegation did not call Captain Archer here, then who *did*?" said Thoris, his antennae thrusting forward in an apparent mix of curiosity and querulousness.

"First Minister T'Pau of Vulcan," Soval announced in his customary matter-of-fact tones.

Thoris and Gral harrumphed in unison, almost as though they had rehearsed the joint maneuver in advance.

"Proceed," the Tellarite growled with a defeated sigh before dropping ungracefully back into his chair.

Once more unto the breach, Archer thought. He cleared his throat again, screwed up his courage one last time, and plunged forward.

"The Romulans," he announced as his preface. "Maybe we've all been a bit too busy lately arguing among ourselves to focus on the threat they pose to every world in the Coalition and beyond. The attack on Coridan was only the first catastrophe to emerge while we've been preoccupied with politics."

"How can you be so certain that the Romulans are to blame for Coridan, Captain?" Gral asked, interrupting.

Archer paused and thought of Trip, who had been behind enemy lines for the past several months, covertly risking his life. *I wish I could tell you the plain unvarnished truth, Gral.*

"Indeed," said Soval. "The Klingons are equally likely to be the responsible parties."

"Or a rogue asteroid strike, for that matter," Thoris said.

Archer shook his head. "With respect, Minister Thoris,

asteroids don't travel at multiwarp speeds. And I've never seen a natural impact produce an antiparticle flux capable of igniting half a world's underground dilithium supply."

"But you cannot deny the occurrence of a number of recent border skirmishes between Coalition vessels and warships from the Klingon Empire," Thoris said.

Archer nodded. "Of course not, Minister. But the occasional up-front fight with the Klingons over territorial jurisdiction isn't what I'm talking about here. Sneak attacks on dilithium freighters are something else entirely."

Soval raised an eyebrow. "The Klingon Empire is a starfaring civilization, like each of the Coalition worlds. They require dilithium just as we do."

"Blatant piracy just doesn't fit the Klingon Empire's profile, Minister Soval," Archer said. Addressing the entire room, he continued. "You're all aware of the recent attacks on Coalition cargo vessels. We've found the energy signatures of disruptor fire wherever we've recovered debris after one of these incidents. This is certainly consistent with Romulan technology."

"The Klingons have disruptors as well, Captain," Soval said.

"True enough," Archer said, spreading his hands before him. "But would the Klingons ambush our ships while we're still trying to negotiate the boundaries of the Neutral Zone between Coalition space and their own empire?" He held up a hand to forestall any interruption. "And again, everything I've learned firsthand about the Klingons tells me that sneaking up on unarmed freighters just isn't their style."

"I must agree with *that* part of your assessment, Captain," Soval said, stonily calm. "However, ambushes using disruptor weapons are also characteristic of the

Orions, as well as a number of other races that you
have, so far, been fortunate enough not yet to have encountered. The Breen, for example."

*After all we've been through together over the past four
years, he still sees us as poor relations*, Archer thought,
biting back a sharp verbal retort. *Even now, he just can't
resist rubbing my face in how much more Vulcans know
about the rest of the galaxy than we do.*

Then, doing his best to emulate Soval's damnable
coolness despite the concerted glowers of his superiors,
Archer began methodically outlining the facts concerning the so-called pirate raids of the last several weeks,
taking care to reveal nothing that might compromise
the secret of Trip Tucker and his present critically important covert activities behind enemy lines, or the secret kinship of the Romulan and Vulcan peoples.

But the impassive demeanor of the assembled delegates immediately told him that only definitive firsthand
evidence—information that would almost certainly
compromise Trip's ability to contribute to the continued
survival of the Coalition, and maybe even that of Earth
itself—would suffice to persuade the assembled wise
heads of four worlds to set aside their many differences.

And to act on something other than the ever-shifting
internal politics of their fractious, fragile new alliance.

Archer wondered, not for the first time, whether he
had embarked on a fool's errand by coming here.

Archer's main recollection an hour after he'd presented
his case before the Coalition Council was that his audience had listened attentively for the most part, but
had nevertheless seemed either unwilling or unable to
deal head-on with the coming Romulan threat. Sitting
in the copilot's seat of Shuttlepod One beside Travis
Mayweather, Archer silently dissected his own perfor-

mance before the Coalition's massed powers-that-be as he watched the fog-shrouded San Francisco skyline drop over the horizon. He felt almost robotic as he went through the motions of assisting his helmsman in taking the small auxiliary craft back up into the parking orbit where *Enterprise* awaited.

Travis checked in with Lieutenant Donna "D.O." O'Neill, *Enterprise*'s third watch commander, who confirmed the shuttlepod's approach vector. Then Archer secured his console and rose from his seat to face the rest of his senior officers, all of whom were seated aft of the cockpit area. T'Pol regarded him with an all but unreadable expression, while both Phlox and Hoshi watched him as well, their gazes radiating quiet concern. Malcolm stared distractedly out of one of the small portside windows, apparently lost in his own thoughts.

Archer took the empty seat beside his tactical officer. "Looks like my speech must have come off as badly as I think it did."

Reed turned toward him, displaying a bemused expression. "Sir?"

"You seem to be brooding, Malcolm. Just like the rest of my audience."

"I wouldn't say I'm exactly *brooding*, Captain," he said in his clipped British accent. "I was just thinking about these Breen that Minister Soval mentioned."

"Ah." Archer nodded. "What about them?"

"I just wonder why the hell we've never heard of them before, sir."

Archer had considered that as well, but had already decided that he had to place some limits on his capacity to worry about the future, the unknown, and what might be the unknowable.

"Perhaps the Breen are obscure to humans because so little is known about them," T'Pol said. "Even the

Vulcan Security Directorate possesses very little hard information about that species."

Archer nodded, accepting T'Pol's explanation at face value. "There's no point in jumping at shadows, Malcolm," he said. "For all we know, the Breen are really just Soval's favorite breed of saber-toothed Vulcan puppies, and he was just jerking our collective chains. Besides, we've got the annual inspection of the Altair VI outpost ahead of us, and then it's back to the commercial freight corridors to prowl for pirates, Romulans, or whatever else turns up. We've already got enough on our plate without borrowing any *more* trouble."

Reed smiled ironically. "Worrying just might be the biggest part of a tactical officer's job description, sir."

Sir, he thought, nodding a silent acknowledgment of Malcolm's commendable vigilance. *Captain.* When had his crew begun sounding so excessively formal in his presence?

It started after Trip left, he realized in a rush. Despite the fact that his working relationship with T'Pol had grown more close, open, and cordial than he had ever imagined possible, there was nobody aboard *Enterprise* who could fill the cold void created by Trip's open-ended absence. Though he knew Trip's death was merely a ruse—as did T'Pol, Phlox, and Reed—it felt real enough to inspire genuine mourning.

Captain. Sir. Captain. Nobody here feels comfortable just calling me Jonathan. Not even T'Pol, who had to have been grieving over Trip's absence even more intensely than Archer was, her Vulcan emotional makeup notwithstanding.

He suddenly felt more disconcertingly alone than he had since he'd first accepted command of *Enterprise*.

THREE

Vulcan Year 8737 (2135 A.C.E.)
Trilan (Vulcan outpost settlement)

T'POL FLATTENED HERSELF against the moist wall, struggling to keep her ragged inhalations under control. She wasn't certain what had happened to the others. It had been at least a quarter of an hour since she had heard any screams, or anything other than the sound of her own heartbeat and rushing blood—life-giving fluid that she felt certain might be betraying her even now.

She had been one of six agents of the V'Shar—the Vulcan Security Directorate—that had undertaken this mission, but she knew that their prey had already dispatched at least two of the others. Their squad's leader, Denak, had disappeared down a hole in the ground; the fact that the hole had sealed itself almost immediately lent credence to the idea that Denak had been *taken* and had not fallen victim to a simple misstep.

The two other V'Shar agents had similarly disappeared as they'd made their way through the dank caverns that housed the Fri'slen, but T'Pol had nimbly managed to avoid capture. She tried to tamp down the voice inside her that fairly screamed, *You haven't been taken* yet. In this context, the feeling of fear was less an emotion than a primal survival instinct. She allowed it to settle upon her like a warm but ill-fitting cloak.

To catch something as primal as these creatures, I must think like them, T'Pol reasoned. It was, in fact, one of the most basic lessons of intelligence and espionage work; to infiltrate, one had to learn to think like one's opponent, even to the point of becoming one of them if necessary.

She knew that she could never *become* one of the Fri'slen, unless she contracted the contagion that had ravaged them. From what the Security Directorate's files had indicated, that would require both intimate sexual contact and a significant blood-to-blood transfer; the majority of the Fri'slen's victims were not transformed, however, but served instead as food for their cannibalistic appetites.

Despite their savagery, the Fri'slen were apparently not without technological defenses, as the V'Shar team had learned shortly after disembarking here. A targeted electromagnetic pulse had rendered not only all of their scanning and communication equipment useless, but their weaponry as well. The pulse should have been their cue to leave, as T'Pol and Eskren had reasoned, but Denak had ordered them to move into the caves that apparently housed the Fri'slen. They were armed now only with smaller weapons barely suitable for hand-to-hand combat, although T'Pol knew that she could throw the hand-length *tricheq* on her belt with deadly accuracy. *Once, at least.*

T'Pol felt her boots come into contact with something on the floor, and she crouched defensively, peering into the darkness around her. One hand moved forward, and her fingers connected with something crust-covered and tubular. Further exploration told her that what she had stumbled upon was the skeletal remains of . . . something. She couldn't be certain what it was. It wasn't humanoid, but it was too large to be one of the smaller creatures that were indigenous to this world.

A sehlat, she finally reasoned, exploring further and

finding not only clumps of fur and gristle, but also the sharp tusks that were indicative of adolescent-to-fully-grown members of the urso-feline species that this forbidding world's Vulcan settlers had brought with them.

Her mind racing, T'Pol quickly began removing certain parts of the *sehlat's* skeletal structure. She winced as she broke several of the bones—the sound of the cracks was like cannon fire in the tunnels—but her fingers told her that she had guessed correctly about the brittle condition of the remains.

A short while later, T'Pol heard sounds nearby. She couldn't tell from which direction they had emanated, but she assumed she was now being stalked anew. Crouching lower, curled almost into a ball, she quickly finished making her preparations, then stood. Shaking, she used a bone fragment to scratch the top side of her shoulder, where the fabric of her *sedmah* had already been torn. She felt the blood well up immediately; she had been cut deeply enough to bleed, but not enough to cause nerve damage—nor, she hoped, to affect her defensive abilities.

Knowing that the Fri'slen could detect her scent even more strongly than before, T'Pol sprinted forward into the darkness, barely able to see the tunnels around her. She sensed movement behind her, but dared not whirl around to face her pursuers. The only thing she knew for certain was that the farther into the caves she got, the closer she would come to their nest.

The floor abruptly gave way in front of her, and she pitched forward, falling into a shallow fissure or ravine—or a trap—and she felt the creatures leap on her the next moment, their hands pummeling her over and over again, their nails slashing at her. She struggled against their powerful limbs, but after an indefinable length of time allowed herself to go limp. She focused her conscious mind inward, ready to wake up fully with the speed of a charging *le-matya* from behind her meditative shield against both mortal terror and physical pain.

They carried her with them instead of dragging her, and she was grateful for that, even as she continued to focus herself on what was to come. Eventually, she heard screams she could identify as coming from Vekk'r, but as they came closer, the wailing subsided into guttural cries and moans. She hoped silently that if she should survive the mission, she would be able to find the strength to deliver a painless death to any of her comrades who had become infected.

She remained limp as a rag doll as her captors unceremoniously dumped her against something hard, allowing her to land in a semiseated position. Vekk'r was mostly silent now, though in her meditative state, T'Pol could hear several of the other sounds that were reverberating through the dark, rocky chamber. Within her mind, she withdrew, as if she were a hungry, ravening Underlier waiting to strike from below the baking sands of Vulcan's Forge.

A rough hand grabbed her face, its jagged fingernails digging into her chin. T'Pol allowed herself to come back to full consciousness, but willed herself not to tense up into a defensive posture that the creatures might notice. She opened her eyes, however, and found herself staring into the ravaged face of what appeared to be a female humanoid.

Her features were vaguely similar to those of Vulcans, but her eyes were more prominent and seemed to have multiple lids, nictitating from the sides as well as from top to bottom. The woman's ears tapered to graceful points at their tips, but everything else about her external pinnae struck T'Pol as less than aesthetically pleasing; they were flattened backward, were roughly the same size as the woman's entire face, and were covered in bulging greenish veins.

In a movement that might have been a smile had she had lips, the Fri'slen woman allowed her mouth to tilt upward on the sides as she noticed T'Pol studying her. Four rows of rotted teeth—which included sharpened, predatory incisors—filled her oral cavity.

"You will be mine, I think," the woman said, speaking in a perfect Vulcan Standard dialect.

T'Pol was less interested in what the statement meant than she was in keeping the woman talking. As naturally and fearfully as she could—she didn't really have to feign the trembling that had overtaken her—she peered around the woman into the dimness of the cavern beyond. She saw three more of the Fri'slen, as well as the remains of Yekda, and the body of Vekk'r, on top of which lay a fifth Fri'slen, who was moving languidly, almost as if in a drunken state.

"What are you planning to do with us?" T'Pol asked, hearing the quaver in her own voice.

"You will be *mine*," the woman said again. "That one belongs now to Grom'stl," she said, gesturing toward the creature atop Vekk'r. "The others," she added, sweeping a clawed hand toward a grate in the floor that apparently covered a prisonlike pit, "will be food. Or fun. Or they will *belong*, too."

T'Pol understood that the woman's emphasis on the word "belong" meant that she intended to infect T'Pol.

"Why are you preying on the people here?" T'Pol asked.

The woman tilted her head, a scabrous tongue sliding against one of her forward rows of sharpened teeth. "To survive. To feed. To procreate. To be a reminder, always."

T'Pol didn't know what the woman meant, but needed

to keep her talking until the time was right to move. "A reminder of what? That savagery exists in the worlds we inhabit? That sentient beings can debase themselves to the level of carnivores or parasites?"

The woman pushed T'Pol's head back roughly and rose to a crouch as she released a noise that might possibly be interpreted as laughter if it hadn't sounded so much like howling. She looked around at the others, then returned her gaze to T'Pol, who had gathered her arms close in around her torso, clutching herself the way a frightened child might.

"Perhaps one of these days we should allow someone to *return* to tell the others what we really are," the woman said. "The origins of what you call the 'Fri'slen.' Before the experiments, the mutations, the banishment."

The woman leaned in close, fixing T'Pol with her dark, predatory eyes. "They would tell how *we* were once *you*."

In that moment, T'Pol allowed her entire being to suffuse itself with every bit of energy she had kept in reserve. Flashing her arms out, she pulled the broken *sehlat* ribs out from where she had concealed them inside her sleeves, tight against her forearms. With a quick slashing motion, she used the jagged tips of the bones to cut the throat of the woman, rolling herself aside even as the ichorous green blood began to spray.

As the dying Fri'slen woman clutched at her throat, T'Pol drew the short *tricheq* from the boot where she had hidden it and threw it at one of the other creatures in the cavern. It pierced his forehead, dropping him instantly.

T'Pol had barely managed to regain her footing before one of the remaining Fri'slen roared toward her, on the attack. She swiped her foot out in a wide kick, hoping that her second makeshift weapon would work as well as the first. The *sehlat* tusk she had strapped to the side of her boot sliced through her attacker's torso, and before his forward momentum had entirely spent itself, the Fri'slen's innards were spilling out upon the rough cavern floor.

A keening sound swiftly filled the chamber, and T'Pol whirled again, expecting to be attacked by the other two creatures. But the one making the sound was exiting the room through a tunnel, his body slipping effortlessly into the darkness. The other one, the creature atop Vekk'r, seemed neither alarmed nor particularly conscious of what had just transpired nearby.

T'Pol noticed only now that she could hear the voices of Denak and Ych'a calling out to her. Pushing aside the still bleeding body of the Fri'slen woman whose throat she had cut, T'Pol looked down into the pit below the grate. Despite the darkness that enfolded the pit, she could see her comrades, at least in silhouette. She quickly cut through the improvised twine that held the grate in place, moved it aside, then reached down to grasp the hand of Ych'a.

The green blood that still rained down on them from the dying Fri'slen woman made getting a grip difficult, but within a minute, T'Pol had finished extracting both her fellow agent and her mission leader.

Denak quickly counted the corpses, and listened as T'Pol told him about the Fri'slen that had escaped into the adjoining chambers. "There are many more of them than we've seen so far," Denak said gravely, pointing toward numerous cavelike openings that could have served as berths for sleeping or hibernation. "We probably don't have much time before we're beset again. And they'll be *angry* this time, instead of merely hungry."

He pointed to some fabric remains that still clothed

skeletons in a shady corner. "Get some torches going with those scraps."

As Ych'a scrambled to comply, T'Pol retrieved her *tricheq* from the Fri'slen's forehead. A quick scouting of the cavern revealed several of their party's other fallen weapons: both the useless depowered component devices and a few other *tricheq*s and bladed weapons.

As she returned Denak's weapon to him, she saw him holding one of the sharpened *sehlat* bones over the back of the Fri'slen who lay atop Vekk'r. The creature hadn't even noticed that anyone else was nearby, much less the danger that loomed above. Under its form, a bloodied Vekk'r lay unconscious, or worse.

Denak stabbed the weapon down through both figures, piercing through their hearts almost simultaneously. The creature atop Vekk'r thrashed for a moment, then twitched in its death throes; T'Pol's ravaged comrade hadn't moved at all.

"Even had Vekk'r lived, he would have been infected," Denak said simply to T'Pol. "He would have become one of *them*."

Ych'a came over with torches, and the dry fabrics ignited quickly.

Weapons in hand and torches held aloft, the trio swiftly plunged into the caves and, T'Pol hoped, toward their freedom. Should they make it, T'Pol knew that Denak would probably call in a military air strike on the region, to bombard the caves with some kind of contained plasma fire. Nothing that lived down here would survive such an attack, nor would any trace of the Fri'slen—or their crimes—remain.

Sparing one final glance backward as they departed, T'Pol pondered exactly what the cryptic words of the Fri'slen woman had meant.

"They would tell how we *were once* you."

How different was the statement from Denak?

"He would have become one of them."

Even from her brief time in the Vulcan Security Directorate, T'Pol knew that the Vulcan people had buried many dark secrets in their past. As they moved through the blackness, she understood with perfect clarity that the Fri'slen woman had believed herself to number among those secrets.

What other secrets have we hidden? And when will another one come out of the darkness to consume us?

T'Pol shivered, telling herself that she might never discover the answer to that question if she didn't concentrate on getting out of this place, *now*.

Sunday, July 13, 2155
Enterprise **NX-01**

Though she knew it was illogical, T'Pol shivered slightly. She finally moved over to her bed and pulled the neatly folded gray blanket from the end of it, wrapping it around her shoulders. She returned to stand near the viewport, outside of which the blackness of space and the bright streaks of stars had become almost monotonous in their constancy.

Although the temperature in her quarters was certainly high enough that she needn't have bothered with the blanket, its presence around her provided an immediate and undeniable sense of comfort. The feel of the finely woven synthetic fabric between her fingers evoked a vivid tactile memory of Trip and the time they had lain together on her bunk, the sweat cooling on their naked bodies after they had made love; Trip had pulled this same blanket up, over the pair of them, though he'd smilingly lamented all the while having to remove any portion of her beauty from his vision.

The Vulcan science officer and the human engineer, the High Command and Starfleet, a highly unlikely pair. "The ice princess and the good ol' boy" were among the nicknames she had heard whispered more than a few times, as they walked through the corridors of *Enterprise*, though she thought that the Starfleet and MACO personnel who had uttered them would have been both appalled and embarrassed had they known that she had heard them. And she sometimes wondered whether they might have been more appalled and embarrassed still had they known that she and Trip had actually consummated their now-undeniable mutual attraction.

The self-absorbed direction of her own ruminations surprised her, though she couldn't deny having had similar thoughts before. But today she could identify no convenient infirmity or injury upon which she might blame this private lapse, no obvious reason behind her increasing fixation on the irrecoverable past. She knew that her emotions were always close to the surface, however deeply she had meditated last evening. She could only wonder whether that night with Trip had had a far more profound impact upon her than she could have known.

Is this what humans experience when they "fall in love"? she thought.

Thanks to Trip's protracted absence, her memories of their brief time together had become as irrepressible as they were bittersweet. And the fact that the last year had brought her more than enough reason to grieve apart from Trip's departure hadn't helped; she had lost her mother, T'Les, during a raid against the Syrrannite sect at Vulcan's Takarath Sanctuary, then had faced the death of Elizabeth. It didn't matter that her infant offspring had been a cloned hybrid created with her and Tucker's DNA by the rogue geneticists of the Terra Prime separatist movement; little Elizabeth had nevertheless been *their* child. And now both T'Les and Elizabeth were interred beneath the broiling sands of Vulcan, on the grounds of the rebuilt sanctuary.

T'Pol had not been back to Vulcan since the funeral ceremonies for Elizabeth, only a few months ago. Trip had been with her then, his arm still immobilized in a neurotherapeutic sling to treat the wound he'd received during the fight against the Terra Prime terrorists. T'Pol had pushed him away at first, fighting the pain that had threatened to bring all of her carefully suppressed emotions surging to the surface. But their mutual loss of little Elizabeth had eventually brought them closer together in spite of her reticence.

What they had attempted to build between them afterward was torn asunder a short while later, when Trip had taken an assignment for a covert Earth intelligence agency that was connected in some remote fashion to Starfleet. In order for him to infiltrate the Romulan Empire, he had been forced to fake his own death, with the aid of Captain Archer, Doctor Phlox, and Lieutenant Reed. T'Pol had not been told the truth until later, when Trip visited her on Earth, just prior to Archer's speech at the signing of the Coalition Compact.

Trip had given Archer a note for her, and she had subsequently met him in a chamber underneath the stadium where the signing ceremony was being held. There, she had learned of his mission, and had seen that he had been surgically altered to resemble a Vulcan. It was only during their talk that she realized that if he was actually supposed to be a Romulan infiltrator, then the old stories of Romulans and Vulcans being kindred species must be true.

Oddly, T'Pol found herself unsurprised by the revelation; from past experience, she knew that Vulcan history was teeming with secrets, and that the Romulans were not the only Vulcanoid race to have become separated from the ways of its forebears. The Syrrannite sect had had it easy compared to what she had learned about the Fri'slen decades ago . . . and about other races, during the time since.

That knowledge of the connection between the Romulans and the Vulcans carried with it an awful burden, however; if the secret connection between the Vulcans and the aggressive Romulans were ever made public, the distrust of other Coalition members toward Vulcan could split the fledgling alliance apart, thus rendering all of its members more vulnerable to dissension from within, attacks from without, and war from either direction.

Trip had assured her that the secret of the Romulan-Vulcan connection would be safe with him, and that as few others as possible would learn of it. Archer had since discussed the matter with T'Pol, having come to many of the same conclusions that she had. But they hadn't discussed it as much as they might have before Trip's "death," even if Archer had taken obvious pains to leave both Phlox and Reed out of those particular discussions.

Having once worked as an intelligence operative for the V'Shar, T'Pol fully understood the need for subterfuge and secrecy in espionage, but she nevertheless couldn't deny that her exclusion from the initial plan to fake Trip's death had created a fracture in her relationship with Archer and the others. She had sacrificed everything to join the crew of *Enterprise*, even resigning her position in the Vulcan High Command. What more could she have done to prove her loyalty to Archer? She'd always admired the captain, even if she did sometimes disagree with his often emotion-laden decisions.

He, however, apparently had felt that he could not trust her quite as fully, and therefore had initially denied her the peace of knowing that Trip wasn't, in fact, gone, but rather was simply . . . away.

Archer had tried to become more friendly with T'Pol since Trip's "passing," but she felt that those efforts had sprung as much from his own lack of people close to him—an innate loneliness that accompanied any command position—and from his feelings of personal guilt as they did from any specific desire for friendship. She couldn't deny that there was a certain logic to his actions, and she therefore allowed some degree of camaraderie to develop between them as they worked together. But until Trip returned—or she found a way to reconcile Archer's betrayal of her trust—she knew that an emotional wall would continue to stand between her and Archer.

That wall stood even higher between herself and both Phlox and Reed. It wasn't as if either of them had reached out very much to her socially anyway, and the distance they both kept from her was consistent with the fact that their spheres of daily responsibility aboard *Enterprise* overlapped either very little or not at all with her own. Only during briefings or interdepartmental meetings were they generally all in one place, and during those times, T'Pol put forth an extraordinary effort to keep herself on point and focused on ship's business.

T'Pol grasped at the IDIC symbol that she wore on a chain around her neck at all times, even under her Starfleet uniform. The pendant had been a gift from her mother, and it served as a constant reminder of the Vulcan credo, "Infinite Diversity in Infinite Combinations." T'Pol *was* that symbol aboard *Enterprise*. Certainly, humans of virtually every imaginable color and background served aboard this vessel, but besides herself and Phlox, no other nonhumans were present.

It wasn't that she wanted to isolate herself from others, even taking into account her sometimes ambivalent feelings toward Archer, Phlox, and Reed. T'Pol had cultivated friends and companions when she had lived and worked on Vulcan. But they were like her, suppressing their emotions, putting logic at the forefront. Only with Trip had she found on *Enterprise* a human whom she felt accepted her Vulcan attitudes, even if he did not share or necessarily even understand them. To the others, she must have seemed inscrutably alien.

The device attached to her desktop terminal let out three short beeps, pulling T'Pol out of her morose reverie. The irony behind the fact that she had been preparing to send a scrambled subspace transmission to Denak at the Vulcan Security Directorate—and thereby covertly breaking Starfleet's communications protocols—was not lost on her. In fact, it seemed somehow fitting, given that the last several years of her life aboard *Enterprise* had brought her into multiple secret arrangements, clandestine and covert operations, governmental and religious subterfuges, and more. She hoped that one day in the future, *Enterprise* and her crew might resume the pure exploration of the cosmos. Today, however, galactic politics in the known regions of space were simply too unstable to allow for that possibility, and Trip's ongoing spy mission in Romulan territory stood as mute proof of that unhappy fact.

She pulled out her chair and sat before the terminal on the desktop, composing her thoughts. She hoped that she could still trust Denak, but until she knew for certain, she remained determined not to give too much away. Tapping the viewscreen, she took note of the tiny digital countdown screen linked to the subspace com-scrambling device. She had approximately four minutes before her activities might be discovered by anyone monitoring outgoing signals from *Enterprise*.

The man's face that appeared on-screen looked significantly more haggard than the one in T'Pol's memory, and sometime in the last several years, Denak had apparently lost an eye and part of an ear. He was standing outdoors on a balcony of some sort, the shifting red sands of their homeworld visible in the distance behind him.

"I am surprised to hear from you, T'Pol," Denak said. *"It has been twenty years since the* Kish'altriq *celebration, has it not?"*

T'Pol nodded, knowing that it had, in fact, been longer. But the fact that Denak had mentioned *Kish'altriq* meant that he was in a safe position to talk. "I hope you and your wife are faring well," she said. That was her verification response, since they both knew that Denak was not only a widower at present, but was also fast approaching the age when not even the fierce hormonal firestorms of *Pon farr* could furnish any real impetus to seek a mate. T'Pol understood his insistence that she adhere to such time-honored security protocols whenever they communicated; if either of them were under duress, or not in a safe zone, the personal banter would have seemed innocuous enough to anyone who might be listening in.

Denak nodded curtly, his expression bland. *"I truly am surprised to hear from you. Once you resigned your commission, I expected you would sever ties to—"*

"I am Vulcan, Denak," T'Pol said, interrupting her erstwhile superior. "And I have only a brief time to communicate with you. Speaking plainly, I need to know about any anomalous military or intelligence activity that Vulcan may be undertaking within the Romulan Star Empire."

Raising an eyebrow, Denak shook his head slightly. *"Such things are somewhat out of my immediate area of knowledge, T'Pol, though it is not an entirely unknown subject to me. I do know that we have taken Captain Archer's theories about imminent Romulan aggression far more seriously than has the Coalition Council. With this in mind, we have agents investigating all the various acts of interstellar piracy, as well as every recent outworld attack."*

T'Pol nodded, choosing her next words with extreme care. She didn't know whether or not Denak knew about the relationship between the Vulcan and Romulan peoples, nor did she want to jeopardize any mission that Trip was currently involved in during his covert tenure inside the Romulan sphere of influence.

"Are your agents working from . . . within Romulan circles . . . or are they investigating only in a defensive sense?"

Denak's eyes narrowed—his ocular implant made for a fair approximation of his missing eye—and he seemed to study her closely for a moment. " *'We are engaging in purely defensive maneuvers' is the answer most anyone in the Vulcan intelligence hierarchy would give you, T'Pol. But because you've saved my life on more than one occasion, I shall simply say that it would be illogical for us not to attempt to understand the goals and capabilities of the Romulan Star Empire by studying them from within. Precisely how that is being done is a matter somewhat beyond my clearance level, but I know that such operations are indeed under way. And that they are being done at tremendous personal risk to the individuals involved."*

"Could you enlighten me as to *which* individuals may be involved?" she said.

He paused for a moment, then added, *"You might look into associates of Captain Sopek of the Vulcan High Command."*

She frowned. "Don't you mean the *late* Captain Sopek, Denak?"

Something that almost resembled a small smile came to the older man's lips. *"Reports of Sopek's death may have been . . . greatly exaggerated."*

"I appreciate the information, Denak," she said, wondering precisely how Sopek might be involved in Romulan espionage; only two years ago, following the Andorian attack on P'Jem, Sopek had used his influence with the Vulcan High Command to keep T'Pol aboard *Enterprise*. She resolved to investigate Sopek whenever time and duty permitted it.

"I only have a few moments more before the subspace scrambler may be detected," she added quickly. "Please contact me again at this frequency should you discover anything further that you think would be helpful." She tapped the screen, sending him a specific frequency graph.

"I will expect you to do the same, T'Pol," Denak said. *"As I noted, many of us believe that the Romulan threat is* significantly *more dire than even Vulcan's government officials and representatives seem to understand. Or will admit. If you learn anything that might help raise awareness within the new administration, you have my word that I will contin—"*

The screen went blank as the timer reached zero, and T'Pol knew that the scrambling device was already erasing any trace of the transmission from the ship's com logs and computer backup subroutines. She wished that she had been able to speak to Denak for just a little longer. But for now, she had some slim threads to follow.

It seemed clear that at least *some* Vulcan military or intelligence operatives were working covertly within the boundaries of the Romulan Star Empire, which meant that at least some knowledge existed on Vulcan of the connection between the two long-sundered peoples. She had no reason to believe that Denak was aware of that connection, however; nor did she feel that he was holding back any important information.

Which meant that he also didn't have any information concerning Trip, or the specifics of his mission for the covert Earth-based intel bureau. T'Pol cared intensely about the future of Vulcan, as well as that of the Coalition of Planets and the safety of the *Starship Enterprise*. But she also knew that deep within her, no matter how much she tried to repress her emotions, her actions were being guided, illogically, by fear.

And by loss.

Where is Trip now, and what kind of danger is he facing right at this moment? And when will he be back?

T'Pol knew she couldn't rest until she found the answers.

FOUR

Day Twenty-nine, Month of K'ri'Brax
Romulus

With more than an hour to spare before his next scheduled check-in with Captain Eric Stillwell, Charles "Trip" Tucker III left his small suite of rented rooms for a brisk sunset walk downtown.

Of course, downtown Dartha wasn't just *any* downtown. Even by the standards of the Romulan capital's venerable Government Quarter—which had been built, and was even today continuously being rebuilt, over the bones of one of the oldest settlements on the planet—the ancient streets seemed absurdly narrow. Moving with a confidence instilled by having lived here continuously for the past several weeks, Trip wended his way along the tightly packed warren of constricted roads and footpaths, all of which curved gently to conform to the generally round, concentric style that characterized even the oldest Romulan urban planning. As he walked, the remnant of the neighborhood's daily throng of assorted shopkeepers, clerks, laborers, and retail customers moved past, either ignoring him entirely or favoring him with wordless nods or perfunctory greetings of *"Jolan'tru,"* the local equivalent of "Have a nice day."

He turned sideways to allow a middle-aged man and woman to pass him on a narrow sidewalk. *These people don't smile much more than the Vulcans do*, Trip thought,

suppressing an ironic grin so as not to attract any un-
wanted attention; he knew from firsthand experience just
how dramatically the sometimes explosively passionate
Romulans differed from their more contemplative—if
sometimes equally standoffish—cousins on Vulcan.

The slow trickle of passersby inexorably slowed further, dying off entirely as the yellow Romulan sun finally completed its long horizonward arc, its present
low angle giving it the hue of human blood. Trip paused
to take in the spectacle of the bloated, ruddy orb as it
settled behind the phalanx of centuries-old structures
that comprised the squat Old City skyline. Caught between the waning rays and lengthening shadows, the
venerable illuminated spires of the kilometers-distant
Hall of State rose belligerently, war pikes poised over
the Romulan capital, the anthracite-black waters of
the Apnex Sea at their backs. It told Trip a tale of the
fearsome martial past that T'Pol's people shared with
the Romulans, a way of life that could return to the
presently peace-loving Vulcan people should the star-
spanning empire's dreams of conquest ever reach fruition. The tableau could have been the work of a painter
determined to limn the contradictory streaks of beauty
and savagery of the galactic civilization that radiated
from this very city.

A civilization, he reminded himself, whose crash
program to develop a warp-seven-capable stardrive
still posed a direct and mounting threat, not only to the
world of his birth, but also to its allies. Putting a definitive stop to that program was the reason he had come to
this alien place. It was also the reason he had allowed
all but a handful of the people in his life to believe the
official reports of his death in the line of duty. His par-
ents, his brother Bert, and Owen, the child that Bert
and Miguel had adopted a few years back—all of them

believed what Starfleet had told them about his death in an apparent pirate raid.

He ached to finish his mission, to return home and see them all again—to put his life and the lives of his loved ones back together. *Thank God that at least T'Pol knows the truth,* he thought, briefly wondering if he could ever mend that particular relationship. Ever since the death of their daughter Elizabeth a few months back, he tended to doubt that he and T'Pol would ever recapture whatever spark had once passed between them, even though their relationship had been headed that way very shortly before his "death."

The narrow street upon which Trip stood seemed to become even more constricted as the evening settled in, covering the sky like a bejeweled raven-colored canopy and bringing with it a chill, foggy breeze tinged with Apnex Sea brine and the faint but acrid scent of what might have been shore-dwelling *mogai* or *nei'rhh,* or perhaps some other kind of local predatory bird. Illuminated only dimly by the greenish glow of the lanterns that topped the district's widely spaced, age-pitted stone lampposts, his surroundings quickly began to suggest menace rather than beauty. Cinching his brown travel robe tightly against the rapidly falling temperature, he turned and began retracing the route he'd taken from his apartment, hoping the terrain wouldn't appear too different in the baleful semidarkness.

The pavement beneath one of his feet suddenly became soft and yielding, and he nearly fell backward before regaining his balance. A stench, wholly alien yet also somehow distinctly familiar, assaulted his nostrils not half a heartbeat later.

"Ugh," he muttered as he leaned against a wall, squinting to get a good look at the semisolid foulness into which he had just stepped. *Damn it. There's one thing that's the same on any planet that's got cities on it, pointed ears and green blood notwithstanding.* Doing his best to ignore the stink, Trip stepped over to the nearby brick-lined gutter, against which he scraped the bottom of his shoe until its sole once again looked reasonably clean. Then, after breathing a pungent Rihannsu curse upon those who failed to curb their pet *set'leth*s, he resumed walking, quietly rounding a corner.

Trip suddenly found himself standing between a pair of youthful male Romulans, neither of whom appeared to be any older than perhaps sixteen or seventeen. Both teens distinguished themselves immediately from everyone else he had encountered so far this evening, and not merely because of their age.

They were smiling.

Maliciously.

The solitary streetlamp across the street shed just enough pale light to make the blade in the shorter teen's hand gleam menacingly.

Trip offered them a sideways grin of his own. "*Jolan'tru,* boys," he said in his best conversational Rihannsu, relying on the translator mounted inside his artificially pointed ear to smooth out whatever difficulties his persistent Alabama-Florida accent might pose. "Maybe I'd better warn you up front: I left my wallet back at the hotel."

The kid holding the knife took a fateful step forward, evidently not about to take Trip at his word.

Trip sighed. This was shaping up to be a complicated evening.

"You're twenty minutes late checking in, Commander," said a frowning Captain Stillwell, imaged on the little security-scrambled subspace transceiver that Trip had

just retrieved from its strategic hiding place beneath one of his bedroom floorboards. Stillwell paused, blinking at his own screen as he studied the image there. *"What the hell happened to you, anyway?"*

Trip grinned, ignoring the slight twinge of pain that lingered in his jaw. "It's all right, sir. Just ran into a little bit of trouble while I was walking home tonight, that's all."

"Looks like you were injured," Stillwell said, leaning forward slightly as he squinted at Trip from across the light-years. Despite the extreme distance, the visual channel looked exceptionally crisp today, probably because of the adjustments Trip had just made to the official subspace array on the roof of Ehrehin's lab, which lay only a few klicks away. On several occasions over the past month, Trip had succeeded in quietly piggybacking his own narrow-beam, amplitude-modulated subspace signals onto those of the lab's multiband transceiver; this enabled him to send messages that blended in undetectably with both the never-ending torrent of incoming and outgoing lab data and the natural background static of subspace—so far, at least.

"Let's just say you oughtta see the other guy." Although in actuality he had faced two attackers, Trip didn't want to sound as though he were bragging. Fortunately, the toughs who had tried to jump him had only been aggressive teenagers; since they hadn't had the benefit of Starfleet training, they'd been fairly easy to persuade to move on in search of easier prey. On the other hand, even young Romulans had a pretty significant advantage over humans in terms of sheer physical strength. . . .

Stillwell appeared to be scrutinizing Trip's bruised face in minute detail. *"You'd better tend to those scrapes and bruises carefully, Commander. We can't afford to let these people see you shedding red blood, now can we?"*

I'm so very touched by your concern, Trip thought, though he knew his new superior in the spy bureau was making an excellent point. Nevertheless, Stillwell made Harris, the enigmatic spymaster who had originally recruited him into the bureau, seem almost cuddly in comparison.

It's his job to develop Earth's version of the warp-seven drive before the Romulans manage to pull off the same trick, Trip reminded himself. Having spent four years laboring to keep *Enterprise's* frequently beleaguered warp-five engine running with its matter/antimatter needle always necessarily oscillating somewhere between *off* and *kaboom,* Trip had some natural sympathy for Stillwell. It wasn't hard to imagine what the crushing weight of so much high-stakes responsibility might do to any man's sense of humor.

"I've still got a good supply of sulfatriptan salted away, Captain," Trip said, nodding. Thanks to the drug's property of harmlessly binding its sulfur compounds to the human hemoglobin molecule, no cursory glance at Trip's blood, mucus membranes, or internal organs would give him away as a red-blooded Terran—even after the new red cells produced by his bone marrow had overwhelmed the initial green-blood treatment he'd received on Adigeon Prime. Regardless, he knew he had to remain vigilant about not making anybody curious enough about him to subject him to deep-tissue scans or DNA tests of any sort, or else the jig would truly be up.

"I just took a booster dose," Trip continued. "By tomorrow my blood and innards will look as green as the Chicago River on Saint Patty's Day." *I just hope I can avoid spilling any more of it any time soon,* he added silently, with no small amount of gallows humor.

"*Good,*" Stillwell said with a sober nod, apparently as

unmoved as ever by Trip's witticisms. *"Now let's discuss your progress monitoring and regulating the activities of your target."*

Trip suppressed a wince. *Target.* He hated that word. "I'm still keeping very close tabs on Ehrehin," he said.

"I can see that, Commander. So close, in fact, that you and Doctor Ehrehin i'Ramnau tr'Avrak now seem to be on a first-name basis."

Trip's frown appeared unbidden, and he felt it creasing the artificially constructed brow ridge that formed a subtle V shape across his forehead. He hoped that Stillwell found it an imposing sight.

"That's hard to avoid when you're posing as a scientist's assistant." And he wasn't posing as just *any* assistant; thanks to the skill of the plastic surgeons of Adigeon Prime, Trip had been passing himself off for months now as Cunaehr ir'Ra'tleihfi tr'Mandak, Ehrehin's most beloved and valued aide. "It's part of my cover, remember?"

"Then I trust I don't need to remind you not to let it become anything more *than that, Commander. The old man's work poses the most clear and present danger to Earth since the Xindi came gunning for us. It's a threat to the entire Coalition. Never forget that."*

"You're worried about me going native, like my old pal Sopek," Trip said, not asking a question. Though he had recently almost died at Sopek's hands, he still wasn't entirely certain whether Sopek's primary allegiance had been to Vulcan or Romulus.

"It's a very real hazard every deep-cover agent has to consider, Commander. You'd do well to face that possibility honestly."

Trip's jaw hardened in resentment, his sympathy for Stillwell notwithstanding. "Look, Captain. Ehrehin wants to rein in his people's war making just as much as we do."

"The old man may be a genius whose expertise you admire," Stillwell said, a scowl creasing his already hard countenance. *"But he's also a loyal Romulan. You'd do well not to forget that either, Commander."*

You just can't admit the possibility that a Romulan could be the same as we are, can you? Trip thought, though he managed to hold his tongue.

"If Ehrehin believed in the aims of the Romulan military, he could have completed a working warp-seven prototype long before now."

"Maybe. Or maybe that's just what you'd prefer to believe. Whatever he hasn't achieved yet for the Romulan military might not be for lack of trying. Remember, Commander, I also have a pretty damned thorough understanding of just what has to go into any crash high-warp research program," Stillwell continued.

"Starfleet *did* put you in charge of it," Trip said, keeping his expression guarded. Trying his best to be charitable, he supposed that Stillwell's annoying tendency to try to micromanage and second-guess his work on Romulus was an outgrowth of his management of Earth's warp-seven program, in addition to his covert duties seeking out related information from alien worlds under the auspices of the bureau. He didn't envy the man his job. Still, he couldn't help but wonder how badly Stillwell would have screwed up Trip's task on Romulus were the two men to trade places.

Stillwell nodded. *"They did indeed. And I find it hard to believe that I could fool them for any length of time into believing that my team was making significant progress if it really wasn't."*

A sinking feeling developed deep in Trip's belly, but

he tried not to show any discomfiture. Had Stillwell just admitted that Earth's warp-seven research had reached some sort of impasse?

"How *is* the project going, Captain?" Trip wanted to know.

Stillwell's scowl deepened. *"That's not a data point that you need to know at the moment, Commander."*

Trip's shoulders suddenly felt heavier as the weight of his own responsibilities bore down on him.

"My point is that I seriously doubt that the old man's superiors are fools either," Stillwell said. *"Just as I doubt his claim that he's deliberately taking his research team down a blind alley to contain his people's militarism. But if he is . . . if . . . then sooner or later Admiral Valdore will spot the lie and replace Doctor Ehrehin with somebody who will get the job done."*

"For whatever it's worth, Captain, I don't think there *is* anybody else here capable of getting the job done," Trip said. "I'm a pretty fair warp engineer myself, and I can't make heads or tails of the technical gobbledygook he's been putting in his progress reports. I can't see how Valdore's people will do any better."

"Let's hope you're right. Maybe Doctor Ehrehin is, as you once so colorfully put it, 'baffling Valdore with bullshit.' But the old man knows who you really are. He knows your agenda. And he knows how impressed you are by his credentials, as well as by his alleged ideals.

"Therefore you must face the possibility that he is playing you, Commander. He may be conducting real warp-seven research behind your back as we speak. He might actually be making solid progress toward the creation of a prototype stardrive. Progress that you are unaware of, at least so far."

Trip fumed quietly. "If anything like that was going on, we'd both know about it by now."

"I have no doubt of that, Commander. If you discovered it."

Trip was finding it increasingly difficult to avoid delivering a sharp retort. "So now you're worried that I'm incompetent. On top of maybe having gone native."

Stillwell paused, then chuckled, his frown suddenly melting into a look of almost fatherly concern. *"Not at all, Commander. But as long as you have vulnerabilities, I'm going to remind you of them from time to time. Making the good-faith error in judgment of trusting someone too much and the problem of 'going native' are very similar pitfalls. It's very hard to know precisely when you've stepped into the former. And once you've done it, it's deceptively easy to slide from there to the latter. The difference is a matter of degree, a line along the same continuum."*

Hoping both to contain his own rising ire and to change the subject, Trip forced a smile and said, "You know, Captain, one of the main reasons Harris recruited me into this cockamamie secret bureau of yours was because I'm a 'people person.' A big part of that is being able to tell when somebody is lying to your face."

"I certainly hope your faith in your own judgment is justified, Commander. As well as your faith in the old man's motivations. But if it turns out it's not, you'd better be prepared to do what's necessary."

Trip frowned again. "You know all my contingency plans, Captain. If I find the plans for a *real* warp-seven prototype here, I'm gonna take it. Failing that, I'll destroy it, and wipe every computer I can find that's carrying the files."

"Very good. But you'll need an additional contingency plan as well."

"What do you mean?"

"Wiping computer files is an incomplete solution at

best," Stillwell said. *"You can never be sure you got to all the backup copies. Computer techs can often reconstruct files unless you out-and-out vaporize the hardware substrate. And original research can always be reconstituted as long as it still exists inside somebody's head."*

Trip didn't like what he was hearing one bit. "What are you saying, Captain?"

Stillwell spoke in a voice as sharp and cold and unforgiving as a guillotine execution on a January morning. *"I'm saying, Commander, that you'd better be prepared to kill Doctor Ehrehin i'Ramnau tr'Avrak."*

Trip could only nod his head numbly. He felt some sort of "spy autopilot" take over for him during the remainder of his check-in with Stillwell, as both men crossed a few routine matters off their respective lists for the next few minutes before the captain signed off.

Trip wasn't sure how long he just sat there afterward, simply staring into the dead black screen of his subspace unit. Had Stillwell allowed the weight of responsibility to crush the humanity out of him, to the point where he saw paranoiac conspiracies that didn't exist? There was no question in Trip's mind that the man was entirely too jingoistic to see the universe as it really was, in all its subtle complexities and nearly indistinguishable shades of gray.

But Trip also knew that he had to face the possibility that Stillwell had judged Ehrehin correctly. He searched his soul. Had he allowed his own humanity, his own willingness to believe the best about people, to put the very existence of the human species in jeopardy? He truly didn't think so. Despite the fact that Ehrehin was unquestionably still a loyal Romulan, a man whose main priority was the welfare of his own people, Trip felt certain that the elderly scientist's commitment to the larger morality of peace was a sincere one as well.

But he also knew that he'd have to face squarely, sooner or later, the main question that Stillwell had raised: What if the security of Earth and the Coalition required the destruction of more than just Ehrehin's research records?

FIVE

**The Year of Kahless 781
The Klingon-Romulan border**

BENEATH HIS LONG MUSTACHE, Nah'tan smiled, displaying the grin of a *toQ* vulture. Today was a glorious day. His *D'Vagh*-class battle cruiser, the *I.K.S. Veqlargh Jajlo'*, was in top shape, having just undergone a thorough refit and overhaul at the shipyards orbiting Praxis. His complement of weapons was full, and his crew was rested and ready for a battle.

And now they had one.

"Ready disruptor cannons!" he ordered, standing up from his chair in the center of the ship's bridge and stalking closer to the main viewer. Around him, the warriors at his service bustled to comply.

On the screen was a *RomuluSngan* vessel, though it wasn't a ship of the type most commonly seen in his ship's database. They had first encountered the enemy vessel via long-range scanners within the past *kilaan*, while searching for two missing Klingon battle cruisers, the *I.K.S. SIm'yoH* and the *I.K.S. Mup'chIch*.

"What progress have you made with the scans?" Nah'tan asked, stalking to the workstation of Nevahk, his most intelligent technician.

Nevahk barely glanced his way, concentrating instead on moving his blunt fingers over a multitude of blinking tactical screens. "They have been successful at blocking most of the scans, but we captured some fragmentary information nonetheless." He pointed a dusky-hued finger at a diagram that was uploading to a hull-mounted monitor to his upper left. "They have shields and weapons comparable to ours, though their skill in utilizing them no doubt pales beside the strength of the Empire."

He pointed to another area of his console, upon which the screens appeared blank. "We are unable to scan *this* section of the vessel, which seems to be shielded heavily."

"Then that section shall be our first target," Nah'tan growled, turning on his heel and striding back to the center of the bridge.

"Open channels again!" he commanded, casting the most intimidating glower he could muster toward the central viewer. "Romulan vessel, you will stand down and prepare to be boarded. You stand accused of piracy and sabotage, and will answer to the laws of the Klingon Empire!"

He waited for several moments before turning his gaze toward Dekk'ven, his communications officer. The young warrior, a *bekk* who had recently lost most of his lower teeth in a brawl over a spilled bowl of *gagh,* shook his head. "No response, Captain," he said, his words slightly lisped around his injuries.

"Repeat the message and continue sending," Nah'tan barked. He knew that if he were to fire on the other ship unprovoked, it could be seen as an act of cowardice. But by openly accusing the *RomuluSngan*—even giving them a chance to surrender without a fight—he was protecting himself both tactically *and* politically. But soon, he would have no choice but to follow through on his threats. Other than that, his only concern now was whatever it was the Romulans were trying to conceal from his ship's sensors.

"Captain, the Romulan ship is polarizing its hull

plating," the comely Kori'nd said from her station at the left of the viewer. "Its weapons tubes are powering up."

"Prepare to attack," Nah'tan growled loudly, feeling his pulse quicken with the exhilaration of imminent combat. He felt certain that his crew was as excited as he was; they had done without the glories of battle for far too long.

"Tracking another ship coming out of warp," Kori'nd said, even as the main viewscreen split into two images. On the left side was the Romulan ship, but on the right was a far more familiar vessel.

"The *Mup'chIch*." Nah'tan was surprised but pleased. No trace of either of the missing Klingon ships had yet been found; no one had yet assumed the worst, though both vessels had been overdue long enough to cause some concern among the fleet's command hierarchy.

Grinning with satisfaction, Nah'tan now felt certain that he would see unequivocal and absolute victory this day. No Romulan vessel had ever been captured whole, and certainly not with its crew alive. But the enemy craft before him now was hopelessly outgunned, and might therefore be overwhelmed and seized intact. If the *RomuluSngan* were smart, they would turn and run back to their sovereign space like a whipped *targ* while they still stood any chance at all of doing so. The only choices that remained to them now were to display their cowardice, blow themselves up, or admit *Doghjey*— unconditional surrender—and await their just fate as *jegh'pujwI'*, lawfully conquered alien prisoners of the Klingon Empire.

"Hail the *Mup'chIch*," Nah'tan said. "Invite her commander to share the spoils of our conquest."

"Communications are jammed, Captain," Dekk'ven said, his voice rising to a slightly higher than normal register.

Nah'tan muttered a curse that might have shocked even his own brother. "Get them back online!"

Abruptly, the yellowish lights on the bridge winked out, and the blood-hued emergency lights replaced them. Nah'tan whirled toward Nevahk's station, where the technician was moving his hands across multiple screens, almost in a panic. "*QaStaH QI'yah nuq jay'?*" Nah'tan roared, desperate to discover the cause and meaning of whatever malevolent influence was afflicting his ship.

"We've just lost life support!" Nevahk shouted. "Other systems are beginning to fail, shipwide!"

A sound like a gong reverberated through the *Veqlargh Jajlo'*'s hull, and Nah'tan felt the hollow, dropping sensation of the artificial gravity cutting out beneath his boots. He scrabbled to grab hold of his chair as a variety of surprised shouts, random clatterings, and other less identifiable noises reverberated from across the bridge and from other parts of the vessel.

"Shields are down, and we have explosive decompression on three decks, from *Soch* to *Hut!*" Kori'nd screamed, her voice raised to a nearly frantic pitch as she drifted upside down and clutched at the console at her station for stability.

Suddenly, the central viewscreen switched images, showing a trio of what appeared to be *vulqangan* staring forward from what was obviously a Klingon bridge. The female in the center smiled viciously, uttering but a single short phrase before the image disappeared.

"Boch ghIchraj," the woman said just before vanishing. "*Your nose is shiny.*"

Captain Nah'tan of the *I.K.S. Veqlargh Jajlo'* barely had time to wonder why a Vulcan had hailed them with Klingon taunts from the *Mup'chIch*'s bridge, or why the viewscreen now showed the *Mup'chIch* firing its disruptors directly at the *Veqlargh Jajlo'*.

His final thought, just before the smoke and fire and darkness took him, was one of disappointment. *Perhaps today was not to be such a glorious day after all.*

Day Twenty-nine, Month of K'ri'Brax
Dartha, Romulus

The holographic image of the Romulan captain flickered lightly in the air as a small insect flew through it. The *kekla*-gnats were ever-present in the Romulan capital at this time of year, when the *grekekla* trees were in fragrant bloom. Even here, within Admiral Valdore's spacious office in the Romulan Hall of State, this tiniest member of the insect orders had insinuated itself.

Seated behind his heavy sherawood desk, his hands steepled under his chin, Valdore listened to Commander Dagarth's report with barely contained glee. The first full-scale test of the Romulan Star Empire's new tactical system—conceived by Valdore and designed and realized by the scientists under his command—had been an outstanding success.

There had been some trepidation on all fronts, given the earlier failure against the first *klivam* vessel that Dagarth's bird-of-prey, *Nel Trenco,* had attempted to seize, but their system reportedly had worked flawlessly in capturing and maintaining control over the *Mup'chIch*—which Dagarth's crew had then used to destroy the pursuing *I.K.S. Veqlargh Jajlo'*. Had any serious operational errors occurred—or had the Klingons somehow managed to summon reinforcements—the considerable risk of causing an ill-timed war with the Klingon Empire would have loomed. Instead, as matters stood now, the best evidence available would show that one Klingon vessel had been responsible for the destruction of the others. The Klingons would be more interested in concealing their embarrassment than in engaging in another war against Romulus.

"Your service will be commended," Valdore said, gesturing toward the holographic image of the female captain of the *Nel Trenco*. "History will mark this day well."

"*I serve the Empire,*" Dagarth said, bowing her head. The image rippled slightly again, then disappeared.

On the other side of the desk, Doctor Nijil, Valdore's chief technologist, approached, a triumphant smile playing upon his lips even as his hands were clasped behind him in a show of submission.

"*You* have done well, also," Valdore said, pointing toward the scientist with one hand as he reached into a recessed area under his desk with the other. He noted that Nijil flinched just a little in response to the maneuver, as though Valdore might have been retrieving a concealed disruptor pistol rather than a celebratory bottle of *carallun* wine.

"Relax, Nijil," Valdore said in a deep voice intended to inspire calm, uncorking the wine as he spoke. "You're in no danger from me." He stood and hoisted the bottle above the level of his head, allowing the light from the tall windows to glint through the green *ehrie'urhillh* glass of the bottle.

"I know that you don't normally drink, but you *will* share a toast to our success." Valdore took a swig of the tart liquor, not bothering to stop to look for drinking vessels. Then he passed the bottle to Nijil, who wasted no time following Valdore's lead. The scientist seemed to try not to make a face at the bitter taste, but with little success.

Valdore stoppered the bottle again and returned it to its dusty spot beneath his desktop. A few *khaidoa* ago, he had made a point of leaving that dusty spot undisturbed by *not* celebrating the Romulan Star Empire's devastation of Coridan. Even though he had played a part in the execution of the attack, it had not been a proud moment for him. Not only had it seemed a dishonorable action, it had also failed to disrupt the peace pact that now united the worlds of the fledgling Coalition of Planets. The sneak attack had, however, greatly curtailed the Coalition's supply of dilithium, a material that had long been crucial to the operation of Coalition starships. Many in the Romulan military thus saw the action as a success, and Valdore was happy to accept the resulting laurels and accolades, finding such unearned praise infinitely preferable to once again facing the prospect of political disfavor, imprisonment, or even execution. He reflected that his longtime friend and former senator, Vrax, who languished in Praetor D'deridex's dungeons during the long *khaidoa* that had followed the Romulan military's most recent significant tactical defeat, might not be so fortunate.

Looking beyond Coridan, Valdore was glad to focus on his other plans for furthering the military goals of the Romulan Star Empire's ambitious Praetor. The half-crazy Doctor Ehrehin was still working on a singularity-powered stardrive prototype, and Nijil and his team had been engaged with multiple projects, including a stable cloaking device capable of rendering large manned vessels effectively invisible to both scans and visual observation. Unfortunately, the invisibility cloaks that had been tested so far worked only to conceal small objects, or ended up quickly overtaxing the power-production capabilities of large vessels—invariably with explosive results. It appeared that significantly more time—or an unexpected breakthrough—would be necessary to find a truly workable solution to the cloaking problem.

Recently, however, Nijil and his team had succeeded in developing a new technology, one based in part on the principles that governed the operation of the tele-pathically controlled drone ships, whose recent failure had resulted in Valdore's brief imprisonment alongside Vrax. This new tactical system was able to intuitively bypass ships' control mechanisms, allowing the Romulans to seize control of enemy vessels.

Thanks to Valdore's association with the former Vulcan Administrator V'Las, Nijil had already succeeded in confirming that the tactical system would work well enough if deployed against Vulcan software, and the just-concluded field experiments against the Klingons showed that their vessels were vulnerable as well.

"We must bring our new *arrenhe'hwiua* telecapture system to bear against Coalition vessels," Valdore said, emerging from his reverie. "Other than those of the *thaessu*, that is: our distant Vulcan cousins. But we must do so in a way that does not implicate the empire."

Nijil nodded, then spoke. "It is easier to unravel a weave when one has pulled a single thread. If we target a Coalition vessel that is of little intrinsic importance, something that is not likely to be missed immediately, we will have grasped the very thread that leads us to other, more consequential ships."

Valdore raised one eyebrow as he considered his chief technologist's words. The time to strike against the Coalition was coming, but to assure victory, whatever specific blow he was going to deal would have to be carefully considered and flawlessly planned.

He smiled. When the hammer finally fell, the Coalition would not even have time to wonder about what had hit it.

SIX

Monday, July 14, 2155
Enterprise **NX-01, near Altair VI**

To ARCHER, the regulation-required inspection of the United Earth Space Probe Agency's port facilities at Altair VI had seemed all but interminable. The fact that the planet's surface gravity, at least in the areas not outfitted with artificial gravity plating, was fifty percent higher than Earth normal didn't help matters any. And despite the protective eyewear that he and Malcolm Reed and everyone based at the Altair VI colony donned whenever the inspection checklist had required them to venture outside, the intense brightness of the sun had given Archer a nearly equally intense yearning for a welding mask.

Archer was thankful, at least, that the proceedings had gone largely without incident, and that the few areas in the central compound and its surrounding outbuildings that weren't quite up to Starfleet standards and UESPA code hadn't affected any critical systems. Fortunately for everyone concerned, Altair VI's mild and relatively Earth-like climate, particularly at the high northern latitudes where the bulk of the settlements had been established, rendered the planet's few thousand human colonists safe from pressure-dome blowouts and other similar technological catastrophes, if not from distant Altair's intense, ultraviolet-heavy brilliance. The few small problems that had been discovered during the inspection had been put right within a couple of hours with the aid of *Enterprise*'s new chief engineer, Lieutenant Mike Burch, and his able crew.

After he had finally finished with the inspection and the final exchanges of pleasantries with the port's command staff, Archer and Reed returned to Shuttlepod One and took it back into the green-tinged sky that overlooked the northern seaside port facilities. Archer turned the shuttlepod as it gained altitude, allowing him to take in the welcoming vista of the Darro-Miller settlement that had risen over the carbon dioxide–infused Altair-water aquifers to the south. The pioneer town was still growing quickly, already home to nearly twenty-two thousand humans; more than a few of these settlers would no doubt soon participate in the creation of other settlements, either elsewhere on this world or on the even more challenging surface of the system's still largely untouched fourth planet.

The magenta-and-white mountains beyond Darro-Miller rolled into view next, fronted by an enigmatic jumble of ruined stone columns and temples that had been left behind untold eons ago by some long-extinct sentient race. Archer looked on wistfully as the tantalizing ancient vista quickly vanished over the horizon and the shuttlepod arced upward toward a standard orbital insertion.

"They say the statues the archeologists found down there look almost human," Reed said, almost as though he'd been reading Archer's mind.

"It's amazing to find traces of anything that looks so much like we do almost seventeen light-years from home," Archer said as he returned his full attention to the console before him. "I wish we had at least a solid week down there to go picking through those ruins." The mysteries of where those ancient people had gone, where they had originated—and whether they were cosmic cousins of humanity or had arisen independently—were enticing almost beyond measure.

"A few uninterrupted days of shore leave for the crew wouldn't go down badly either, sir," Reed said, wearing an expression that was somehow both hopeful and fatalistic.

"Time and tide are impatient mistresses, Malcolm," Archer said with a weak smile. "Duty calls. Starfleet says we've got pirates and raiders to catch."

Roughly forty minutes later, Archer found himself back on *Enterprise*'s busy bridge, along with Reed, Mayweather, and Sato. After confirming that the engineering repair team was also back aboard and ordering Ensign Mayweather to break orbit for the starship's next destination, the captain leaned back in his command chair and watched Altair VI begin making a swift descent into the void. Presented on the main viewer in an aft view, the blue-green orb quickly began to shrink in apparent size, like a pebble falling in slow motion into a dark and bottomless pit.

Now he had to get *Enterprise* back to the main civilian shipping lanes of Coalition space. It was time to resume the interminable vigil, patrolling for pirate vessels that only very rarely deigned to put in an appearance. Which really meant that it was time to go back to simply waiting around passively for something, *anything*, to happen, while the Romulans, and maybe the Klingons as well, continued drawing their plans behind the slumbering backs of the Coalition's perpetually distracted movers and shakers.

"On course and steady on half impulse power, Captain," Mayweather said as he entered several commands into his console, refining the starship's flight path.

"Thanks, Travis," Archer said. "Engage warp drive,

warp factor five. Let's not keep our pirates and raiders waiting any longer than we absolutely have to."

Mayweather turned and favored him with a brief but rueful grin before facing front once again. "Aye, sir," he said, then pushed the throttle stick purposefully forward. The feel of the deck plates suddenly changed beneath Archer's boots as the increased output of the vessel's powerful matter/antimatter reactor sent subaural vibrations racing throughout *Enterprise's* superstructure.

"Captain!" Reed's sudden exclamation from the tactical console at the bridge's aft section startled Archer out of his reverie. The keening wail of a proximity alarm pierced the air at almost the same moment.

Archer turned his chair around, then rose to his feet in a single swift, fluid motion. "What is it, Malcolm?"

A frown of concern crumpled the ever-vigilant weapons officer's forehead. "The long-range navigational sensors have just made contact with a small object in our flight path. It fits the general profile of a manned space vessel."

Archer motioned to Hoshi to cut off the klaxon, whose nerve-jarring noise abruptly ceased a moment later. "Collision danger?" he asked, facing the tactical console.

Reed shook his head. "Correction, sir: The object doesn't lie *directly* in our flight path. We should clear it by a hundred kilometers or more."

"So why the alarm?" Hoshi asked. "A hundred klicks is a pretty wide berth, isn't it?"

"In deep space, that's like practically trading paint jobs," Mayweather said, frowning as he studied the console before him. "If this thing's a ship, then why isn't it using a standard navigational beacon?"

Donning a frown that matched the helmsman's,

Archer nodded. "That's exactly what I intend to find out, Travis. Match velocity and intercept."

"Aye, sir," Mayweather said, adjusting the stick with one hand as he touched a series of buttons and switches with the other. "Dropping out of warp."

"What about our pirates and raiders, sir?" Reed asked as the deck plates beneath Archer's feet resumed their usual subwarp feel.

Archer turned toward his weapons officer, noted his ironic grin, and returned it. "Let's just say it's *their* turn to sit around and wait."

"Unless they've decided to come to us," Mayweather said, nodding in the direction of the unknown and not yet visible vessel.

Archer was already considering that possibility—along with the possibility that the mystery ship might be a Romulan or Klingon vessel, here to probe Coalition defenses surreptitiously.

"It's definitely a ship, Captain," Reed said. "I'm reading hull metal."

"Visual?" Archer asked.

"Coming up now, Captain," Reed said.

Archer faced the forward viewer, upon which a long, slender shape was already beginning to resolve itself, obviously with the help of a good deal of low-illumination image enhancement. Whatever this vessel customarily used for running lights had been either disabled through mishap or deliberately turned off.

Archer's frown deepened. "It's a ship, all right. She's either rigged for silent running, or else she's a derelict. I don't think I've ever seen that exact configuration before, though." He turned back toward the tactical station. "Malcolm?"

Reed was already studying something on his console that only he could see. "Already on it, sir."

The aft starboard turbolift doors hissed open and T'Pol stepped purposefully onto the bridge, a look of concern overlaid upon her otherwise stoic Vulcan features. Archer nodded to her in greeting, and she returned the gesture before becoming completely absorbed in the image that had just formed on the forward viewer.

"The ship configuration databanks recognize the design," Reed said, his eyes abruptly widening.

"And?" Archer said sharply, struggling with only partial success to subdue an intense surge of impatience.

"It's Klingon, Captain," T'Pol said calmly, beating the saucer-eyed tactical officer to the punch as she moved gingerly to one of the aft science consoles.

"Tactical alert," Archer said, and the bridge lighting dimmed automatically in response.

"For a Klingon ship, it doesn't look all that dangerous," Reed said, sounding surprised.

"Guess they can't all be battle cruisers," Travis said. "Even the Klingons must have freighters and tugs and garbage scows."

Archer nodded in agreement as he studied the image on the screen. Like the few Klingon battle cruisers he had encountered over the past few years, this vessel possessed a long, narrow midsection, which terminated on its forward end at a small oblong command-and-control structure that abutted a much wider aft section, to which a pair of engine nacelles were attached. Unlike those other vessels, however, this craft's hull seemed to display the wear of long, hard toil rather than the scars of combat, and was conspicuously bereft of overt weaponry.

"The vessel conforms to the general configuration of a *Hasparath*-class military cargo vessel," T'Pol said. "Two hundred thirty-seven meters in length, one hundred eleven meters at the beam. Mass of approximately two hundred thousand metric tons."

Archer nodded appreciatively. The other ship was nearly fifty meters longer than *Enterprise,* and considerably more massive. *Hell of a thing to just leave lying around,* he thought.

Speaking in clinical tones, T'Pol continued her report. "The vessel appears to have been modified to carry neutronic fuel and other volatile chemical compounds, judging from both the visible deviations from design norms and the vessel's sensor signature."

"Is she a derelict?" Archer asked. "Or is anyone alive aboard that ship?"

"Scanning," the Vulcan woman said. After a brief pause she said, "I'm picking up nearly four hundred strong lifesigns." She paused again as she raised an eyebrow and fixed her dark gaze upon Archer. "Predominantly *human.*"

Archer's jaw fell open involuntarily. "Humans. Operating a *Klingon* cargo ship. In Coalition space."

"And without a functioning navigation beam," Reed grumbled.

Anger drew Archer's mouth closed again, hardening his jaw like quick-drying thermoconcrete as he turned to stare at the enigmatic image on the viewer. "Hail that ship, Hoshi. T'Pol, assemble a boarding team. Travis, I want you to warm up Shuttlepod One."

He turned again, facing T'Pol while Hoshi busied herself signaling the other ship. "That ship's captain has got one hell of a lot of explaining to do," he said.

"Capture," Mayweather said, allowing himself to feel no small amount of relief as he heard the repressurization valve on Shuttlepod One's portside hatchway give a reassuring *whoomph.* "We've established a hard dock with the freighter."

"I've always hated that sound," said Lieutenant Reed,

who was seated directly behind Captain Archer's co-pilot's seat, to Mayweather's left. "It makes me expect to have to start sucking bloody vacuum at any moment."

"That, Malcolm," the captain said as he put the console before him into "safe" mode, "is only the sound of two mutually compatible airlocks making beautiful music together."

"Perhaps the airlocks ought to get a room, sir," Reed said quietly.

Mayweather turned in his seat and cast a sidelong glance at the aft portion of the shuttlepod's small crew cabin, where Chief Engineer Burch chuckled as he unhooked his flight harness. Reed nodded toward the captain as he unstrapped himself from his seat, checking the charge on his phase pistol as Burch and the two MACOs seated nearby did likewise before moving swiftly toward the hatch. Mayweather thought he saw the tactical officer suppressing a gratified smile as the ranking MACO trooper, Sergeant Fiona McKenzie, eyed the airlock with evident suspicion while the much younger and greener Corporal Matthew Kelly held his phase rifle in a white-knuckled death grip.

"Don't worry, guys," Burch said, evidently beating down an ironic grin of his own. "I packed a big roll of duct tape in my toolkit, just in case the airlocks decide to give us any real trouble."

"I suppose the airlocks would be one of the first things a human freighter captain would modify on a Klingon tub, Captain," Reed said, not sounding terribly reassured. "I just wish we'd brought the captain of this free-falling disaster aboard *Enterprise* instead of agreeing to come aboard *his* ship."

Archer shook his head. "You know as well as I do that it's standard Starfleet procedure to board and inspect any problem vessel we encounter, Malcolm," he said.

"And judging just from what I've seen so far, this bucket is a textbook example of a problem vessel."

"Fair enough, Captain," Reed said, raising his weapon to a ready position as the hatchway hissed open. "I just have a bad feeling about this ship."

Mayweather felt his ears pop slightly the moment the hatch cleared its seals, a sensation that punctuated the short-lived movement of a slight breeze as the small pressure differential between the shuttlepod and the freighter abruptly equalized. Having grown up on a freighter not so vastly different from this one, the sensation didn't trouble him in the least. As he followed the MACOs, Captain Archer, and Lieutenants Reed and Burch into the familiar narrowness of the gray, utilitarian corridor that lay beyond the shuttlepod's hatchway, he felt a pang of nostalgia that bordered on homesickness.

It's been way too long since I've been in touch with Mom and Paul and everybody else on the Horizon, he thought, drawing in a deep draft of the freighter's recycled, faintly metallic air. *I should at least get a letter off to them soon.*

"Where's the welcoming committee?" Archer asked, his phase pistol drawn and at the ready. The MACOs flanked him as he took the point—Mayweather knew he wouldn't have agreed to bring the troopers along had either of them insisted on taking the point—and moved steadily forward down the conduit-lined corridor toward a bend some ten meters distant.

"They knew we were coming," Mayweather said, his voice echoing along the otherwise silent corridor. Unlike the captain and Reed, he had left his weapon holstered, though he wasn't allowing his hand to venture far from its handle. Somewhat encumbered by the half-meter-long toolkit he carried, Burch had likewise left his phase pistol at his side.

"Maybe they're baking us a cake," Reed said with a weak smile.

The sound of multiple footfalls approaching from beyond the bend in the corridor prompted Mayweather finally to grasp his phase pistol and raise it defensively. Despite the results of Commander T'Pol's sensor scans, he half expected to bump into a group of angry Klingons at any moment.

Three figures suddenly strode into view.

"Halt!" McKenzie cried as both MACOs raised their weapons in a clear gesture of warning.

The trio, which consisted of two men and a woman—all apparently human—abruptly stopped in their tracks. Each of the three raised their hands, their faces displaying expressions of pure shock.

"Oh, crap," said the middle-aged Asian man who stood at the front of the trio, his colloquial speech belied by an accent worthy of an Oxford English Lit professor. "Looks like we've been boarded by bloody pirates again."

Mayweather nearly snickered out loud at this as he appraised the other man's ruffled white shirt, black buccaneer-style boots, and bright paisley-printed waist sash. All that was missing from the stereotypical image of an ancient Caribbean freebooter was an eye patch, a parrot perched on one shoulder, and perhaps a peg leg, though an open jug of rum and a hook hand would have been nice touches as well.

"Easy, Sergeant," Archer said to the female MACO. She nodded to her fellow trooper, and both took a step backward, their rifles lowered slightly. Mayweather continued holding on to his own weapon, as did Reed.

The captain holstered his phase pistol, took a step toward the olive-skinned Asian man, and extended his right hand. "Captain Jonathan Archer," he said. "Commanding the *Starship Enterprise*, from Earth."

"Captain Kojiro Vance," the man said, accepting Archer's handshake and flashing a brilliant, and apparently somewhat relieved, smile. "Master and commander of the merchant vessel *S.S. Kobayashi Maru,* based out of the port of Amber on Tau Ceti IV. Welcome aboard."

Archer released his grip on the other man's hand and took a moment to exchange introductions of the other members of the boarding team and Vance's officers, both of whom were clad in light blue jumpsuits more characteristic of flight engineers or other technical personnel than of pirates. Vance introduced the woman as Jacqueline Searles, his chief engineer, and the man as Arturo Stiles, his first mate.

Once the initial pleasantries were completed, Reed said, "We used our searchlights to read your hull markings and looked up your vessel in the Earth Cargo Service registry." From beneath a disapproving scowl he added, "The records show her as a Class-III neutronic fuel carrier, one presumably manufactured by an Earth firm or one of the Martian contractors."

"Imagine our surprise at discovering that she's actually a rehabilitated Klingon military freighter," Archer said.

Vance sighed, staring off at a bulkhead as he gathered his thoughts. "So you've noticed that," he said at length. "The port authorities tend to overlook such things in some of the more remote places. I suppose that's one of the advantages of adopting Tau Ceti IV as a home port, rather than carrying the flag of Earth or Alpha Centauri or Vulcan."

Or even Altair VI, for that matter, Mayweather thought, wondering if the still relatively new frontier settlement there had already acquired slightly too much law and order for the freighter captain's taste. The fact that Tau Ceti, whose human colonies lay about five light-years closer to Earth than did Altair, could allow someone like Vance to operate with impunity seemed to Mayweather a testimony to just how much work lay ahead for the nascent Coalition of Planets. Vance and his ship seemed to be an object lesson in how desperately the interstellar neighborhood needed the law and order the Coalition promised—including, apparently, those parts of the galaxy that were in Earth's backyard.

"What's your point, Captain Archer?" Searles asked, folding her arms defensively across her chest. The corners of her eyes crinkled as she frowned, revealing the subtle, scar-like lines characteristic of long-term exposure to low levels of delta radiation, which was still a common pitfall in the space freight business. Mayweather guessed she was probably ten to fifteen years younger than her apparent age, which might make her his contemporary.

"You don't think flying around in Coalition space in a *Klingon* ship is a problem?" Mayweather said, holstering his weapon. *No wonder these people prefer to ship out with their lights turned off,* he added silently.

Searles waved one of her hands dismissively. "Captain Vance has had the *Maru* retrofitted extensively since he acquired her. Except for her gross hull configuration, she's about as much a Klingon vessel as your *Enterprise* is."

Stiles, the fortyish jumpsuited man who stood at Vance's other side, spoke up in clipped, almost angry tones. "Thanks to those modifications, the *Maru* conforms to every regulation in the UESPA rulebook governing the equipment and capabilities of Class-III neutronic fuel carriers."

Vance nodded, looking pleased at the point his exec had just made. "For all intents and purposes she's precisely as advertised in your ship registry, as well as in our current ECS flight plan, and in our own logs: a

Class-III neutronic fuel carrier with eighty-one hands on board."

Archer raised an eyebrow. "Eighty-one? Our sensors picked up quite a few more lifesigns than that."

"In addition to the *Maru*'s crew, we're also carrying about three hundred colonists, engineers, and various other technical experts and tradespeople," Stiles added, thrusting his chin out in Archer's direction in a silent *so there* expression.

Vance nodded cheerfully. "All of them qualified, ready, and eager to carry the blessings of civilization to the farthest reaches of the galactic hinterlands. Where no man has gone before, as it were."

"Of course, you're welcome to verify all of that for yourselves if you're not content to take our word for it, Captain Archer," Stiles said in stilted tones.

Archer smiled humorlessly. "I'm afraid Starfleet doesn't give me the option of taking *anything* at face value, Mister Stiles. Especially not after we've found such a flagrant violation of ECS and UESPA navigational regs."

Vance once again looked confused. His expression would have been comical had the matter before him not been so very serious. "Come again, Captain?" he said.

"Captain Vance, *why* is this vessel running dark and silent?" Archer said.

Vance shifted his weight from one buccaneer-booted foot to the other in obvious discomfiture. At length, he said, "Lately we've been experiencing a few small . . . technical problems, Captain Archer. But it's nothing that Miz Searles can't handle. We're already well on our way to putting all of it to rights."

"Do you need any help?" Mayweather asked.

"We could use our grappler," said Burch. "Give you a tow to the port at Altai—"

"Thank you, but that won't be necessary," Vance said quickly, interrupting. "We've just had to shut down a few nonessential systems temporarily in order to make some . . . in-flight repairs."

Archer glowered. "Are you telling me that you consider something as basic as your navigation beam a 'nonessential' system?"

Though Vance looked no less uncomfortable than he had before, he now seemed to have no trouble returning Archer's glower. "Frankly, the only thing I consider truly essential, Captain Archer, is getting my ship back under way as quickly as possible. My passengers and cargo have to reach their destinations on time."

"And where might those destinations be?" Archer wanted to know.

"The first one on this voyage is the Gamma Hydra system," Vance said around an avaricious leer. "Those planets and most of the surrounding sector are extremely resource-rich, with huge deposits of everything from deuterium to pergium to the dilithium everybody's been so worried about running out of ever since the Coridan disaster. We're transporting a crew of mineral-extraction experts and other specialists to the outposts that have been popping up all over the vicinity over the past few years."

Gamma Hydra, Mayweather thought, recalling that the *Horizon* was scheduled to bring some technical and commercial cargo out to one of that sector's rapidly proliferating new outposts sometime in the not-too-distant future.

"Gamma Hydra," Archer repeated as he stroked his chin thoughtfully. "Judging from what I've heard, that's a pretty rough neighborhood."

"Meaning what?" Searles said.

"Meaning the Gamma Hydra sector is immediately

adjacent to space claimed by the Klingon Empire, Captain Vance," said Reed.

Archer nodded to Vance. "I'm pretty sure that the Klingons are every bit as interested as you are in developing the very same resources that you're salivating over."

Expecting Vance to start pushing back harder against Archer's increasingly challenging tone, Mayweather was surprised when the freighter captain merely threw his head back and laughed.

"My crew and I are probably responsible for a goodly number of those stories about dilithium-hungry Klingon raiders plundering the Gamma Hydra sector," Vance said after he'd finally gotten his breathing back under control. "Spreading those kinds of tales tends to encourage my competitors to drill their wells somewhat closer to the safe green hills of Earth, as it were. Which leaves more profits for me to spread around the fleshpots of Rigel X and Risa."

"I suppose plying your trade in a Klingon-built ship could lower your profile quite a bit out in places like Gamma Hydra," Reed said in a tone that suggested he was beginning to appreciate the other man's tactical instincts. "At least as far as any real, live Klingons you might bump into out there might be concerned—as long as they don't find out who's driving, that is."

"Very well reasoned, Lieutenant Reed," Vance said with an engaging smile. "Tell me, have you ever considered seeking your fortune in the private sector?"

"Captain Vance, I didn't come here to bring my crew to a job fair," Archer said, his voice edging into noticeable testiness.

Vance sighed again, then nodded. "No. I don't suppose that you did. In any case, we're not expecting a lot of trouble from the Klingons. At least not with the

United Earth government and its Coalition of Planets allies working so hard to protect Gamma Hydra from the Klingons with that 'Neutral Zone' idea—a no-man's-land that your Starfleet will no doubt defend with great ferocity once it's established."

Evidently losing patience with the topic of galactic politics, Archer said, "Captain, my immediate concern is defending Coalition space from *this* vessel."

"I'm sorry?" Vance said, his expression going abruptly blank.

"The *Kobayashi Maru* is a menace to navigation, Captain," Mayweather said.

Vance tipped his head to the side and blinked in evident bewilderment. "Beg pardon?" he said.

"Again . . . you're not using a navigation beam," Archer said, speaking with exaggerated slowness, like an Academy instructor trying to get through to a particularly thickheaded cadet.

"Or even a bloody night light," Reed added without smiling.

"Captain Vance already *explained* about all of that," Searles said, frowning and speaking with the same slow meter Archer had used. "I had to take the navbeam offline for a few hours, just for the duration of our other repairs."

"That's why I took the *Maru* somewhat off the beaten path, Captain Archer," Vance said, holding up a hand in an obvious effort to prevent Searles from aggravating Archer any further. "Out of consideration for any other vessels that might happen by while our trousers are still down, so to speak."

"How very considerate of you," said Archer.

Vance didn't appear to have noticed the jab. "On the other hand, space is bloody *huge*. I hardly think we're posing any serious danger to anyone, navbeam or no."

"Then humor us, Captain," Archer said. "And remember, the sooner we complete the inspection the regs require us to make, the sooner you can get back to carrying, as you put it, 'the blessings of civilization to the farthest reaches of the galactic hinterlands. Where no man has gone before, as it were.'"

Vance appeared to be making a careful study of Archer's expression, which was resolute. Then he spread his ruffle-fringed hands before him in an almost theatrical concession of defeat. "So be it," he said, turning and retracing his earlier steps down the corridor. "Follow me."

Mayweather found the nearly two-hour inspection tour both tedious and nostalgic. Tedious because there was precious little for a pilot to do while the more engineering-oriented portions of the inspection proceeded, and nostalgic because the freighter's interior, in which he found himself wandering, was so much like the one in which he had grown up.

He passed part of the time in a surprisingly congenial conversation with Arturo Stiles, who also had found himself with little to do for nearly two hours other than to hang around the freighter's crowded, ramshackle crew lounge, awaiting Mike Burch's detailed assessment of the freighter's condition.

"I tried getting into Starfleet once," Stiles said, leaning against a bulkhead near one of the battered coffeemakers, from which he had just poured himself a full cup. "Couldn't quite pass the physical, though." His tone sounded vaguely resentful of the fact, though he offered no further explanation.

"I'm sorry," Mayweather said, his elbows resting on a dull stainless steel table as he sipped at a cup of coffee that tasted as though it once might have been used to cool old-style plutonium fuel rods. He felt stupid that he hadn't been able to come up with anything better to say.

"I'm from a Starfleet family, though," Stiles continued, apparently unfazed by Mayweather's well-intentioned gaffe. "I have a niece who's just earned her lieutenant's commission, a grand-nephew who's a freshly minted ensign, and a couple of cousins who made it as far as lieutenant commander. At least one of 'em's bound to make captain sooner or later."

"You must be very proud," Mayweather said, pushing the nasty-tasting coffee to one side, taking care not to spill any lest it eat through the table, the deck, and the *Maru*'s ventral hull.

Stiles chuckled mirthlessly, then looked around as though to make sure he wouldn't be overheard by any of his shipmates. "I'm just glad I can take pride in *something* while I'm serving aboard this tub."

While Stiles was speaking, a small group of men and women brushed past Mayweather's table on their way to the freighter's self-service galley area. Most of them looked somewhat weather-beaten, though they all seemed strong and fit, fairly radiating both confidence and competence. As Mayweather quietly watched them going about their meals—they all seemed to be doing their best to avoid any contact with the Starfleet intruders who had temporarily disrupted their ship's routine—he reflected that these people represented the true cutting edge of the permanent expansion of humanity's presence throughout the galaxy. This crew reminded him of the stories his late father had told him of the hardy professional survivors whose livelihoods had required them to drive incredibly heavy multiaxle trucks over the treacherous ice roads of the remote Alaskan wilderness. Like those survivors, these people were the strong backbone of the human species' ongoing effort to make a permanent mark on the eternal stars themselves.

Pioneers, as it were, on a wagon train to the stars.

"So you're bound for Gamma Hydra next," he said, turning back toward Stiles in the hopes of directing the conversation toward a happier topic than career regrets.

Stiles nodded. "If we ever get this inspection business out of the way so we can finish our repairs."

Mayweather tried to defuse the thinly veiled complaint with more small talk. "You know, my family's in the interstellar hauling trade, too, working with the Earth Cargo Service. I was born on a freighter, in fact."

Stiles chuckled around a sip of his own coffee. "Ah. A Boomer, huh?"

"Better believe it," Mayweather said, grinning. "The family is still doing business in the ship I was born in. That boat has to be at least as old as this one. In fact, family legend has it that the inside of her warp casing was autographed by Zefram Cochrane himself."

"Get outta town," the other man said in an almost bantering tone.

Mayweather grinned. "That's Mom's story, and she's sticking to it. Anyway, the family freighter has a few stops in the Gamma Hydra sector planned for the near future."

"Really? What's the ship's name?" Stiles asked, sounding genuinely interested.

"The *Horizon*."

Stiles's eyebrows rose in surprise. "It's a small galaxy, Ensign. The *Horizon*'s scheduled to make a cargo pickup from us when we get to Gamma Hydra."

Mayweather didn't try to conceal his delight in hearing that. His grin broadening involuntarily, he said, "Do you think I could trouble you to deliver some personal mail to Rianna and Paul Mayweather, care of the *E.C.S. Horizon*?"

Stiles shrugged. "I don't see why not. Assuming we can get there in time to make the rendezvous, that is." He rapped his knuckles against the bulkhead, and the sound made hollow echoes throughout the somewhat squalid crew lounge. The earlier curtain of glumness abruptly descended once again over the first mate's demeanor.

Once again at a loss for a satisfactory reply, Mayweather felt relieved when Captain Archer, Captain Vance, Lieutenant Burch, and Jacqueline Searles chose that moment to step into the room, followed by Lieutenant Reed and the two MACOs.

Burch wasted no time handing Stiles a small padd, which the first mate studied with a steadily lengthening face.

"Here's a copy of my report, Mister Stiles," Burch said as he pushed a pair of old-style reading glasses onto the thatch of graying blond hair at the top of his head. "As I've already explained to Captain Vance, this vessel is going to need some serious repairs before she's back up to UESPA code." Burch shook his head. "Don't ask me what's been holding your life-support system together."

"Clean living and noble intentions, for the most part," Vance said, looking vaguely dyspeptic. "The repairs will be expensive ones, no doubt."

"No doubt," Burch said. "You've either just flown this ship through the flames of hell and back, or else you've been deferring your major maintenance problems and ignoring component-replacement issues for years."

Vance responded with a noncommittal smile. "Let's just say that the vicissitudes of interstellar trade have lately placed some severe limitations on my ability to keep this vessel in factory condition. And all the uncertainty and confusion surrounding the formation of the new Coalition hasn't helped matters any."

Archer's brow furrowed. " 'Uncertainty and confusion,' Captain? It's funny how law and order can make everything look uncertain and confusing. Particularly when you've gotten used to making a living in the *absence* of law and order, that is."

Vance's smile grew ironic. "A pity you weren't here to explain the newly lawful and orderly status quo to the Orions and the Nausicaans. Particularly the last few times they decided to deprive me of my cargo."

Vance's earlier reference to the pleasure worlds he favored when his vessel was at liberty sprang abruptly into Mayweather's mind. Having lived in space all his life, he understood better than most that the interstellar hauling trade favored neither the lazy nor the libertine, though he also knew that brains counted for at least as much as hard work did. And he could see that this self-styled pirate was certainly not lacking in brains. *Maybe if he spent more time working and less time partying,* he thought, *he'd be able to afford to keep his ship from falling apart around his ears.*

"We can tow you back to one of the drydock facilities at Altair VI in just a few hours, Captain," Burch said.

"And I'm to pay for their services with *what*, Lieutenant?" Vance said, sounding angry now that his embarrassing state of financial disarray had at last been laid totally bare. "My credit with the Altair VI port authority is, shall we say, less than sterling at the moment. My cargo is already spoken for, so I can't simply trade it away. Besides, the fine, upstanding citizens of Darro-Miller will want hard currency, and I won't be flush again until after the *Maru*'s current voyage concludes."

"In the state she's in right now, Captain, the *Maru's* voyage is *already* over," Burch said. "I'm sorry."

Though Vance looked deflated, his tendency toward bravado hadn't deserted him entirely. Addressing Archer, he said, "You wouldn't be interested in floating us a temporary loan, would you?"

Except for the faint clatter of metal forks against lightweight aerogel plates, a sudden hush blanketed the room. The crewmen and technicians who were eating at the tables along the opposite wall made a show of ignoring the tableau, though they had to have heard every word. Stiles looked like he wanted nothing more than simply to crawl away somewhere and die with whatever slender shreds of dignity remained to him. Mayweather felt intense embarrassment for the first mate, as well as for his captain.

Archer was the first to disturb the extended silence. "I'm afraid I can't lend you any money, Captain Vance."

Vance now looked utterly defeated. "Then please don't neglect to scuttle us before you get under way for your next assignment," he said very quietly.

"But since the regs require me to render aid to all vessels in distress," Archer continued, "I'll lend you something more valuable than money: my chief engineer and his staff."

"Sir?" Burch said, obviously as surprised as Mayweather was. Reed, Vance, Stiles, and Searles all looked poleaxed as well, and even the two usually impassive MACOs exchanged quiet sidelong glances.

"How much time do you need to get the *Kobayashi Maru* back under way?" Archer asked the engineer.

Burch answered without hesitation. "Forty-eight hours, max."

"Then get busy, Lieutenant. Give T'Pol a list of whatever personnel and matériel you think you're going to need."

"Yes, sir," Burch said, grinning as he contemplated the no doubt unusual challenges that awaited him. Mayweather hoped for his sake that his repair-time estimates would prove as reliable as those his predecessor used to make. After all, as good as Burch had so far proved himself to be, he wasn't Commander Tucker.

Nobody *is at the moment,* Mayweather thought with a profound sense of sadness.

After directing Lieutenant Reed and the MACOs to remain aboard to keep an eye on things, Archer moved toward the lounge's raised hatchway. "Let's head back to *Enterprise,* Travis. I want to get this job expedited so we can get back to chasing *real* pirates just as soon as humanly possible."

"Can never get enough of *that,* Captain," Mayweather said, grinning as he followed Archer into the corridor that led back to the section of the *Kobayashi Maru* to which Shuttlepod One was docked. As they walked, he contemplated still more endless hours of patrolling, watching, and waiting. And the interval that would precede the resumption of those monotonous tasks.

Forty-eight hours. Two days.

Plenty of time to dash off a few handwritten letters home before the *Maru* resumed her voyage toward Gamma Hydra, and a rendezvous with the *Horizon.*

SEVEN

Day Thirty, Month of K'ri'Brax
Dartha City, Romulus

THE LIGHTS SUDDENLY WENT OUT, throwing the entire lab into stygian darkness. Trip knew that the facility had its own emergency backup power systems—which should have kicked in on their own the minute the main power circuits were interrupted—so he was immediately suspicious. His pupils struggled to cope with the night's abrupt intrusion.

Though he was still effectively blinded, his artificially pointed ears nevertheless identified the nearby sound of metal clicking against metal.

A disruptor pistol's safety catch.

"Ehrehin, get down!" Trip shouted.

In the same breath, he tackled the elderly scientist, hoping that the more-than-human strength inherent to Vulcans and their genetic offshoots would keep the old man from suffering a bad fracture when he hit the floor.

Breaking a hip is still a lot better than taking a disruptor blast, he thought as both men's bodies slammed against the unyielding tile floor behind one of the lab's massive bookcases. The transitory brilliance of an energy blast singed the hairs on Trip's neck in the split second before he'd moved out of the immediate line of fire.

That was way *too close,* he thought amid the acrid stench of ozone and fear. He struggled to catch his breath and get his bearings.

"Cunaehr!" The old man could barely wheeze Trip's Romulan cover name, his lungs just having been forcibly and suddenly emptied. But at least he had eluded the assassin's disruptor beam.

For the moment, at least.

"Stay down, Doctor," Trip whispered. "And keep quiet." He hauled himself up onto his elbows, cautiously surveying what little he could see of the lab's work area in an attempt to pinpoint the would-be killer's location.

Then he heard the gentle rustle of something moving beyond the sturdy desk behind which he and the old man had taken refuge. The sound seemed to have come from somewhere near the lab's rear exit. Another muffled noise came from the opposite side of the room. Though his heart raced like a reactor core about to go critical, Trip tried to remain absolutely still.

Shit. At least two of 'em are in here with us.

"Are you armed, Cunaehr?" Ehrehin said quietly, a fearful quaver in his voice.

"Don't talk anymore," Trip whispered back, ignoring the question. Though he didn't, in fact, have an effective weapon within handy reach, he didn't want to admit it out loud. Keeping the bad guys guessing about things like that was always the best policy in this sort of situation.

"Stay here," Trip whispered directly into Ehrehin's ear. Despite the darkness, he was close enough to Ehrehin to see that the old man was beside himself, owl-eyed with commingled fear and outrage.

Trip heard another noise coming from the front of the lab, the direction from which the disruptor bolt had originated. Someone's feet moved slowly and stealthily forward. No one was visible as yet behind the farrago of tables, desks, bookcases, and computer terminals scattered about the room, so the shooter had to be crouching, keeping his profile low.

Taking his cue from the intruders, Trip slowly—and quietly—combat-crawled toward the source of the intermittent sound before him. A moment later, another disruptor blast cleaved the air above him, at perhaps chest level.

Trip grinned as he imagined a pair—he hoped it was only a pair—of assassins, hunkered down on the floor much as he was, at opposite sides of the lab. *They don't know exactly where to shoot just yet. And they have to fire high to protect each other.* He wondered whether the assassins' tactics implied that they lacked night-vision equipment, or were merely displaying an overabundance of caution.

As he inched forward toward the edge of a storage cabinet, Trip's hand brushed against a padd that he'd evidently knocked to the floor when he'd tackled Ehrehin. He picked it up and felt its reassuring heft. It was solid, square, and not too badly balanced. Taking care to remain silent, Trip rose to a crouch, clutching the little device nearly hard enough to shatter it.

More motion, this time coming from the right side in his peripheral vision. Without thinking, he turned and hurled the padd with every ounce of strength he could muster. Moving from a crouch to a full run, he wasted no time chasing the object he'd thrown, shouting as he executed a flying tackle on the source of the movement.

He landed hard and found himself lying directly atop a supine humanoid body—one that was very much alive and struggling. As he tried to grab and restrain his assailant's wrists, he realized his adversary was female.

And as strong as the proverbial ox.

The Romulan woman sat up abruptly in spite of his

strenuous attempt to pin her shoulders to the floor, and forced him relentlessly sideways and onto his back. Hot liquid dripped from her face onto his. He realized it was most likely blood; the missile he'd thrown must have split her lip open, or perhaps clipped her in some other part of the head or face. *Just nowhere near hard enough,* he thought as she kept pushing him steadily backward and downward in spite of his best efforts to push in the opposite direction.

The room's scant illumination gleamed at the threshold of visibility against the disruptor pistol she still clutched in her right hand—and whose barrel he saw she was trying to point directly at his head. His arms trembled with exertion as he tried to push back against her and keep the weapon away, succeeding only in slowing its inexorable progress toward him. He remembered his bureau colleague, a deep cover field agent named Tinh Hoc Phuong, who'd been killed elsewhere in Romulan space by a blast from a nearly identical weapon. He forced that horrific recollection aside with an absurd transient thought about T'Pol, and how much fun an encounter like this might be in an entirely different context. If, that is, he ever got to see her again.

Trip felt as though he were in an arm-wrestling contest with a piece of farm machinery. His biceps, triceps, and forearms quivered as fatigue toxins began to accumulate in his tissues. He knew he was getting tired out. And that she wasn't. Though he probably outweighed her by more than a few kilos, she nevertheless seemed to be at least marginally stronger than he was, no matter how much effort he expended. And in terms of endurance she appeared to have him flat-out beaten. He was uncomfortably aware that even the most marginal advantage in a contest like this could end it quickly and decisively in favor of the least exhausted opponent.

Unless he changed the rules of the game, and damned quickly.

A number of small, hard objects clattered to the lab's floor, presumably after having fallen from some pocket in the woman's dark, formfitting garment. Taking full advantage of the momentary distraction, Trip suddenly stopped resisting her efforts to push him backward. Her disruptor hand swung directly toward Trip's face, overshooting it before she could press the trigger even as both combatants abruptly crashed to the floor.

He exploited her surprised state further by delivering a savage head butt. She dropped her weapon, though he couldn't immediately see where it had fallen. He breathed a silent "thank you" to Adigeon Prime's avian plastic surgeons for the durable cranial implants they'd installed in his forehead when they'd altered his appearance to enable him to pass as a Romulan.

The woman shook her head, dazed, but nevertheless tried to get her feet back under her. Rising to a crouch, Trip responded with a rabbit punch and a hard right cross in rapid succession, both of which landed squarely upon the Romulan woman's face.

She fell back to the floor hard, apparently unconscious.

Trip knelt to feel about on the floor for the woman's fallen disruptor, but found only a handful of data chips, apparently the objects she had dropped just before losing her weapon.

These two didn't come here just to kill Ehrehin, he thought, realization dawning on him. *They wanted to steal Ehrehin's files after getting rid of us.*

But there was no time at the moment to consider their assailants' motivations, or on whose behalf they might be acting. He groped about the dark floor for a few agonizingly long moments until he found the assassin's pistol, which he immediately snatched up and brought before him in a two-handed combat grip.

The other one isn't on top of me already, Trip thought. *Which has to mean that he* doesn't *have night-sight gear, same as his partner.*

Which also meant that these people most likely weren't career military personnel. They were acting on behalf of passion or politics, or perhaps simple greed.

Trip heard the sibilance of another disruptor blast, accompanied by a momentary nimbus of light that originated from the opposite side of the room. He caught sight of the shooter's silhouette and took aim just as another searing bolt of energy tore through the cabinet beside him, reducing it to a collapsing heap of burning shards. He hit the floor in a diving shoulder roll, hanging on to the disruptor pistol like the precious lifeline it had become. He rolled up into a crouch and kicked over one of the worktables before him, sending a computer terminal and several stacks of paper flying. He immediately opened fire from behind the cover he'd just created.

Trip's weapon illuminated the room just long enough to confirm that he had indeed hit his target, taking the shooter full in the chest. He ran to a control pad that was mounted on a nearby wall and quickly activated the lab's emergency backup lights.

A voice croaked weakly from somewhere behind him, down low. "Cunaehr."

"Sit tight, Doctor," Trip said as he hastened to disarm both attackers, confirming their condition in the process. The man he'd just shot sported a disruptor burn that had thoroughly cooked every organ in his chest, killing him instantly. *Damn these bastards for not believing in the "stun" setting,* he thought, not for the first time since his arrival in Romulan space. Although he knew full well that the gunman had left him little choice, he nevertheless couldn't deny the guilt he felt in situations like this one.

The woman, however, was only unconscious, not dead.

"Cunaehr," Ehrehin repeated, far more weakly this time. Trip rushed to the old man's side.

"You're going to be all right, Doctor," Trip said as he knelt on the debris-littered floor not far from the spot where he'd left Ehrehin. He blanched as he noted that the old man was anything *but* all right, but he did his best not to display his feelings of shock and fear.

"I'm sorry, Cunaehr," Ehrehin said, wincing as he cradled the badly burned right side of his torso. "I'm afraid I didn't follow your advice about staying down. I got up to trigger the silent security alarm."

Trip tucked the disruptor into his belt. Very gently, he helped the old man into a more comfortable-looking, half-reclined position up against the leg of one of the lab tables. Ehrehin's charred tunic was stained emerald with blood.

"I'll call for the medics, Doctor," Trip said, rising to his feet.

"They'll never get here in time," Ehrehin said, shaking his head and coughing. Sea-green froth bubbled at his lips. "Promise me something, Cunaehr."

Trip knelt again beside the old man and took his frail hand in a gentle two-handed grip. "Anything."

"Don't let Valdore finish this project."

Tears stung Trip's eyes. "Of course."

"And you can't let the *Ejhoi Ormiin* have it, either."

Trip frowned. The *Ejhoi Ormiin* was the Romulan dissident group from which Trip had recently helped rescue Ehrehin. Phuong had died on that mission. The *Ejhoi Ormiin* wanted to prevent Admiral Valdore from indulging in his imperial ambitions by stealing the warp-seven drive project that Ehrehin had undertaken on behalf of the Romulan military.

The only problem with the dissidents' plan was that they intended to keep the secrets of the revolutionary new stardrive for themselves—presumably to fulfill their *own* imperial ambitions. And what those ambitions were was anybody's guess, given that their leader was a murderous Vulcan turncoat known alternatively as Sopek or Ch'uihv.

"You think the *Ejhoi Ormiin* had something to do with this?" Trip asked.

"Who else?" The voice was barely audible.

Trip had to admit that that was a damned fine question, one to which he could provide no easy answer.

The life was beginning to fade from the old man's rheumy eyes. "Cunaehr," he whispered. "Trip."

The old man had made it his habit *never* to use Trip's real name, even though he had discovered it very early in their association.

"Yes," Trip said.

"Everything . . . everything is up to you now."

Trip felt Ehrehin's hand go slack at that moment. The old man's final breath came a heartbeat later, laced with green bubbles as his lungs emptied for the last time.

A crushing weight of responsibility settled squarely upon Trip's shoulders. Whether war or peace came in the next few weeks might well depend on whatever he decided to do, or not to do, next.

Moving with extreme care, Trip lowered Ehrehin's body back to the floor from where it leaned limply against the table leg. Tears shrouded the old man's image as he knelt beside him and took his hand for the last time. They had indeed become close, particularly since Ehrehin had saved his life at the *Ejhoi Ormiin* compound on Rator II, and had helped him find a place in Romulan society after their chaotic escape. The old man's motivations had never been entirely clear to Trip—Ehrehin was certainly no Coalition sympathizer, despite his strong advocacy for peace—but Trip's resemblance to the late Cunaehr might have been a factor. As well as Ehrehin's respect for Trip's talents as an engineer.

After an uncountable interval, Trip released Ehrehin's hand. Anger brought him to his feet and he stalked back to the front of the lab, where the surviving assassin still lay unconscious. Reaching down to grasp the lapels on the front of her black jacket, he hauled her up roughly.

"Why did you do this?" he shouted into her slack face. "Who do you work for?" She made no response, and her body lolled before him like a rag doll. Dark green blood slowly trickled down her lightly ridged forehead, which sported a nasty gash, as well as from her split lower lip. He saw that she was still breathing and briefly considered remedying that before dismissing the thought in horrified disgust.

Crap. Maybe I am *going native,* he thought with an inward shudder.

The lab's front and rear doors suddenly crashed open nearly simultaneously, admitting at least half a dozen uniformed and helmeted Romulan military troopers, each of whom carried disruptor pistols, several of which were being pointed directly at Trip.

"This woman is a saboteur," Trip said, suddenly feeling oddly detached both from his emotions and his body. Numbly, he realized that this must be what pure shock feels like. "She's still alive," he continued. "Her partner murdered Doctor Ehrehin. I had to kill the shooter, or he would've burned me down next."

One of the soldiers who had evidently come in

through the rear of the lab shouted a terse confirmation of Trip's report. Then another one, a broad-shouldered, dour-faced man whose uniform baldric bore the single wedge-shaped insignia that denoted the rank of centurion, separated himself from his fellows and approached Trip closely.

"Set the woman down," he said in a deep and dangerous-sounding voice. "Carefully."

Despite the weapons that were directed at him, and the centurion's obvious authority, Trip was unimpressed. He continued clutching the front of the unconscious woman's garment in both hands. "Just who the hell are you?" he demanded.

The centurion's tone was surprisingly patient. "Terix. Centurion of Admiral Valdore's Fifth Legion, in the service of our glorious Praetor D'deridex. And just who in Erebus are *you*?"

Trip began to realize that he was not only in a crime scene, but also that he was challenging a phalanx of armed and perhaps trigger-happy Romulan military personnel, none of whom had reason to deal gently with defiance or disrespect. And he was doing all this while operating behind enemy lines under an assumed identity.

Stupid, he told himself.

"Cunaehr," Trip said quietly, having regained enough presence of mind to avoid blurting out his real name. "Doctor Ehrehin's chief assistant."

Terix laid a large gauntleted hand on Trip's shoulder, the apparent gentleness of the gesture only barely concealing a grip of hard, cold steel. "We will take charge of this . . . perpetrator now, Cunaehr," the centurion said.

"I think this woman and her partner were working for the *Ejhoi Ormiin*," Trip said, not yet quite able to will his arms to move or his hands to open. "They wanted to take for themselves the new stardrive we've been developing for Admiral Valdore. And they wanted to make sure that Doctor Ehrehin couldn't re-create it later."

Trip realized that they had succeeded, at least, in the latter goal. It also dawned on him that they had accomplished one of the objectives of the bureau that had sent him here to Romulus, using means that probably wouldn't have much bothered the spymaster Harris, and probably would have made Captain Stillwell do a football quarterback's end-zone victory dance.

Except, of course, for the fact that Trip hadn't managed to seize a working warp-seven drive for Earth and the Coalition. Without the brilliance of Doctor Ehrehin on tap, the likelihood of that eventuality coming to pass now seemed vanishingly small, his own engineering skills notwithstanding; while Trip had tremendous faith in his own abilities, he harbored no delusions of being Ehrehin's peer.

"Let *us* take charge of the prisoner now, Cunaehr," Terix repeated. "We will interrogate her thoroughly about her ties to any political dissident groups." Although Trip still could hear something like compassion and sympathy in Terix's voice, the centurion's grip on his shoulder felt progressively more stern with each passing second.

Trip nodded, then allowed a pair of Terix's troopers to take the unconscious woman from his nerveless hands.

"Do not worry," Terix said as the troopers carried the woman away and began securing the room as a crime scene. "You may continue Doctor Ehrehin's work secure in the knowledge that he will be avenged."

Continue Ehrehin's work, Trip thought, aghast but trying desperately not to show it. *Work that Admiral Valdore expects to produce a working warp-seven stardrive soon. So that Praetor D'deridex can grab even more new elbow room for his galactic empire.*

Trip Tucker had never before felt more alone and isolated than he did at this very moment. Only now was he beginning to understand, in a deep, visceral way, just how dependent he had become upon Ehrehin, not only for the accomplishment of his mission on behalf of Earth and the Coalition, but also for simple survival in such a strange, faraway land.

Long before he had allowed circumstance to sweep him into the spy trade, all Trip had ever wanted to do was to be an engineer. For the first time in his career, he wished he'd never picked up a tool, never gone into space, served on a starship, or so much as laid eyes on the Starfleet Charter.

Particularly Article Fourteen, Section Thirty-one.

Day Thirty, Month of K'ri'Brax
The Hall of State, Dartha, Romulus

The intercom on the desk buzzed in a broken tone that denoted an incoming communication from a particular source. Chief Technologist Nijil placed the secured privacy earpiece carefully into his right ear before opening up the channel.

"Go ahead."

"The deed has been done," said the deep but flat voice on the line's other end.

A triumphant smile slowly began to spread across Nijil's vulpine features.

"There has, however," the voice continued guardedly, *"been a slight complication. . . ."*

EIGHT

Tuesday, July 15, 2155
E.C.S. Horizon, **Gamma Hydra Sector**

PAUL MAYWEATHER HEARD the noise of the creaking deck plates behind him as it rose slightly above the background buzz of the ancient freighter's computers and air-circulation fans. Turning toward the familiar sound, he watched as his mother and chief engineer, Rianna Mayweather, approached the middle of the aft section of the small hexagonal bridge that she had always insisted on describing as "cozy" rather than "cramped."

Gesturing toward the image of the uncannily Earth-like globe that turned slowly on the bridge's large forward viewer, she said, "The people down there really surprised me."

"I'm just happy they turned out to be friendly and willing to deal with us," Paul said.

Rianna nodded. "Of course. But isn't it amazing how quickly they picked up English?"

"I thought that was pretty remarkable, too," said Charlie Nichols, who seemed delighted to be back behind his helm console after his brief sojourn dirtside. He looked happy to hear that the last few repairs had finally been completed, no doubt because he was raring to perpetrate yet another one of the sudden, kidney-damaging lurches directly from space-normal speed to warp two for which he was so renowned.

Paul nodded silently in response to the observations of

his mother and the helmsman before facing forward again to study the stately turning of the blue-and-white-streaked world on which he and the *Horizon*'s crew had just completed the bulk of their emergency repairs. He had to admit that the natives' facility for languages was remarkable, if indeed they had been telling the truth about never before having played host to a visiting Earth vessel.

But even more remarkable was the lucky happenstance that this world's barely industrial-age inhabitants had been able to furnish sufficient supplies of the metals and organic polymer precursors necessary to allow Mom, Nora, and Juan to get the *Horizon*'s propulsion system up and running again after that damned micro-meteoroid swarm had crippled the *Horizon*'s aging Bussard collectors and navigational deflectors.

Juan Marquez and Nora Melchior, who served in the freighter's small merchant crew as junior engineer and Jill-of-all-trades respectively, were in the process of replacing a burned-out navigation sensor module in one of the starboard consoles. Although they'd seemed utterly absorbed in their work, they both evidently had been following the desultory conversation every bit as closely as Paul had done.

"I'll grant you that they're quick learners," Nora said, grunting as she strained to free a slightly balky hydro-spanner from the awkward tight space between consoles into which she'd gotten it stuck. "But none of the natives I dealt with seemed all that big on original thinking."

"I don't know about that," Juan said. Paul quietly watched as the junior engineer looked askance at Nora's handling of the spanner, as though expecting it to come flying out at any moment, like Excalibur suddenly freed from the stone. "Sure, they seemed a bit imitative, but that probably just reflects their method of absorbing new languages."

Nora grimaced as she put more of her weight into the task of trying to extract the spanner from where it had become lodged. "Maybe," she said. "Maybe not. It might be fun to come back here in twenty years," she said, pausing momentarily to grunt with another burst of futile effort to extract the spanner, "to see if they've started trying to build their own J-type interstellar freighters."

Rianna folded her arms and shook her head skeptically. "They're still trying to get a handle on steam technology, Nora. I wouldn't expect them to get anything off the ground for at least another hundred years or so."

"Probably true," Juan said, his dark eyes still riveted to Nora's trapped spanner. "Careful with that thing, Nora," he said, his expression showing vicarious pain for the abused tool. "You're gonna break it if you're not careful."

"Helping is good, Juan," Nora said, scowling slightly as she continued fruitlessly coaxing the stubborn instrument. Her tongue was sticking out of the corner of her mouth as she worked. "Kibitzing, not so much."

Juan shrugged and looked toward Paul and Rianna, perhaps to avert his eyes from Nora's flagrant abuse of the innocent spanner. "Anyhow, the natives really didn't seem nearly as interested in that sort of thing as they were in the cultural stuff, anyway."

Paul couldn't help but agree with Juan, though he thought that Nora definitely had a point as well. In fact, he had already characterized the natives as very bright and imitative people in the log he had recorded for later transmission to Earth Cargo Service Central. Even in the merchant service, which arguably made more of an imprint on the galactic neighborhood than did Starfleet, detailed reports about all first contact situations were a regulation-required necessity. It made no sense to allow the next Earth ship that happened by this world to rediscover these people purely by accident.

"I'm still just happy that they seemed so eager to help out a bunch of stranded strangers," Paul said. Had the *Horizon* been forced down in more hostile surroundings, the outcome of their just-concluded adventure might have turned out far less happily.

"Don't forget that they expected to be paid for the stuff we needed," said Rianna, her gaze locked on her younger son's. "I think their cultural leanings saved our asses at least as much as their sense of altruism. We're just damned lucky they were willing to accept some of the stuff we were carrying in the hold. What exactly did you give them, anyway?"

Paul chuckled quietly. "A few of the vintage amusement items from Earth that I was hoping would pay most of the bills during that stopover we have coming up at Denobula Triaxa."

Rianna's eyes narrowed. "Which 'vintage amusement items' are you talking about?" she asked in a voice that seemed to lower the ambient temperature by at least a good two degrees Celsius. Paul could only hope that he hadn't accidentally traded away any of Mom's favorite nifties in his haste to acquire the materials the crew needed to get the *Horizon* back under way.

He concentrated for a moment, staring off at a bulkhead as he assembled a brief mental inventory. "Analog music recordings pressed on vinyl disks," he said sheepishly. "Along with a couple of old hand-cranked players. Some flatvid movies recorded on celluloid, and a projector. A mechanical arcade game I think they used to call a 'pinball machine.' Oh, and a couple of boxes of books."

Her eyes narrowed further still. "*Which* books?" she said, her tone evoking childhood memories of the moments immediately preceding the occasional "time outs" he'd had to spend alone in one of the empty cargo holds.

Wait *a minute now,* he told himself. *Since Dad died, she's* my *chief engineer. Which makes me* her *captain.* It was damned difficult to remember that at times like this.

Paul felt nothing but gratitude for Nora's spanner when it chose that moment to come free, its gripping surfaces apparently shattering in the process.

"Told you," Juan said, shaking his head.

"Oh, be quiet," Nora muttered as she knelt to pick up the little bits of hydrospanner that now lay scattered about the deck.

"Never mind us," Juan said, addressing Paul. "In spite of appearances, I think we're actually ready to shove off whenever you give the word."

Couldn't have timed it better myself, Paul thought as he turned toward the man who sat fidgeting impatiently behind the helm, awaiting the order to break orbit.

"Set us on a course for Gamma Hydra, Charlie. Warp two. Take us out when you're ready. And try not to shake our fillings loose this time."

Charlie grinned. "Aye, aye, Cap'n," he said, then immediately began updating the navcomputer with his left hand while entering velocity data with his right.

Rianna began moving toward the open archway at the aft part of the bridge. "If we're heading out now, I'd better keep an eye on my babies down in the engine room."

"Find something to hang on to," Paul said to her departing back.

"Just remember," she said over her shoulder. "If I find out you gave away my big book about old-time Chicago, I'm gonna make you walk the plank." And with that she disappeared into the access corridor behind the bridge.

"The Chicago book," Nora said, now apparently done

clearing away the mess she'd made and discreetly disposing of the wreckage. "Wasn't that the big old white hardcover that the village elder fell in love with?"

Oh, crap. Paul swallowed hard. He wasn't sure, but that book—which told the story of a crucial time in the history of Mom's hometown—just *might* have gone out with the trade goods that circumstances had forced him to sacrifice. He hoped that Travis still had *his* copy of the book with him in his billet aboard *Enterprise*.

And that he would be willing to rush it over to the *Horizon* on short notice to save his little brother's life.

"Hang on to your butts," Charlie said. A moment later he pushed the throttle forward.

Paul grabbed the back of the big chair in the center of the busy little control area as the *Horizon* lurched into motion. The freighter's forward surge launched squadrons of butterflies deep in his guts, but they flew only for the split second it took for the inertial damping system to catch up to the warp drive's sudden burst of superluminal acceleration. The blue-and-white world on the viewer immediately shrank to a small pinpoint of light before losing itself amid the myriads of other celestial fires scattered throughout the boundless interstellar deeps like so many grains of sand on a beach.

The ship roared and rattled, but held together. Charlie grinned up at him from the helm. "Warp one point six. One point seven. One point eight. One point nine.

"Warp two."

The rattling and shaking gradually evened out, and after a seeming eternity Paul realized that he had been holding his breath. He released it in a great relieved rush.

"You're gonna get it," Nora said, shaking her head gently at Paul.

"Come again?" he said.

"Your mom's book, remember? Since we didn't get

vaporized in a warp core breach just now, you're going to have to deal with that."

He nodded glumly before pushing that problem off to one side. "We'll just have to find a way to divert that particular asteroid before it hits us."

Nora grinned mischievously. " 'We'? 'Us'?"

He sighed. "All right. It's *my* problem. Yours is transmitting my first contact report to ECS Central."

"I'm all over it, Skipper," she said, turning toward the port communications console.

"Please don't call me that," he muttered under his breath, sighing as he sent the log files from his chair console to Nora's station.

"Message transmitted to ECS Central," Nora reported a few moments later.

"No, it isn't," Juan said.

"What are you talking about?" Nora said, scowling. "My console shows the message as sent."

Paul walked over to Nora's station and confirmed that fact with a glance.

"True enough," said Juan, who was staring at the com interface from the opposite side. "But look at the frequency bands the transmitter used."

"Hell," Nora said. "I didn't tell the damned thing to use the snail channel."

"Looks like the transmitter's subspace capabilities must have gone down," Juan said with a cool, appraising nod, his hitch aboard the *Horizon* evidently having inoculated him against finding any sort of technological glitch surprising. He turned toward Paul. "The computer must have automatically enabled the regular EM radio antenna as a backup. So ECS Central isn't going to receive *that* transmission for over a century, Jefe."

"You know, I think I like 'Jefe' even less than I like 'Skipper,' " Paul said.

"Sorry, boss," Juan said as he returned to scrutinizing the com console. Paul wasn't sure whether he was talking about the title or the balky transmitter.

Regardless, he knew there was no point in chewing anyone out over this little setback. After all, virtually instantaneous interstellar communication via the subspace bands was still a relatively recent innovation, at least for humans, and therefore wasn't yet completely trouble-free even under ideal circumstances. And that micrometeoroid swarm that had forced the *Horizon*'s most recent unscheduled layover couldn't exactly be described as an ideal circumstance; the crew might continue to encounter yet-undiscovered meteoroid damage for weeks to come.

"We'll have to take the entire com system offline for a few hours at least while we get this problem sorted out," Juan said.

"The sooner you two get those subspace bands tuned back in," Paul said, "the sooner I can cross that report off my list."

Perhaps ten minutes after Nora and Juan had pulled open the bridge's primary com system access panel, Charlie pointed directly toward the main viewer.

"What the hell is *that*?" he said with a puzzled frown.

Looking at the forward screen, Paul could see for himself that his helmsman wasn't simply imagining things. A long, tapered shape had indeed suddenly appeared like an apparition before his startled gaze, seemingly materializing out of nowhere.

Nora and Juan both abruptly set aside their com system repairs, transfixed by the approaching ship.

"Must have roared in pretty damned fast," Juan said. "I'd guess she must have been doing warp four or better before she went sublight."

"What kind of ship is she?" Nora wanted to know.

"I hope it's not what it looks like," Charlie said, his eyes suddenly going nearly wide enough to see in the radio spectrum.

Paul swallowed hard as he nodded in silent agreement with the *Horizon*'s pilot. The bulbous projection at the nearer end of the incoming vessel's long, narrow body marked it as something no freighter captain wanted to encounter. As did its two widely spaced, ventrally curved engine nacelles.

The dull glow Paul saw emanating from the depths of the newcomer's forward weapons tube wasn't exactly an encouraging sign, either.

"What's a Klingon battle cruiser doing way out here in the Gamma Hydra sector?" he said, addressing nobody in particular. "We're a hell of a lot closer to the Romulans' stomping grounds right now than we are to Klingon space."

"Let's just hope they keep right on going without noticing us," Juan said, standing beside the com console, transfixed by the image on the screen.

Equally absorbed by the approaching apparition, Charlie said, "Not much chance of that. What are the odds they'd just happen to drop out of warp almost right on top of us?"

"I'm receiving a hail," Nora said. "Audio only."

"Put it on speakers," Paul said, nodding.

A deep, gravel-coated voice resounded through the small bridge. "Nov Duj. Pejeghbe' Duj. Ghuh tIjta pagh QIH."

"Dunno what he's saying," Charlie said. "But it doesn't sound friendly."

Paul was forced to agree. "Run that through the translation matrix, Nora."

"Already on it," she said as she finished entering a brief series of commands into her console.

A few tense heartbeats later, the computer substituted a synthetic English-speaking voice for that of the Klingon who was hailing them. *"Alien vessel. Surrender your ship. Prepare to be boarded or destroyed."*

Paul sighed. "That's pretty much what I *thought* you were going to say," he muttered under his breath. He flipped a switch on his chair console, opening an intercom channel to the engine room. "Mom, I'm going to need all the speed you can give me."

"You don't seriously expect to outrun that monster, do you, son?" Rianna said, evidently having already monitored the developing situation from her station.

"We've got a better chance of doing that than we do of winning a straight fight," Paul said. Even though his brother had persuaded him of the wisdom of upgrading the *Horizon*'s weaponry during his last visit more than two years earlier, a Klingon battle cruiser was nowhere near as easy to dissuade from using force as was your garden-variety pirate ship.

"All right, son," Rianna said. *"I've got my hand on the throttle. You just give the word."*

"Consider it given. Charlie, take us back down into the gravity well of the system we just left, pedal down all the way. Maybe we can lose 'em in one of the asteroid fields."

"Hang on to your butts," Charlie said again as he entered the appropriate commands. Paul felt his stomach lurch once more as the freighter accelerated and the inertial dampers again took a few microseconds to catch up. His lunch seemed to desire escape nearly as urgently as he did, but he somehow held on to it until the mercifully brief peristaltic impulse passed.

"Nora, send a distress signal," Paul said once he'd found his voice again. He knew that transmitting a Mayday via ordinary EM-band radio—the only option available with the subspace gear still down—would be about as useful as waving semaphore flags. But he had to do *something*.

"It's no good," Nora said, shaking her head in evident frustration. "They're jamming us!"

"Then launch the log buoy," Paul said, swallowing hard.

"Done," Nora said a moment later.

Paul felt a subtle change in the vibrations coming through the deck plates. Something wasn't right.

At the helm, Charlie seemed to be beating back panic, but only barely. "The helm just went dead. Navigation is completely offline."

Paul's heart raced. "Did the log buoy get away?"

Nora slammed her fist down on her console, then closed her eyes and took a deep breath as though struggling to compose herself. "Afraid I can't tell. My station just went down, too."

Darkness suddenly enfolded the bridge. Paul heard a brief chorus of startled cries and gasps.

"Life support, too," Charlie said. Only then did Paul notice the sudden total absence of the ubiquitous background hum of the air-circulation fans.

Paul fumbled for the intercom controls. "Engine room! Mom!" Nothing. Despite the failure of the helm and just about everything else, the ever-present aural backdrop created by the warp engines was gradually intensifying.

Then an eerie but welcome reddish glow slowly began to suffuse the chamber as the battery-powered emergency backup circuits dutifully yawned, stretched, and began to wake up.

"At least *something's* still working," Paul said.

"We still don't have any control over anything up here," Juan said, speaking from the gloomy shadows near one of the port stations.

The vibration in the deck plates shifted yet again. Paul knew the ship was accelerating.

"We're still generating warp power," Nora said.

The deck rattled and vibrated. The effect was very different from anything he had ever experienced before. More powerful, and more out of control. Deck segments slammed into one another like a planet's tectonic plates suddenly cranked into absurdly fast motion, a billion years crammed into a few fleeting heartbeats.

"We'd better get the escape pods ready," he said, raising his voice to be heard above the din. "Just in case."

Charlie entered a command, checked a readout, then cursed. "Not functioning."

Why doesn't that surprise me? Paul thought, struggling to remain calm, or at least to sound that way the next time he spoke. "Nora, get that viewer back up. I need to see what that Klingon ship is up to."

"Working on it," she said, a keen edge of terror audible in her voice. "But I can't seem to—"

She stopped abruptly when the forward viewer suddenly winked back to life, displaying an aft view. Looming against the star-bejeweled blackness of deep space, the Klingon battle cruiser was still closing in inexorably on the *Horizon*'s retreating stern.

"Good work," Paul said, thankful for whatever small miracles might appear.

"I didn't do it," Nora said, sounding flummoxed. "I still haven't figured out why the hell the lights went out in the first place."

They're *why*, Paul thought, staring straight ahead at the approaching harbinger of death. *They must have a new weapon that can cripple us without having to blow us full of holes first. And the screen came up just now because they* wanted *us to see whatever's going to happen next.*

"Charlie," he said aloud as renewed determination and plain, old-fashioned anger stiffened his spine. The *Horizon* was both his home and his livelihood, and he wasn't going to give up either without one hell of a fight. "We're going to have to get clever with these guys."

I.K.S. Mup'chIch

"The remote system is working flawlessly so far, Commander," Centurion T'Vak said, his gaze still riveted on the broad bank of gauges and indicators that stretched across three bridge workstations.

Of course, the still experimental *arrenhe'hwiua* tele-capture weapon had worked somewhat less than flawlessly during its initial outings, Commander T'Voras recalled; still, it had enabled the capture of the *klivam* cruiser he was currently using as the system's test bed, and had done so in fairly short order. And thanks to the Romulan Star Empire's long and acrimonious association with the Klingon Empire, the translation device that the chief technologist's office had integrated into the prototype had succeeded in transmitting a convincingly barbaric-sounding *klivam* hail.

It was a pity that it couldn't also do something about the lingering stench of the hirsute, overly armored animals that had once infested this otherwise adequate vessel.

"We have achieved complete control over the Terran freighter's propulsion, navigation, and life-support systems," the centurion said as he entered a few adjustments into the system interface.

"Very good, Centurion," T'Voras said. "Admiral Valdore and Chief Technologist Nijil will both be pleased indeed. I shall not neglect to mention your diligence to them."

The centurion immediately stood at attention and offered the traditional salute, his clenched right fist raised to high chest level just below the left shoulder, his bent elbow positioned precisely above the lower abdominal ribs that protected his heart. "You do me honor, Commander," the junior officer said.

Let us hope that this device will prove as effective against Terran military vessels, T'Voras thought, *as it has thus far against their civilian freighters and the* klivam *warship that now carries us.*

An ominous blood-green light on the device's central console suddenly began flashing rhythmically, matching the staccato wail of a klaxon. The centurion immediately returned his full attention to his readouts.

"The freighter crew is attempting to bypass both its primary and secondary systems," he said, sounding surprised at his opponent's apparent ingenuity.

T'Voras nodded, taking the revelation in stride. "They're no doubt trying some novel method of recovering their console functions. Respond accordingly, Centurion, and maintain control."

The centurion's brow ridge crumpled with concern, as though he'd suddenly become worried that the commendation he had been expecting earlier might suddenly metamorphose into a reprimand. Or perhaps something far worse.

T'Voras placed a hand gently on the hilt of his razor-sharp *dathe'anofv-sen,* his Honor Blade. *That shall be entirely up to him,* he thought.

E.C.S. *Horizon*

"Damn it!" Nora shouted.

"What's wrong?" Paul said. *Apart from the obvious.*

"Almost had helm control rerouted and recovered.

Then I lost it again. It's like the Klingons have found a way to monitor everything we try to do, using our own systems against us."

Paul nodded. That was no doubt *exactly* what they were doing, though he was completely at a loss as to how to explain it. Fear gnawed at his insides, like an animal trying to escape.

But he was no less determined to get his crew—his *family*—out of this mess.

"You and Juan keep at it," Paul said, trying his best to conceal his steadily increasing desperation. "Charlie . . . just keep pushing those buttons."

I.K.S. Mup'chIch

"Control recovered," Centurion T'Vak said, looking intensely relieved after several *siure* of genuine uncertainty.

After the struggle he'd just witnessed, T'Voras wasn't entirely certain that the centurion's renewed confidence was justified. But he was nevertheless satisfied that today's activities had garnered enough operational data to produce real, substantive refinements to the equipment. And he knew it would not do to linger here any longer than necessary, lest any transient vessel from Vulcan, Andoria, Tellar, or even Earth discover anything about the operation being conducted here today—or even begin asking questions about what a Klingon vessel might be doing so far from home.

"Is the test data safely recorded, Centurion?" T'Voras asked.

"It is, Commander."

"Very well," T'Voras said. "Dispose of any evidence that we were ever here. Including the small distress beacon the freighter launched."

"Immediately, Commander." T'Voras watched as the centurion deftly entered a series of commands into his primary board.

T'Voras turned toward the young female decurion who was serving at the communications station.

"Get me Admiral Valdore on a secure frequency," he said.

E.C.S. Horizon

The deck plates shuddered even more violently than before, signaling further acceleration. The engine noise continued to increase along with it, rising to a nearly ear-splitting roar.

"I dunno how, but we're *still* gathering delta vee," Charlie said. "Warp three point two and steadily climbing. Didn't think this tub could *go* this fast."

"I noticed," Paul said. "What's our heading?"

Charlie turned toward the center of the bridge. The harsh, ruddy-tinted shadows that fell across his face did nothing to soften the terror Paul saw etched across his usually placid features.

"We're locked on a ballistic course directly for Sigma Iotia!" he shouted, his voice nearly drowned out by the ever-escalating whine of the engines.

Sigma Iotia. The primary star of the world the *Horizon* had just departed.

Paul Mayweather turned and saw Rianna Mayweather standing by his side. He could see from the haunted look in his mother's brown eyes that engine control was a lost cause. There was no point in asking whether a warp-core jettison was even possible. Besides, the din of the engines had become so loud as to make conversation essentially impossible except in the form of top-of-the-lungs shouts. He took both of her hands between his own as he looked at the forward viewer.

The dazzling golden-orange brilliance of Sigma Iotia overwhelmed the screen, prompting the automatic imaging system to damp the light down to a tolerable level. Paul imagined he could already feel the searing heat of the photosphere toward which the *Horizon* was falling at multiwarp speed. Time seemed to stretch, and he truly didn't want to know precisely how many seconds remained to him and his crew.

His family. Paul Mayweather gently put his arm around his mother's shoulders. She had brought him into the world. Protected him from the occasional teasing of his older brother Travis. Taught him how to fly a ship. Comforted him after Jaliye had left him for another pilot.

And now she would die beside him.

He suppressed a morbid laugh as he drew some comfort from a final absurd thought: *At least I won't have to 'fess up to her about giving away that damned book.*

NINE

ADMIRAL VALDORE FROWNED, his face creasing sharply.

"What do you mean, you *believe* that it was destroyed?" he asked, displeasure fairly dripping from his lips as he spoke.

The holographic image of Commander T'Voras didn't blink, though Nijil did note that he cast a sidelong glance—presumably at some unlucky guilty party, or his corpse—before he answered. *"It seemed prudent to destroy any elements that might relate to this attack. The log buoy was following the same general trajectory of the Coalition ship when we sent it into the sun. But unlike the ship itself, we were unable to ascertain either its destruction or its safety."*

Nijil cleared his throat slightly, and glanced over at Valdore. They had worked together for so long on and off over the years that most gestures between them were unspoken, though Nijil was always aware of the need to appear appropriately obsequious before the admiral in the presence of lower-ranking officers.

"Were the *klivam* sensors unable to target the buoy effectively?" Nijil asked. "I was under the impression, from your reports, that their ship's sensor systems were rather similar to those of our own vessels."

The holographic T'Voras turned slightly to favor Nijil with his answer. *"There is significant spatial debris ob-*

scuring close scans of the system's sun. Once the Coalition ship entered the photosphere, we could not easily
locate a device as small as a log buoy."

Valdore put his knuckles to his forehead, clearly
vexed. "So, what you're saying now is that the buoy
might have been sent on an unknown independent trajectory, or it might possibly have dropped into the sun?"

Now, T'Voras looked a bit more nervous. "*Yes . . . The
orders were . . . I was unclear on protocol, sir. In all of
our previous attacks on the* klivam *vessels, we specifically
jammed their communications and prevented them from
sending out messages. It was . . . It seemed prudent to do
the same here. And, if I may remind you, Admiral, every
other aspect of this operation was a complete success.*"

Valdore leaned forward, sighing. "*You* do not need to
remind me of anything, Commander. Nor do I authorize
you to punish *any* of your crew for this . . . lapse in judgment. But to be clear, Commander, we undertook all our
previous attacks on *klivam* ships for two reasons: to test
the *arrenhe'hwiua* telecapture system, and to seize some
of their battle cruisers, *both* for technological study and
covert sabotage.

"*You* were engaged in both a technological test *and*
an act of covert sabotage. The log buoy of the Coalition
ship you destroyed would have furnished our adversaries with positive *proof* of Klingon aggression. It might
even have been enough to spark a war between the Klingon Empire and this 'Coalition of Planets.' Instead, we
are left with no proof of any Klingon attack."

"*But the test of our tactical system on the Coalition
ship went flawlessly, Admiral,*" T'Voras said. Nijil imagined he could see beads of sweat appear on the commander's heavily ridged brow.

"That is the reason you do not face disciplinary action, Commander," Valdore said, standing. "Yet," he

added, his voice lowering to a near growl. "The next mission you undertake will answer whether or not you have a future with . . . well, let's just leave it at that."

As Valdore stabbed his finger down upon a button on the desk-mounted com system, the holographic T'Voras saluted nervously, but the salute wasn't even finished before the image winked out of existence.

"I don't believe that Commander T'Voras's error in judgment will create any lasting repercussions for your plans, sir," Nijil said, hoping to soothe Valdore, whose head was bowed and shadowed.

Valdore lifted his face, smiling. "Neither do I, Nijil. We still have other tests to conduct, and there will be more than enough time and opportunity to implicate the Klingons or, conversely, to convince the Klingons that the Coalition has destroyed one of *their* ships. But Commander T'Voras had gotten a bit too cocky after our last several triumphs; I needed to remind him that he is fallible, and can be replaced."

Nijil nodded, smiling at Valdore's cunning. Although he had designs on furthering his own standing in the power structure of Romulus, for now, Valdore was the right man to back. Of all the officers in the Romulan military, Valdore appeared to be the one who was most adaptable to changing technologies, and to the myriad possibilities of the future.

Despite Valdore's failure with the initial telepresence drone-ship remote-control units, which had required telepathic Aenar to operate them, the concept had led to this latest technological breakthrough. Nijil had been ecstatic when he'd been moved from the mostly stalled project charged with the creation of a functional large-scale cloaking device—a unit capable, in theory, of rendering even large war vessels effectively invisible to an adversary—to his present post. Despite the best efforts of some of the finest minds on Romulus, the power needed to cloak a large ship still invariably resulted in a complete loss of fuel containment—and therefore the utter destruction of both a test ship and a hugely expensive cloaking-device prototype. By contrast, the prospect of overcoming an enemy by using direct subspace contact to remotely seize his own consoles and control computers had proved to be a much more fruitful area of research.

Nijil now felt extremely confident that the recent telecapture breakthroughs over which he had presided for the past couple of *khaidoa* had proven to Valdore that he had decided to back not only the right technology for the next war, but also the right technologist to bring the Praetor's dreams to fruition.

Now, after the convenient death of Ehrehin—at the hands of Nijil's own agents, though no one seemed to have discovered this inconvenient fact as of yet—and the success of the *arrenhe'hwiua* telecapture system, Nijil was all but certain that a place of honor in the annals of Romulan scientific and military history awaited him.

Once his ideas had been thoroughly tested and properly deployed, of course.

As had often been the case during the last few months he had spent both on and off Romulus, Trip Tucker was feeling exceedingly ill at ease. Playing his public role of the junior engineer named Cunaehr, he was attending the funeral services for Ehrehin i'Ramnau tr'Avrak. Trip had discovered only today that the old man had no surviving relatives; his five sons and one daughter had all been killed in action during various Romulan military incursions. This revelation certainly made Ehrehin's having balked at completing his warp-drive project easier to understand.

As he stood beneath the midday shadows cast by one of the great stone archways of Dartha's ancient mausoleum district, Trip found he had little to do other than to concentrate on not making a public spectacle of himself. After all, none of his pre-mission intelligence cramming, or any of his other studies to date, had brought him up to speed on Romulan funerary customs, a fact that was especially unfortunate given that his covert persona was supposed to be *quite* familiar with *all* Romulan customs. Whenever he hadn't been working alongside Ehrehin, Trip had spent a great deal of his time poring over Romulan texts, which he absorbed as quickly as he could translate them. He had even gone so far as to improvise a text-scanning-and-conversion device, which read to him aloud in standard English through the translation units the Adigeons had mounted inside his ears.

Lucky for me there aren't too many people here, Trip thought. Less than a dozen others had come to the crypt, and most of these were fellow scientists or lab assistants with whom Tucker was already familiar, having worked alongside them fairly closely for the past few months. A few uniformed centurions and other military officers were present as well, the most conspicuous of which was a tall, broad-shouldered brute who seemed to be scrutinizing all the mourners very carefully as they came and went.

Trip recognized the man as the same brusque centurion who had been in charge of the security team that had come to Ehrehin's lab after the *Ejhoi Ormiin* assassins had attacked. He had taken the lone surviving assassin away, promising to interrogate her. *So what's he doing here, giving the stink-eye to all of us?* Trip wondered, his hackles rising.

Trip watched as the others began to approach the

raised granite bier upon which stood the half-meter-high ceramic *tibulec* vessel that contained Ehrehin's mortal remains; per Romulan custom, the scientist had been cremated within an *eisae*—a single revolution of the imperial homeworld—after his death. Each person who approached the urn performed an intricate series of hand movements while simultaneously murmuring words that Trip interpreted as some sort of ancient prayer. He couldn't see exactly what the other visitors were doing, or hear their words precisely, but the whole business strongly resembled the burial ritual he had learned a few months earlier, when he and T'Pol had interred the body of their infant daughter Elizabeth at the T'Karath Sanctuary on Vulcan.

I should be able to fake my way through this easily enough, Trip thought, his confidence rising as his turn neared to mount the few narrow steps that led up to the highly decorated, tubular vessel. Despite his covert mission, he still had every reason to pay his heartfelt personal respects to Ehrehin—the man had saved his life and taken him under his wing even after discovering that Trip was actually a non-Romulan spy—and he needed to do whatever he could to send his fondest, most positive thoughts toward whatever afterlife Ehrehin might have anticipated. As he approached the raised bier, prepared to make a quick—but not *too* quick—run-through of the gestures and murmurs he'd seen the other mourners make, he redoubled his concentration on remaining as inconspicuous as possible.

As he moved forward, Trip caught a flash of movement to his left, and his newly acquired confidence sank like a stone dropped into a canyon.

"Please, feel free," Ehrehin's young laboratory assistant said, making an "after you" gesture.

Centurion Terix studied the young man again carefully, just as he had done earlier in today's *animaur'olhao*, the Ceremony of Respect. Something seemed out of place with the man, and he couldn't quite put his finger on it. The dead scientist's assistant seemed nervous; perhaps the loss of his colleague was the sole reason for his apparent discomfiture, or maybe it was something else, something less than seemly.

"No, you were closest to Technologist Ehrehin," Terix said. "You may perform the rite of *pizan'ris*."

The young man seemed to swallow hard before he nodded and walked up the small steps that led to the *tibulec* of his slain mentor. His back angled away from Terix, he began to speak, his voice low, and his hands moving in the time-honored manner. Finally he quit speaking and touched his index finger and pinkie to the base of the *tibulec*.

The gesture brought a rush of insight to Terix, as well as certainty about what he had to do next.

As the assistant turned away and descended from the bier, he pulled up the hood on his mourning cloak. Terix looked over to Sweba, the *uhlan* who stood guard at the rear of the mausoleum district's ceremonial arena; Terix jerked his chin up sharply, directing the *uhlan*'s attention toward the departing young man.

After seeing Sweba's curt nod of acknowledgment, Terix turned back to the *tibulec* and concluded the ceremony swiftly, using a fusing device and a military seal to specify that this vessel contained the physical essence of one who had given his life in service to the Romulan Star Empire and Praetor D'deridex. Although Technologist Ehrehin had a checkered past—like so many of the greatest scientific and military leaders of Romulus—his work and service had nevertheless furthered both the strategic and the tactical goals of the Empire, and the

Praetor who personified her. And as he'd learned yesterday, the murder of the scientist had been far larger than the simple act of burglary that appeared to have precipitated it. Terix felt certain that Doctor Ehrehin had been a martyr to a conspiracy whose existence was known, as yet, to perhaps no more than a handful of others.

Stalking away, Terix saw that Sweba had properly detained the assistant—a man whom Terix believed was *not* who he pretended to be.

"And what makes you so certain that this Cunaehr is a *Vulcan* spy?" Valdore asked, squinting up at Terix from behind his vast desk, atop which sat numerous reports and other paper documents. On the wall behind the admiral was mounted the *dathe'anofv-sen*—the Honor Blade—that usually hung at the admiral's side.

"During Doctor Ehrehin's *animaur'olhao*, he performed several movements that I know to be specific to *Vulcan* tradition, rather than ours," Terix said. He had hoped that Valdore would have received the news of this discovery a bit more favorably.

"I had no idea you were so well versed in Vulcan traditions, Centurion," the admiral said, lofting an eyebrow.

The admiral's stare made Terix feel like a bug in a jar. "I performed two covert intelligence missions there right out of the Academy."

"And you find this man's . . . 'Vulcan movement' to be proof that Cunaehr is a Vulcan? Have you interrogated him? Tested his blood?"

Terix nodded. "We *have* interrogated him, sir, though not as thoroughly as we might without authorization from your office. Our admittedly cursory medical tests on him revealed that he has a very unusual mutative blood type, with traits common to both Vulcan and Romulan genetics."

Valdore held up a hand, palm outward. "Do not force further interrogation on the prisoner yet. Your . . . allegation may require further investigation first. Doctor Ehrehin was working on a *very* important project for the Praetor's fleet when he died, a project whose ultimate goal remains unfulfilled. This Cunaehr may hold the key to reaching that goal. If you damage him, or do anything to make his mental state more . . . fragile than it may be already, you may seriously jeopardize that prospect."

"Then, do you wish me to release him?" Terix asked. He had hoped for permission to use every tool at his disposal to extract the truth from the scientist, but it appeared that Valdore wasn't about to grant him that.

"Not yet," Valdore said, looking thoughtful. "Let me think on this for a night. Keep Cunaehr in custody for now, but keep him sequestered away from Ehrehin's assassin. I must consider all of my options. But if I don't find a way to make him useful—or if we find hard evidence that he really is somehow involved with the Vulcans—then *you*, Centurion, will be allowed to choose the method of execution."

Terix saluted and favored his superior with a rare smile.

TEN

Wednesday, July 16, 2155
Enterprise **NX-01**

T'POL WASHED HER HANDS CAREFULLY, looking in the mirror as she did so. It was something she rarely did—whatever her many failings might be in following Surak's teachings, she did not number vanity among them—but she could see in her reflection that she looked tired.

She hoped that none of her colleagues on the bridge had noticed this, or any fatigue-related errors she might have made. She regarded the chance of the latter as relatively minuscule, given that she generally triple-checked her work; on the other hand, she had been up for most of the last forty-eight hours, applying her off-shift hours to her ongoing surreptitious search for more information about Sopek, emphasizing anything that might connect him with the Romulans.

She moved through the open secondary hatchway inside the sanitary facility the humans referred to as "the head," entering the tiny interior chamber in which puffs of aerosolized sanitizer attacked any bacteria or other dirt that might be present, on either bodies or uniforms. Some of the crew occasionally joked about the head's "decontamination chamber," but T'Pol—with her heightened sense of smell—was grateful for it.

Exiting the head, she found herself immediately disoriented. Instead of being back on the bridge, she now stood in a corridor whose walls and floor and ceiling exuded an almost painfully brilliant white light. To her right, T'Pol saw that only a few meters down the corridor the light ended, dropping abruptly off into the inky, star-strewn vastness of space.

T'Pol turned her head and saw two figures, both of them far enough away to appear somewhat indistinct. One seemed to be slumped on the floor, while the other stood above the first in a threatening stance. The standing figure leaned over and picked up the slumping one by grabbing a handful of its dark hair and dragging the body to which it was attached to a nearly upright position.

Running toward them, T'Pol wasn't sure if she should announce her presence to the aggressor or not. She chose to stay silent, at least until she knew what she might be facing. But the distance between her and the pair seemed to elongate as she moved, even as the taller figure began to beat on its prey.

T'Pol heard a roar behind her, a cacophony louder than anything she'd ever heard before. Despite its unnatural volume, she recognized it instantly, just a split second before the blast of wind struck her. The sound and fury of massive decompression spurred her on, and she barely glanced back to see the white corridor breaking apart behind her, the vacuum of space seeming to hurtle toward her in a headlong, predatory rush.

"Stop!" she shouted, throwing caution to the grasping winds around her as she forced herself nearer to the two figures, perhaps relying on the power of her will alone. The aggressor turned and roared at her, its Vulcan features distorted and angry. With flattened ears and sharpened teeth, it resembled one of the Fri'slen mutants that she had battled some two decades ago.

With the corridor tearing asunder behind her, T'Pol used the last of her declining strength to launch herself at the monster, tackling it at its midsection. The thing writhed and screamed, and through the flying tatters of its robe T'Pol finally caught a glimpse of what the monster had been beating.

Or rather *whom*. Despite the extensive surgery he had undergone to help him blend into Romulan society, and the bruises and contusions that swelled his face, she knew it was Trip. His eyes looked unfocused, but he seemed to see her nevertheless.

"T'Pol," he said weakly. The escalating roar of cold, empty space swallowed up anything else he might have said.

The corridor behind him crumbled a heartbeat later, and Trip went tumbling into the void, his voice gone, though she was certain he still carried her name on his blood-flecked lips.

Marshaling all her remaining strength, T'Pol continued to grapple with the monster, determined to end its life before it managed to do the same to her.

"T'Pol!" The voice was closer now, louder, despite the intensifying rush of white noise. "Commander T'Pol!"

Abruptly, the white corridor and the void beyond it vanished, displaced by the bridge of *Enterprise* and its startled beta-watch crew. Lieutenant Mack McCall was in front of her, grasping her shoulders, concern etched deeply on his features. "Commander T'Pol, can you hear me?"

T'Pol turned her head, blinking away the vision that had just filled her mind, willing her racing heart to slow down.

"Yes, Lieutenant," she said slowly, focusing first on the distraction of the man's salt-and-pepper goatee before looking directly into his brown eyes. "I . . . I'm not sure what just happened."

"Neither are we," McCall said, his demeanor softening

a bit. "You exited the head, stopped in the middle of the deck, and yelled, 'Stop!' You seemed to be in some kind of . . . trance." Very gently, he grasped her wrists and pulled her hands up. "And you did this to yourself."

T'Pol looked down at her hands, both of which were balled into fists, her fingers clenched so tightly that her short-cropped nails had pierced the flesh of both palms. Emerald-hued blood welled out onto her wrists and dripped from between her knuckles.

"Perhaps I should pay a visit to Doctor Phlox," T'Pol said.

"That's what I was going to suggest," McCall said, sighing in apparent relief that he wasn't going to have to try to force the issue on a superior officer—one who might be going insane right before his eyes, for all he knew. "Why don't I have Ensign Ko accompany you to sickbay?"

T'Pol also didn't miss the trepidatious look on Ko's face as he accompanied her into the bridge turbolift, where he stood as far away from her as possible. She wasn't offended by his quite logical impulse toward caution, nor by the unusual alacrity with which he exited sickbay once he had finished conducting her inside.

A moment after she finished offering an awkward greeting to Phlox, the sickbay doors slid open again. T'Pol turned in time to see Captain Archer enter, looking every bit as concerned as McCall had. *No doubt Mc-Call notified him*, T'Pol thought. She would have done the same in his position.

As T'Pol attempted to describe to both Phlox and the captain what had just happened to her on the bridge, Phlox treated the cuts on her hands with a disinfectant, then quickly and expertly bandaged them. Phlox then activated one of his small medical scanners, which he used to check both her blood pressure and the dilation of her pupils.

"Please lie back on the bed," he said, his voice exhibiting just a hint of concern.

"And you're certain that it was Trip that you saw?" Archer asked as T'Pol walked to the bed and settled back onto it, placing her head underneath the wall-mounted medical display panel.

"I am certain," T'Pol said.

"I'd certainly like to see what Mister Tucker looks like *now*," Phlox said. He hadn't been present when Trip had come to her during Archer's speech at the Coalition Compact signing ceremony; on that historic occasion, the Denobulan physician had spent most of his time with his three wives.

"As I have already explained, Doctor, he now resembles a Vulcan, though he lacks most of the emotional control that my people usually exhibit," T'Pol said. "If you like, I could search through the database to find you an appropriate image to view."

"Not necessary," Phlox said, smiling down at her benignly.

T'Pol turned her head slightly to look up at Archer. "I am concerned, Captain. I believe that Commander Tucker is presently in grave danger."

Archer rubbed his right eyebrow, scrunching up his face. "You believe that because of a *hallucination*? That's not a very sound source of information."

"I do not believe it was merely a hallucination, sir." T'Pol paused for a moment, aware that she was going to have to reveal something of an intensely private and personal nature. "When Vulcans join minds, they sometimes forge a . . . mental bond. I believe that I may have formed such a bond with the commander shortly before his 'death.' I have had another experience similar to this, though it was of a far less violent nature."

Phlox touched her shoulder. "You may sit up now,

Commander. I've heard of many such bonds between mates in many species, including, as we know, the Andorians. However, I've never heard of it crossing species boundaries."

As she moved to a seated position at the edge of the bed, T'Pol felt a bit embarrassed. "Trip and I are . . . we *were* something of an anomaly, Doctor. Our genetic codes were commingled to create a baby that should never have been possible. Our brief . . . romantic entanglement was in itself unique; can you really rule out that in our . . . pairing, we might have created an entirely new interspecies phenomenon?"

Phlox's tufted eyebrows lifted. "Not at all. It is *entirely* possible." He held up a datapad whose screen displayed ranks of slowly scrolling data. "It is, however, also possible that you are still suffering from the aftereffects of your addiction to trellium-D. Or even a delayed reaction from your repeated exposures to the Romulan telepresence unit last year, during the first Aenar crisis. Either way, the extreme certainty you seem to feel about the reality of these hallucinations—or whatever they ultimately prove to be—could be an artifact of residual neurological damage."

T'Pol wasn't convinced. "Conversely," she said, "as we have learned from the heightened emotional states I have experienced occasionally during the time *since* my addiction, those same aftereffects may merely have opened up neurological or emotional pathways that had previously been *closed*."

"Hmmm," Phlox said agreeably, nodding. "Either answer could be, as you're fond of saying, logical."

"T'Pol, I'd be the last one to deny the validity of Vulcan telepathy," Archer said, folding his arms before him. "Hell, I once shared my skull with your people's most revered philosopher. And even if none of his logic rubbed off on me, I'd still have to question how a link like that could work over interstellar distances."

"The Aenar had that capability," T'Pol said.

Phlox shook his head. "Aenar telepathy is somewhat more powerful than Vulcan psi abilities," the doctor said. "With a very few exceptions, your people are touch-telepaths."

T'Pol turned to face Archer directly. "Captain, I *knew* that Trip wasn't dead before I was told the truth. I was aware of his living consciousness at a time after *you* had told me he was dead. In my previous mind encounter with Trip, I even became aware that his appearance had been altered. At the time, I was unable to understand it. But later, when I saw him in person on Earth, my . . . 'hallucination' turned out to be true."

She paused, swallowing the unbidden emotion that was even now creeping into her mind. "My behavior is *not* irrational, nor emotional. I know this to be true: Commander Tucker is in mortal danger."

Placing a bandage-covered hand gingerly on Archer's sleeve, T'Pol implored him. "You are Trip's best friend, Captain . . . Jonathan. I *am* connected to him. We *can* find him. Rescue him."

Archer pulled away from her, his face crumpling in obvious anguish. "I'm sorry, T'Pol. You *know* we can't." He swept at the air angrily with one hand. "We're *one ship*, damn it! Even if I did take *Enterprise* into Romulan territory, we'd be overwhelmed within minutes. We'd never even *reach* Romulus! And we'd be sacrificing an entire crew for the life of one person, not to mention leaving the security of Earth and the Coalition at risk, *and* very possibly starting a war as well.

"I can't do it, T'Pol. I can't sacrifice this ship, this crew . . . *everything*, for Trip, no matter how badly any of us would like to. I just can't."

He walked away from her, toward the door. "Please don't ask me again."

Once the captain was gone, Phlox cleared his throat as he looked up from the datapad he had been studying so intently for the past several minutes.

"Did you really expect Captain Archer to give you any other response?" His tone sounded more curious than judgmental.

T'Pol shook her head. "No, Doctor. The captain has always had to strike a balance between the demands of his superiors, interstellar politics, and his desire to lead this ship based on something purer than either one. But more often than not, he opts to follow the rules out of necessity."

"For what it's worth, I believe that there *is* more to your mental link to Mister Tucker than most other physicians and scientists would admit," Phlox said. "That said, I also am fully aware that you are in a state of exhaustion. And the heightened emotions you *are* exhibiting are no doubt draining your strength even further.

"I'm going to strongly suggest that you take some time off . . . some *significant* time off, to meditate, rest, and clear your mind." He smiled wryly, but his ice-blue eyes were otherwise inscrutable. "Perhaps *away* from the others in the crew for a time, you will be able to find the answers you need."

T'Pol stared at him for a moment, wondering at the intent of Phlox's words, and surprised at the kindness she saw in the Denobulan's gaze. But that part of her that had been trained long ago, before *Enterprise* even existed, instinctively told her not to ask for clarification.

"Perhaps you are right, Doctor," she said after several moments of silent reflection. "Thank you for the advice."

*   *   *

"You know that what you're asking is in gross violation of a score of laws?"

T'Pol stared at Denak's face on the viewscreen. She had signaled him several hours earlier, and his response had finally come only a few minutes ago.

"I also know that *you* have operated outside the law *numerous* times when circumstances required it," T'Pol said. "I worked at your side on some of those occasions. You have done things that will never be written into Vulcan history . . . or even in the most secret files of the V'Shar."

Denak raised one of his eyebrows, but only slightly. *"A lesser man might think you were threatening me in some manner, Commander. But I know better. I also know that I owe you my life, several times over."*

T'Pol glanced over at the timer attached to the subspace scrambling device on her desktop. Her time was fast running out.

"Denak, you were the one who told me to look into Captain Sopek—"

"The late *Captain Sopek,"* he said, interrupting her.

"—and while I have been unable to find concrete evidence, I have followed up on a number of rumors about Sopek working within the Romulan sphere of influence."

"Why is it so important for you to learn about Sopek now?" Denak asked, squinting as though with enough effort he might read the answer to his question on her forehead. *"Or is there another reason behind this request that you're not sharing with me?"*

"I'm sharing as much with you as I can. At least until you comply with my request." T'Pol looked again at the timer.

"'Comply with my request'? That's an oxymoronic statement if I ever heard one," Denak said. *"What you're*

asking would be difficult under normal *circumstances, and I'm not certain it's even* possible. *But if it is, you'll hear from me at my next opportunity."*

T'Pol held up five fingers, and folded them into her wrapped palm as the timer counted down. "If you do this for me, Denak, all debts will be considered paid."

"Understand that if I do this for you, all—" The screen went black, cutting Denak off in mid-sentence.

T'Pol sat back in her chair, exhaling. She was aware that she had been tightly clenching her other fist again only when her concentration ebbed and she felt the pain in her hand. As she got up to find a fresh bandage, the chime at her door sounded.

Quickly pushing the scrambling device behind a small stack of datapads, T'Pol said, "Enter."

She hadn't expected the hatch to open on the face of a very worried-looking Hoshi Sato.

"May I speak with you?" Sato asked as she stepped inside.

"Yes, Ensign," T'Pol said. "What can I do for you?"

Sato sighed heavily. "As part of my bridge duties, I am assigned to monitor all subspace messages sent to or from this ship." She shifted from foot to foot, nervously. "As you've probably noticed over the last four years, however, I'm a *bit* of an overachiever. I regularly make spot checks on the systems even when I'm *off*-duty."

"I see," said T'Pol evenly. She sat at the edge of her table, further blocking her computer from Sato's view. "And have you discovered something that should be brought to my attention?"

"Technically, it should be brought to Captain Archer's attention," Hoshi said, clasping her hands behind her back. "But before I do that, I felt that perhaps asking *you* why you were sending an unauthorized, unlogged, scrambled subspace transmission a few minutes ago would be the more prudent thing to do. In case you have . . . a reasonable explanation."

T'Pol studied the young woman for a moment. A fleeting thought crossed her mind that a mind-meld might allow her to influence the young woman's mind, just enough to induce her to forget having noticed T'Pol's transgression. But apart from the ethical implications of the act, she also wasn't certain whether or not Sato had already informed others, or had left some tangible evidence in her personal logs or her quarters. *Better just to tell her the truth,* T'Pol thought. *Or at least,* a *truth.*

"Please review the beta-watch duty logs. You will discover that I suffered a brief . . . emotional attack on the bridge earlier today," T'Pol said. "I found the incident to be most . . . demoralizing. And embarrassing. I have already been examined by Doctor Phlox, and have discussed the matter with Captain Archer as well. If you were to bring this matter to their attention, they would both undoubtedly tell you that my private affairs are none of your concern, Ensign."

T'Pol slumped her shoulder slightly, in an attempt to lose the bearing that she knew read to humans as "stick-up-the-ass-Vulcan" in the words of one Charles Anthony Tucker III. She hoped that the mannerism would make her appear more vulnerable in the ensign's eyes.

"I am confiding in you, however, Hoshi, woman to woman. There are certain Vulcan . . . *things* that I am going through right now. Things that are . . . difficult to discuss with humans, or even with a Denobulan doctor. I used the scrambled transmission because I was already ashamed at what the beta crew had witnessed on the bridge; it would shame me even further if any revelations about my private health were intercepted *accidentally* by another crew member. Yourself included."

Sato looked sad, and approached T'Pol with her arms outstretched, gathering her in for a hug.

"I understand, Commander. And I'm certain that Captain Archer will as well. I'll check with him to verify that he's okay with you using the scrambler, but unless he tells me otherwise, your secret is safe with us. And if you ever need to talk, just know that I'm here for you."

"Thank you," T'Pol said, stiffly allowing herself to submit to the somewhat awkward hug the younger woman offered. She felt guilty for misleading the ensign, but she knew it was necessary. And T'Pol felt confident that Archer would believe her excuse as well were he to confront her about the matter.

Just as she felt confident that Jonathan Archer would never suspect what she had *really* just requested of her old friend Denak.

ELEVEN

Day Thirty-three, Month of K'ri'Brax
The Hall of State, Dartha City, Romulus

"I HAVE BROUGHT THE VULCAN SPY, Admiral, per your orders," Centurion Terix said, standing at attention in the open doorway to Admiral Valdore's office. A pair of armed *uhlan*s, members of the Hall of State's ceremonially dressed yet highly trained security contingent, stood vigilantly behind him. The *uhlans'* sidearm disruptors were conspicuously visible, as were their sheathed Honor Blades, and the guards' dark eyes gleamed alertly from beneath their shiny silver helmets.

A somewhat shorter man, clad in a rumpled, deep-green detention jumpsuit, stood at the centurion's side, his wrists tightly shackled together before him. The bruises that marred the prisoner's face did nothing to dampen the fires of defiance that burned deep within his eyes.

Valdore looked the captured spy up and down for a long and silent moment. *This is indeed a dangerous one,* he thought without any irony. *He will certainly bear close watching wherever he goes from now on.*

Nodding a curt acknowledgment to Terix, Valdore rose from the chair behind his heavy sherawood desk. "You may remove his restraints, Centurion."

"Sir?"

Valdore scowled. "Perhaps you pulled your helmet straps a bit too tightly around your ears this morning,

Centurion. I said that the prisoner's restraints will no longer be necessary. Remove them. *Now*."

A look of surprise briefly crossed Terix's usually hard and stoic features. "At once, Admiral." He turned and nodded to the nearer of the two *uhlan*s, who retrieved a small electronic key from his belt, stepped forward, then opened and took the restraints before resuming his previous position.

During the entire process the spy simply stared at Valdore, his expression now displaying a sort of defiant curiosity. The man stared in silence as he rubbed his wrists where the shackles had chafed them.

"What is your name?" Valdore asked the prisoner.

"Cunaehr ir'Ra'tleihfi tr'Mandak," he answered slowly, pronouncing each syllable as though his tongue had grown swollen and heavy. "I have been Doctor Ehrehin's assistant for the past twelve *fvheisn*."

Valdore nodded, not bothering to challenge the spy's professed identity despite the fact that his own research the previous evening had already conclusively put the lie to it. Cunaehr, the longtime apprentice, assistant, and amanuensis of Doctor Ehrehin i'Ramnau tr'Avrak, died some three *khaidoa* ago on Unroth III during an ill-fated static test of an early prototype of the *avaihh lli vastam*, the still-elusive warp-seven stardrive. Therefore, Cunaehr was the only person in the entire vast expanse of Romulan Star Empire space that this spy could *not* be.

Who is *he, really?* Valdore wondered, as he had done for the past nine *dierha*. *And how did the Vulcans manage to place one of their spies in such a sensitive position?*

Valdore knew he couldn't discount the possibility that his own instincts had been compromised more than he had realized by his own recent political imprisonment following the drone-ship fiasco of the previous *fvheisn*.

Or perhaps the spy had gained his initial foothold on
Romulus during the several long *khaidoa* of Valdore's
incarceration.

But Valdore allowed all such questions to go unasked,
at least for the moment. He knew that there was nothing to be gained by letting the spy understand the extent
to which his assumed identity had been compromised.
Far better to allow him to continue operating with impunity, all the while keeping him under close but discreet scrutiny. This Vulcan might be put to considerable
productive use for the Empire, whether knowingly or
not.

"On behalf of all the military forces of the Romulan
Star Empire," Valdore said, "please accept my apologies
for your confinement."

"I'm sorry?" the spy said, looking nonplussed.

Valdore assayed a smile he hoped the man would find
reassuring. "No. *I'm* sorry. For having allowed you to be
arrested and imprisoned, and so soon after the slaying
of your mentor. You are free to go, Cunaehr."

"Sir?" said Terix, who was still standing with the
*uhlan*s near the office doorway.

"I wasn't addressing *you*, Centurion," Valdore said,
using a tone that brooked no further argument. He kept
his gaze fixed upon the spy, whose blunt response took
him by surprise.

"Why?"

Valdore chuckled. "Contrary to what many of our officers believe, not even the Romulan government is in-
fallible. I stand before you as proof of that. I, too, was
once imprisoned. Until my superiors thought better of
that erroneous decision, that is."

"I was arrested," the spy said quietly, looking more
puzzled by the moment, "by *mistake*?"

"We thought you were someone else," Valdore said,

nodding. "It appears you were the victim of a simple case of mistaken identity. Nothing more."

The spy nodded, a look of hesitancy bordering on suspicion displayed across his face, as though he feared falling victim to some devious psychological trick. "It's a real relief to hear that, Admiral," he said at length.

"I hope this unfortunate incident will not significantly slow down your progress toward accomplishing Doctor Ehrehin's objectives."

The spy's earlier hesitancy abruptly vanished. "I live only to serve the Empire, Admiral," he said in his hard-to-place, possibly rustic accent.

And serve the Empire you will, my Vulcan friend, Valdore thought. *Regardless of your real intentions.*

"My chief technologist's office will furnish whatever you require to continue the good Doctor Ehrehin's work," Valdore said aloud. "You will find that the laboratory in which you and Doctor Ehrehin worked has already been repaired." *And it will be under much heavier surveillance from now on,* he added silently.

"Thank you, sir," the spy said, lowering his gaze contemplatively in a way that made him look vaguely troubled.

"You may speak freely here, Cunaehr," Valdore said, hoping to inspire the other man's confidence.

"Have you learned the identities of the ones responsible for Ehrehin's murder?" the spy asked. Valdore noted with some surprise that the man's expression of concern for the dead mentor whose legacy his very presence threatened appeared as authentic as it did. It was a fine performance. Or perhaps he really had developed some genuine affection for the old man, his Vulcan emotional repression and political predilections notwithstanding. After all, despite all their pretensions to the contrary, Vulcans were no less emotional than their Romulan cousins; they were merely far more repressed, and therefore arguably far less sane—and thus more dangerous—than the typical Romulan.

"Centurion Terix," Valdore said, his eyes still riveted upon those of the spy. "Since we have established that this man is indeed a loyal Romulan, I believe his question deserves an answer. What have you learned so far about the assassins?"

Terix made flustered noises. "Admiral, these are sensitive security matters. I shouldn't—"

"What you *shouldn't* do, Centurion, is disobey a direct order," Valdore said, stepping down hard on the young officer's protestations. "Give me the general outlines of your report. Now."

Terix nodded, apparently hastening to focus his concentration and gather his scattered thoughts. After a momentary pause, he said, "So far as my people can determine, Doctor Ehrehin was killed by terrorist revolutionaries whose larger goal is to compromise the stardrive project."

"The *Ejhoi Ormiin*, I'll bet," the spy said, his eyes now riveted upon Terix.

"Why are you so certain of that, Cunaehr?" Valdore asked, raising an eyebrow and using a tone of voice that had been known to make first-year *uhlan*s—and occasionally even sublieutenants and decurions—soil themselves during inspection tours.

The spy didn't appear to be cowed in the least as he faced Valdore again. "Let's just say I know they're highly motivated to go after Ehrehin a second time. It's got to be the same dissident group that I helped rescue Ehrehin from in the Rator system two *khaidoa* ago." Addressing Terix, he added, "I tried to explain that to you when you and your men arrived in the physics lab—just a little bit too late to save Ehrehin's life."

Terix nodded impassively, not rising to take the obvious bait. "My men immediately began investigating the *Ejhoi Ormiin*, beginning with a most thorough interrogation of the lone surviving assassin. It was a far more intensive questioning than any such terrorist operative is capable of coping with. Or surviving, as we discovered during last night's, ah, interview session."

As Valdore nodded his dispassionate acknowledgment, he noticed that the spy seemed to flinch ever so slightly at Terix's description of standard military interrogation procedures, which the intelligence experts in the much-feared Tal Shiar had refined almost to an art form. The ousted Vulcan leader V'Las, with whom Valdore had once quietly conspired, had had no such compunctions about the prosaic realities inherent in transacting the sometimes-bloody business of espionage. It seemed odd that even the largely peace-loving Vulcans would not have selected someone equally sanguine about the use of *aelhih'druusmn* equipment for direct mind-scans and other such things to employ as a deep-cover spy inside the Romulan Star Empire.

You should handle that font of compassion with great care, my covert friend, Valdore thought as he studied the spy. *It can be as hazardous as raw antimatter in a profession like yours.*

"Please give me a summary of the results of your investigation, Centurion," Valdore said.

"We have a high degree of confidence," Terix said, "that the *Ejhoi Ormiin* terrorists have already managed to acquire a good deal of classified data concerning the *avaihh lli vastam* stardrive project. We will need to infiltrate their organization directly in order to determine their precise capabilities pursuant to that stolen data."

"I suppose that such an operation would require a great deal of highly specialized expertise in warp-field theory and related fields," Valdore said, stroking his clean-shaven chin. His gaze drifted to the tapestries that adorned the far wall, as was his wont whenever he was deep in consideration of weighty strategic or tactical matters.

"Indeed, Admiral," the centurion said. "I will need the help of personnel capable of recognizing every possible permutation of the stolen data if we are to succeed in tracking down the thieves and their confederates. And if we are to prevent what they have taken from becoming a direct threat to state security."

"The level of expertise required would have to be comparable to that of the late Doctor Ehrehin himself," Valdore added as he fixed his stare back upon the spy, whose face was beginning to pale as understanding appeared to dawn upon him.

Despite his evidently discommoded emotional state, the spy's next utterance surprised Valdore yet again. "As I said before, Admiral: I live only to serve the Empire."

"I believe the admiral has just ordered you to accompany me on a field mission to infiltrate the *Ejhoi Ormiin* terrorists," Terix said, his words tinged with no small amount of incredulity. "The very same people who once took you and your mentor prisoner."

"Correct, Centurion," Valdore said as he studied the spy's reactions. "You've just been drafted to serve the Empire in a way you doubtless hadn't anticipated, Cunaehr."

"I'm an academic," the spy said, his jaw setting in apparent determination as he paused and regarded both Terix and Valdore for a long and sober moment. "But I think I can handle that. The stakes in this particular game of *trayatik* are way too high to do otherwise, Admiral."

Valdore's initial surprise at the spy's sentiments

dissipated after a moment's consideration. Being an operative from one of the worlds allied with the fragile young Coalition of Planets, this man almost certainly had no more desire than did Praetor D'deridex himself to permit a group of self-styled renegades and revolutionaries to gain control of the most potent stardrive ever conceived.

Cunaehr, or whatever his name really was, offered a clumsily executed Romulan military salute. "When can I get started?"

Valdore suppressed a victor's smile. "Centurion Terix, please take Cunaehr to your computer terminal. I want you, personally, to familiarize him with the briefing materials I'm about to transmit there." Those materials contained everything "Cunaehr" would need to know. The success of the rest of the coming mission would hinge largely upon Terix's suspicious nature; Valdore knew he could rely on the centurion to keep a weather eye on his Vulcan charge, regardless of any superior's orders.

After Terix and the *uhlan*s had escorted the spy away, Valdore smiled in his otherwise empty office. As he activated the terminal atop his desk and transmitted the files he had prepared in advance for Terix's mission, he quietly savored a feeling of triumph.

He always felt this way whenever a significant new weapon came into his possession.

When the guards had thrown open his cell door and dragged him abruptly to his feet, they had awakened Trip Tucker from a fitful sleep and an *extremely* convincing dream about T'Pol. As he awakened, he had been convinced then that he was finally about to die. *Well, I guess I've had a good run,* he thought, wondering precisely what he'd do during his final moments before the fatal disruptor blast, or sword slash, or guillotine—or whatever the hell they were planning on using—finally carried him off to glory.

The last thing he'd expected his captors to do was to offer him an apology, a job, and the freedom to move about Dartha as he pleased during the few hours that remained before he was to embark on his first mission on behalf of the Romulan Star Empire's military, under the supervision of one very dour-faced Centurion Terix. He found the situation almost laughably complicated: here he was, a human masquerading as a Romulan, but mistaken by the Romulans for a Vulcan; all the while, he'd be working with the Romulans to catch people who might actually *be* Vulcans infiltrating the Romulan Star Empire.

Reasonably sure he hadn't been surreptitiously followed back to his small rented suite of rooms near Dartha's central commercial district, Trip carefully checked the apartment for listening devices. Once he felt satisfied that no one was about to kick his door down, he removed his small subspace transceiver unit from its hiding place beneath his bedroom floorboards. For the first time during the two days since he'd called in to make the initial report about Ehrehin's untimely death, he activated the heavily shielded unit's battery pack, powering it up.

Stillwell thought he needed to worry about me going native before, Trip thought as he waited for his unscheduled transmission to wend its way across the light-years and negotiate the labyrinth of the bureau's clandestine two-way audio-video communications protocols. *I wonder what he's going to say about* this *report.*

As he'd expected, Stillwell had seemed fairly bowled over by Trip's revelation about his most recent change of plans.

"So you're just charging off to some remote part of Romulan space alongside one of their military officers," Stillwell said, looking doubtful as he digested Trip's initial bare-bones report about his arrest, his temporary confinement, and the mission briefing that had followed his sudden and unexpected release. *"Just like that."*

Trip smiled ironically at the image on his screen. "Sure beats a summary execution, Captain."

"You still have plenty of time to stumble into one of those, Commander. I just hope you haven't forgotten that Romulans can turn on you like rattlesnakes. I'm sure you haven't forgotten what our 'friend' Sopek did to your partner on Rator II. Treachery seems to be these people's national pastime. I give you the Romulans' own Ejhoi Ormiin *dissident group as People's Exhibit Number One to prove my point."*

The Romulans are hardly alone on that *score,* Trip thought. He was sorely tempted to remind his superior that Sopek might have been about as Romulan as T'Pol was, and to mention the xenophobes of Terra Prime, a human terror group that had nearly succeeded in strangling the infant Coalition of Planets in its cradle a few months back. Even after the death of its founder, the fading remnants of Terra Prime were still a thorn in the Coalition's side.

But because he didn't want to get bogged down in an ideological argument, Trip skirted the issue. "Valdore didn't leave me a lot of other options, good or bad," he said. "Anyway, you have to admit that this is one time when what we want and what Valdore wants fit together like spoons. Letting a bunch of rogue dissidents have the potential to build their own warp-seven-capable starships won't do a damned bit of good for us *or* for the Romulans."

Stillwell considered the matter in thoughtful silence

for several moments. Then with a sigh and a nod he said, *"For whatever it's worth, I've always found it damned difficult to get toothpaste to go back into the tube. But I'm forced to agree that you have to at least try. Good luck."*

Trip wondered what Stillwell would say if he told him he'd planned on going on the mission anyway, regardless of the bureau's input. "I appreciate that, Captain."

"I do have another concern, Commander," Stillwell said.

I'm all alone on Romulus, the center of a hostile galactic nation-state, a place where I don't dare trust anybody, Trip thought. *What the hell is there to be concerned about beyond that?*

"And what's that, sir?" he said aloud.

"I have to consider the possibility that the Romulan intelligence apparatus has compromised your disguise, and is deliberately allowing you to continue to operate."

Trip frowned. "Why would they do that?"

"To feed you disinformation to report back to us, of course. You must have considered the possibility that something other than good luck intervened on your behalf."

"Of course I have. I just seriously doubt that Admiral Valdore thinks I'm stupid enough to fall for a gag like that. Especially when you can test at least some of the information from my mission briefing independently."

"What kind of information?" Stillwell said, raising an eyebrow.

"Okay, why don't you take a close look at a detail from the written report I'm about to file?"

"All right, Commander. But give me the short version now."

Trip nodded. "A Romulan outpost recently observed what appeared to be an Earth Cargo Service freighter being attacked and destroyed by a Klingon battle cruiser.

The attack occurred somewhere in the Gamma Hydra sector, where the ECS probably doesn't have very many ships operating at any one time. It shouldn't be too hard to check this out, or at least get confirmation if any freighters in Gamma Hydra are overdue or missing."

"My people here will run that down immediately, Commander," Stillwell said. *"I'll transmit our findings via a subspace burst as soon as possible. In the meantime, let me wish you Godspeed on your mission.*

"Stillwell out."

Trip continued staring into the screen for long, uncounted moments after the display had faded to black. All he could do at this point was hope that Stillwell could verify the data he'd been given before the time came to embark on an extremely hazardous mission.

A mission that would be dangerous enough if it were completely on the level, rather than merely part of some hypothetical trap set for him by a wily Romulan admiral.

"I am ready to begin the next sequence of real-time tests, Admiral," Nijil said, gesturing toward the lab's central holo-projector, which had created a free-floating three-dimensional representation of one of the three Klingon battle cruisers his long *khaidoa* of continuous effort had finally succeeded in acquiring for the illustrious Praetor's fleet. "The remote-control tactical system should be ready for practical operation very shortly thereafter, should everything go according to plan during the next round of trials."

Valdore watched the virtual ship as it slowly turned through every conceivable degree of pitch, roll, and yaw, and silently thanked all the gods of Erebus for the coming culmination of his painstaking work. Both Praetor D'deridex and First Consul T'Leikha had lately been applying an uncomfortable amount of pressure on him to produce results.

They would soon see results beyond their wildest expectations. Valdore was beginning to feel sure of it, even though years of finely honing his instincts gave him a general distrust of such complacent certainties.

"Very good, Nijil," he said, nodding appreciatively at his chief technologist. "But remember, both the *klivam* vessels and the personnel we captured along with them are to be considered expendable should anything go wrong after we launch the attack."

"Of course, Admiral," Nijil said, fist clenched and elbow bent in a crisp salute. "I will see to it that their brutish lives are spent profitably in the defense of our Empire. And that theirs are the only identifiable fresh corpses anyone will be able to recover from the wreckage."

Soon, Earth and her Coalition partners would have all the proof they might need that the slope-browed *ahlh* who infested the Klingon Empire represented a far more imminent danger than did the Romulan Star Empire. Despite his ingrained, pragmatic aversion to wish-fulfillment fantasies and his hesitancy to believe in best-case scenarios, Valdore grinned as he considered what was to come.

Particularly once the Coalition weaklings set their vigilant eyes upon the wrong part of the sky and became preoccupied with the phantoms that would shortly be planted in their distracted field of view.

With a little help, he thought, *from my newest loyal servant, Cunaehr.*

TWELVE

Thursday, July 17, 2155
Enterprise NX-01

ALTHOUGH SHE HAD APPEARED on the bridge during the alpha watch just long enough to request that Captain Archer excuse her from her duties for unspecified personal reasons, T'Pol had really done so to show Ensign Sato that the captain had no issues with her earlier unauthorized transmissions. As she had anticipated, he had honored her request that he refrain from prying into the specifics that lay behind it. That was perhaps for the best, since T'Pol knew she had never mastered the fine art of lying. Misdirection seemed more credible, at least in theory, but had proved only marginally easier in practice.

Though he didn't insist on it, Archer nevertheless seemed to wish to discuss the matter further; T'Pol ignored the instinct that impelled her toward forthrightness and duty and walked away from him. He had already made it abundantly clear in sickbay that he had no intention of rescuing Trip, which meant that her plans simply didn't fall into line with the captain's.

The feeling was odd. She had defied authority before, but usually in the service of the needs of the many. This time, however, she knew that she was acting largely to satisfy her own deeply personal needs, no matter how she might seek to justify them using arguments about the urgency of the encroaching Romulan menace.

Life calls to Life, she thought, using the immortal words of the *Third Analects* of Surak to validate her all but irresistible compulsion to come to Trip's aid. In doing so, she knew she was brushing aside one of the ancient Vulcan philosopher's even more fundamental axioms: *The needs of the many outweigh the needs of the few.* She didn't care.

Once safely within her quarters again, T'Pol triggered a subspace signal burst to Denak, who had signaled already during the brief time she had been on the bridge. Even with the knowledge of her transmissions shared now by Archer and Sato, T'Pol still took the precaution of activating the scrambling device as Denak's incoming signal announced itself with a series of beeps on her desktop computer terminal. *It's preferable for them to think I'm discussing personal medical issues with a doctor on Vulcan than to learn what I'm really doing,* she thought.

Denak appeared on the screen, his eyes tinged with green and his skin visibly ashen even across the many light-years that separated them; he clearly had not been sleeping well. *"I've succeeded in getting you a ship, T'Pol, but it has not been easy. Let's just say that you've exhausted every debt I've ever owed you."*

T'Pol nodded slowly, acknowledging her old friend's implied warning without allowing herself to appear intimidated by it. "Will the ship be capable of getting me into Romulan space?"

"It can get you in, but not out," Denak said ominously. *"You will need to rendezvous with this vessel using a ship of your own near the periphery of Romulan space. I presume you will not be using* Enterprise *to do this."*

"I feel certain that I will be able to find some kind of craft," T'Pol said, ignoring Denak's sarcasm as her mind quickly worked the problem of acquiring a small auxiliary craft on short notice.

"The ship I have secured for you can take both you and whatever small craft you arrive in well past the Romulan Star Empire's borders. As long as you don't encounter any Romulan patrol vessels along the way, you should be fine."

"Where should I rendezvous with the ship, and when?"

"I've arranged for the vessel to be diverted from its regular course and mission," Denak said. *"Neither of which is known to anyone outside the V'Shar . . . and even then, it is known only to a handful. I am transmitting to you the rendezvous coordinates and timetable, along with a brief profile of the ship. You will have* one *contact on board, and you will be required to remain confined to whatever sections of the ship she specifies."*

T'Pol stared at him inquisitively. "Why?"

"The vessel carries . . . sensitive matériel to which you have not been granted access."

T'Pol saw a file open in the corner of her screen and was surprised to see that it was the image of a familiar face, even if it was noticeably older than the last time she had seen it. "Ych'a? *She* is my contact?"

"We both risk much with this, T'Pol," Denak said.

"I appreciate the trust you have placed in me, Denak," T'Pol said.

Denak raised an eyebrow, giving her the look that had made her feel so very uncomfortable during her years as his underling in the V'Shar. *"I wish you would extend me the same courtesy. I know that you are hiding things from me about the true purpose of this mission. But I also sense that you are acting . . . outside the purview of both Starfleet and the Coalition of Planets. Perhaps even against direct orders."*

He paused, leaning slightly closer to his own com unit. *"Before you were even born, a wise woman once told me that sometimes it takes those who will travel past*

the boundaries—without regard to arbitrary rules—to dis-
cover what truly lies beyond the horizon."

T'Pol had heard her mother express the same sentiments before, and suspected that it was she to whom
Denak was referring. She offered him a slight nod of acknowledgment. "Whatever I must do, I have no intention of causing any harm either to the Coalition or its
member worlds. I act to preserve life, and to protect our
people. You have my word on that."

Denak settled back in his chair again and steepled
his hands and fingers underneath his chin. T'Pol saw
that the thumb and forefingers were still missing from
his right hand; he had lost them during a mission years
ago, and had been unable to receive appropriate medical attention in time to save the nerves that would have
allowed them to be regrown successfully.

"While you might not harm the Coalition, T'Pol, re-
member that your actions may have consequences for
those who have placed their trust in you. You must be
prepared for that eventuality." Denak held up his good
hand, splitting his fingers into a salute. *"Live long and*
prosper, T'Pol."

T'Pol returned the salute as her viewscreen went
black.

Denak's words stung her, but she still felt certain that
her mission was absolutely necessary, even if it might
not be entirely logical. Assuming, of course, that the
encounters she had experienced with Trip in her mind-
scape were not, in fact, hallucinations.

Launch Bay Two seemed unnaturally quiet as T'Pol
quickly went about her work. Her fingers moved
smoothly over the computer panel as she input data
and observed the results. The subroutines she had ac-
cessed were complicated, and one wrong keystroke

could signal her actions to someone on the bridge, or elsewhere.

The gamma watch commander, Lieutenant O'Neill, and those on her shift were used to quiet "nights" aboard ship, and T'Pol knew from experience that this would be the best time to set her plan into motion—not because O'Neill's bridge crew was any less capable than the alpha watch team, but because nobody would even suspect the borderline sabotage she was engaged in at such a late hour. With the likely exception of Doctor Phlox, all of those aboard *Enterprise* who were closest to her would have been asleep for hours by now.

An alert light blinked on the computer viewscreen, prompting T'Pol to curse under her breath. She realized she must have run afoul of a security subroutine for which she had not prepared; perhaps Lieutenant Reed had installed a new code. She wondered briefly if he had done so because he'd anticipated her present course of action and felt the need to preempt it. *Illogical*, she told herself. There was no way Reed could have anticipated her plan. The captain, maybe the doctor . . .

Her fingers hovered over the keypad as her mind raced. She could back out of the subroutine, but that would mean taking care to erase every step she had already taken. Worse, her failure to beat *Enterprise*'s security measures tonight would force her to miss the rendezvous that Denak had so painstakingly arranged.

"Enter code alpha-two-epsilon-seven-niner-niner-tau-nu," said a voice from the shadows behind her in distinctively accented English.

Malcolm Reed's voice, to be precise.

"And what will happen then?" T'Pol asked, not turning around to face him. Despite her lifelong Vulcan training, she felt fear turn her spine to ice.

"That command will reroute the new security subroutine," Reed said. "Once that's out of the way, you can finish carrying out your plan to bypass the entire security system and commandeer one of our shuttlepods," Reed said. She heard his footsteps as he approached her. "That *is* what you intended, isn't it?"

T'Pol tensed, then ducked, sweeping her leg out quickly in a low, wide arc. She felt it connect with Reed's calves, and as she spun around she saw him collapse backward, a look of intense surprise on his face.

He's not carrying a phase pistol, she thought with a start. *And he's not even in uniform.* In fact, Reed was wearing what appeared to be a dark robe, similar to the attire of a civilian Vulcan merchant.

Reed quickly rolled backward, regaining his footing and springing to a crouching defensive stance. "Do you want to fight me, T'Pol, or do you want my help? Because Vulcan or not, I'll kick your ass, plus you'll miss your chance to input the code I just gave you. If you don't do that in the next twenty seconds, the security alarms will go off and we'll *both* have some heavy explaining to do."

T'Pol's mind raced, but her decision came quickly. She tapped the code into the datapad, and was rewarded with a green light.

"Now, we have ten minutes of safe time to get away from *Enterprise* before the system stops running the redundant program I wrote to conceal our little act of piracy," Reed said, cautiously moving closer.

T'Pol turned to him, reflexively raising an eyebrow. *"Our?"*

"Whatever your plan is, I'm coming with you," Reed said.

"Why?"

"I'd rather save the detailed explanation for after

we've gotten safely under way," Reed replied, a hint of sarcasm in his voice. "Suffice it to say that I know your intention is to rescue Trip. And he wouldn't be in this mess if it weren't for me."

T'Pol knew that Reed had worked in the past for the same secretive Starfleet organization for which Trip had since become an agent. She also knew that after Reed had told them he would no longer work for them, they had recruited Trip. She didn't know how or why they had convinced Trip he could be an effective spy— she hoped he'd tell her after they extracted him from Romulan space—but she assumed they had their reasons. She was surprised, however, to learn that Reed felt so guilty about Trip's recruitment.

"Did Captain Archer put you up to this, Lieutenant?" T'Pol asked. Had the captain's reticence about helping her merely been another secret maneuver, a tactic akin to the deliberate disinformation that still concealed, from most people, the fact that Trip wasn't really dead? Were Archer's earlier protestations simply an official gesture intended, as Trip might have put it, to "cover his ass"?

"I'm afraid not, Commander," Reed said, looking a bit crestfallen. "In fact, I suspect this may be my final straw with the captain. I've had to lie to him before because of my relationship with the bureau, and he believed me afterward when I told him I was through with all of that."

"My hope is that we will be able to retrieve Trip, and that the information he has gathered will be directly useful in mounting a defense against the Romulan Empire's encroachment on Coalition space," T'Pol said. "The ends would justify the means in this instance, and Captain Archer would understand, especially if we keep him insulated from our actions."

"That's a great hope," Reed said. "We can also hope

for ticker-tape parades, commendations from our superiors, and free hot fudge sundaes for life. But I suspect that even if we're successful, most of those wishes won't be coming true."

"Then why come with me?" T'Pol asked, fixing Reed with an inquisitive gaze.

He offered a wan smile. "Because you're not the only one who cares about Trip, Commander. We didn't start out as friends when this whole journey began, but there are few men I've met before or since whom I hold in higher esteem."

He pointed toward the viewscreen on the console where T'Pol had been working. "We have four minutes left before our departure window closes. Time to get packing."

T'Pol pointed toward a small traveling case she'd left leaning against a nearby bulkhead. "I have already packed."

Reed shook his head. "It's a human expression, T'Pol. Don't take it literally."

"Like 'kicking my ass'?" T'Pol asked, grabbing the case and heading toward Shuttlepod Two. "Why are humans so fixated on the gluteal muscles?" she said.

Reed fell into step beside her, snorting slightly. "Perhaps it's because we've all got 'em, Commander. Even Vulcans, I suppose." He reddened visibly as he moved to open the shuttlepod's hatch. "Not that I take much notice of such things."

"Indeed," T'Pol said in the most frostily polite tone she could muster. "And just so we're clear, Lieutenant, you could *not* have kicked mine."

THIRTEEN

Friday, July 18, 2155
Columbia **NX-02, near Draylax**

"*Please assist us! Our defenses cannot hold much longer against the hostiles' weaponry!*" Even without the bridge's linguistic translation matrices rendering the incoming message into intelligible English, the static-laced voice that carried it would have conveyed a crystal-clear message of desperation and fear all on its own.

Captain Erika Hernandez leaned forward in her command chair as she listened to the plaintive distress call and stared straight ahead into the star-flecked infinitude displayed on the large forward viewer.

"Origin point of the transmission?" she said, turning her chair slightly toward the portside com station.

"Looks like it's coming from the Draylax system, Captain," said the redheaded Ensign Sidra Valerian, her Scottish burr thickening into a heavy brogue as it often did during times of heightened tension. The youthful senior communications officer had gotten busy tracing the Mayday signal immediately after its arrival a few moments ago.

"Maybe it's lucky for the sender that he isn't farther away, Captain," said Lieutenant Reiko Akagi, from the helm console. "Draylax is very close to our current position. At maximum warp, I can get us there in just a few hours."

"Lucky for *them,* maybe," said Commander Veronica

Fletcher, *Columbia*'s executive officer and Hernandez's second in command. "For us, not so much."

"Especially if we're expected to stop a threat that the entire Draylaxian defense fleet can't cope with," said Lieutenant Kiona Thayer, the senior tactical officer. She stood in the bridge's starboard section, studying the readouts on her station as Lieutenant Commander Kalil el-Rashad, *Columbia*'s second officer and sciences expert, analyzed the same data on his own console.

"Not necessarily," Hernandez said. "From what I've seen, Draylax's defenses are nothing to write home about. In fact, their defensive capabilities have always been weak enough to make me wonder why they've been so uninterested in joining the Coalition."

"I wonder if they might be a bit more friendly to a Coalition sales pitch after this," Fletcher said, her New Zealand accent sharpening her words.

If they're still around afterward, Hernandez thought, recalling the horrible devastation that had been visited upon Coridan Prime not so very long ago. Aloud, she said, "I'll leave that sort of thing to the diplomats. Our main concern is putting an end to this assault, if we can. Reiko, make best speed to Draylax. Sidra, get me Starfleet Command. Advise Admiral Gardner of our diversion to Draylax."

Brushing a lock of her blond hair away from her eyes, Fletcher stepped close to the command chair and leaned toward Hernandez. "Gardner's not gonna be happy about this," she said in an almost conspiratorial tone. "After all, we're supposed to be protecting the Coalition shipping lanes from pirates and litterbugs, aren't we?"

Hernandez favored her exec with a wry smile. "Weren't you just complaining about how much patrol duty bores you?"

"Let's just say that boredom is infinitely preferable to reenacting the Charge of the Light Brigade," Fletcher said quietly.

"Don't worry, Veronica," Hernandez said with a grim chuckle. "We'll scout out the situation first and assess the odds. Then whether we stay or fall back will be up to the captain's discretion."

Fletcher's reply was preceded by a bantering smirk. "That's very reassuring, Captain. You have always been the very soul of discretion."

An excited exclamation from Ensign Valerian interrupted Hernandez's rejoinder. "Admiral Gardner's on the line," the com officer said, looking surprised.

"Very efficient, Sidra," Fletcher said.

The com officer's brogue thickened even further. "Commander, I didn't raise *him*. *He's* calling *us*."

"He must have a spy aboard," Fletcher said quietly, her voice obviously pitched for the captain's ears alone. Hernandez couldn't always quite tell when she was kidding. "Or maybe he's bugged our helm console."

Hernandez ignored the comment. Nodding to the com officer as she rose from her command chair, she said, "I'll take it in my ready room."

"Admiral Gardner," Hernandez said as she seated herself at her small and perpetually cluttered desk. Fortunately, she had taken the liberty of pushing the stacks of paper, books, and two coffee cups safely out of the admiral's line of sight. "Please go ahead, sir."

The subspace-transmitted image of the stern-faced man displayed on her ready-room terminal began speaking without any preamble. *"Captain, an emergency situation has arisen."*

"Draylax," she said.

Gardner nodded soberly as he ran a hand across his

duranium-colored crew cut. *"It's a potentially explosive situation."*

"We're already on our way there at maximum warp, sir. My com officer was about to advise you of our course change. We'll reach Draylax in less than four hours."

Assuming we don't get sent back out on pirate patrol in the meantime, she added silently.

"Outstanding, Captain," Gardner said with the faintest hint of a smile. *"The Draylaxians are in considerable danger, given their relatively limited defensive and tactical capabilities. Even a single NX-class starship could make all the difference."*

"We'll do everything we reasonably can to assist the Draylaxians," Hernandez said, nodding. "And to limit the loss of life."

"Of that I have no doubt, Captain. Nevertheless, I need to emphasize just how critically important Draylax is to the Coalition."

Unbidden, a frown creased Hernandez's brow. "I thought the Draylaxians had refused Coalition membership." Like the government of the nearby Porriman civilization in the Gamma Virginis system, with whom Hernandez had recently concluded a series of negotiations that had proved both lengthy and fruitless, the Draylaxians remained stubbornly determined to protect their sovereignty by avoiding large-scale diplomatic entanglements.

"They have," Gardner said with a grave shake of his head. *"Which is a damned shame for us."*

"I'm not sure I understand, Admiral," Hernandez said, blinking involuntarily.

He leaned forward slightly. *"I've just conferred with Minister Samuels. He and I are in agreement that if Earth could get another nonhuman civilization or two to apply for Coalition membership right now, Captain, it would go a long way toward smoothing the ruffled feathers of the Vulcans, the Andorians, and the Tellarites over Earth's position favoring full membership status for Alpha Centauri. Our intervention in the current crisis might persuade the Draylaxians that joining the Coalition is in their best interests after all."*

"My only interest is in saving lives, Admiral," Hernandez said, shaking her head. "The galactic political horse-trading behind all of this really doesn't concern me all that much."

"I'm afraid it has *to concern you* now, *Captain,"* Gardner said, his voice evoking the cold solidity of hull metal. *"We're involved in this matter regardless. Even though Draylax isn't a Coalition member, it has recently entered a mutual defense pact with one of its closest neighbors: Alpha Centauri."*

"And we're already committed to the defense of Alpha Centauri," Hernandez said. A slow, sinking feeling began tugging her guts inexorably downward.

The admiral nodded. *"Alpha Centauri is one of the United Earth government's Coalition partners, which has its own separate mutual defense compact with Earth. Therefore Starfleet is legally required to treat an attack on Alpha Centauri as if it were an attack on Earth. We are obliged to protect Alpha Centauri's treaty partners as well."*

"So we have to treat an attack on Draylax as though it were an attack against Alpha Centauri," Hernandez said. Her stomach was now in free fall.

"Or against Earth itself," Gardner said, nodding.

Hernandez recalled a history course she'd taken at the Academy, in which she had studied the complex diplomatic cat's cradle of mutually interlocking defense agreements that had bound the European nations of the

early twentieth century. With so many countries prepared to deploy their armies in defense of so many allies, all it had taken was the assassination of one man in
an obscure Balkan country to plunge most of the planet
into the bloodiest war humanity had ever experienced
up to that time.

*"So I'm afraid you may have to do a bit more than
whatever you 'reasonably can,' Captain,"* the admiral continued, his gaze hard yet also sympathetic. *"You* have *to
defend Draylax. To the death, if that's what it comes to.*
Columbia *is therefore to be considered expendable so long
as Draylax remains in jeopardy."*

*And while the Coalition's nonhuman members remain
in a snit over the Alpha Centauri business, or Draylax
continues to stay out of the alliance,* Hernandez thought
sourly. She could only hope that something other than
the blood of her crew would become the coin that pur-
chased peace within the Coalition, if such a thing was
even possible.

"Aye, aye, sir. Do we know who the attackers are,
Admiral?"

"Klingons," Gardner said after a pregnant pause.
*"Three battle cruisers, according to the reports we've just
received."*

Hernandez nodded, though she wasn't encouraged.
"I hope we arrive in time to do some good. Once we get
there, we'll hold them off as long as we can, Admiral.
I'm sure Major Foyle and his MACOs will give the Klingons one hell of a fight."

She could only hope that Doctor Metzger's sickbay
would be spared the baptism of fire that the MACOs
were about to face.

The admiral nodded again, his eyes glistening with
unshed moisture. *"I know you* all *will do your best,*

Captain Hernandez. Godspeed to you and your crew. Gardner out." And with that, his image vanished.

Oh, well, she thought. *"Captain's discretion" has always been overrated anyway.*

She reached across her desk and punched a button on the compad built into the desk beside her computer terminal.

"Hernandez to engineering," she said.

The Austrian chief engineer replied in his customary blunt Teutonic tones. *"Lieutenant Graylock here, Captain."*

"We need to get to Draylax as quickly as possible, Karl. I need you to push it a little bit past the redline. Again."

"I suppose my engine core can manage warp five point two for an hour or so without vaporizing us completely," he said, an undercurrent of dour humor buoying his grim words. *"Anything else, sir?"*

"Just try to keep us in one piece, Karl."

"That complicates things a bit, Captain, but ja, *I think my people can handle it. I'll make Biggs and Pierce get out and push if I have to. And I'll set Rivers and Strong to running in the hamster wheel."*

Smiling, she said, "Thanks, Karl. Hernandez out." She pressed another button. "Hernandez to com."

Ensign Valerian's crisp reply came half a heartbeat later. *"Bridge, Captain."*

"Sidra, isn't *Enterprise*'s patrol route supposed to take her into this sector about now?"

"Aye, Captain, I believe it is."

That struck Hernandez as suspiciously like a good omen, though she was far too experienced an officer to put much stock in such things. "Try to raise them. I need to speak with Captain Archer as soon as possible."

"Aye, I'm on it, sir," the com officer said. *"I'll transfer the connection to your ready room once it's established."*

"Thank you, Sidra. Hernandez out."

She hadn't decided yet whether she was calling because she wanted to ask for Jonathan's help, or because she merely needed the emotional closure of a last farewell.

FOURTEEN

Friday, July 18, 2155
Enterprise NX-01

CAPTAIN JONATHAN ARCHER COULD FEEL his pulse accelerating as he left his ready room and stepped onto the bridge. His conversation with Erika Hernandez had crossed over the time of *Enterprise*'s early-morning shift-change, so while most of his alpha-watch crew were already on deck, his gamma-watch commander, D.O., was still seated in the captain's chair, going over reports on a datapad.

"Ensign Mayweather, your console should be receiving a set of coordinates near Draylax in a moment," Archer said before acknowledging O'Neill or any of the others. "Set a course there immediately, maximum warp."

He spoke up then, looking around at the other members of the bridge crew. He noticed that a few faces were missing; T'Pol's absence was to be expected, but he had assumed he would see Malcolm Reed at his usual place behind the tactical station. "It appears that the Klingons have launched an attack near Draylax," he announced loudly. "Captain Hernandez is taking *Columbia* there now. *We* are going to be her backup."

"Is this the first strike of a war?" O'Neill asked, surrendering the captain's chair to Archer as she stood. Alarm was etched on her features.

"We're not sure yet, D.O.," Archer said. "All we really

know so far is that three heavily armed Klingon warships are fighting their way toward the Draylax system's main population centers. Draylax's entire defense fleet may not be up to fending them off, and Admiral Gardner has ordered *Columbia* to assist them."

"And *Enterprise*?" O'Neill asked warily.

"Gardner hasn't given us any new orders yet, but I expect that to change soon enough."

"Forgive me, sir, but isn't sending Starfleet's two best ships to deal with this a bit of overkill?" Mayweather asked, turning from his console. "Draylax isn't even part of the Coalition of Planets."

"That may be, Travis, but Earth has a mutual defense arrangement with Draylax," Archer said, taking his seat and toggling a switch on one of its arms. "Burch, I need full warp capability. We have to push this ship to her limits. And make certain all weapons ports and hull-plating polarization protocols are triple-checked. We may be seeing some action soon."

"Right away, sir," Burch replied, his voice issuing from the com unit on Archer's chair.

Archer reached for a datapad that O'Neill was patiently holding out to him. "How was the night shift, D.O.? Did I miss anything interesting?"

O'Neill, a petite redhead, smiled grimly. "Not really, sir. We encountered a cloud of debris at about oh-three-hundred. Drifting ice crystals that must have been the remnant of some long-dead comet. But they apparently weren't substantial enough to even fog up the windows."

"Where's Malcolm?" Archer asked, gesturing toward the tactical station that the enthusiastic Englishman usually manned during the alpha-watch hours.

"He called in sick earlier," D.O. said, her smile slipping into a frown. "Said he must have had a bad reaction to some of Chef's food. Unless we wanted to have him hitting the head every five minutes, it didn't make sense to have him on duty."

Archer grinned and lowered his voice. "Malcolm and his sensitive stomach . . . it's a wonder he's ever able to fly at all sometimes. I assume Phlox will have some kind of antidiarrheal to settle him down." He squinted for a moment, scrolling through a personnel roster in his mind. "Who do we have to replace him? Yoc? Beaton?"

"If you don't mind, sir, I'll take Reed's post myself," O'Neill said. "I didn't really have any plans for my off-duty time today, and I'm not terribly tired."

Archer clapped a hand on the lieutenant's shoulder and stood. "Suit yourself, D.O. Have some food ordered up from the mess though; can't have your stomach rumbling so loudly it drowns out the com system. But before you take over that post, I have a call to make from my ready room. You have the bridge again until I'm done with that."

Turning toward the communication station, Archer saw that Hoshi Sato was frowning as she studied her com-system displays. "What's wrong, Hoshi?" he asked, moving toward her.

"I know you said it was all right for a *certain* crew member to make private subspace transmissions off the main system," Sato said, keeping her voice low even as she glanced sideways to make sure that none of the other bridge crew were standing near enough to overhear her. "But I think we should put them in the official logs."

Archer frowned. "Do any of these transmissions pose a problem?"

"I'm not sure," Hoshi said, shrugging. "But another, significantly *longer* transmission went out last night."

"And?"

"*Enterprise*'s clocks happen to be roughly synchronized with the region on the planet to which the transmission was sent," Sato said, carefully leaving out the name of the planet they both knew they were discussing: Vulcan. "The transmission went out at about oh-three-thirty hours. That seems like an odd time to be dealing with personal business back home."

Archer waved his hand to one side. "I've given up on what seems 'odd' when it comes to those particular people, Hoshi. Thanks for alerting me, but I'm not overly concerned about it."

"Yes, sir," Sato said, though her expression showed that she wasn't entirely placated.

"Besides, we have bigger fish to fry right now," Archer said. "I need you to raise Admiral Krell of the Klingon Defense Force. Pipe it through to my ready room after you set up the connection."

Minutes later, Archer found himself pacing in his small ready room office, wishing that any of his closest companions aboard the ship were present to consult with him regarding the trials that lay ahead: T'Pol, Trip, Malcolm . . . even Porthos was good for counsel from time to time. It wasn't that he couldn't make decisions on his own, but he'd always found it best to bounce ideas off his trusted friends, even if, ultimately, he went with his own gut feeling more often than not. But at the moment his most trusted friends were either "dead," hallucinating, running to the bathroom, or sleeping on the pillow at the foot of his bed.

Two chimes sounded from the com unit mounted on the wall. *"I have Admiral Krell,"* Sato's voice announced from the speaker.

Archer crossed back behind his desk, tilting the desktop viewscreen up even as he remained standing. The visual pickup would be looking up at him, giving him a subtle if slight psychological advantage. "On-screen," Archer said.

Less than a year had passed since Archer had first tangled with Krell, when the hostile fleet admiral had been intent on destroying the Klingon Empire's own Qu'Vat colony, including its inhabitants: Klingons who had been infected with genetically mutated augment virus. Although Doctor Phlox had succeeded in synthesizing a cure for the plague—partially by using Archer as a guinea pig to create antibodies—Krell still attempted to go ahead with the colony's destruction, personally leading a trio of Klingon battle cruisers against both *Enterprise* and *Columbia*.

It was only after a canister containing the metagenic Qu'Vat virus ended up aboard the admiral's ship—dispersing an aerosolized virus and infecting the Klingon leader and his crew—that Krell called off the attack on Qu'Vat in favor of perfecting a cure to the illness.

The viewscreen before Archer melted to black for an instant before the shadowed face of the Klingon fleet admiral appeared to replace it. Archer recognized the mane of white and brown hair, and the white goatee with a center braid that defined Krell's aggressive appearance. But something seemed subtly different about him. When Krell leaned forward, the difference immediately became clear.

"What do you want, Archer?" Krell asked. He sounded as angry as he had during the confrontation at Qu'Vat, and a pair of large hooked teeth still protruded from beneath his upper lip, but the dusky-hued ridged Klingon that Archer had seen before was gone. In his place was a more human-looking Klingon with less pronounced ridges. He looked more like a swarthy human pirate from Earth's South Sea islands than he did a Klingon warrior.

"Why have your ships attacked Draylax, Admiral?" Archer said, not allowing his expression to convey any shock at the change that time and retroviruses had wrought upon the warrior whose visage once could have made children cry.

"*I have no idea what you're talking about,* human," Krell said, emphasizing the final word as if it were a curse.

"Three of your vessels have attacked Draylax without provocation. *You* have command of the fleet, Admiral. Order them to withdraw."

Krell sneered and leaned back again into the shadows behind him. "*You credit me with too much power, Captain. There are* many *admirals and generals who wield authority in the Klingon Empire, and my . . . influence has been reduced of late due to . . . certain* changes *that have occurred.*"

"Changes within the Klingon military, or changes to *you*?" Archer asked, pressing the point. "I can't imagine that you'd let anybody take any authority away from you, Krell. It was always my impression that *you* were one of the most powerful warriors who ever drew a blade on Qo'noS."

Krell wound his beard-braid around one finger, tilting his head to crack his neck languidly. "*Your flattery is noted, Captain, but your understanding of a warrior's place in our society is lacking. Especially when such a warrior has been infected with a pernicious disease.*"

"But you helped to bring an end to the disease, and stability to the Empire," Archer said, exaggerating the truth to almost elephantine proportions. "That should have brought you commendations and honors."

"*Perhaps if I had not been changed by the virus, that would be true,*" Krell said, leaning forward again and growling into his monitor. "*Your physician is responsible for my shame. His perfidy has bought him my undying enmity. I will one day paint the walls of my cabin with his blood.*"

Archer stood his ground. "What does *your* shame have to do with Draylax? Are you so spiteful that you would be willing to strike the first blow of a war in a system that can barely defend itself? Is *that* the legacy you would leave to your children?"

"First, even if the Empire were to engage in the attack you speak of, it should be no cause of concern for you humans, or your so-called Coalition of Planets," Krell said, all but growling his words. *"You are meddling in interstellar affairs that are beyond your grasp.*

"Second, the Klingon Empire has ordered no hostilities against Draylax. If we had, I would know about them."

Krell moved in closer, until his angry face nearly filled the monitor completely. *"I have not sworn a blood oath against you, Archer, but that can change. Whatever tenuous honor you have accrued inside the Empire in exchange for your help in curing the metagenic virus is balanced on the tip of a* d'k tahg. *Be careful that you do not slip down the edge to your doom."*

The screen abruptly went black, and Archer realized a few seconds later that he was holding his breath. Even across light-years and through a viewscreen, an angry Klingon could be both formidable and intimidating. He hoped he wouldn't have to encounter Krell in the flesh any time soon.

More importantly, he hoped that the fleet admiral hadn't been lying to him. But if the Empire really had not authorized the hostilities now being directed at Draylax, then what was really behind the danger toward which Erika Hernandez and *Columbia*'s crew were hurtling at this very moment?

To say nothing of his own people, who were speeding toward the very same fate just as quickly as Henry Archer's mighty warp-five engine could carry them. . . .

FIFTEEN

Friday, July 18, 2155
Columbia **NX-02**

"WE DON'T HAVE any other choice," Captain Erika Hernandez said, feeling a single cold bead of sweat escaping her hairline and moving down between her shoulder blades.

Sitting at the edge of her captain's chair, she spoke to her senior helm officer in a steady voice. "Evasive maneuvers, Mister Akagi. Every salvo you dodge will earn you an extra hour of sack time every day for a week."

"*Hai*, Captain," said Lieutenant Reiko Akagi. Hernandez didn't need to see the pilot's face to know that she was smiling broadly even as her hands deftly moved over the ship's helm controls.

Hernandez turned partially around, catching the worried glance of her XO, Commander Veronica Fletcher, before her own gaze settled on Lieutenant Kiona Thayer, her senior tactical officer. "Kiona, bring to bear everything you've got. I have a feeling this could be the fight of our lives."

As hyperbolic as that statement might have sounded, Hernandez suspected it would prove not to be an exaggeration once the battle was through. *I hope we're still around then to debate that,* she thought grimly.

But the odds didn't look good. Even as *Columbia* had arrived at Draylax, the three Klingon battle cruisers began firing on the planet below, even though several expanding clouds of glittering metallic debris provided mute testimony that they had already dispatched Draylax's defense ships some time ago. Fletcher had noted that the Klingons appeared to have been holding back, as though they had been waiting for *Columbia* to decelerate into orbit around the principal inhabited planet of the Draylax system. Hernandez had to admit that the tableau before her looked suspicious as hell.

Damn, I wish Archer was here along with his ship, she thought. The last time they had faced a trio of Klingon cruisers—above the Qu'Vat colony—it had been *she* who had helped *him*. At least two Starfleet ships against three Klingon vessels had seemed a fairer fight; this time it would be three against one.

She toggled a switch on her chair's com unit. "Lieutenant Graylock, whatever you do, don't be stingy with the power to our hull plating. We're about to take some heavy fire." She didn't wait for his affirmative reply; she didn't need to. He was as good a chief engineer as Tucker had been during his brief time aboard this vessel, before he'd been billeted back to *Enterprise*.

"Take her down to block the disruptor cannons," Hernandez said. "Polarize the hull plating, and double it up here on the bridge and in engineering."

She turned toward Fletcher. "Veronica, get Major Foyle and the MACOs ready for a ship-to-ship transport. I know it'll be risky, so let them know that it's not mandatory. Volunteers only. But if we can catch even *one* of their ships with its proverbial pants down, we might be able to get our guys on board and take over."

Fletcher nodded and moved swiftly to a com station to call Foyle. Hernandez knew that there probably would be few volunteers. *MACOs might be brave to a fault once they get to the battle, but I doubt that many of them trust the transporter enough to risk buying the farm with it before they get close enough to see the whites of the enemies' eyes,* she thought gloomily.

Still, she had wanted to try that maneuver for a while now, and the time to try seemed to have arrived at last. The Klingons might not suspect such a bold gambit when they so clearly outnumbered their opponent. *Just imagine what we could learn if we actually manage to capture one of their cruisers,* Hernandez thought. The idea sent an added jolt of adrenaline surging into her veins.

"Coming into effective weapons range in forty seconds, Captain," Akagi said. The bridge's main viewscreen showed one of the battle cruisers directly in *Columbia's* flight path.

"Give me one more hail, Sidra," Hernandez shouted back to her communications officer, Ensign Sidra Valerian. When she saw the red "go ahead" light appear at the bottom of the viewscreen, she squared her shoulders and put on her best "scolding teacher" face.

"Klingon cruisers, this is Captain Erika Hernandez of the United Earth *Starship Columbia*. You must cease fire immediately, or we will open fire on *your* vessels. Your continued aggression will be considered an act of war not only against Draylax, but also against Earth and Alpha Centauri."

"The central ship is charging her weapons," Thayer shouted.

"Then so do we," Hernandez said, leaning forward in her chair. "Employ evasive maneuvers, and send them a full phase cannon salvo, maximum intensity." The tactical alert lights activated even as she gave the command, casting the bridge into forbidding shadows.

The viewscreen image changed as the ship arced between the central Klingon cruiser and the blue-white planet below it, as the hull-mounted sensors realigned the sweep of their imagers. Hernandez saw two bright greenish arcs exit the belly of the Klingon ship, and she braced herself for their arrival, digging her fingers into the arms of her chair.

Columbia shuddered as the disruptor beams struck the primary hull, causing the viewscreen image to crackle and waver momentarily.

"Hull plating down fifteen percent," Lieutenant Commander el-Rashad shouted from his science station. "The other two ships are altering their trajectories. Looks like they're going to try to catch us in a crossfire."

Hernandez studied the main viewer, where the other two enemy ships were indeed moving toward positions flanking *Columbia*. "You know that tactic you've been wanting to try for far too long, Reiko? The Niagara Barrel Roll?"

She thought she heard a gulp of surprise coming from the woman at the helm. "Are you certain now is the time?"

"If not, we might not get another chance," Hernandez said. She toggled her com unit, tying into the shipwide intercom system. "All hands, brace yourselves. We're gonna have a bit of a tumble." Tapping another button, she said, "Karl, you're gonna need to make *sure* that the inertial dampers hold up."

Akagi had once told her that despite her Japanese heritage, the one thing she loved more than anything else on Earth was quintessentially North American: roller coasters. Hernandez couldn't stand them herself, and thought the simulation rides she had endured in Starfleet's flight training program had to be more than realistic enough to satisfy whatever death wish seemed to motivate roller-coaster aficionados.

"They're charging their tubes, ready to fire," el-Rashad shouted. "All three cruisers!"

As the viewscreen showed the first hint of green energy coming from a disruptor bank on one Klingon ship's ventral side, Hernandez heard herself give an order. "Roll it, Reiko!"

The words seemed to leave her lips in slow motion, but the reaction to them was anything but slack. As Akagi manipulated the controls, *Columbia* began to twist in a corkscrew fashion. The ship's hull groaned as it spun, and Hernandez felt almost as though she were trapped in a high-speed centrifuge despite the accelerated inputs to the artificial gravity plating and the inertial compensation system. The maneuver overwhelmed the hull sensors, transforming the image on the central viewscreen into a jumbled and pixelated mess, but the fact that the ship hadn't encountered a disruptor blast—or six—in the several seconds since the cruisers had opened fire seemed to imply that the maneuver had worked.

At least for the moment.

"Get us steady and return fire!" Hernandez shouted. A few moments later the ship seemed to lurch toward its port side, pulling everyone on the bridge a bit off balance.

"Firing now," Thayer said emphatically, as gravity and inertia returned to their proper ratio, and the viewscreen rebooted to display a short-lived blue wash of outgoing phase-cannon fire.

The image cleared quickly; just ahead was the battle cruiser that had been farthest from *Columbia* at the outset of the battle. Hernandez could see clearly that *Columbia*'s phase cannons had communicated very clearly with the hostile vessel's aft engine areas.

An instant later, the Klingon warship's impulse engines exploded, sending a bright sphere of plasma expanding into space as the interior gases escaped and ignited. The conflagration quickly caught on throughout the hull-ruptured cruiser, and in moments both the secondary and primary hulls exploded as well, sending jagged hunks of debris and the remains of the vessel's burning nacelle pylons and long, fractured neck tumbling in random directions, with some pieces falling toward the planet while others tumbled outward into space.

"Good shooting, Kiona," Hernandez said, excited despite the fact that she would have preferred to avoid the engagement with the Klingons entirely. Good intentions aside, Hernandez knew that she was committed now to fight to the finish—and that the two remaining cruisers would be even tougher to stop now that blood had been drawn. *There will be no negotiating now.*

"Bring us about, and let's see if we can keep the other two off-kilter." She realized that even though her stomach was still lurching a bit from the spin maneuver, it had worked very well indeed. She didn't expect it to become a standard maneuver, however.

"We're receiving a hail," Ensign Valerian said from her station at the rear of the bridge.

"Are the Klingons finally coming to their senses?" Hernandez asked with a smirk. She knew better; the most likely reason they were calling was to spew invective and to make threats about feasting on her entrails or some other such macho nonsense.

"Not exactly," Valerian said.

The image of two menacing Klingon cruisers set against the star-flecked blackness beyond Draylax vanished, to be replaced by a far warmer and more welcoming sight: Captain Jonathan Archer and the bridge of *Enterprise.*

"Think you could use a hand, Captain?" Archer said, a grim smile on his lips.

"Well, I haven't been able to talk any sense into them so far, Captain," Hernandez said, gesturing outward as if toward the Klingons. "In fact, they've ignored all our hails and warnings. We had to destroy one of their ships before you got here."

"That makes the odds a bit more even," Archer joked. *"Two against two is a* much *fairer fight."*

"What's your ETA, Captain?" Hernandez said, eager to make the coming fight an even-money proposition.

"We're nearly right on top of you already," Archer said. He turned his head slightly, speaking to someone off-screen. *"Fire to disable."*

Hernandez tapped a button on her chair's arm-mounted console, and the forward viewscreen switched to a view of the other ships. *Enterprise* was thundering forward, having apparently just dropped out of warp, and its pulsed phase cannons threw a series of blasts toward the central Klingon aggressor that had been pouring the heaviest fire onto the surface of Draylax.

The beams arced over the enemy vessel's hull, and it visibly shuddered, but did not move further. Instead, the Klingon launched a salvo of projectiles at the swift-moving *Enterprise*.

"Bring us to bear against the third ship," Hernandez said. "Try hailing them one last time, but prepare to fire again at my signal."

Looking at the viewer, Hernandez saw that Archer was making a pass toward the other ship as well, essentially trapping the vessel between *Enterprise* and *Columbia*. The Klingon cruiser arced to starboard, attempting to flee—Hernandez thought she understood Klingon pride well enough to imagine the ship's captain would no doubt claim the maneuver was really only a means of "regaining the defensive high ground"—but Hernandez knew that *Akagi* was already matching the hostile's new course.

"Still no answer," Valerian said.

"Target their nacelles," Hernandez ordered.

Suddenly, the Klingon vessel slid off the viewscreen, as if vanishing.

"What happened?"

"They *braked!*" Fletcher shouted, staring goggle-eyed from a computer station she was using. "They just cranked their reverse-thrusters all the way up. We just overshot them!"

"*Shit!*" Hernandez ordered, "Polarize the aft plating! Get Archer back on the—"

A moment later, the ship shuddered violently, and Hernandez had to grab the arms of her chair to avoid being tossed to the deck. The rest of the bridge crew were similarly jostled, but they had all braced themselves solidly just prior to Akagi's earlier evasive maneuvers.

"Status?"

"Our starboard nacelle took a hit, Captain," el-Rashad said, a hint of panic in his voice. "We're venting quite a bit of plasma."

The viewscreen image switched perspective to the aft end of the ship's saucer section; from that vantage point, Hernandez could see very clearly the extensive damage the starboard nacelle had sustained, and the energetic plasma that was rapidly escaping from it. Beyond the nacelle, she saw the sapphire glow of Draylax, the Klingon cruiser, and something else.

Enterprise firing.

A heartbeat later, the phase-cannon blasts from *Enterprise* ignited the impulse drive module at the aft end of the Klingon ship's secondary hull. Within seconds, the second cruiser turned inside out as the resulting explosions tore it to pieces, its decompression as spectacularly violent as the conflagrations that had taken apart the first vessel.

"*Is your ship okay, Captain?*" Archer asked, his worried face reappearing on the forward viewer.

"It's nothing a little time and baling wire can't fix," Hernandez said through a wry but grateful smile. "But we still have one more ship to deal with first. Let's see if we can get *them* to surrender in one piece."

"*They're Klingons,*" Archer said. "*I'm not sure their language even has a word for 'surrender.'*" His gaze shifted to his right for a moment as someone spoke to him.

Fletcher spoke up then as well. "Captain, it's *not* just one ship."

"What?"

"Three more Klingon battle cruisers have just dropped out of warp. They're flanking the surviving vessel."

"*Damn,*" Archer said, his image frowning into his own central bridge viewer. "*So much for trying to stack the odds in our favor. Are you seeing what we're seeing, Captain?*"

"On-screen tactical," Hernandez said. "*Enterprise* to audio-only."

There were now indeed four Klingon vessels orbiting Draylax, and not a one of them showed so much as a dented fender's worth of damage.

"Hail the newcomers, Sidra," Hernandez said.

"They're priming their weapons," Thayer shouted, her voice ragged.

"All available power to hull plating!" Hernandez barked. She wondered if the system's remaining power would be enough to resist even the first shots of the new arrivals, or if this was to be *Columbia*'s last stand.

A moment later, all four of the Klingon vessels fired, but only one seemed to be taking aim at either of the Starfleet ships.

The other three had directed their disruptor blasts at the fourth cruiser, the last of the original trio that had attacked Draylax.

Caught in a withering crossfire, the cruiser erupted instantly in a series of conflagrations that might have been brilliant enough to damage every optic nerve on *Columbia*'s bridge had the main viewer's luminal filters not intervened to prevent it.

"What the . . ." Hernandez couldn't even finish her thought.

A moment later, the newly arrived trio of Klingon cruisers abruptly turned about and sped away, accelerating to warp almost instantly on a direct heading toward Klingon space.

Hernandez looked around at her bridge crew. "What the hell just happened here?"

"I was hoping you could tell me," Archer said from the audio speakers.

Focusing on the screen, Hernandez watched as the last molecular fires from the destroyed Klingon ship's expanding debris field silently burned themselves out several hundred kilometers over Draylax.

Something extremely strange had just happened here, and the only people who might supply the answer to the mystery—the Klingons aboard the three just-departed battle cruisers—were gone, leaving nothing but destruction and questions in their wake.

SIXTEEN

THE AFTER-BATTLE REPAIRS, which mostly centered on *Columbia*'s rather extensive but thankfully nonfatal damage, had made for a long day that had challenged the combined engineering teams of both *Enterprise* and *Columbia*. And now, despite the lateness of the hour, Jonathan Archer found that he couldn't sleep. Lying on the bed in his night-dimmed quarters, he felt a desperate need, almost a physical hunger, to talk to someone about his current problem with the Klingons.

At least someone other than Porthos, whom he noted was still watching him in the semidarkness, his large black eyes alert as he lay on the pillow in the corner he used for sleeping. Though he knew he was anthropomorphizing, Archer couldn't help but read the beagle's vaguely quizzical expression as one of canine concern about the current pensive state of his human.

Still recumbent, Archer reached across the bed to the small com panel mounted on the wall nearest to the bed. He hesitated as his fingers made contact with the button.

Archer paused for a moment. While he certainly had the authority to interrupt his senior officers' off-duty activities when circumstances warranted, even in the dead of ship's night, he didn't consider his personal feelings of isolation and loneliness to be sufficient cause.

And despite the unprecedented emotional closeness he and his first officer had come to share over the past few months, he hadn't forgotten the ingrained tendency of Vulcans toward a certain standoffishness. He also knew how emotionally stressed T'Pol had been lately, perhaps as much by Trip's feigned death as by the need to keep the truth behind it concealed from all but a small handful of her crewmates and friends. Considering all she'd been through since she'd first set foot aboard *Enterprise,* she deserved to be allowed to continue doing whatever she needed to do in order to keep body and *katra* together.

He resigned himself to dealing on his own with the Klingon problem.

He sat up with a sigh, and Porthos regarded him with an expectant look and a wagging tail for a moment before launching himself into Archer's lap. Scratching the dog's head behind the right ear, he said, "Porthos, how do you feel about trading jobs with me?"

Porthos tipped his head and whined, and his swiftly wagging tail abruptly dropped out of warp.

Archer chuckled. "Sorry. You're way too smart to fall for that. Get some sleep. *One* of us should."

He patted Porthos near the rump, and the dog jumped back down and returned to his sleeping corner while Archer finally gave up on the idea of slumber entirely. Sometime during the few minutes it took Archer to doff his bathrobe and don his standard blue duty uniform, the beagle had closed his eyes and drifted off into what looked like a bottomlessly deep slumber.

Archer looked on wistfully as the sleeping animal's paws jerked three times, probably in response to the appearance of a sprawling dream-pasture, a wish granted by some merciful canine Morpheus. Until he got to the bottom of this mess with the Klingons, he seriously doubted he'd be able to follow Porthos's wise example.

Moving quietly, he crossed the small room to his desk and took a seat in front of the computer terminal there. He entered his personal com access code manually, along with a particular subspace frequency, and then drummed his fingers on the desk for several seconds while the screen's ship status updates vanished.

Archer ceased his drumming when a blood-red Klingon trefoil emblem appeared, standing out starkly against a background as black as space itself. A moment later, the alien sigil was replaced by the scowling visage of a middle-aged male Klingon dressed in a warrior's battle armor. For an absurd moment, Archer wondered whether everybody on Qo'noS dressed like that, right down to the receptionists in the lobby who answered the incoming com transmissions and whoever came in at night to mop the floors and empty out the wastepaper baskets.

"NuqneH, Tera'ngan?" the frowning warrior said as *Enterprise*'s linguistic translation matrix took a beat to calibrate before beginning its continuous real-time translation stream. *"What do you want, Terran?"*

Noting that the man on the other end of the com-link had a conspicuously smooth, humanlike forehead, Archer knew he would have to proceed with no small amount of caution. After all, any Klingon who bore a permanent reminder of that particular crisis was bound to have a chip on his shoulder when it came to dealing with humans.

But he also understood Klingons well enough to know that they preferred plain talk to beating around the bush.

"I am Captain Jonathan Archer of the *Starship Enterprise*. I must speak with Fleet Admiral Krell immediately regarding the Draylax situation."

"I am Captain Qapegh, Fleet Admiral Krell's adjutant," the Klingon said with a pronounced sneer. *"You have already been privileged to speak with the admiral very recently. Why should I permit you to do so again so soon after the previous occasion?"*

Although Archer never broke eye contact with the Klingon on the monitor, his hands moved busily across his desktop keyboard as he composed a covert text message just out of the line of sight.

Can't afford to let myself look like a timid beggar, Archer told himself as he fixed the other man with his hardest, most withering stare.

"I called before to seek an explanation for the Klingon Empire's hostilities against Draylax," he said, discreetly hitting the "transmit" key as he spoke. "Admiral Krell has yet to provide a satisfactory one."

Though Qapegh bared his sharpened teeth aggressively, he appeared impressed by Archer's audacity nevertheless. *"You risk much, human."*

"It's all part of the service, Sparky."

The Klingon suddenly broke off from Archer's stare, apparently not out of intimidation, but rather because something outside the Klingon com system's field of view had just demanded his attention.

"You have targ-*backed a text transmission onto the subspace channel you used to reach this office,"* Qapegh said, his face adorned in undisguised surprise as he looked back in Archer's direction.

"Uh-huh," Archer said, nodding.

"It is coded," Qapegh said in truculent tones.

"That's right. For the admiral's eyes only. And I expect he's going to be pretty damned unhappy with anybody who delays his seeing it. Needless to say, it's fairly time-sensitive stuff. Admiral Krell can contact me on the secure frequency specified in the message header to receive the encryption key."

Archer closed off the channel before the goggle-eyed Klingon could finish drawing breath to make a reply that was doubtless now being delivered at a full-throated shout before a blank screen. After all, the last thing he needed was to have some pissed-off Klingon waking up his dog in the middle of the night.

That certainly felt good, Archer thought as he leaned back in his chair and waited patiently for the inevitable return call. He listened to the gentle susurration of Porthos's snoring in his otherwise dark and silent cabin.

He was a little surprised that it had taken six whole minutes for the incoming call indicator on his companel to light up. Suppressing a grin, he transmitted the encryption code in response to the text message that scrolled up his screen, and then allowed nearly another whole minute to pass. The incoming light came on again, and he sat up straight and assayed his best parade-ground military bearing just before toggling the "accept" key.

"Thank you for contacting me so soon after our last conversation, Admiral," he said to the older, gray-bearded Klingon whose glowering face and almost human-smooth forehead now filled his viewer like a looming mountainside. "You do me honor."

"Do not play games with me, Archer," Krell said. *"You know as well as I do that my decision to respond to your summons has little to do with honor, either yours or mine."*

Archer suppressed a smile, as well as any further comment regarding matters of honor. Krell was obviously making a veiled reference to Archer's encrypted text message, which had intimated that Krell might want to cooperate, lest the admiral's covert cooperation with a human espionage bureau during the Qu'Vat affair the previous year become generally known throughout the Klingon Empire.

"Your honor remains safe with me, Admiral Krell," Archer said carefully. "As well as other matters that are best never spoken about again."

"I can see that a RomuluSngan might envy your skill in the dark art of blackmail, Archer," Krell said with a grunt. "You spoke to my aide of the Draylax incident. Why can you not leave the matter alone?"

"Because I'm still having trouble making sense of it, Admiral," Archer said. "Perhaps if you were to help me shed a little more light on what really happened here at Draylax—and why—I might be able to see my way clear to talking about it a whole lot less from now on."

Krell's eyes narrowed as he stroked his grizzled chin in apparent contemplation. With another grunt, he said, "Your threats aside, you have proved trustworthy with confidences thus far, Captain. Perhaps I can afford to trust you somewhat further. Particularly if doing so makes you less of a pain in the 'o'yoS. And makes you go away as well."

Archer smiled, though he was even less sure about the meaning of 'o'yoS than the translator evidently was. "Nothing would make me happier, Admiral. You, too, I expect."

"Very well, Captain," Krell said, nodding. "But I shall add only this to what I have told you already: The three battle cruisers that attacked Draylax were commanded by rogue captains. Men who were operating without the legitimate authorization of either the High Council or the Klingon Defense Force. They were killed during the commission of their treachery. Their Houses, as well as the Houses of the craven subordinates who followed their un-

lawful orders, have since been dispossessed and discommended for their lack of honor and discipline."

Archer had no pretensions to serious expertise about Klingon culture. Nevertheless, he felt more than justified in assuming that virtually everyone in the Empire who might know anything about the Draylax affair was no longer available for questioning. *At least,* he thought, *not without an extremely sensitive Ouija board. One that's tuned in to* Sto-Vo-Top, *or whatever the hell the Klingons call their version of the hereafter.*

"Forgive me for making this observation, Admiral," Archer said aloud. "But that sounds awfully convenient."

Krell leaned forward and displayed a pair of curved and wickedly sharpened incisors. *"That is as may be, Captain Archer. But it is also my final word on the subject. Admiral Krell out."*

And with that, Krell's image vanished, replaced for an instant by the Klingon trefoil emblem, which yielded to the ship's status screen a heartbeat or so later as the subspace channel closed.

He sat alone in the darkness, staring into the empty blue glow of the screen. *"Naghs,"* he muttered, thinking that mastering the Klingon spoken language might not be as difficult as he'd once thought.

Still lying in the corner, Porthos came out of his apparent slumber, raised his head slightly, and released a low growl that might have done a Klingon captain proud. Archer chose to take it as a noise of solidarity rather than a reprimand for his rude use of Klingon vocabulary.

"I agree completely, Porthos. I can't buy what Krell's trying to sell, either."

He knew that the Klingon Defense Force ran on discipline just as much as Starfleet and the MACOs did. Perhaps even more so.

Three trained Klingon captains wouldn't just suddenly go rogue for no apparent reason, he thought. *Krell still knows a hell of a lot more about this than he wants anyone else to find out. And he's prepared to sweep it all under the rug to make sure that nobody does.*

Once again, Archer felt an all but overwhelming need to talk to someone he could trust. Somebody with fewer than four legs.

He toggled open the intercom switch on his desk. "Archer to T'Pol."

No answer. His second try wasn't any more successful. Despite the lateness of the hour, and his knowledge of T'Pol's habit of retreating behind a veil of Vulcan meditation, a small worm of suspicion began to turn in his guts. He rose and crossed to the hatchway, letting himself out into E deck's main corridor, and onto the tubolift to B deck, determined to prove that suspicion unfounded.

After a brisk trot nearly a quarter of the way along the hallway's gentle curvature, he came to a stop before the door to T'Pol's quarters and buzzed the keypad to announce his presence.

Still no answer. The suspicion in his belly was quickly congealing into an awful certainty as he entered his override code into the controls. The hatch hissed obediently open, and he slowly stepped into the darkened chamber beyond.

It only took a few moments to determine that T'Pol wasn't in her quarters. The pattern of T'Pol's recent behavior—particularly her recent insistence that Trip was in urgent need of rescue, and her even more recent withdrawal behind the impenetrable veil of "Vulcan meditation"—suddenly began to make sense.

He sincerely hoped the conclusion to which he had just jumped was wrong. Crossing to a desk illuminated only by the wan light of a neutral monitor screen and the distant stars beyond the viewport, Archer toggled open another com channel.

"Archer to Launch Bay One."

"Launch Bay One," came a young crewman's crisp, almost instantaneous reply. If he sounded surprised to be hearing directly from Archer, particularly at such a late hour, it didn't show. *"Ensign Nguyen here, sir. What can I do for you?"*

"I need a status report on Shuttlepod One and Shuttlepod Two, Ensign."

"Shuttlepod One is fueled and ready to go," Nguyen said.

"And Shuttlepod Two?"

"I can give you a detailed status report on her just as soon as she returns to Enterprise."

Goddammit! Archer thought, kicking himself, hard. *Why didn't I see this coming?*

Struggling to keep any trace of anger out of his voice, he said, "When did Commander T'Pol depart, Ensign?"

"Let me check the log, sir." A pause. *"Yesterday evening at eleven-hundred hours, nine minutes."*

"Thank you, Ensign. Archer out."

T'Pol had no doubt wanted him to believe that she'd been in meditation continuously since around that time, Archer reflected. Now he understood clearly the *real* reason she hadn't been on the bridge when *Enterprise* had received *Columbia*'s report about the Klingon attack on Draylax. *So much for that renowned Vulcan inability to lie,* he thought. *That little whopper has got to be the most useful lie the Vulcans ever got us to swallow.*

And as a partial consequence of that lie, T'Pol was now off on a foolish quest in hostile territory.

All alone.

He keyed the com again. "Archer to Reed." He paused

to await a response, but none came. Though he hated to bother a man afflicted with the sort of nasty gastrointestinal trouble that had sidelined Malcolm—especially at such a late hour—he pressed on. "Malcolm, I need to talk to you. Even if we have to chat through the bathroom door."

Still nothing.

Oh, no, he thought, shaking his head as he struggled to tamp down a rising tide of anger. *Well, at least she hasn't charged off to oblivion alone.*

It occurred to him that at least one of them would have left him a note before doing something so damned stupid. Taking a seat before T'Pol's monitor, he started searching the com logs.

The desktop terminal brightened a few moments later, then suddenly displayed the serious-miened faces of *Enterprise*'s exec and weapons officer. They were standing awkwardly side-by-side in a cramped, dimly illuminated cabin that Archer immediately recognized as the interior of his missing shuttlepod. Both were out of uniform, clad instead in dark, nondescript clothing devoid of any visible insignia linking them to Starfleet, Earth, or the Coalition.

"*Captain Archer, by the time you view this recording, Lieutenant Reed and I will probably be deep inside Romulan territory,*" T'Pol began without preamble. "*Please accept my apologies for the rather . . . unorthodox actions we have taken. However, our mission is one of the utmost importance. And not merely for the safety of the man we both know as 'Lazarus.'*"

Lazarus, Archer repeated silently, recalling the code name Trip had used when he had delivered his last-minute warning about the attack on Coridan.

"*I must also protect the vital work that Lazarus is performing inside the Romulan sphere of influence,*" T'Pol continued. *"Should we fail, the repercussions will be incalculably larger than the life of any one person."*

"Or even our lives, I suppose," Malcolm said.

Something written millennia ago by the Vulcan philosopher Surak, a long-dead man whose living spirit had nonetheless once briefly shared the space inside his skull, sprang unbidden into Archer's head, soothing his roiling emotions: *The needs of the many outweigh the needs of the few.*

Reed added, *"I know I once promised you that I was finished with this kind of subterfuge, Captain, and that my first loyalty was to you and to* Enterprise . . . *I understand the consequences of my actions. But I wouldn't be doing this if I thought we had a better alternative."*

As he listened, Archer felt a renewed surge of anger begin to sweep away the calming memory of once having been in close proximity to Surak's peaceful, orderly mind. *How could the two of them leave* Enterprise *at a time like this?* he thought. Regardless of T'Pol's vehement certainty that Trip was in mortal danger, her actions were a far cry from what he'd come to expect from his logical first officer. Reed, yes. Trip, certainly. But not T'Pol.

"If it is at all possible," T'Pol's image said, *"we will return to* Enterprise *at our earliest opportunity, to take responsibility for our unauthorized actions. And to face whatever disciplinary consequences await us."*

She raised her right hand in a familiar split-fingered gesture. *"Live long, and prosper."*

The message abruptly ended.

Slumping backward into T'Pol's chair, Archer sighed into the semidarkness that surrounded him. Whatever qualms he had about what his subordinates had just done, he knew there could be no changing any of it now. The die was cast. Railing against what was done would do absolutely no good.

"Godspeed," he whispered to the blank screen.

Even before he'd heard the recording, the main reason behind T'Pol and Malcolm's clandestine stunt had been glaringly obvious to him.

Trip.

And because this entire business revolved around a man believed dead by all but a handful of people, there was only one person currently aboard *Enterprise* with whom Archer could speak freely about what T'Pol and Malcolm were trying to do.

His frustration welled up again, and he slammed his fist down on another com button, striking the console nearly hard enough to shatter it. He found the pain that shot through his hand strangely calming.

"Archer to Phlox," he said, addressing the one crew member who would be awake regardless of the lateness of the hour. "Doctor, I have a *huge* problem on my hands."

SEVENTEEN

Friday, July 18, 2155
83 Leonis V

TRIP FOUND HIMSELF adrift in a borderless white nothingness that seemed to stretch out into infinity.

He tried to calm the terror that clawed his guts. *I must be dreaming,* he thought, though the vivid clarity of his senses argued otherwise. As did the fact that he had been to this very same nonplace before.

A familiar voice behind him spoke urgently. "Trip."

Though he didn't understand how his feet were able to find purchase in this insubstantial netherworld, he nevertheless planted them solidly and turned toward the sound.

T'Pol stood before him, attired in a Starfleet uniform. "Are you safe at the moment?"

He chuckled and waggled his hand back and forth. "Safe enough to fall asleep about a sword's length away from a Romulan soldier who thinks I'm a Vulcan spy. Or maybe I'm just tired enough to hallucinate."

"You're not asleep, Trip. And you're not hallucinating or dreaming."

He shrugged. "Then I guess I'm as safe as safe gets here in the belly of the beast. Unless my watchdog decides to turn on me, that is."

The only thing he felt fairly certain about was that Admiral Valdore wasn't deliberately feeding him disinformation. At least not since he'd received independent confirmation from Captain Stillwell that an Earth Cargo Service freighter had indeed gone missing from its pre-filed course, a fact that was consistent with the Klingon attack that a Romulan outpost had reported having witnessed in the Gamma Hydra sector.

T'Pol nodded, a look of concern threatening to overwhelm her usual Vulcan stoicism. "Help is coming, Trip. In the meantime, please be careful."

He smiled at the dream-image of the woman with whom he'd once thought he might build a future. But he knew enough about nostalgia and wish-fulfillment fantasies to resist believing that she was really communicating with him telepathically and in real time across all the boundless light-years that separated them.

And he knew enough about life not to expect any hairbreadth rescues or other miracles to intervene on his behalf.

"I promise to wear my mittens until the cavalry comes," he said, not quite suppressing an ironic smile.

She raised an eyebrow in a classic expression of Vulcan perplexity. "Stay safe, Trip," she said after a seemingly uncertain pause. "And remain vigilant."

I know, Trip thought wistfully. *I guess I still love you, too.*

The real world returned to Trip in a disorienting rush of sensation. "Cunaehr!" a stern male was shouting into his ear, startling him back into wakefulness. The fathomless white expanse around him vanished like fog, taking T'Pol with it. The face of Centurion Terix, whose aquiline features were creased with both concern and frustration, now nearly filled his vision.

"I had feared you dead for a moment," Terix said, releasing his grip on Trip's bulky Romulan travel robes and backing away to his own nearby barstool.

Trip allowed his gaze to drift momentarily around

the crowded, noisy, and dimly illuminated gambling establishment that surrounded them both as he regained his psychological bearings. The barstool that had somehow kept him from tipping over backward during his apparently brief episode—he no longer felt entirely certain that it had been a mere dream or hallucination—reminded him that the seat hadn't been designed with the Terran backside in mind. That single tangible reality jolted him the rest of the way back into the real world.

"I'm fine, Terix," Trip said. "Just a little tired, that's all. It was a long flight out here."

"Sleep *during* the flight next time, Cunaehr," the centurion said in a low growl. "I didn't bring you all the way to the Empire's southern galactic limits for you to doze off while so much work still lies ahead of us."

Right, Trip thought as he discreetly eyed the telltale bulge beneath Terix's otherwise unassuming dark travel robes. *I should just take a catnap right next to a man who's convinced that I'm a Vulcan spy.* He knew that the centurion's deliberately nonmartial garment was intended to conceal both a disruptor pistol and a razor-sharp military Honor Blade, though he didn't think it was accomplishing that objective particularly well with regard to either weapon—and that was to say nothing about Terix's aggressive stance.

He wondered which Terix would grab first, the gun or the blade, once he decided that he finally had an adequate excuse to follow his instincts.

"I'd be happy to get started, Terix," Trip said. "I'm just hoping not to die of sheer boredom while we're sitting around waiting for our contact to turn up."

Terix's eyes narrowed dangerously. "Be patient, Cunaehr. And remain alert."

Trip nodded as he reached toward the bar on which he'd set his now half-empty mug. His first impression of the surprisingly potent blue ale had been that it probably ought to be illegal. The sip he took now only confirmed that initial opinion.

Several more minutes passed, during which Trip ever so slowly drained his glass. "What makes you so sure we're even waiting in the right place, Terix?" he said as he contemplated whether or not ordering a refill would make him more or less likely to experience another vivid hallucination.

"This place is more a frontier outpost than an established colony, Cunaehr. Therefore relatively few places like this exist on all of Cheron, since the Rihannsu population here numbers only a few thousand at most."

Cheron, Trip thought, reminding himself yet again that it would be a bad idea to slip up and call the place by its Earth astronomical designation, 83 Leonis V.

Aloud, he said, "But I saw huge cities when we were making our approach from orbit."

Terix shook his head. "No. You saw but the *skeletons* of those cities. Their builders preceded the Rihannsu presence on this world by many millennia. They died out before our people arrived and gained a toehold here, perhaps centuries before. If they died by their own hands, they did quite a thorough job of destroying themselves."

Terix's statement roused Trip's curiosity. "What do you mean?"

Terix paused to quaff some of his own drink. "I take it you've never wandered about in the unexplored sectors of this city."

"No. I've never been here before. And I didn't think you wanted to take the time for a sightseeing tour today."

"Well, I *have* been here before, Cunaehr, when time was not so pressing. I have seen the results of whatever plague felled these people, whether it came from happenstance or biological warfare. Whatever the cause, it killed all but a few of the hardier lower species of plants and animals. Even most of the natural microbiological processes that should have rotted away the remains of the dead eons ago have been crippled, or even stopped altogether."

The centurion's eyes grew distant and haunted. "This world is like an unburied corpse, mummifying alone and forgotten in an uncaring desert."

Trip shivered inwardly. "Then why would anyone want to come to this planet, much less establish a permanent outpost here?"

"For the strategic value of the place, of course," Terix said, studying him as though he were an exotic butterfly awaiting an unpleasant end in some oversize killing jar. "This system provides an almost completely unobstructed view of the world of our most remote ancestors." He paused, cranking up the amperage of his already accusing stare. "As well as those of their degenerate allies."

A beachhead, Trip thought. *The beginning of an invasion route that'll take bastards like this straight on to Vulcan.*

And then Earth.

A hand gripped his shoulder, startling him into nearly falling off the awkwardly contoured barstool. He turned and dismounted clumsily from the seat, expecting combat.

Instead Trip stood facing a smiling Romulan woman who appeared to be about his age. She was dressed much as both he and Terix were, in simple, dark traveler's robes.

"Who's your new friend, Terix?" the woman said to the centurion, her eyes moving appraisingly up and down Trip's body in a manner that made him feel distinctly uncomfortable. *No wonder Vulcans are so hard to get along with,* he thought. *I'd be cranky, too, if I had to try to keep a libido like theirs reined in all the time.*

"His name is Cunaehr," Terix said in a tone that implied that he still wasn't absolutely convinced of that fact.

"Cunaehr. Good, solid name," the woman said, her dark eyes now fixed on Trip's, although she was still pointedly addressing the centurion. "And does he know how to talk?"

"Ma'am—" Trip began.

"It's not *his* job to talk, T'Luadh," Terix said, interrupting. "We came to this necropolis of a world to hear what *you* have to say."

"So much for formal introductions," the woman said, looking disappointed. "It's always right down to business with you, isn't it, Terix? Perhaps you should have another round of *kheh'irho* brews before we proceed." She raised a clear glass full of a sapphire-blue liquid, which she seemed to have conjured out of thin air. Trip wondered if he was drinking the same stuff she was.

"Do not play games with us, T'Luadh," the centurion said. "The *Ejhoi Ormiin* cell we seek could be putting many *liorae-eisae* of distance between themselves and lawful pursuit even as we speak." He reached into his robe, and Trip feared for a moment he might draw one of his weapons.

Instead, Terix pulled out a small cloth sack and gave it a gentle toss. The little bag jingled as it landed heavily on the bar, and the woman wasted no time snapping it up, hefting it, and tucking it inside her own robe.

"Aren't you going to count it?" Trip asked.

She displayed an ironic half-smile. "The centurion knows better than to cheat his prime intelligence sources. After all, the last thing he wants is to cause them to dry up. Or give them a reason to send him off hunting *mogai* in downtown Dartha."

Even without prompting from his translation gear, Trip recognized the Romulan idiom for "wild goose chase." Despite the fact that the Romulan equivalent of wild geese were as large as people, on top of being rather nasty carnivores.

"Where are the *Ejhoi Ormiin* we're pursuing?" Terix said, his right hand straying again toward the robe-shrouded shape of his Honor Blade.

The centurion's less-than-subtle movement had obviously not escaped T'Luadh's notice, any more than it had Trip's. *"Kroiha,"* she said in a tone that contained both fear and warning. "They were seen on Taugus III as recently as yesterday morning, Dartha ch'Rihan Standard Time."

Drawing on his recent studies of the Romulan star charts he'd obtained from Ehrehin, Trip tried to get a fix on the location of the new Romulan place name in relation to their present position. Unless he was very much mistaken, Taugus—known on UESPA star charts as Gamma Equulei—was probably at least several weeks away from Cheron. Trip could only hope that he and Terix would have a reasonable chance of running the dissident technology thieves to ground during that time, reaching them before they vanished into the woodwork permanently and put their ill-gotten gains to the worst possible use.

"And what is the name of their present leader?" Terix asked.

The woman took a short swallow from her glass, then looked quickly around the bar as though she feared she might be overheard. None of the other carousers or gamblers present appeared to have taken any particular notice of her.

"They answer to a man named Ch'uihv," she said at length, speaking in a voice so quiet that Trip had to lean toward her to hear her words clearly.

Trip barely managed to avoid knocking over his drink when he recognized the name she'd just dropped.

"You've dealt with this Ch'uihv before, Cunaehr?" Terix asked, his curiosity clearly piqued.

Trip nodded, not seeing any point in trying to paper over his initial reaction. "Yes, in a way."

Terix scowled at Trip's uncertain pause. "Out with it, Cunaehr."

After taking a moment to decide just how much to reveal, Trip said, "He was the leader of the *Ejhoi Ormiin* group that captured me and Ehrehin a few *khaidoa* ago. The doctor and I both barely managed to escape from them with our lives."

He restrained himself from blurting out the additional fact that Ch'uihv was known to have worked on both sides of the Romulan territorial border, having once been Captain Sopek, the commander of the Vulcan *Starship Ni'Var. But how could I know anything about that,* he thought, *unless I really* am *the Vulcan spy that Terix already suspects I am?*

Still holding her drink, the woman used her free hand to toss a small object toward Trip. He instinctively caught it a split second before he managed to identify it as a standard Romulan data module.

"You need to learn not to be so trusting, Cunaehr," she said around another appraising leer. Then she nodded toward the finger-sized bit of plastic in Trip's hand. "For all you knew, that might have been something dangerous."

I'm sure it is, he thought. Aloud, he said, "Thanks for

the advice." He did his best not to sound sullen and resentful, even though he couldn't help but remember how
angry he'd felt whenever his older brother Bert would
aim a finger at his chest, then flick Trip's nose when he'd
look down to see what he was pointing at.

"Are you going to tell us what's on this thing," he
said, "or am I going to have to see for myself?"

"The module contains the precise coordinates of
Ch'uihv's base in the Taugus system," she said. "Hand
delivered to you rather than transmitted in order to
maintain your element of surprise."

Unless you're as trustworthy as Ch'uihv and have al-
ready warned him that we're coming, Trip thought as he
pocketed the chip.

Terix rose from his stool and tightened his cloak
about him. "Let's waste no more time, Cunaehr," he
said. "We must make haste to Taugus."

"You're *welcome*," T'Luadh said with what Trip
thought was an overly theatrical pout.

Terix exited the saloon without so much as a backward glance, and Trip followed a short distance behind
him. As they wended their way through the rough and
shopworn spaceport district toward the austere launch
pad where they had left their small scoutship, Trip considered what might await them in the Taugus system.
They would either root out the thieves who had raided
Ehrehin's lab, or else walk right into a trap set for them
by T'Luadh and the *Ejhoi Ormiin* dissidents.

Life or death, to be determined by capricious fate
as much as by their own brilliant improvisations. As
they strapped themselves into their seats in the vessel's
cramped cockpit and worked their way through the pre-
launch checklist, Trip hoped the former would take a
back seat to the latter.

"*Scoutship* Drolae," said a tinny voice from Cheron's

spaceport traffic control facility. *"You are clear to depart from launch pad khi'der."*

"Scoutship *Drolae* acknowledging," Terix said after toggling open the channel. He entered a brief series of commands into the console before him, and a moment later Cheron's broken and silent mausoleum cities fell away into the infinite night as the chase resumed.

"Leaving Cheron orbit," Trip said, casting a sidelong glance at Terix. The centurion acknowledged him with a silent nod before returning his attention to his console and the star-sprinkled blackness that filled the forward window above it.

Trip continued studying his traveling companion surreptitiously, and wondered what would happen in the event their mission succeeded. After all, he still couldn't allow the Romulan military to obtain the secret of the warp-seven stardrive. And he felt certain that Terix still regarded him merely as a useful enemy—a resource to be exploited, but tolerated only for the duration of the current circumstances.

Am I going to have to kill this guy before he gets a chance to turn on me?

Prepared to remain alert and vigilant throughout the entire voyage to Taugus III, he gazed forward into the boundless void and hoped he was betraying no outward sign of his internal turmoil.

He wondered if Stillwell and Harris would be reassured by his newfound paranoia.

Enterprise NX-01

"Sometimes venting at a computer screen just won't cut it," Archer said as he stepped into sickbay. "Phlox, you're the only other person aboard I can really talk to about this."

"Captain," Phlox said. in a gently bantering tone. "You know I only sleep six days per year, whether I need it or not. And unless I'm very much mistaken, I won't need to do it again for another seven or eight of your months." The doctor busied himself feeding one of the exotic alien animals he kept in his small therapeutic menagerie.

"I need T'Pol and Malcolm *here*, Phlox," Archer said. "Captain Hernandez and I need their help sorting out this Draylax business. We still don't have a clue about the real reasons behind the Klingon attack. Or why the Klingons felt it necessary to destroy their own ships to stop it."

Phlox adopted a patient expression, as though he were ministering to a particularly challenging patient. "But you said yourself that Commander T'Pol and Lieutenant Reed left *Enterprise* prior to the Draylax crisis."

"I did," Archer said, almost snapping despite his best efforts to remain calm. "But that doesn't do us any good at the moment."

Phlox nodded. "You're angry because they left without official authorization."

"Of *course* I'm angry about that!" Again, frustration seemed to be getting the better of him, but he felt too damned tired to fight it off any longer.

"That's certainly understandable, Captain," Phlox said, unfazed. "Would you like a mild sedative?"

"Thanks, but no," Archer said as he rubbed at eyes that felt as gritty as a sandlot baseball diamond. "I should have seen this coming. And kept a closer eye on T'Pol. I can't *believe* I missed the warning signs!"

Phlox closed up the container that housed his specimens, then focused his icy blue eyes on Archer's face. "Captain, when T'Pol makes up her mind, she doesn't take 'no' for an answer very easily."

"And Malcolm's got an independent streak about half an AU wide, too," Archer said, nodding. "But that's no excuse." *I'm going to be even more disappointed if they get themselves killed,* he thought.

He preferred to reserve that privilege as one of a captain's most sacred prerogatives.

"If I had suspected that Commander T'Pol would actually abscond with a shuttlepod and head out into Romulan space on her own authority," Phlox said, "I suppose I could have ordered her confined to sickbay. But I didn't do that. So it appears that I missed the very same 'warning signs' that you did, Captain."

The Denobulan stepped toward Archer and placed a gentle hand on his shoulder.

"The question you have to answer now," he said, "is what do you intend to do about it?"

Archer felt a great empty chasm open up in the pit of his stomach as he realized that he had no answer to Phlox's question.

EIGHTEEN

Saturday, July 19, 2155
San Francisco

"Gannet, something's happened at Draylax."

The intrusive voice in Gannet Brooks's earpiece carried with it the same unmistakable end-of-the-world quality that she recognized from all the other times the end of the world had seemed imminent—and yet had somehow failed to arrive—since the Xindi sneak attack of 'fifty-three.

Sitting alone at a sidewalk table in front of Madame Chang's Mandarin Café, Gannet paused in the midst of her current rather urgent search of Earth's datanets and the Coalition networks to which they were already partially linked via the subspace bands. She smiled to herself. As usual, Nash McEvoy had gotten wind of the story well after she had. *That,* she told herself, *is what separates a good reporter from a merely competent editor.*

"I'm way ahead of you, boss," she said, subvocalizing into her throat mic to guard against the possibility that anybody within earshot—such as the half-dozen or so Starfleet personnel she'd seen entering the eatery since her arrival—might overhear what she was about to say. "I know about the alien ships that opened fire on the Draylaxians."

"Is it still going on?" McEvoy said, sounding shrill in her ear.

"Can't say," she said as she scrolled through the text

messages recorded on her data padd. She would have paid serious coin for a knowledgeable and talkative Starfleet officer to share her table right now, but none of the carefree 'fleeters nearby seemed likely to fill the bill. "My sources say it's been taking everything Draylax has to stand up to the assault. Assuming that's even possible."

"Did your sources say anything about who the attackers might be?"

"Still working on that, boss."

"What about that significant other of yours in Starfleet? Do you think he could shed any light on the matter?"

"That's *ex*–significant other, remember?" she said aloud, apparently startling a young busboy who had begun clearing a nearby empty table of a spent coffee urn and several other remnants of a previous customer's meal. Catching herself, she resumed her outwardly inaudible subvocalizing.

"As if it's any of your business anyway, Nash," she said as she pushed an errant lock of her otherwise straight brown hair away from her eyes. "Besides, Travis Mayweather and I have barely been on speaking terms all year."

Although she and Travis had parted company on friendly enough terms after Terra Prime's poop had finished hitting the ventilator, Gannet hadn't forgotten Travis's suspicions that she was in league with Terra Prime in their failed assassination plot against Nathan Samuels, and she suspected that he hadn't forgotten either; he hadn't believed her when she'd claimed to be doing spook work on behalf of Starfleet Intelligence, even though her journalistic career made it a professional necessity to forge and maintain close working relationships with certain key intel operatives. Travis's distrust during that crisis still stung, and it fueled her continued determination to resist any impulse to ask him for favors—even if it seemed as likely as not that he'd grant them.

A new line of text scrolled into view on her padd's display, as if summoned by her thoughts. She recognized it immediately as a reply from one of the clandestine sources Travis hadn't believed she sometimes worked with.

She gasped when she read it, once again momentarily startling the busboy.

"What's wrong, Gannet?" McEvoy murmured.

"Looks like one of my best sources knows who attacked Draylax," she said, still subvocalizing.

He sounded impatient, though she could hardly blame him. *"And?"*

She paused long enough to pick up her sweating water glass and raise it to her lips in the hopes of moistening her dry throat enough to make an intelligible reply. "It's the Klingons," she said a moment later.

"The Klingons?" he said, sounding quizzical. *"Those motorcycle-gang types with the big knives and the shell-fish attached to their foreheads?"*

Gannet replied with a sigh and a resigned shake of her head. Nash McEvoy sometimes stood as a talking, breathing object lesson proving the Vulcans right in questioning humanity's readiness to move out into the galaxy.

"The hostile ships are of Klingon configuration," she said. "Three heavily armed battle cruisers. And their attack began sometime yesterday."

"Klingons," McEvoy repeated, his tone again oscillating back toward the shrill end of the spectrum. *"From what little I know about them, it sounds like it's going to be a slaughter. If it isn't all over for the Draylaxians already, that is."*

Gannet could only wish that her intelligence source had been able to provide a more up-to-the-minute report on that score.

Another chill thought occurred to her then.

Whatever happens next, Enterprise *is sure to be in the middle of it.*

With Travis behind the wheel.

NINETEEN

Saturday, July 19, 2155
San Francisco

NATHAN SAMUELS NEARLY jumped out of his chair when his office door flew open and slammed into the wall behind it with a resounding thud.

"Have you looked at the newsnets?" Haroun al-Rashid said, holding up a large sheet of gray e-paper. The black text that dominated the page was so large that it all but screamed at him.

Samuels couldn't remember the last time he'd seen Earth's interior minister appear so agitated. On the other hand, it wasn't every day that he saw headlines like this one:

KLINGON EMPIRE ATTACKS DRAYLAX

"Contact the sergeant at arms, Rashid," he said, swallowing hard. "Tell him to round up every available delegate immediately. And call Ambassador Li on Centauri III.

"The Coalition Security Council is going into emergency session."

The last time Minister Soval had seen such a grim mood descend upon the Coalition Council's spacious assembly chamber, half the planet Coridan Prime had been engulfed in flames.

Today, Vulcan's senior representative couldn't help but wonder whether the nascent Coalition of Planets might not be about to undergo a similar immolation, succumbing to the fires lit by the all but ungovernable passions of some of its small but extremely variegated membership.

"Never before have the Klingons made such a bold incursion so deep behind the Coalition's boundaries," said Andorian Foreign Minister Thoris, who stood behind his world's designated section of the room's curved central table between a pair of his aides. The minister's twin antennae lay flat against his white-maned scalp, pointing forward in a conspicuous display of outrage. "This body has no choice other than to respond in kind, and to do so *immediately*."

Minister al-Rashid rose from behind his own section of the table almost directly opposite the Andorian delegation, and spread his hands in a placating manner. "There are *always* choices other than war, Minister Thoris," the human said.

"Not when you're talking about the Klingons," Gora bim Gral of Tellar growled in a rare display of agreement with his Andorian counterpart. The hirsute diplomat remained seated at a position at right angles to both the human and Andorian parties, where he was flanked by a pair of Tellarite junior functionaries, both of whom were nodding in vociferous agreement with their superior. "You starry-eyed humans simply haven't been out in the galaxy long enough yet to take such basic realities at face value."

To his credit, al-Rashid sidestepped the Tellarite's verbal jab without offering any provocation of his own. "There's still a lot we don't know about the Draylax situation, Ambassador Gral," he said. "And I have to point out that the Coalition's boundaries are a relatively new addition to the galactic map. Perhaps the Klingons weren't aware they were violating them."

"Klingons care little for such niceties," Gral said. "Indiscriminate expansion through conquest is their way. When the Klingons decide to go after you, your choices usually amount to either surrender or war. Therefore we would do well to teach them some respect for our boundaries, and to do it in the most direct fashion possible."

Thoris nodded grimly. "Photonic torpedoes can be excellent educators in situations such as these."

"I grant you that Klingons respect strength," al-Rashid said. "But—"

Gral interrupted him. "And do you also grant that the security of nearby nonaligned worlds such as Draylax has a direct bearing on the security of the Coalition members?" The Tellarite leaned forward across the table, his hairy knuckles supporting his weight. "Indeed, on the Coalition's continued existence?"

The human's eyes narrowed as he appeared to struggle to keep his internal emotional fires carefully banked. "I understand that all too well, Ambassador."

Seated beside al-Rashid, Prime Minister Samuels nodded in agreement, though he maintained as emotionally neutral an expression as Soval had ever seen on a human face. "Earth's delegation believes very deeply in maintaining peace and security in the local systems. Indeed, we would hope that the assistance Earth is already providing to the Draylaxians would convince them to finally join the Coalition. We hope it will entice other nearby worlds as well, such as Porrima V."

Soval couldn't help but agree, even though he was well aware that additional alien recruitment into the Coalition suited the humans' own self-interested political purposes; after all, the inclusion of more nonhuman worlds in the Coalition's roster would go a long way toward blunting the ill feelings that persisted among the rest of the current membership because of Earth's insistence on granting not only Coalition member status but also full Security Council voting rights to the human-inhabited Alpha Centauri system.

"A stout blade and a fully charged disruptor pistol will get far better results with a ravening Klingon than will any amount of hope," Thoris said, punctuating his declaration by pounding his cerulean fist upon the tabletop several times. "We must waste no more time mounting a full counterattack!"

"The last thing we should do is allow ourselves to be drawn into an all-out war," al-Rashid said. "At least not until our fastest frontline starships gather more first-hand information about what really happened at Draylax. We still don't know, for instance, precisely why the Klingons apparently resolved the situation themselves by destroying their own warship."

Thoris appeared unmoved. "With respect, Minister, the Klingons have never shown much interest in resolving anything. Were it otherwise, they would not have made the additional brazen move of destroying an Earth freighter in the Gamma Hydra sector."

"We've seen no definitive evidence of that so far," said Samuels. "But I can see that your intelligence bureaus must be listening to the same rumors as ours do."

"No one has heard anything from the *E.C.S. Horizon* for several days," Thoris said. "That is no mere rumor."

"True enough, Minister," Samuels said, crossing his arms before him. "But I'm not prepared to go to war over what might turn out to be only a faulty com system."

"The Andorian government does not require the permission of Earth, or of this Coalition for that matter, to take whatever action we deem justifiable and prudent in the face of this grave danger," Thoris said, his antennae flattening backward against his scalp.

"Nor does Tellar," said Gral. "The provisions of the Coalition Compact notwithstanding."

Remaining in his seat, Samuels made an admirable display of equanimity in the face of such vehement opposition. "Of course not. We're a body of equals, meeting as equals. That's why nobody is addressing anybody else from up there, especially today." He paused to gesture toward the empty speaker's podium that stood upon the unoccupied raised dais at the front of the room. "But must I remind you both that your governments' actions will reflect on *all* the members of this body?"

Gral huffed. "And must *I* remind *you* that Earth and Alpha Centauri are entangled with Draylax in a webwork of mutual defense treaties? You do your entire species a disservice by leaning on diplomacy during a time that demands soldiery instead."

Gral pushed away from the table, as did Thoris a moment later. Soval watched as his Tellarite and Andorian counterparts stalked angrily out of the room, heading for separate exits, their respective aides following closely on their heels.

Soval was grateful that neither the press nor any members of the general public were present in the gallery that overlooked the formal debating chamber; the participants in today's meeting had agreed to convene behind closed doors. Presently a tense and uncomfortable silence stretched between the human and Vulcan contingents, the only Coalition representatives who now remained in the room.

Haroun al-Rashid was the first to break that silence.

"May nobody do anything stupid over the next few days, *inshallah*," he said.

"Hear, hear," Samuels said, looking crestfallen and small.

Soval recognized al-Rashid's last utterance as a word from the human language known as Arabic.

Inshallah. If God wills it.

Though Soval himself espoused no specific deity of any sort, he couldn't help but agree with the minister's overall sentiment. Just as he concurred with Gral's and Thoris's general contention that the Klingon Empire did indeed pose a potentially grave, if not an immediate, danger. *While we've debated the issue of Romulan aggression,* he thought, *we have allowed ourselves to become blind to the Klingons.*

Nevertheless, both logic and simple decency dictated that war could never be a first option.

"Even the Andorian and Tellarite governments must engage in a deliberative process of sorts before going to war independently of the will of the Coalition," Soval said, intent on offering his human colleagues at least some small degree of comfort.

Samuels and al-Rashid both nodded in agreement. "We'll stand adjourned until tomorrow," Samuels said, finally rising from behind the table.

"I suppose we ought to be thankful that Gral and Thoris aren't the final decision-makers on their respective homeworlds," al-Rashid said.

Soval rose from his seat, thereby signaling his aides that it was time to leave the chamber. Addressing the humans, he said, "We must maintain hope that—how do the humans put it?—cooler heads will prevail on both Andoria and Tellar."

But that hope felt nearly as forced as Thoris's smiles, or Gral's table manners.

Sunday, July 20, 2155, 7:22 A.M.
Montgomery, Alabama

When Charles Anthony Tucker II saw what he had just finished downloading onto the e-paper, he nearly spit his morning orange juice across the kitchen.

"Elaine!" he shouted when he'd finally managed to stop sputtering.

His wife emerged from the hallway into the kitchen nearly at a run, pulling her bathrobe sash tightly about her slim waist. Wet hair framed her face, which was a study in concern at the moment, as though she'd half expected to find him dying on the kitchen floor. Considering everything the Tucker family had endured over the past few years—the loss of their two adult children still felt like an open wound to Charles, and probably would continue to feel that way for whatever span of time remained to him—he could hardly blame her for believing the worst.

"What's wrong, Charles?" Elaine said.

He held up the e-paper and coughed again before croaking out a single syllable. "Look," he said.

Maybe Trip and Lizzie were the lucky ones, he thought. *They never saw things come to* this.

Charles watched Elaine's eyes widen even further as she silently absorbed the bold, thumb-high morning headlines:

COALITION COUNCIL DEBATES WAR RESOLUTION
AGAINST KLINGON EMPIRE
ANDORIAN AND TELLARITE FLEETS
MOBILIZING FOR BATTLE

TWENTY

Sunday, July 20, 2155
Enterprise **NX-01, near Draylax**

"DOCTOR PHLOX TO THE TRANSPORTER," Archer said, turning away from the viewscreen to regard *Enterprise*'s beta-watch commander, Lieutenant Commander Mack Mc-Call, with a half smile. "Good job, Commander."

McCall grinned under his graying close-cropped mustache and goatee. "The credit really belongs to several members of the bridge crew, sir. The lifesigns were so faint that it took eight sensor sweeps to zero in on the Klingon's escape pod. I'm not even sure how she stayed alive out there, given that the atmosphere in the escape pod had almost completely vented by the time we located it."

"Well, let's hope our Klingon castaway can shed some light on what the hell those battle cruisers were really up to at Draylax," Archer said, turning to exit the bridge. "Have Sergeant McKenzie and two of her MACO troopers meet me in sickbay immediately. And call over to *Columbia*; let Captain Hernandez know what we've found."

"I've already notified Captain Hernandez," McCall said. "She'll be coming aboard *Enterprise* as soon as she can."

Archer let out a sigh as the turbolift doors slid closed behind him and the car began to descend. He reflected on the fact that he still hadn't told anyone other than

Phlox about T'Pol and Reed's abandonment of their posts, or their unauthorized departure in Shuttlepod Two, predominantly out of a desire to avoid further exacerbating Trip's predicament.

A question flitted across his mind regarding T'Pol and Malcolm's dereliction of duty: *Are their actions really any worse than my own?* He knew that his hands weren't entirely clean, and that made condemning the actions of his officers even more difficult. How many times had he disobeyed orders himself, stretched the limits of a mission, disregarded Starfleet's code of honor, engaged in some deception all in pursuit of a higher goal?

The turbolift arrived at E deck, and Archer exited, feeling glum as he stalked into sickbay. Seeing that the MACOs had beaten him there cheered him somewhat, as did the fact that one of the troopers was already deployed outside the doors of Phlox's sickbay, his pulse rifle at the ready.

Inside, Phlox was moving quickly around the biobed on which lay a Klingon woman, her body—still inside a battered pressure suit—twisted into an almost fetal position, probably as a consequence of the decompression injuries she had suffered. Phlox strapped a mask to her face, and the warrior woman offered no resistance.

With a nod, Archer acknowledged Sergeant McKenzie and another MACO trooper nearby, then spoke up. "Does it look like she'll pull through, Doctor?"

Phlox barely spared him a glance, his orange-hued fingers tapping on some of the medical controls. "Hello, Captain. I'm not certain yet. She *has* been breathing intermittently on her own for some time now. But it is likely that she will *not* regain consciousness."

Archer moved closer to Phlox. "Do everything you can for her, Doctor, but understand this: the Klingons may have struck the first blow in a war against the Coalition, and we need to know *why*. Do whatever you have to—*whatever* the cost—to get her back to consciousness."

Phlox regarded him with a curious expression. "I imagine you must consider her a prisoner of war then, Captain. I hope you're not suggesting that I take any measures to awaken her that might further jeopardize her life?"

Archer clenched his jaw for a moment, letting out a heavy breath through his nose. "We don't know if she's a prisoner of war or not because we do not know if we are *at* war. What I *am* suggesting, Doctor, is that we need to question her. *That* is your imperative, beyond doing everything in your power to save her life."

Phlox nodded noncommittally. "I will do my best to accommodate you, Captain. So long as doing so does not threaten the life of my patient."

The doors to sickbay whisked open, and Archer turned to see Hernandez, escorted by another MACO, enter the room.

"Will she make it?" Hernandez asked.

Archer pulled her aside and updated her, explaining the instructions that he had just given Phlox.

"It's understandable that Phlox might question the ethics of your order, Jon," Hernandez said, "but these *are* extraordinary circumstances. If you need my CMO to take over, I can arrange that. Doctor Metzger will have the same concerns, but she *will* act as ordered."

"That's a tempting offer, Erika," Archer said, his voice low. "There's been a bit too much free thinking among my command staff lately."

Hernandez gave him a puzzled look, but before she could question him further, the wall-mounted com unit beeped, and McCall's voice promptly issued forth. *"Bridge to Captain Archer. We've received a Prior-*

ity One communiqué from Starfleet for you and Captain Hernandez."

"We'll take it in my ready room," Archer said. "Thanks, Mack."

As he moved toward the door, he looked back in Phlox's direction. "Interrupt me the moment you have her stabilized enough to answer some questions, Doctor," Archer said.

Phlox affirmed the command, but did not look up from his work.

As Archer and Hernandez strode across the few meters that separated sickbay from the central turboshaft, Hernandez spoke quietly. "You can discuss with me what that 'free thinking' comment meant whenever you're ready, Jon. No pressure, though. I have a feeling you're carrying the weight of the world on your shoulders right now."

"*Worlds*, plural," Archer said with a small smile.

As the turbolift doors closed around them, Hernandez put her hand in the center of Archer's back.

For the moment, he was grateful to have received even that modest gesture of human contact.

"So you're letting them off with a *slap on the wrist*?" Archer said to his ready-room viewscreen, his words charged with far more anger than Hernandez thought was wise to display before a Starfleet admiral.

Hernandez watched as Gardner leaned forward slightly in his chair. "*Archer, you and I have been through a lot together, and you know that while I disagree with you from time to time, I still respect you. That's why I'm not shouting my strong suggestion that you adjust your tone.*"

Hernandez nudged Archer gently aside, effectively pushing him out of Gardner's line of sight. *Whatever's bothering Jon has to be immense,* she thought. *And a lot bigger than what just happened at Draylax.*

As if anything *could* be bigger than the brink of war.

"Admiral, does the Coalition Council realize that the Klingon ships not only opened fire on Draylax," Hernandez said, "but that they also engaged both *Columbia* and *Enterprise* in battle, refusing to explain their actions or even answer our hails?"

Gardner nodded, settling back again. *"The Coalition Security Council has resolved that we are to give the Klingon Empire one final warning. They are to cease hostilities against all Coalition worlds and/or their allies. If they cross this line again, or engage any Coalition or allied vessel in battle, the Coalition will issue a formal declaration of war."*

"You *know* that the Klingons will be honor bound to return that declaration tenfold," Archer said, stepping back into Gardner's field of view. "Hell, they'll probably welcome it. And you don't even know half of the savagery that the Klingons are capable of."

"The Council hopes that this resolution will broker a truce, however tenuous, and thus stave off a war."

Archer sighed heavily. "And of course, nobody is paying attention to what the Romulans might be doing while we're all distracted by this Klingon business."

Gardner's expression turned to one of angry incredulity. *"Unless I'm missing something here, Captain, the Romulans had nothing to do with this attack. And no evidence has turned up yet linking them to the other recent—"*

"Except for Coridan," Archer said, interrupting.

Gardner closed his mouth, and Hernandez thought she could hear the grinding of his teeth across the gulf of light-years that separated them. *"There are some on the Council and in Starfleet who agree that your warn-*

ings were vindicated by the attack on Coridan. But at this time, the Council has voted that the most clear and present threat currently emanates from the Klingon Empire. That is where the Council feels our priorities should lie, and for eminently understandable reasons."

The room's intercom let out a bosun's whistle a moment before Phlox's voice announced, *"Sickbay to Captain Archer. My patient is regaining consciousness, but I can't guarantee how long it will last."*

Archer leaned in toward the viewscreen. "That's the sole survivor from the destroyed Klingon battle cruisers, Admiral. She might be our only chance to get to the bottom of what's really been going on here."

"Go," Gardner said, testiness still slightly audible in his voice. *"And good luck, Archer."*

Before they exited the room, Archer tapped the com panel once more. "Ensign Sato, meet me in sickbay. On the double."

Moving quickly to follow Archer out of the ready room and into the turbolift, Hernandez spoke in low tones. "I don't get why you set out to antagonize the admiral, Jon. He's not an idiot, and he's probably trapped by the politics of the situation. And as my father used to say, you catch more flies with honey."

As the turbolift doors opened onto E deck, Archer grinned humorlessly. "I'm not interested in catching flies, Erika. And duty or not, the things *my* dad used to say about the top brass in Starfleet would have made an Andorian blush."

"Admiral Krell is lying. Captain Vesh'tk was . . . neither a traitor nor a rogue," the Klingon woman said, her words rendered into standard English by one of Lieutenant Sato's pleasant-voiced universal translator units. The Klingon's natural voice came as a kindling-dry rasp that

Archer found painful to hear. Every word she uttered had to be causing her excruciating pain.

"She says that Admiral Krell is lying," Hoshi said, listening directly to the woman's Klingon speech in order to confirm the accuracy of the electronic translation. Archer didn't want to leave any of the Klingon survivor's inflections or half utterances to chance. "She says that her commanding officer, Captain Vesh'tk, was not a traitor, and that he wasn't operating as a rogue agent."

"Then why did they attack Draylax without any official authorization?" Archer asked, waiting anxiously for Hoshi to translate his question for the woman. Nearby, Phlox frowned, tapping away at his monitor consoles. Archer saw that he was pumping sizable quantities of painkillers into the woman's system.

As before, the electronic translation device spoke on behalf of the Klingon woman before Hoshi did. *"We were on patrol . . . and something seized control of our ship. Our guidance systems . . . our gravity, even our life-support systems . . . nothing would respond to us. I barely got into . . . a pressure suit in time. The others were still alive, but barely . . . and we were unable to do anything but . . . float in the air while our ship acted as though . . . it had a mind of its own."*

"She claims that something remotely gained control of their ship while they were on patrol," Hoshi said. "It took over their guidance systems, artificial gravity, and even the life-support systems. This woman was able to don an environment suit, but the others were kept just barely alive. Apparently the artificial gravity system remained disabled while the ship was being controlled."

"How could something like that happen?" Erika asked after Hoshi had confirmed the machine translation.

The Klingon woman responded to Erika's question with a series of halting rasps that Hoshi's equipment quickly transformed into English. *"The first thing they did was . . . to use some remote means of seizing and deactivating each of our systems, one by one. They started with life-support . . ."*

"Who seized control of your ship?" Archer asked. "Was it someone aboard one of the other two Klingon vessels that attacked Draylax?"

The woman moaned loudly, coughing up purple-hued bloody mucus as Hoshi questioned her in the Klingon tongue. But the look on the patient's face—even through her pain—was one of surprise.

"I was not even aware of the other ships until . . . the battle began. The screens on our ships . . . showed me the carnage. I tried to return your hails . . . or stop the weapons from firing, but I . . . was unable. The others on the crew were . . . too far gone."

"Does she have any idea *who* it was that took over her ship?" Archer asked.

The woman's body suddenly began to jerk, her back arching up off the bed as her hands clawed feebly at the air. Purple blood spouted from her nose, and she coughed up a darker fluid.

"Move back, Captain," Phlox said, his manner grim and urgent. He punched a few buttons, and the movements of the woman lessened somewhat, though the blood still flowed. For a moment, her gaze seemed to focus on something distant, then moved back toward Hoshi and Archer.

"RomuluSngan."

The word was clear, but final. The woman's eyes rolled back in her head, and her body fell limp.

Phlox lowered his head. "She's gone, Captain."

"You did what you could to ease her pain," Archer said softly. "You didn't do anything to contribute to her death."

Phlox stared at him, but Archer couldn't quite read the tightly coiled emotion that showed in the Denobulan physician's blue, recessed eyes. "No, I did not. Her survival until now was, frankly, a miracle. She might have lived longer had I not . . . induced consciousness . . . but probably not for more than another day or two."

Hernandez stepped forward, looking toward Hoshi. "Was her last word what I thought it was?"

Hoshi nodded, her expression glum. "*RomuluSngan*. It's the Klingon word for—"

"Romulan," Archer said, interrupting her.

Archer reached down to scratch Porthos between the ears, then took a sip of the Skagaran Lone Star tequila he had poured for himself and Erika from the bottle Trip had left behind. He had brought Hernandez back to his quarters, rather than to his ready room, to discuss what to do next. "I'm just sick of sitting behind that ready-room desk and waiting for more orders and more news that I know will take us down the wrong path," he said before taking another swallow.

Hernandez stopped pacing and sat on the edge of the small desk across from Archer's bunk, where she stared contemplatively at the amber fluid that covered the bottom of her own glass. "So what do we do now? The only proof we have that the Romulans *may* have been involved with this is the dying declaration of a Klingon who had enough morphine in her to tranquilize an elephant."

"If the Romulans *are* somehow behind the attack on Draylax . . . if they've managed to gain control of at least these three Klingon ships, then who knows what other surprises they might have in store for us?" Archer said, trying not to let the despair he was feeling creep into his voice. "If we're being tricked into going to war against the Klingons, then the Coalition may be about to pick a fight with the wrong enemy. That would leave us vulnerable to ambush from the *real* enemy. We might even find ourselves surprised by another Coridan-style sneak attack. . . ."

"Or the Romulans might just wait until the Klingon and Coalition forces have worn each other down in battle," Hernandez said. "They could swoop in then and start picking up the pieces while nobody's fleets are in any shape to do much to stop them."

"But you already know what the higher-ups will say about that theory," Archer said. "'Where's your *proof?*' We can't change our entire defense posture based on nothing but assumptions and speculations."

Hernandez set her glass on the desktop, then moved to sit down next to Archer, who was perched on his bed. "If you were in Admiral Gardner's shoes, would you have it any other way, Jon? It seems we're rushing headlong toward an interstellar war, and we've only just started getting out into the galaxy in the first place."

"And the galaxy has turned out to be a much more dangerous place than any of us realized," Archer said, staring down into his nearly empty glass. On the other side of the room he could see Trip's tequila bottle.

He immediately regretted having let his last few words slip out.

"You still miss him, don't you?" Erika said quietly, backing away slightly, giving him some room.

He nodded silently.

"I know how close the two of you were," she said. "Commander Tucker didn't serve aboard *Columbia* all that long, but I worked with him long enough to know what a good sounding board he could be. And that's something a captain needs almost as much as air and gravity. That big chair on the bridge can be a very lonely place."

Archer chuckled, but without any humor. "Especially lately. But I don't suppose either of us needs any lessons about how isolating command can be."

"No, we don't. But it does sounds as though *I* need to remind *you* to reach out to some of your other senior officers for guidance. You're pretty tight with your tactical officer, Lieutenant Reed, right? And I'd be willing to bet that even your Vulcan XO would be a good listener in a pinch."

He shook his head. "They've both been a bit . . . pre-occupied lately."

Erika frowned then, and for a moment Archer feared she might ask why she hadn't seen either of them during the past days of repair and recovery layover that had followed the fight over Draylax. Instead, her frown softened. With a small shrug, she said, "Well, there's always Doctor Phlox."

Archer raised his glass, and some of the tequila nearly splashed out. "To Phlox. Maybe Starfleet won't post bartenders aboard our ships, but a chief medical officer is usually the next best thing."

And there's always Chef and Porthos to fall back on if Phlox ever decides to steal the other shuttlepod and pull a disappearing act of his own, he added silently as he downed a considerable fraction of what remained of his drink.

He noticed a beat later that her frown had returned with a vengeance. "I'm a little worried about you, Jon. I haven't seen you like this since we went rock-climbing right after the Xindi crisis."

No more eager to discuss that topic than he was to open up to her about what was really going on with Trip, T'Pol, and Malcolm, he said, "You don't have to worry about me, Erika."

She folded her arms across her chest, her eyes narrowing in that familiar look of *you-can't-kid-a-kidder* skepticism. "Oh, good. I'm glad *that's* settled. I'm *completely* reassured now."

Archer spread both arms and one hand in a gesture of peace, nearly spilling the remnants of his drink in the process. "Sorry. Look, I just don't do the whole self-revelation thing particularly well. Maybe T'Pol has been rubbing off on me."

He paused for a moment, grateful for her patience while he tried to gather his thoughts. "It's just that I came out here to explore the galaxy," he said at length. "I didn't sign up to become a soldier. That's why I joined Starfleet and not the MACOs, for Christ's sake." He raised his drink again.

She gently took the glass from his hand before he could finish emptying it. "You're right, Jon. We *should* be explorers and ambassadors, seeking out the things no one has ever seen before. In peace, and with open hands. And I have faith that we *will* do that, one day." She offered him a wan smile. "If not our generation, then the *next* one, or the one after that."

Archer looked into her dark eyes, which were as soulful and sympathetic as he remembered. At that moment he wanted nothing more than to kiss her, to hold her, to be held by her. But that ship had left spacedock long ago. Besides, he was a canny enough drinker to realize that the impulse might have originated in the depths of Trip's bottle of Skagaran tequila.

"I'm glad *one* of us is still optimistic enough to hang on to a little hope," he said after the silence had stretched for a while.

Hernandez moved her hand to his shoulder, squeezing it gently. "As long as we breathe, Jonathan Archer, there will always be hope."

TWENTY-ONE

Romulan *Scoutship Drolae*

ALTHOUGH THE SCOUTSHIP'S DAMPING SYSTEM effectively canceled out any noticeable inertial-acceleration effects, Tucker found he couldn't keep his heart from lodging itself firmly in his throat. As he contemplated the velocity gauge on his copilot's console, it occurred to him that he had never before traveled so fast in his life, not even aboard *Enterprise*. In fact, he might just have become the fastest human who ever lived.

Trip had picked up enough of the Romulan Empire's dominant written language to understand the meaning of the text displayed on the speed readout before him. In his mind he pronounced the sounds that the blocky, angular Rihannsu script would make had he chosen to speak them aloud: *avaihh fve ehr rhi.*

Warp six point five, he thought, translating those alien sounds into English. *Plasma flow is up to eight thousand* kolem, *with twenty-two thousand* melakols *of pressure in the intermix chamber. Damn.*

Even during the *Drolae*'s swift voyage from Romulus to Cheron, Terix had not pushed the little scoutship's warp drive nearly so hard as he was doing now. Once the Cheron mission had revealed Taugus III to be the most recent known location of the *Ejhoi Ormiin* cell responsible for Doctor Ehrehin's murder and the theft of his warp-seven data, the centurion had seemed absolutely hell-bent on either reaching the dissidents' enclave as quickly as possible or perishing in the attempt.

The little ship shuddered briefly, revealing what was probably an eddy of turbulence in the tiny, barely stable warp field that surrounded the vessel. He could only hope the unaccustomed vibrations didn't portend some impending catastrophic failure; at such high speeds, a sudden warp-field collapse could reduce a vessel to a light-year-long string of vaporized debris in a matter of moments. And with the propulsion systems under so much obvious strain, the margin for error within that superluminal bubble of survival was probably too small even to measure.

"Do we really have to ride this poor beast so hard, Terix?" Trip asked, taking care to keep both Alabama and Florida out of his diction.

"We have no way of knowing for certain how long the *Ejhoi Ormiin* we seek will remain at the coordinates T'Luadh provided," the centurion said. His gaze was focused straight ahead at the warp-distorted vista that rushed ceaselessly, and at unimaginable speeds, toward the scoutship's forward windows. "We must reach the Taugus system before they find another hiding place."

"All this speed won't do us much good if we blow ourselves clear to Erebus getting there," said Trip. "Besides, if we can generate this much speed with such a small warp core, I have to wonder why it's worth taking such risks to recover the data these dissidents stole from Doctor Ehrehin in the first place."

Terix turned to face Trip and looked at him as though he was being deliberately obtuse. "Look at the readouts on this ship's support systems, Cunaehr."

With a shrug, Trip did as the centurion asked. A moment later he realized that both the life-support and structural integrity systems were redlining—or rather greenlining, since the emerald-blooded Romulans had their own unique take on which color best signified imminent danger.

He realized all at once that he'd been playing the spy game so long that he'd momentarily forgotten to think like a warp engineer. The *Drolae*'s extreme current speed—which nearly rivaled that of Ehrehin's yet-unrealized dream of a warp-seven stardrive—came at a trade-off cost that a larger, better-armed vessel could never sustain. Terix's current speed-at-the-expense-of-everything-else use of the *Drolae* reminded Trip that Ehrehin's research hadn't been about merely reaching the upper reaches of the warp scale; it had been about doing so in a sustained fashion without sacrificing every scrap of a starship's non-propulsion-related functionality.

"I understand," Trip said, nodding. He didn't relish the prospect of having a long conversation about the calculus of power utilization curves with the centurion.

Unfortunately, Terix seemed to be one of those martinet types who enjoyed lecturing those he regarded as his inferiors. "We can't very well assemble a viable war fleet out of ships configured like this one," he said. "An armada that has to expend all of its energy resources just to reach the battlefield is useless from a tactical perspective. *Unless* your ship needs only to deliver one or two men very quickly to a target by stealth."

"All right. So maybe taking a few risks to neutralize the *Ejhoi Ormiin* is a worthwhile thing after all. But I still say that blowing ourselves to quarks on the way there is a spectacularly bad idea."

"We have little time to waste, Cunaehr. And for reasons other than our urgent errand in the Taugus system."

Trip frowned, wondering whether his own time might not have just become even shorter than he'd feared. "I'm afraid I don't understand."

"Taugus will not be our only stop on this voyage," Terix said.

That's assuming we don't smithereenize ourselves en route, Trip thought. *Or get killed by Ch'uihv's people once we reach Taugus.*

Aloud, he said only, "Oh?"

The centurion offered a grim nod. "Once we put an end to the dissidents in the Taugus system, we shall head directly to the Sei Paehhos'aehallh sector."

It took Trip a beat or two to translate the Romulan place name into the words that appeared on the star maps with which he was most familiar. *Sei Paehhos'aehallh. That's what the Romulans call the Gamma Hydra sector.*

"Why aren't we heading back to Romulus?" Trip wanted to know, almost as much as he wanted to know why Terix hadn't seen fit to mention this little detour before now.

"Our intelligence operatives have uncovered evidence that the Coalition has recently set up a small surveillance station near the Tezel-Oroko star system. We must find that listening post and take it out."

"Oh," Trip said, still suspicious. "Well, I suppose we'd better get on with Taugus, then." *Pedal to the metal,* he thought as he faced forward again and stared out into the relentlessly approaching cosmos.

Since the bureau wasn't in the habit of deliberately giving itself vulnerabilities by briefing its operatives beyond what they needed to know for a given assignment, Trip knew he could neither confirm Terix's intel about a Coalition spy base in the Gamma Hydra sector nor dismiss it out of hand. He desperately wished for enough time alone with the *Drolae*'s subspace transmitter to allow himself to touch base even briefly with his superiors, or at least to send a burst transmission to warn them to take precautions at Tezel-Oroko. That might not only protect anyone who was stationed there monitoring the Romulans, but could also keep him from being killed by friendly fire coming from the alleged listening post's defenders.

It occurred to him then that he was already more than six hours late for his regularly scheduled check-in with what he liked to think of as "the home office." Unfortunately, that couldn't be helped. At least not so long as circumstances forced him into close quarters with a Romulan soldier who probably already harbored enough suspicion about him right now to justify blowing him right out the nearest airlock—and at warp six-point-five, no less.

Okay, so I don't get to check in with Stillwell or Harris while this guy's looking over my shoulder, Trip thought, hoping, as always, to make the best of a bad situation. *But at least he can't file any reports about* me *to* his *home office without my knowing about it.*

Nevertheless, the continued inescapable presence of Centurion Terix gave Trip an intermittent but highly uncomfortable sensation.

He kept imagining he could feel Admiral Valdore's hard, vigilant stare drilling into the back of his neck like a pair of white-hot mining lasers. . . .

TWENTY-TWO

Sunday, July 20, 2155
Enterprise **NX-01**

ARCHER COULDN'T QUITE BELIEVE what Admiral Gardner was asking him to do. "You do realize that the only reason I was able to help with the crisis on Qu'Vat was because I was used as a guinea pig for the cure, and my ship's doctor blackmailed the fleet admiral?"

The image of Gardner on the ready-room viewer nodded. *"Nevertheless, the best xenoanthropological minds of the Coalition scientific community feel that you may be the one human to whom the Klingons are most likely to listen. On Qu'Vat, after all, you* did *become partly Klingon."*

Archer shook his head, still incredulous even though the admiral's reasoning made a crazy sort of sense. "Sure, the therapeutic retrovirus Phlox injected me with left some Klingon genes in my DNA. But I also spread the infection to the fleet admiral himself, not to mention several dozen of his crew. Admiral Krell has, by the way, practically sworn a blood oath on Doctor Phlox over the whole damned thing, and I suspect he'd cook and eat me in a heartbeat if he could. Or maybe he'd even skip the cooking, take me straight to his dining room, and do the deed raw."

"I never tire of your flair for the dramatic, Archer," Gardner said, traces of both bemusement and condescension mixing in his voice. *"The Klingon High Council*

has agreed to grant you an audience, authorized by Chancellor M'Rek himself."

"This is the same chancellor who sent Duras to kill me for busting out of Rura Penthe. Just so we're clear that *you're* aware you're sending me to face an extremely unfriendly crowd."

Gardner sighed. *"Among many warrior societies, opposing leaders would often meet on neutral ground, setting aside their hostilities in order to discuss terms. Our xenoanthro experts believe that the Klingons will be much too honorable to do anything to you while under a flag of truce."*

"Permission to speak freely, sir?" Archer said, struggling to keep calm.

"Of course," Gardner said, nodding.

"Admiral, you're already talking as if we *are* at war."

"We will be at war if the Klingons ignore this message, Captain," Gardner said, his voice grave. *"Our formal 'cessation of hostilities' ultimatum will be better received—and discussed—if one of our own is there to hand it to them personally."*

"Have you ever heard the phrase 'shoot the messenger,' Admiral?"

Gardner offered a slight smile. *"Archer, from what I've been told, the Klingon High Council holds you in much higher regard than you think. Although the resolution that you and your CMO brought to Qu'Vat's metagenic virus crisis didn't make those affected by the cure terribly happy, the virus you helped cure would have decimated the Empire, and perhaps even destroyed it if you'd left it unchecked. According to some intelligence we've gathered, a few influential Klingons have stopped just short of calling you a hero."*

"Joy," Archer said under his breath. It wasn't that he minded having these people regard him as a hero—it would be far preferable to being one of their targets—but Klingon warriors were tremendously mercurial and unpredictable. And, as he had learned from *Enterprise*'s very first mission, it was a mistake to assume that members of an alien society would think, act, or react the way that humans did.

"Have you reviewed the security recording I transmitted of the Klingon woman we recovered from the wreckage here at Draylax?" Archer asked.

Gardner nodded. *"We did. All of us at Starfleet Command did. And we cannot support your theory that the Romulans were really behind the attack on Draylax. Just because one dying Klingon suspects it does not make it so. Your scans of the ships before they were destroyed showed Klingon crews—live Klingon crews—and despite the actions of the second cadre of battle cruisers, it is more likely that there have been intramilitary squabbles about hostilities related to the Coalition than it is that they were covering up Romulan involvement. Why would they not want to expose the Romulans? Or are you suggesting that the Klingons are also somehow in league with the Romulans?"*

Archer clenched and unclenched his fists under his desk, wanting so badly to strike at something. "The Klingon woman *specifically* said that the crew on the ships that struck at Draylax were kept barely alive, but unable to act. That would explain our sensor readings. And the second wave of Klingon ships may indeed have been trying to eradicate any trace of Romulan involvement. Whether that's because they suspect it, or because they don't want to be framed for the actions of those ships—"

"Exactly," Gardner said, interrupting him. *"The second wave of vessels—ships whose actions Krell apparently authorized—was acting in our favor. For whatever*

reason, they were trying to stop further attacks against Draylax, Enterprise, and Columbia."

"Or they were trying to cover up the initial attacks."

Gardner shook his head. *"If they wanted to cover this thing up—if they didn't care about how their actions would be interpreted—then they probably would have destroyed you as well."* He held up a hand, palm facing the screen. *"Enough, Captain. The formal message you are to deliver to Qo'noS has been transmitted to Enterprise via subspace radio already. It is now your duty to bring it before the High Council and present it."*

"What about *Columbia*?" Archer said, squaring his jaw while trying not to look defensive.

"Two Daedalus-class ships—the Essex and the Archon—will arrive at Draylax within the next few hours. They will continue to assist Columbia with her repairs, and render assistance on Draylax as well."

Gardner's look softened a bit as he leaned forward. *"Archer, whether you want to believe it or not, I do listen to what you have to say, and weigh your concerns, and present your arguments to my superiors. But you are just a part of this organization. So am I. Starfleet is bigger than either of us. And the Coalition of Planets is immensely bigger, even though it's only been around for a few months now. You have been on the edge of discovery, have encountered new civilizations and seen things that most humans would never dream of outside of fiction. I have no doubt that history will record great things about you. Probably a hell of a lot greater than whatever it might say about me eventually.*

"But for now, you have your orders, and you will carry them out. Go to Qo'noS. Impress the High Council. Make certain that we don't go to war. And down the road, when and if the Romulan threat really does become more apparent, you will be able to use all the experience you've

*gained out there on the edge of the unknown—as well
as the strength of a more unified Coalition—to stand up
to it."*

Archer saw Gardner move his hand toward the
switch on his desk as he prepared to end the transmission. *"Good luck, Captain. And Godspeed."*

The computer screen went black

With a roar, Archer smashed his fist into the screen,
sending it tumbling off his desk in a short-lived shower
of sparks. It crashed into the wall before falling to the
floor, where it lay broken and dead.

Archer knew it was a stupid, brutish gesture that
T'Pol would have found appalling. Nevertheless, it made
him feel better, at least for the moment. Still, he realized that the isolation and anger he felt now would be
nothing compared to what he would experience when
he entered the lion's den on Qo'noS to deliver the Coalition's ultimatum.

When he faced *that* challenge, he would be utterly
and terrifyingly alone.

TWENTY-THREE

Monday, July 21, 2155
Qam-Chee, the First City, Qo'noS

THE OTHER TWO TIMES that Jonathan Archer had visited the Klingon homeworld had taught him little about the civilization other than the fact that their architecture looked as foreboding and militaristic as nearly every Klingon he had ever encountered. He wondered if there was any room for nonmartial culture and beauty among these severe, warlike aliens. But although high art here seemed largely confined to the production of elaborate edged weapons, he knew there had to be more to the Klingon people than that; even the savage Hun tribes of ancient Earth weren't complete strangers to art and culture. When discussing this very matter once with Trip, the engineer had said with his understated Southern humor, "Hell, even cannibals can make some beautiful bone necklaces."

Archer had left *Enterprise* under the watchful eyes of Lieutenant Donna O'Neill. She didn't ask why he was not taking Commander T'Pol or Lieutenant Reed along, he noticed. By now, the missing shuttlepod had been noted, though Archer had yet to log the incident officially. D.O. wasn't stupid, nor were any of the other bridge personnel; they probably figured that Malcolm and T'Pol were off on some secret mission—which, in truth, they were. *It's just not a mission that anybody authorized*, Archer thought glumly.

He had also decided to leave Phlox behind, given the threats Krell had made. It was better to know that the Denobulan was safe aboard *Enterprise* than potentially imperiled on the surface of the Klingon homeworld. Archer had left a grateful Hoshi Sato at her post as well; a small, communicator-sized translator unit clipped to his uniform jacket would ensure that he got his point across, and that he wouldn't misunderstand the Klingons when they made theirs. He hoped they wouldn't succumb to the temptation to communicate via their cutlery.

Which left Archer alone except for the two MACO troopers who had accompanied him, Corporals O'Malley and Ryan, both of whom had been trained in multiple unarmed fighting techniques, including the Vulcan disciplines of *Suus Mahna* and V'Shan. Even though all three humans had been disarmed immediately upon entering the outer foyer of the Klingon High Council citadel, Archer knew he could count on the two MACOs to give a good accounting of themselves if it came down to a fight.

They had not been able to offer much in the way of moral support during the interminable shuttlepod ride down from orbit, however. Archer knew he was on his own in the Great Hall, for better or worse. As the huge iron doors before him opened with a groan and a clang, Archer stepped into the expansive inner sanctum. This wasn't the same High Council Chamber he had visited on *Enterprise*'s first mission, during which he had returned an injured Klingon named Klaang to his homeworld. He was thankful as well that it was not the forbidding multilevel courtroom on Narendra III, where a Klingon magistrate had once sentenced him to a year mining dilithium in the frozen depths of the asteroid penal colony Rura Penthe.

Just because this place wasn't that hellish chamber of summary judgment, however, didn't make it any less intimidating, and Archer felt the hairs on the back of his neck rise like a phalanx of fighters adopting a defensive stance. Seated around the deeply shadowed, torch-lit room in a semicircular, two-level observer's arena were some two dozen Klingons—all but one were male—none of whom looked particularly pleased to be present. At the apex of the semicircle sat the man whom Archer recognized as having thanked him—though Hoshi had implied it was more of a threat—when he had returned Klaang to his people. The Klingon chancellor's hair and beard had become even whiter than they had been four years ago, but the form underneath the august warrior-leader's bulky leather and armor seemed as formidable now as it had then.

Archer stepped forward, holding out a data module in one open hand. "Chancellor M'Rek, honorable High Council members and warriors of the great Klingon Houses, I bring you an urgent message from the Coalition of Planets."

M'Rek gestured to one of his guards, who strode forward and snatched the data module from Archer's hand. The soldier handed it to the chancellor, who held it out, then closed his hand around it, crushing it.

"Starfleet sent *you* to deliver the message, human," M'Rek said, his voice a low snarl. "It is only because you have aided the Empire in the past that you were not executed on arrival. Deliver the message *yourself*, and we shall see if your stay of execution merits an extension."

Having half expected such a response, Archer had already rehearsed his answer. He stepped forward, keeping his hands at his sides in a simultaneous show of defiance and submission; he hoped his body language wouldn't distract the Klingons from the importance of his words.

"Three days ago, three Klingon battle cruisers attacked the planet Draylax, crippling its defenses and causing thousands of casualties on that world's surface. The aggressor ships did not respond to warnings from the Starfleet ship *Columbia,* or from my vessel, the *Enterprise*. They opened fire on *our* ships when we drew close enough for a confrontation. Our ships defeated two of the attackers, but the third was destroyed by a *second* trio of Klingon ships that arrived during the battle. These vessels did not engage either our ships or the colony. Afterward, Admiral Krell told me that the original three attacking Klingon ships were manned by rogue captains and crews."

"And your Coalition leaders do not believe his words? They think we are trying to incite war with them?" M'Rek said, his voice rising in both pitch and volume.

"Not all of them do, Chancellor. But the Coalition Council is a democratic parliamentary body." Archer wasn't used to apologizing for democracy, but as he'd learned over the last four years, human cultures and mores were not predominant in the galaxy.

Another older Klingon stood and shouted. "Draylax is not a member of your so-called Coalition, is it?"

"Not currently, no," Archer said, addressing him for a moment, before turning his gaze back to the chancellor. "However, Draylax is one of Earth's allies, and is a signatory, along with Earth and Alpha Centauri, to a mutual defense pact. Draylax is therefore under Earth's protection."

"Under Earth's protection?" another Klingon snarled. "Were you not barely able to *begin* interstellar travel only a few short years ago?"

Archer ignored the man's hyperbolic comment,

concentrating instead on addressing the High Council's leader. "Chancellor, the Coalition does *not* wish to jeopardize the relative peace this part of the galaxy has enjoyed for so long. But understand that some in the Coalition *may* choose to authorize *retaliation* if the Klingon Empire initiates any further unprovoked attacks against—"

"You *accuse* the Empire? Do you think us a race of honorless *taHqeq?*" M'Rek stood and stalked toward the captain. "If we were going to *attack*, you would know it from the screams of your dying, from the rivers of blood that would drown your cities, from the stench of charred and burning flesh."

He glowered, lowering his voice as he neared Archer. Archer could feel the tension in the MACOs flanking him, and was grateful that they were trained well enough to know to avoid making any overtly threatening gestures.

"What happened over Draylax was directed neither against that world nor yours, Captain," the chancellor said after his face came to a stop only a few centimeters away from Archer's. "Apart from a few minor Klingon-human skirmishes—including those in which you and your crew were involved, Captain—the Empire has spilled no *Tera'ngan* or Draylaxian blood. At least, not in sufficient quantities to merit a declaration of war."

Archer nodded, hoping that the sweat beading on his forehead wouldn't be visible in the firelight of the chamber—and wishing that M'Rek's most recent meal had been less aromatic. "I believe that, Chancellor, and have tried to convince my superiors of that. However, the Coalition Council requires—" He stopped himself for a moment, then quickly regrouped. "The Coalition Council *requests* assurances that the Klingon Empire understands its warning that any further hostilities will be treated as cause for war. We also ask you to furnish objective proof that your government neither planned nor ordered the assault on Draylax."

"You request *assurances?* You require *proof?*" M'Rek turned his back on Archer. He laughed loudly, as did most of the other Klingons in the room. "And what is it *we* are getting in return? Other than your Coalition's promise not to initiate a suicidal war with us?"

"What is it you *want?*" Archer asked, aware that he might regret that question more than anything he had said in this chamber so far. He recalled that on the day he had first seen a Klingon, the Vulcan ambassador Soval had warned him, *"The last thing your people need is to make an enemy of the Klingon Empire."* Those words of wisdom reverberated in his head now.

M'Rek turned back again to face him. "When our children are young, they learn to befriend the lowlier creatures of our world. *Targ*s, *qogh*, *qa'Hom* . . . they play with them, sleep beside them, find allies in them. And when they attend to the Rite of Ascension, they learn that they must *kill* the animals that trusted them and *feast* on them. The animals are not *Saj* any longer, weaker creatures kept at our sufferance. They exist to be sacrificed." M'Rek smiled, showing his pointed teeth. "You are a *Saj* today, Captain Archer. You must decide whether your Coalition Council sent you here *knowing* you would be sacrificed . . . or whether your sacrifice is born of their stupidity."

"Any act against me *or* my ship or crew will be considered an act of war as well, Chancellor," Archer said, trying not to imagine what was going to happen next. He was aware that the two MACOs with him were even now assessing every possible mode of attack—as they more than likely had been doing from the moment the three of them had entered this chamber.

"You ask us for *proof*, Captain," M'Rek said. "We have already given you every answer you will get without cost. Anything further you will have to earn through *vItHay'* combat against a warrior of my choosing. If you truly wish to avoid war with the Empire, *you* may prove it . . . by fighting for the truth."

M'Rek gestured to the back of the chamber with a flourish, and Archer saw a figure standing in the shadows behind the chancellor. "If you are not a craven *bIH-nuch*, then you will cross blades with the very person you most accuse of being a *taHqeq*."

The man stepped forward, and Archer saw the swarthy skin, the braided goatee, and the smooth forehead.

Unless he backed down—a choice he doubted was in any way a realistic possibility—the warrior he was to face in a battle to the death was none other than Admiral Krell.

TWENTY-FOUR

Romulan *Scoutship Drolae*

THE ALREADY OVERSTRAINED ENGINES shrieked in protest at suddenly being thrown into full reverse. The half-illuminated, blue-green limb of a planet suddenly appeared in the formerly empty space directly in front of the slender sheet of transparent aluminum that protected the cramped crew compartment from the unforgiving vacuum of space.

"Damn!" Trip shouted, momentarily forgetting to avoid using human idioms in the presence of Romulans. The planet that had suddenly appeared before him grew steadily and quickly until it filled the viewer's field of vision almost completely. One moment he had been calmly studying the nav display on his copilot's console; the next, an entire world threatened to fall directly on top of him like the mother of all rockslides.

"Terix, I know we need to sneak up on these people," Trip said, grateful for the flight harness that prevented his bucking seat from ejecting him like the Romulan equivalent of a cowboy tavern's mechanical bull. "But did you really have to cut it *this* close?"

Seated at the pilot's console to Trip's left, the centurion only laughed indulgently as he pulled back on his control yoke with one hand while entering attitude corrections with the other. If he was at all concerned about Trip's outburst, he showed no outward sign.

"As you have already noted more than once, we must

provide our quarry with as little advance warning as possible," the Romulan said. His words were punctuated by loud bounces and vibrations as the sturdy little ship's belly slammed hard into the planet's rarefied upper atmosphere.

Trip attempted to draw some comfort from the clear evidence he'd just seen that human pilots had no monopoly on insanity. Before today, he had never brought a ship out of warp so close to the surface of a planet. Starfleet regulations strictly prohibited such stunts except in the direst of emergencies, presumably not only because they were hard on ships, but also because they could cause untold havoc planetside. The still-burning surface of Coridan Prime stood as a mute testament to the wisdom of those flight regs. He breathed a silent prayer of thanks that the Romulan recon vessel had not only survived the punishing high-warp voyage all the way from Cheron to Taugus more or less intact, but had also somehow resisted being torn to molecule-sized pieces by the stress of Terix's brutally abrupt deceleration.

Now he feared that the *really* dangerous part of this mission still lay ahead.

Terix quickly leveled out the *Drolae*'s descent as he continued to bring her down. The propulsion system gradually quieted, though its din was replaced by the nearly deafening howl of the steadily thickening nimbus of ionized atmosphere that surrounded the friction-superheated hull's ventral surfaces. Still trading velocity for heat as it plunged ever deeper into the atmosphere, the scoutship roared across the terminator, passing very quickly from impenetrable night into a cloud-decked but brightly illuminated dayside.

The scout punched through the bottom of the cloud deck moments later; despite the deep band of haze beneath the clouds, the planet's upper mesosphere evidently admitted more than enough light to allow Trip to see that what he'd thought of only moments earlier as Taugus III's western limb had now become its sunward horizon. Only about fifteen kilometers of intermittently turbulent atmosphere now separated the little vessel's still-glowing hull from the planet's forbidding rocky surface.

"Do you have a fix yet on the dissidents' camp, Cunaehr?" Terix asked, the rest of his attention completely absorbed by his buckboard-style piloting.

Trip had already been fully engaged in trying to pinpoint their target before the centurion had asked the question. "The passive scans are giving me some ambiguous results. I'm not sure it's a good idea to risk tipping these people off by putting the sensors into active mode, though."

Terix nodded. "I agree. I'm locking in on T'Luadh's preprogrammed coordinates to make our approach. Can you handle the sensor controls?"

"I think so," Trip said, though he was wary of rousing Terix's suspicions by appearing to be *too* familiar with Romulan military hardware.

"Good," said the centurion. "Continue making passive scans. Be on the lookout for any heavy concentrations of refined metals."

Trip nodded, working his console and keeping a weather eye on the passive sensors' displays as the scoutship continued its rolling, bumping descent. He felt grateful that he wasn't prone to motion sickness.

An orange light flashed, followed by a column of numbers in Romulan script. Trip paused the figures and read them over twice to make absolutely sure he wasn't simply misinterpreting the alien characters to which he was still trying to become accustomed.

"This doesn't make a damned bit of sense," he murmured.

"You've found something?" Terix asked, still preoccupied with keeping the bouncing *Drolae* nearly level and more or less stable.

"I picked up a strong signature of *paesin'aehhrr*," Trip said, using the Romulan word for duranium.

"Was it located at the preprogrammed coordinates?"

Trip shrugged. "I'm not sure. It's gone now, and the sensors weren't in contact with it long enough to localize it. In fact . . ." His voice trailed off as he ran through one of the columns of figures yet again.

"Yes?" Terix said, sounding somewhat irritated.

Trip looked up from his console and faced the centurion. "It might have been a reflection from an object in a low orbit around the planet."

"Another ship?" Terix ventured, raising an eyebrow as he continued making his rapid approach to the surface. "An *Ejhoi Ormiin* vessel preparing to attack?"

Spreading his hands in frustration, Trip said, "This planet has a pretty electrically active ionosphere. Maybe it was only a reflection from the surface, or a sensor ghost." *Or maybe it was an orbiting surveillance drone set up by our friends down on the surface*, Trip thought. *An alarm system that's designed to give them just enough time to roll the welcome mat out for us—and to be just small enough for us to miss on our way in.*

Another light flashed on the sensor console. "There," Trip said, pointing. "Now I'm getting a *definitive* reading of refined metals. Right at the spot where T'Luadh said we'd find our, ah, friends hiding out."

Terix nodded with a grunt. "I'll set us down in the rough country, there," he said, pointing at a tactical schematic displayed on one of the console readouts located conveniently between the pilot and copilot stations. "Our landing site will be only two, perhaps three *mat'drih* from the dissident compound."

That's maybe three, four klicks, tops, Trip thought

after performing a quick numeric conversion in his head. Fortunately, neither the atmospheric composition nor the temperature would require either man to be burdened with heavy environmental gear during the hike to the dissident enclave. Hand-to-hand combat in pressure suits could be damned inconvenient.

Terix set the *Drolae* down with surprising gentleness, and Trip was delighted to note that death had not begun to rain down upon them from their nearby target, or from whatever had created the orbiting ghost the sensors had thought they'd seen.

Not yet, at least.

"Can you handle a hand disruptor, Cunaehr?" the centurion said as he unstrapped himself from his seat and moved immediately aft toward the weapons locker.

"I did a bit of hobby shooting back at the university," Trip said as he undid his own flight harness and followed Terix into the rear of the ship. After watching the centurion open the locker and arm himself, Trip silently accepted the heavy silver pistol that Terix handed him.

"This is the dangerous end, right?" Trip said, pointing at the weapon's tapered, hand-length barrel.

Terix only scowled, then checked and holstered his own weapon before handing Trip an empty holster belt.

Again, no stun setting, Trip thought as he gave the weapon a quick once-over, making certain that the safety was on. He hoped to hell he wouldn't have to fire one of these things in combat again anytime soon, though he knew that was probably far too much to hope for. After all, they were about to raid the stronghold of a cold-blooded killer who had already proved he had no compunctions about killing.

Strapping on the holster belt, Trip thought, *Let's hope my old friend Sopek is getting careless in his old age and left a window open for us.*

TWENTY-FIVE

Shuttlepod Two

SO FAR AS MALCOLM REED KNEW, the name of the aquamarine planet that turned slowly several hundred klicks below the shuttlepod had never been recorded on any Earth star chart. In fact, it was one of the farthest-flung worlds that human eyes had ever beheld.

But if Commander T'Pol was right, another human may already have preceded him to this remote place.

"How can you be so certain we'll find Commander Tucker here?" Reed said.

T'Pol raised an eyebrow as she regarded him with that damnably cool Vulcan assuredness of hers. "My intelligence sources have always proved reliable in the past, Lieutenant."

"I'll grant you that the Vulcan transport vessel you got us docked with did a damned fine job of sneaking us past those Romulan patrols at Alpha Fornacis," Reed said. *Not to mention not reporting our whereabouts to Starfleet,* he added silently. It was obvious that the ship in question had been up to something other than the banal tasks of moving passengers and cargo in order to operate with impunity—sometimes at speeds in excess of warp factor six—more than half a parsec inside territory claimed by the Romulan Star Empire.

He still felt annoyed at having been confined to the shuttlepod for most of their three-day voyage, deprived of even the laconic company of T'Pol, who had been allowed at least partial access to the transport vessel that had carried Shuttlepod Two so close to its destination. But even the usually stoic T'Pol had complained about how little access she had been given to the all but invisible Vulcan benefactor whom her V'Shar contacts had persuaded to grant them covert passage into Romulan space. The Vulcans seemed quite intent on keeping a tight lid on whatever they were really up to so deep within the Romulan sphere of interest. This cloak of secrecy made Reed very nervous about whatever it was that the new, purportedly more transparent T'Pau regime on Vulcan might want to keep hidden from its Coalition partners. And those worries weren't so much for his own safety, or even that of T'Pol, but for that of Trip. A second Coalition-based spy bureau blundering about here among the Romulans could well put Trip's mission and life in jeopardy without meaning to do so or even noticing the damage they'd done.

Of course, he was uncomfortably aware that the very same accusation could well be leveled at both himself and T'Pol.

Putting those matters aside for the moment, Reed continued his conversation with T'Pol: "But the only confirmation we have that we might find Trip here, as opposed to any of a dozen other systems, comes from your . . . visions."

"I do not have *visions*, Lieutenant," T'Pol said, her equanimity apparently shaken but little by Reed's almost accusatory point. "But I remain convinced that I have achieved at least an intermittent telepathic link with Trip—" She paused, apparently catching herself in the act of revealing more than she preferred to reveal. "With Commander Tucker. There is ample precedent for such things, Mister Reed. The Aenar of Andoria, for example."

Reed still didn't feel sufficiently convinced to be able

to stop himself from subjecting T'Pol's reasoning to another round of verbal destruction testing. "The Aenar are *very* strong telepaths, Commander. I thought the esper ability was restricted to touch in Vulcans."

"That is certainly true for the vast majority of us," she said, reiterating a point she had made not long ago to Captain Archer and Doctor Phlox. "However, there have been exceptions. I have become convinced that the link Commander Tucker and I share represents just such an exception."

Knowing what he did about the neurological effects of the trellium-D to which T'Pol had once been addicted, Reed felt a good deal less sanguine than she apparently did about trusting her subjective feelings of certainty.

"Please forgive me for saying this, Commander," he said very gently. "But I think you're putting a great deal of faith in what might turn out to be nothing more than a dream." *Or even some residual effect of trellium-D exposure,* he thought, recalling T'Pol's recovery from an addiction to the neurologically toxic mineral.

She said nothing as she stared straight ahead at the planet.

"It just doesn't seem very scientific to me," he said, uncomfortable with the spreading silence.

Seeming to balance her words very delicately on a bulwark of nettles and brambles, she said, "I am a Vulcan, Lieutenant. And Vulcans do not pursue mere dreams across parsecs of interstellar space."

Never underestimate the power of dreams, he thought. *Or nightmares.*

"Dreams. Visions. Gut hunches. Call them whatever you like, Commander," he said with a shrug. "I just have to ask whether it's entirely . . . *logical* for you to place so much trust in a phenomenon that neither of us can really look at objectively."

To her credit, the only sign of emotion she allowed herself to display was an inquisitive tip of the head as she turned to face him again. "If you truly harbor so many doubts about what we're doing out here, then why did you insist on coming along?"

Now that is a damned fine question, he thought; he had asked himself the very same thing more than a few times since she had first asked it just before they had absconded with Shuttlepod Two. In light of all the subspace chatter they'd subsequently picked up concerning the Klingon-Draylaxian conflict that had broken out since they'd left *Enterprise,* Reed could only hope that their current quest wouldn't prove to be as barmy as it might now look to Captain Archer or the rest of his crew.

"I already told you, Commander," he said at length. "We both want to rescue Trip if he's really in as much trouble as you say he is. Besides, I couldn't just let you go off on your own."

The eyebrow rose again. "Even if this entire endeavor ultimately turns out to be—what is the phrase you humans use?—a wild goose chase?"

He smiled gently. *"Especially* then."

After a pause, T'Pol said, "I am placing a great deal of faith in you as well, Lieutenant. Specifically in your discretion."

"I thought I already proved how discreet I can be when I didn't rat you out to Captain Archer," Reed said.

"Of course, Mister Reed. But that action only required confidence on a relatively small scale. In allowing you to accompany me on this mission, you are almost certain to discover one of my people's most closely guarded secrets. And that knowledge will require a much larger degree of discretion."

Reed found it difficult to imagine the nature of any

secret the Vulcans might be so intent upon protecting. Nevertheless, he shrugged and said, "I used to work for a bureau whose stock in trade was secrets. I think you can rely on me to keep mum when it counts."

A flashing light on the pilot's console interrupted whatever she had been about to say in response. In that same instant, the shuttlepod shook violently before settling back to normal perhaps a second or two later.

"What the hell was *that?*" Reed said as he consulted several conflicting sets of readouts that were vying for his attention across the copilot's console.

"We appear to have encountered an intense warp bow shock," T'Pol said as her long fingers moved across her instruments with almost preternatural speed. "The phenomenon is very similar to a starship's subspace wake."

Reed's own subspace field monitor confirmed T'Pol's observation a moment later. "That must mean we have company here," he said. Though he had yet to locate any other vessel, either by eye or by sensors, his readings had revealed that the already fading subspace concussion fit a particular profile: that of a ship that had suddenly collapsed its warp field bubble, thereby dropping almost instantaneously from high warp speed back to the Einstein-mandated sublight velocities of normal space.

Whoever's behind the wheel on that ship has got to be barking mad, Reed thought, *to perform a maneuver like that so close to a planet.*

"I still cannot pinpoint the other ship's precise location or heading using only passive scans," T'Pol said.

"Maybe the planet's gravity well tore her apart as she decelerated," Reed ventured.

She shook her head. "If that had occurred, then I should be able to detect solid and gaseous debris and hard radiation. Switching to active sensor mode and scanning."

Reed looked up from his console, and he was immediately transfixed by what he saw crossing the half-sunlit world below. "Wait," he said, jabbing an index finger toward the forward transparent aluminum window. "Have a look at that first."

A bright orange line of fire was inscribing itself across the dark side of the planet's terminator, extending at supersonic speeds a rapidly collapsing and steeply descending column of ionized atmosphere. The glowing, meteoric mass at the growing line's forefront hurtled toward the side of the planet that presently stood exposed to the pitiless blue-white glare of this solar system's primary star.

Reed turned toward T'Pol, watching her in silence as she scrutinized the enigmatic trail of fire that bisected the planet's skies. After a moment she checked a scanner readout on her console, and then swiftly rose from her seat to check a secondary monitor located on the port side of the cockpit compartment.

As though responding to some inner will of their own, Reed's eyes dropped toward the portion of T'Pol's anatomy that was, for the moment, in closest proximity.

He thought, *She really* does *have quite a nice bum, doesn't she?*

She turned toward him, abruptly scattering his already errant train of thought. His cheeks flushed with a heat born of something other than atmospheric friction.

"The object is on a precise heading for the coordinates that my intel sources have provided," she said, showing no sign of having noticed his discomfiture as she retook her seat.

Reed wondered again about T'Pol's intel sources,

upon which they had both staked so much. How much did they know about Trip's current mission, or that of Trip's adversaries on this planet? Had the V'Shar allowed them to come here to aid Trip because the Vulcan spy bureau shared Trip's goals, or were they motivated by something else entirely? Were they counting on T'Pol to remove a troublesome game piece from their chessboard?

Or were they banking on the opposite outcome?

Instead of raising any of those doubtless sensitive points, or launching into an infinitely recursive volley of questions, Reed merely nodded and began entering a series of commands into his console. "Plotting an intercept course, Commander. Passive sensors only." There was no point, after all, in shouting their arrival from the proverbial rooftops, as it were, regardless of whether the new arrival proved to be friend, foe, or merely a large meteor or asteroid fragment that had chosen this particular time and place to cross the planet's path.

Judging from both the instruments and the evidence of his own eyes, Reed concluded that whatever was creating the pyrotechnics in the planet's atmosphere was making an extremely bumpy descent. He braced himself to follow it down as T'Pol engaged the impulse drive.

As the shuttlepod lurched into a motion that was almost but not quite in phase with that of his stomach, Reed couldn't help but recall a recent, similarly harrowing descent through the much-thinner atmosphere of Mars. Moving surreptitiously, he reached beneath the copilot's console even as the little ship began to bounce and shake in the planet's steadily thickening blanket of air.

He sighed in relief when his fingers brushed against the motion-sickness bag dispenser.

TWENTY-SIX

ARCHER PUSHED the blade through the air awkwardly, watching as his opponent jumped back.

He might have felt a bit better doing the move if his opponent hadn't been Corporal O'Malley, one of the two unarmed MACO troopers who shared the "preparation room" with him. The three of them had already had a perfunctory discussion about how little a Klingon "preparation room" differed from a jail cell on Earth. But since Archer had actually become very closely acquainted with a Klingon jail cell not so very long ago, he felt he could discuss the special nuances of difference with real authority. For one thing, during his current stay the Klingons had given him the use of one of their curved, arm-long swords; it was a wickedly sharp, two-sided, four-pointed blade known as a *bat'leth*.

Archer had seen Klingons carrying these weapons, both here on Qo'noS and three years ago at the deuterium-mining colony on Yeq, where he and some of his crew helped a group of beleaguered miners repel a raid by Klingon marauders. However, seeing the half-moon-shaped weapon strapped to a man's back or mounted on a wall was a quite different experience from actually handling one—or depending upon the odd-shaped blade in a life-or-death battle.

He regarded the *bat'leth* that rested in his hands for

a long moment, staring down at its double blades. He couldn't quite wrap his mind around the purpose of the secondary pair of blades, the one whose edges lay closest to the weapon's central handgrip. On top of that, the whole damned thing seemed a lot more cumbersome than a straight long sword, given that the *bat'leth* seemed to require a two-handed grip, making it much more a close-quarters weapon than a straight sword of comparable length.

I guess it could be worse, he thought, imagining having to fight off the ravening, *bat'leth*-twirling Krell using the short Andorian *Ushaan-Tor* blades, another weapon he had never used but was forced to wield against Shran in a ritual duel.

A man's deep voice spoke from behind him. "I never thought I'd say this to a *Tera'ngan,* but it's good to see you."

Archer turned to face the speaker, but it took him a moment to recognize the aged-looking Klingon who had evidently just entered the room. The man was missing an eye and part of one foot, and had lost a significant amount of weight, but after some initial doubt, Archer recognized him as the Klingon legal advocate who had defended him when he'd stood trial for allegedly dishonoring Duras, the former captain of the *I.K.S. Bortas.* For his efforts, the advocate had been exiled to Rura Penthe for a year alongside Archer, who had been fortunate enough to escape confinement, unlike his hapless Klingon defender.

"Kolos?" Archer handed the *bat'leth* to Corporal Ryan and rushed over to the older Klingon. "I didn't expect . . . I didn't think—"

"You didn't think I'd survive an entire year on Rura Penthe, did you?" Kolos said, interrupting.

Archer returned the other man's wry smile. "I don't think *I* would have survived that."

Kolos smiled back, his sharpened teeth now showing dull edges. "I told you then that I had a very good reason to survive, Captain. Even if I am but one voice, I am still one voice that can call for honor to be restored to our people through justice rather than violence."

Archer motioned to a nearby bench, where he perched beside Kolos as the frail-looking Klingon sat. "Not to put a fine point on it, Kolos, but I sure could use that 'call for honor' today."

Shaking his head, Kolos looked at Archer with his one good eye. "Chancellor M'Rek is under heavy political fire from those who seek to take his position; your timing *could* have been worse, but not by much. I think that he truly means you no ill will, nor does he— or the Council—*intend* to go to war against the Coalition. But he and his High Council allies see the message you delivered today as an affront. And that cannot go unchallenged."

"But why was it an affront to them?" Archer asked. "If they're telling the truth, there isn't any harm in proving to us that somebody else was responsible for the attack on Draylax."

Kolos smiled. "Do you have children, Captain?"

"Not yet," Archer said.

"Well, I have fathered *many*. And one thing I can tell you that I suspect is true of all cultures—Klingon, *Tera'ngan*, Andorian—is that when a child is embarrassed about something, he will fight all the harder to protect himself than if he is outright lying. Governments are not so different from children, Captain."

Archer shook his head. "What does M'Rek have to be embarrassed about? Is it that the Romulans have found a way to commandeer their ships?"

Kolos did a double take. "Why would you think that?"

"We found one survivor in the wreckage of one of the three battle cruisers destroyed at Draylax. She all but said that the Klingons were being controlled by the Romulans. But she didn't know how, and she didn't survive long enough to give us any more than that."

His expression grave, Kolos nodded. "I don't know that to be true, but if it *were*, that would be something that the military would not want exposed."

"So they'd rather go to war against the Coalition than admit they were vulnerable to the Romulans?"

Kolos shrugged, opening his hands, palms pointed upward.

"Unbelievable," Archer said, sighing heavily. Now he felt even more defeated.

"If that is the case, then you must defeat Krell decisively," Kolos said. "And you must kill him."

Archer stared at the older alien, incredulously. Gesturing toward Corporal Ryan, he said, "I don't even know how to use that weapon properly."

"We have nearly three of your hours before the combat is to begin," Kolos said, standing up. "Let us use the time to find ways for you to use the blade that Krell won't anticipate."

He lowered his voice slightly, moving closer to Archer in order to speak at a volume intended only for the captain's ears. "And let us hope that Krell's strength isn't what it once was because of the changes the metagenic virus has wrought."

Archer's breath was already growing ragged and labored, and it was still fairly early in the match. The gladiatorial chamber that he and Krell were in was ungodly hot; even stripped to the waist, he was sweating profusely. *Probably gonna lose ten pounds in a hell of a hurry,* he thought. *Unless I lose my head first, that is.*

The two of them had been led into the arena ten minutes earlier, wearing only their pants and boots, and carrying only their *bat'leth*s. The chamber was part of a vast, torch-lit underground cavern that had apparently been excavated and enlarged for the sole purpose of conducting combat-to-the-death rituals such as this one. Rising from the ground all around were irregularly shaped stalagmites precipitated out of some hardened mineral that Archer couldn't quite identify; even in the dusky light of the wall-ensconced torches, he could see that many of them were stained a dark purplish-black that was probably the residue of Klingon blood.

About twenty feet up, ringed around the cavern's outer walls, was a secondary level surrounded by waist-high railings, behind which stood the assembled members of the Klingon High Council, various uniformed military luminaries, and a large cheering section comprised of growling, snarling Klingon civilians that might well have included his prospective undertaker and burial florist for all Archer knew.

Krell had barely said ten words since seeing Archer again in the combat chamber, and four of them had not been translatable. Archer knew he couldn't hope to reason with the soldier, but he also knew that even if he somehow managed to prevail, he couldn't find it in himself to kill him, either. *I sure as hell can't afford to let you know that, though,* he thought as he regarded his opponent in much the same way he might a Cape buffalo getting ready to make a lethal charge.

Kolos's accelerated training had been helpful enough to allow Archer to survive this long without injury, though mostly he had been defending himself rather than striking any blows of his own. As Kolos had explained and demonstrated various techniques for handling a *bat'leth*, Archer began to understand that some of the principles were not significantly different from certain types of terrestrial sword fighting, blended with a bit of quarterstaff or *bō* stick combat. Kolos had also provided some guidance in the use of the *bat'leth*'s secondary blades and their multiple serrations; they were used mostly to trap the points of an opponent's weapon. Executed properly, such a trapping maneuver could not only effectively block an otherwise lethal blow, it might also disarm a foe with little more than a simple twist and a yank.

With a roar, Krell attacked again, pulling Archer's focus into laser sharpness. The Klingon's blade swung around in an arc, coming up from below, the tip whistling as it cleaved the air; Archer could tell the move was meant to chop his hands out from under the handgrip. Feeling a stalagmite at his back, he couldn't duck to the side, so he moved his own blade to counter, swiveling his *bat'leth* from an upward-curving angle to a down-turned position.

Krell's blow and Archer's parry brought the two blades together hard enough to strike sparks, and Archer felt the shock reverberate through his wrists as the Klingon's momentum and greater weight rammed his blade upward. Pain lanced his arms, and as Krell attacked again, Archer scrabbled to retreat behind another stalagmite. He ducked, barely evading a horizontal slice that had come uncomfortably close to cleanly decapitating him; instead of Archer losing his head, one of the upturned rocky deposits lost its conical end, shattering into a gray-brown powder as the baakonite blade tore through it with all the force of Krell's offended sense of honor.

As Krell's arms followed through with the blow, Archer charged from his defensive crouch, stabbing the pointed end of his weapon toward his foe's midsection.

Krell sidestepped in time to avoid being impaled right through the gut, but not quickly enough to prevent Archer's blade from inflicting a superficial flesh wound that announced its presence with a small spray of lavender Klingon blood.

Even as Archer continued moving forward, his boot caught on something he couldn't see on the uneven floor, and he suddenly felt himself falling. In the quarter second or so it took his momentum to carry him to the cavern's rocky floor, he willed his arms to move the *bat'leth* out from in front of him.

Notgonnastabmyselftodeathbefore Krelldoes, he thought, his mind racing.

Even as he rolled to the side in an effort to get his feet back under him, he felt a sharp pain in his midchest area, then felt the breath whoosh from his lungs as agony struck him in earnest. He realized in a horrified rush that Krell's *bat'leth* had pierced him at the ribs, and even now, before the red blood had dripped from its tip, Krell was standing above him, a look of rage commingled with triumph flushing his hard features.

Through his pain, Archer wanted to laugh, as in an instant he realized that he was about to die trying to prevent his world and its allies from going to war against the wrong enemy, all while the Romulans were setting Earth up for conquest. Given how little his sacrifice was evidently destined to mean, he hoped that he'd at least leave a good-looking corpse behind for posterity's sake.

Krell brought the *bat'leth* down in a lethal arc straight toward Archer's face, and the captain knew that his final wish would not be granted.

TWENTY-SEVEN

Monday, July 21, 2155
Taugus III

TRIP WAS SURPRISED at how easy entering the dissident complex had turned out to be once he and Terix had located a small, concealed emergency entrance, an aperture that must have been intended to allow easy ingress during times of bad weather outside.

And he was further surprised by just how few of the suspected *Ejhoi Ormiin* dissidents he and Terix had actually found within the indeterminate-sized complex once they'd managed to get inside it. The two middle-aged Romulan men they'd encountered in what looked to be an informal wardroom were thoroughly nonplussed at the sudden arrival of the two armed strangers who had just appeared in their midst, as did the somewhat younger-looking Romulan woman who had been sharing a meal with them.

"By the authority of the battle fleet of the Romulan Star Empire, you are all under arrest," Terix said. He brandished his disruptor pistol, keeping it leveled more or less at all three dissidents, all of whom appeared to be academics rather than soldiers. Raising their hands in barely contained shock and fear, none of these people looked eager to rise from the small round lunch table around which they sat, or to do anything else that might provoke their captors.

"This can't be everybody," Terix said curtly, leaning toward Trip.

Trip couldn't help but agree. Holstering his own weapon, he pulled out the bulky Romulan military scanning device he'd kept strapped to the belt on his simple, black paramilitary outfit, which was a close match for Terix's mission garb.

After consulting the palm-sized display screen for a few moments, Trip said, "There's still no sign of life in this building other than these people and the two of us. Maybe the interference we picked up in the planet's ionosphere is affecting this thing." He shook the scanner as though something broken might have rattled inside it.

"All the way down here on the surface?" Terix shook his head. "That would seem to be a rather convenient technical failure."

Already weary of the centurion's thinly veiled accusations, Trip found it difficult to make his reply sound entirely civil. "I'm not just making this stuff up, you know."

"Of course you're not," Terix said in an ironic tone.

Trip counted slowly to five, trying to calm himself as he turned his attention back to his scanner's readout display. "We have to accept the possibility that Ch'uihv managed to get off the planet before we even got here. Maybe that flash of hull metal I detected on our way in was our man making his escape."

Terix nodded. "Perhaps. But it is equally likely that he has somehow hidden himself *here*. And that he is using his compatriots as a diversion."

Another man's voice spoke up from directly behind Trip at that moment, making him start reflexively. It was a voice he recognized instantly.

"My associates are no diversion. I prefer to think of them more as bait for a trap."

Trip turned toward the man who had just spoken, and found that Terix was already facing him. The centurion was crouching as though he had been about to launch a "spray-and-pray" pattern of fire from his disruptor pistol, but had thought better of it at the last instant—and for very solid reasons.

"Ch'uihv," the centurion said through clenched teeth as he raised the barrel of his weapon so that it pointed harmlessly toward the upper curve of the domed ceiling.

Captain Sopek, Trip thought, mentally correcting Terix. *Well, at least we won't have to waste any more precious time searching for you, will we?*

"*Jolan'tru*, Centurion Terix," the dissident leader said as he strode calmly forward from underneath the very same open doorway arch through which Trip and Terix had entered the room. The man was obviously emboldened by the half-dozen or so armed, paramilitary-garbed young Romulans who had already deployed themselves very swiftly and efficiently around the ten-meter-wide wardroom. Ugly gray pistols were raised and ready, and Trip recalled having seen nearly identical weapons on two earlier occasions. The first was his brief captivity in the *Ejhoi Ormiin* compound on Rator II; the second encounter had occurred in the lab where just such a weapon had been used to assassinate Doctor Ehrehin.

The weapons Trip faced now were no doubt every bit as dangerous as those he remembered, and looked as hostile as the expressions on the pale faces of the men and women who wielded them. Trip harbored little doubt that a single word from Ch'uihv/Sopek, or one false move by either himself or Terix, would suffice to envelop the room immediately in a lethal cat's cradle of crisscrossing disruptor beams.

Despite the death wish that Terix had seemed to exhibit behind the pilot's console, the centurion proved himself eminently more sensible here by allowing the weapon in his hand to clatter to the floor tiles. He had even taken a moment to click a small switch on the disruptor's handle, engaging what Trip assumed was a safety catch, a moment before releasing the weapon and kicking it toward their captors.

A single harsh monosyllable from one of the armed dissidents, punctuated by an aggressive gesture with the disruptor pistol in his hand, persuaded Trip to follow Terix's lead; though he found no safety catch on his own weapon after he slowly unholstered it—he frankly doubted that Terix had allowed him to take a charged and functional weapon in the first place—he obediently dropped the heavy pistol to the floor, then gently tossed his scanning device after it.

Two of Ch'uihv's other troopers knelt briefly to retrieve the discarded gear, which they stowed on the Romulan equivalent of Sam Browne belts.

Ch'uihv came to a stop directly between Trip and Terix. Turning toward Trip, he said, "And *Jolan'tru* to you as well, Mister Cunaehr. Or should I address you more properly as Commander Charles Tucker, late of the United Earth *Starship Enterprise*?"

Ah, shit, Trip thought. *I really, really hate when this happens.* He found himself reflecting, absurdly, that the only moderately enjoyable aspect of this situation was the thoroughly stunned expression on Terix's vulpine face, which had flushed almost to the color of split-pea soup. After all, the centurion had suspected him of being a spy from *Vulcan,* not from Earth.

"Commander Tucker," Ch'uihv said, evidently quite enamored with the sound of his own voice. "Risen from the ranks of the hallowed dead. And now, tragically, fated to return there all too soon." The dissident leader's smirk looked distinctly unpleasant on a face that appeared so outwardly Vulcan otherwise.

Trip felt shock at the sudden revelation of his real identity before Terix, but not all that much surprise. After all, a man like Ch'uihv had to have a talent for connecting the dots, or else he would have fallen into the hands of someone like Terix long ago, on one side of the Romulan border or the other. Besides, if Trip knew about the Romulan dissident leader's other life as a Vulcan, why shouldn't Ch'uihv be able to find whatever skeletons lurked in his closet?

"Ch'uihv of Saith," Trip said, feeling a great deal calmer than he'd expected to feel on the occasions when he had tried to imagine something like his present circumstances. "Or maybe I ought to call you Sopek of Vulcan instead."

Ch'uihv/Sopek raised an eyebrow, a gesture that instantly transformed his appearance from that of a treacherous, scheming Romulan outlaw to that of the logical, dignified Vulcan starship captain who had commanded the Vulcan vessel *Ni'Var* some four years earlier. Trip wondered which of the two identities was genuine, if either one was.

"Well done, Commander," the dissident said. After a brief pause, he added, "I never got the opportunity to thank you for covering my escape when Valdore's forces raided our facility on Rator II."

"Well, I might be willing to call it even," Trip said, his jaw clenching involuntarily as he remembered the bloody chaos that had accompanied his efforts to protect Ehrehin and evade both the *Ejhoi Ormiin* and Admiral Valdore's forces. "But only if you'll agree to let *me* reward *you* properly for what you did to Tinh Hoc Phuong."

Ch'uihv made a brief but infuriating show of pretending not to remember the man he had callously transformed into a pile of smoldering ash on Rator II. At length, he said, "Ah, the man who called himself Terha of Talvath. Your fellow Terran spy who claimed to be a part of the *Ejhoi Ormiin*'s Devoras cell."

Trip noticed the goggle-eyed stares of the three academics; Sopek's revelation had left them all looking as stupefied by this as third-graders poring over a textbook on eleven-dimensional tensor calculus.

Though he knew it was worse than useless, Trip couldn't keep the timbre of accusation and righteous anger out of his voice. "You had him *captured*, Sopek. He was in no position to hurt you. But you murdered him in cold blood."

Ch'uihv scowled, shaking his head in an exaggerated display of mock disappointment. "Mister Tucker, I know that engineering has long been your primary area of expertise. Nevertheless, I thought you'd been in the espionage business long enough to understand the occasional need for thoroughgoing security purges in *any* clandestine organization. I'm certain your friend would have agreed that such things are an unavoidable hazard of our trade."

Although Ch'uihv's lips continued to move, Trip suddenly found that all he could hear was an intense whistling sound. An instant later, the dissident leader interrupted his own monologue, grimacing in apparent agony as he placed his fists over his sharply pointed ears. The armed troopers looked to be suffering every bit as badly; at least one of them dropped his weapon onto the floor.

Moving almost faster than Trip's eyes could follow, Terix leaped on the nearest of the distracted guards, taking her down in a bone-crushing tackle that sent her weapon flying.

Trip wasted no time diving toward the floor. "Get

down!" he yelled toward the owl-eyed academics, none of whom had yet taken the simple expedient of ducking beneath their table for cover.

Ch'uihv/Sopek had already collapsed to his knees, as had fully half his armed people. Of the remaining three, one was unconscious thanks to Terix's quick action. Trip landed a hard right cross on another's jaw before the disoriented man could get his weapon pointed in the right direction.

Terix blew a large, charred hole right through the chest of the last of them even as Trip grabbed up one of the fallen guards' weapons.

"Stay right where you are!" Terix shouted, holding one of the troopers' pistols before him in a double-handed combat grip.

It took Trip a startled moment to understand that the centurion was addressing *him*, rather than Ch'uihv or any of his people. A heartbeat or two later, Trip realized that he and Terix were the only people in the room who were still conscious.

"What the hell happened?" Trip asked. It had all started with that peculiar, transient whistling sound. . . .

"Put the weapon down," Terix said. His weapon's muzzle was pointed straight at Trip's head in a gesture of unambiguous menace. Across a distance of maybe four meters, there was no way the centurion was going to miss if he were to open fire.

"Settle down, Terix," Trip said as he made a careful show of allowing a weapon to fall from his hand for the second time today.

When Terix spoke again, his voice seemed to be unnaturally loud. "That man has my weapon." Pausing, he gestured toward one of the unconscious troopers who lay on the floor nearby. "Lift it out of his belt. Slowly. Then drop it on the floor and kick it over here."

Trip nodded silently, and did as the centurion instructed. From what he'd observed of the weapon, he knew he'd never get the safety setting disengaged before Terix burned him up like a Roman candle. *Or a Romulan candle,* he thought absurdly.

A few moments later, Terix had recovered his weapon. While covering Trip with the trooper's pistol in his left hand, he manipulated a switch on the handle of his own weapon with his right. He then holstered the weapon in his left hand, apparently content to keep it as a backup for the one he kept pointed at Trip's head.

With his free hand, Terix removed two small objects from inside his ears, first the right, then the left.

Understanding began to dawn on Trip. *That was no safety catch on his weapon,* he thought, appreciating the engineering ingenuity involved as much as the tactical genius. *It was some sort of ultrasonic attack. Something that works on a frequency so high that only dogs and Romulans can hear it. Unless they're wearing protective earplugs.*

Or they're not really Romulans in the first place.

"We are *not* leaving together," Terix said as he took a single menacing step in Trip's direction. "Commander Tucker."

I didn't fall down the way everybody else did, he thought. *So he doesn't have to just suspect I might not be the real deal anymore. Now he knows for sure.*

His hands raised and his palms out, Trip tried to put on the same *let's-both-be-reasonable-and-talk-this-over-before-either-of-us-does-anything-rash* grin that had forestalled more than a few bar fights during his undergraduate years.

"I should have listened to my mother when I was in school back in Romii," he said aloud. "She always warned me about playing those Frenchotte recordings with the volume up so high."

Terix appeared unmoved by Trip's improvised excuses. "Once I obtain whatever warp-drive data Ch'uihv has stored in this place," he said, "you will die with everyone else here when I vaporize this complex."

"Is killing me *your* idea, Terix? Or Valdore's?"

"I have made the admiral aware of my suspicions."

"But I'm willing to bet he doesn't share them." *At least he might not until after he hears your next report.* "Otherwise he wouldn't have sent us out here together on this wild *mogai* hunt without another couple of men to watch your back."

Terix's scowl deepened, but Trip could see that doubt was warring with resolve behind the centurion's dark, hooded eyes.

"You are not loyal to the Empire," he said. His weapon remained unwaveringly trained on Trip's head. "And even the *Ejhoi Ormiin* accuse you of being a Terran spy."

"And you *believe* that? Ch'uihv is a pathological liar, Terix. It's how he makes his living." He gestured toward the spot where the dissident leader lay unconscious. "For Erebus's sake, man, he's so crooked he has to screw his pants on every morning."

The weapon seemed to waver ever so slightly in Terix's hand, though Trip couldn't be sure that wasn't merely wishful thinking on his part.

"But you are not even *Romulan*," the centurion said. "You *couldn't* be." He punctuated his point by holding up the protective earplugs he still clutched in his free hand.

Think fast, Charles. "Why? Because my hearing is defective?"

"I find it curious that you have never seen fit to mention this rather convenient 'defect' before," Terix said.

From somewhere far beyond the confines of the

building, Trip could hear the sound of distant thunder. He found it mildly ironic that the keen-eared centurion had shown no sign as yet of having noticed it.

Just as he found it hard not to fantasize that the sound represented the faint and fading hope of a last-minute cavalry rescue. More *goddamn wishful thinking,* he thought, trying but not quite succeeding in dismissing the distracting notion.

"My bad hearing isn't something I'm particularly proud of," Trip said, hoping it wasn't as painfully obvious to Terix as it was to him that he was merely grasping at straws in order to stay alive. "After all, it's kept me out of the military my whole life. And it's kept me from having a career like the one *you've* had. Can you imagine how that feels?" *When all else fails,* he thought, *there's always flattery. Not to mention spadefuls of good, old-fashioned Florida bullshit.*

Another rumble of thunder sounded, much closer this time. Terix obviously noticed it now, and cast a quick glance at the still-empty doorway, to which his right side was now faced.

Jumping Terix remained out of the question. But Trip knew he still had to press forward with whatever advantage he might have just created for himself, however narrow.

"Listen, Terix," he said, trying to sound far more reasonable than worried. "Whatever you might believe about me, I'm the best chance Admiral Valdore has of achieving the goal of creating a working *avaihh lli vastam* stardrive prototype now that Ehrehin is gone. The admiral might be a little upset with you if you do anything to compromise that. Kill me and you set the whole project back by *fvheisn.*"

For an interminably long moment, Terix appeared to mull over the prospect of losing years of hard-fought progress in high-warp physics. Despite his apparent internal debate, he'd lowered his gun only a few centimeters, if that.

More thunder, inside the building this time. A klaxon blared, its repetitive tattoo echoing throughout the complex.

Terix raised his weapon again, pointing it straight at Trip's head. "I believe I can live with that," he said with a snarl.

Trip watched him begin squeezing the trigger with exaggerated, excruciating slowness.

TWENTY-EIGHT

Monday, July 21, 2155
Qam-Chee, the First City, Qo'noS

SOMETIME DURING THE LAST INSTANT of life he expected to experience, Jonathan Archer made a decision: He simply wasn't going to stop fighting.

Even as Krell's *bat'leth* blade descended toward his head, Archer brought his own weapon to bear in front of his face, one hand on the traditional grip, the other grasping the outer blade.

The tip of Krell's *bat'leth* sliced through the gap between the outer and inner blade of Archer's weapon, becoming trapped there, wedged mere inches from Archer's face. He grimaced, ignoring the pain in his punctured side, ignoring the blood that slickened the outer blade beneath his lacerated fingers, and twisted with every ounce of strength he still possessed.

Krell's blade suddenly torqued to the side, and he grunted in anger as one of his hands lost its grip.

Archer kicked upward with his boot, connecting hard with the Klingon's crotch. He knew it was a dirty tactic, but he was already long past observing the Marquess of Queensberry rules.

Krell shouted in commingled pain and rage, his other hand's grip loosening on his *bat'leth* just enough to enable Archer to twist the interlocked blades even further, until the combination of leverage, momentum, and muscle pulled the weapon entirely out of the admiral's grasp. Archer quickly threw the two still conjoined weapons as far across the cavern as he could, then rolled even as Krell moved to tackle him.

Scrambling to get his feet back under him, Archer lunged forward, grabbing Krell's long hair and pulling it hard so as to ratchet the Klingon's head violently to one side. He quickly slammed the palm of his hand into Krell's eye socket, then backed away as the Klingon flailed his arms, apparently disoriented.

Then Archer saw that Krell was headed directly toward the fallen weapons, and dashed toward him to keep him from grabbing the mutually jammed blades. The Klingon crouched, sweeping his foot out and connecting with Archer's ribs. At least one rib broke with a sickening crack.

Now it was Archer's turn to scream as he staggered back and crashed against a stalagmite. The impact knocked Archer painfully onto his belly, and the Klingon instantly leaped onto his back, his knobby hand clawing at Archer's face. Krell dug his fingers into the captain's mouth and pulled at his cheek, as if he meant to rip his face off entirely.

Archer rolled forward, flipping the Klingon over his back, praying that the momentum would make Krell let go of his cheek without major trauma. Krell toppled over the top of him, crashing back against another rocky outcropping. This one, however, was evidently less durable than the one Archer had just struck; it exploded into a spray of dirty powder and chunks of porous rock from the impact.

Moving toward the entangled *bat'leths*, Archer saw Krell scrambling back to him again, swinging his huge right arm in a haymaker punch. Archer sidestepped and ducked, then planted both feet and caught the Klingon's arm as it passed him by millimeters. Archer pulled the arm forward and down very quickly, using the Klingon's own momentum to unbalance and topple him. The simple judo move flipped Krell over, and the admiral's shoulder made an unpleasant-sounding pop as his body slammed into the rocky floor.

Archer stepped toward the *bat'leth*s again, but Krell scissored his legs out, catching Archer's foot. He fell to the dirt, his fingers scrabbling against the ground only centimeters from the fallen blades.

Krell stood up, his right arm hanging limply at his side, his face caked in purplish blood and mud. He swayed unsteadily for a moment, then moved again toward the weapons.

Once again, Archer turned his opponent's own movement against him, though this time he kicked at the back of Krell's knees. One of them blew outward, a shattered shinbone tearing open the Klingon's pants in a spray of purple.

Letting out a sound of pain unlike any Archer had ever heard, Krell fell to the ground. Unfortunately he landed close enough to the entwined *bat'leth*s to wrap his good hand around one of them.

Archer stood, wincing at the pain in his side, his mind racing. Even injured, Krell would be unassailable if he managed to take up both weapons.

Unless . . . I don't use myself *as the target,* Archer thought. Crouching, he scooped up a double handful of the dust the broken stalagmite had scattered on the ground and flung it straight into Krell's snarling face.

The debris cloud momentarily blinded the Klingon, long enough for Archer to slip behind him. With a roar, he tackled Krell, moving his arm smoothly around his foe's neck in a chokehold.

Krell flailed with his good arm—pulling the *bat'leth*s apart and dropping one to the ground in the process—as he tried to dislodge the human clinging to his back. His fractured leg refused to support him any further, however, and he crashed to the ground, with Archer clinging to his back all the way down.

Archer released the Klingon and rolled away from him, grasping for his weapon and finally connecting with it. He heard a whistle in the air as he rolled again, and Krell's blade struck the ground where his leg had been half a heartbeat earlier.

Scrambling to his feet, Archer grasped the *bat'leth* by both grips, raising it as he turned to see that Krell had somehow managed to get up and now stood just a few meters away. Froth flecked the Klingon's lips as he moved to close the gap between the combatants and prepared to deliver another deadly blow with his weapon.

Barely avoiding the *bat'leth*'s impact, Archer sliced his own blade toward Krell, even as the Klingon fell toward him.

For a moment that seemed frozen in time, Archer felt resistance, then saw a violet-hued spray and heard a guttural scream.

Turning, he saw Krell on the ground, writhing in shock and spurting blood from the stump that terminated just below his left shoulder. Krell's severed arm twitched in the dust, its hand still gripping the *bat'leth*.

Archer could feel his head swirling and his side aching as he knelt beside the Klingon. He quickly removed the belt from his pants and cinched it around his dazed foe's stump, slowing the spurt of arterial blood significantly. Krell had fallen too far into a realm of pain and shock to notice, or to resist.

Archer looked up, for the first time in minutes noticing and hearing the screams and cheers and shouts coming from the gallery above. He focused his gaze on one particular section near the front, where he saw the chancellor and several High Council members standing. They didn't look at all pleased by the outcome of the combat.

At that moment, Archer couldn't have cared less about their reactions, their vanity, or their so-called "honor."

"I have defeated Admiral Krell in lawful combat," Archer yelled, aware that his voice sounded hoarse and ragged. "He fought honorably, as did I. But I came to Qo'noS to *avoid* spilling any more blood. Not Klingon blood, not *Tera'ngan* blood."

He pointed to Krell. "This man is a credit to the Empire, and a fierce warrior. He deserves to continue aiding his people, to push the Empire ever forward. I will *not* kill him. *My* people would not consider such an act in any way honorable."

He stared directly at the chancellor as he spoke, hoping that his own waning strength and nearly blinding pain wouldn't overwhelm him entirely before he finished making his point. "*I* have satisfied your challenge. *I* have fulfilled my promise. Now *you* must do the same."

Archer felt his legs suddenly go weak, as though they had in an instant turned to water. His vision grew hazy, and the chancellor appeared to be withdrawing into a dark tunnel, an inscrutable expression on his face as the crowd in the gallery roared incomprehensible things.

Then darkness came, followed immediately by silence.

TWENTY-NINE

Taugus III

TRIP CLOSED his eyes and wondered whether he'd feel the disruptor's searing heat before the weapon broiled his vital organs from the inside out. Or if, just before the end came, he'd hear the sizzle of the pistol's energy discharge over the din of the alarm klaxons that continued to blare and reverberate throughout the *Ejhoi Ormiin* facility.

The klaxon did little to blunt the crackle of a column of disturbed air, which arrived right on schedule. Trip was surprised at how little pain he felt.

In fact, he felt no pain whatsoever.

A familiar male voice spoke from behind him. "Commander Tucker? Is that really you? Are you all right?"

He opened his eyes, which were immediately drawn to the spot on the floor where Terix lay supine, his body crumpled near a pair of the unconscious dissidents and his own fallen disruptor pistol. The blare of the klaxon must have drowned out whatever sound the centurion's body had made on its way down.

Trip turned to face the English-accented man who had called to him—and was further surprised to note that the man hadn't come alone. Both figures wore black paramilitary-type clothing rather than their more familiar blue Starfleet jumpsuits.

Somebody'd better pinch me, he thought, momentarily half convinced that he was experiencing another one of those dreamlike yet almost tangibly real visions that sometimes came to him when his mind straddled the weird twilight realm that lay between slumber and consciousness.

Then he realized that he had rarely, if ever, felt quite so wide awake as he did at this moment. *After all, it's kinda tough to nod off while somebody's got a gun pointed straight at your head.*

"Malcolm," Trip said, still incredulous. "T'Pol. How the hell did you two get here?"

T'Pol paused to glance at the setting on the phase pistol in her hand, then gazed back at Trip with one eyebrow raised in an ironic arch. "Very likely the same way you did, Commander," she said. "In a spaceship."

Trip frowned. "Well, I didn't think you paddled after me in a rowboat." *Can't afford to start getting used to these last-minute reprieves,* he told himself, nettled even though—or perhaps because—he knew he owed his life to the out-of-the-blue intervention of two of his closest friends. But he didn't want to examine this new turn of luck too closely, lest he convince himself either that he was indeed dreaming or that some higher power was quietly guiding his destiny.

Still feeling poleaxed by the cavalry's unexpected arrival—not to mention disoriented by the blaring alarms—Trip could only stand and watch as Malcolm methodically gathered up the disruptor weapons that lay scattered across the floor or were still attached to their unconscious Romulan owners, either holstered on belts or clutched in insensate fingers. Malcolm kept his phase pistol at the ready as he went to work, starting with the fallen centurion, whom Trip noted was still breathing.

Unlike these folks, our *weapons have a stun setting,* Trip thought, relieved that no one had died here as yet. He was bitterly aware, however, that circumstances would still probably require him to kill Terix at some point—probably sooner rather than later—now that he and Sopek had unmasked each other in front of the centurion.

With a start, he became conscious that T'Pol was speaking to him again. "I take it you came here in pursuit of a specific goal, Commander," she said, her voice raised to a near shout to cut through the voluminous background noise.

He nodded. "The dissidents based here stole some of Doctor Ehrehin's warp-seven drive research data. We came to determine exactly what they took. *And* to get it back, to prevent them from putting any of it to use." He realized even as he spoke the words that she probably had no knowledge about Ehrehin, much less anything else he was talking about. But he hoped she would understand the urgency of his task nonetheless; he hoped they'd have time to discuss all the particulars in detail later.

Just as he knew that the mission that he and Centurion Terix had undertaken might already be a lost cause were they to overlook so much as a single copy of the purloined data.

"And have you managed to locate the stolen information yet?" T'Pol wanted to know.

"No," said a groggy male voice. "And he won't."

Trip and T'Pol turned together toward Ch'uihv, who was rather laboriously trying to rise to a sitting position on the floor. Once he had done so, he raised his hands in surrender in response to Malcolm, who stood nearby with his phase pistol aimed straight at the dissident leader's midsection.

"Captain Sopek?" T'Pol said. Trip allowed himself to enjoy the flash of surprise that somehow managed to make a momentary escape to her usually stoic face.

"Small galaxy, isn't it?" Trip said, not quite suppressing a small but determined grin.

"Sub-Commander T'Pol," Sopek/Ch'uihv said, nodding in her direction.

"Commander," she corrected.

The man nodded. "Ah. I'm pleased to see that you've prospered. It would be a pity were you to be less fortunate with regard to the 'long life' part of the traditional Vulcan greeting, however."

"What the hell are you talking about?" said Malcolm, brandishing his weapon.

"Do you understand what the klaxon you're hearing signifies?" After a pause, Sopek said, "It's our automated intruder containment system."

"Let me guess," Trip said. "You're going to blow up the whole building."

Sopek nodded. "You have very little time."

T'Pol brandished her weapon. "You're coming with us, Captain. Your presence here raises a number of questions for which I require answers. I need to determine whether you are acting here at the behest of the V'Shar, or in pursuit of some other agenda."

Sopek nodded, his face now a stony mask of dignified Vulcan equanimity. "Your curiosity is certainly understandable," he said as he rose to his feet.

Trip gestured toward the unconscious centurion. "We need to take this man into custody, too." A few moments later, he and Malcolm hoisted the surprisingly heavy Romulan soldier in a modified fireman's carry while T'Pol covered the three of them with her phase pistol.

"What about the other people?" Malcolm asked, tipping his head toward the table where the academics were seated. "We're not going to just leave them here to die, are we?"

The question made Trip feel a slight twinge of guilt,

but he suppressed it. After all, these people were allied with the craven killers who had murdered Ehrehin.

Turning his back on the academics as he shifted Terix's dead weight, Trip said, "If they're smart enough to poach a great man's research, they ought to be smart enough to find their own ride out of here."

"What about the stolen data?" Malcolm said.

"To hell with it," Trip said. "With any luck, it'll burn up when this place goes *boom*." Thoughts of all the harm the missing data might cause in the wrong hands expunged his remaining guilt over his decision not to extract anyone other than Sopek, Terix, and his friends.

Yet another voice spoke up loudly then, originating from behind the wardroom's small dining table, directly behind Trip.

"No!"

Though he was still burdened by half of Terix's dead weight, Trip turned his head and shoulders toward the speaker, who turned out to be one of the three Romulan civilians whom he and Terix had surprised when they'd arrived. It was the woman—and she held a disruptor pistol that one of the *Ejhoi Ormiin* paramilitary people had evidently dropped earlier; Malcolm must have overlooked it when he'd been rounding up their scattered equipment.

Trip sighed. Yet again, an unfailingly lethal weapon was pointed more or less straight at his head. Only now, there was no guarantee that either Terix or Malcolm wouldn't be killed right along with him should that weapon go off in the woman's shaking two-handed grip. T'Pol—who still held her phase pistol at the ready—might be able to stun the Romulan woman, but probably not before the academic released an energy discharge that would almost surely kill somebody.

"Easy peasy, there," Trip said to the woman. "Why don't you put that down? Let's talk about this, all right?"

"There's no time to talk," she said, keeping the weapon up and apparently ready. "Ch'uihv is our leader, and he must leave with *us.*"

"How much time do we have?" Trip said.

Ch'uihv/Sopek shrugged. "Perhaps enough for you to get back to your rescuers' ship. If you leave now, unencumbered, that is. Put the centurion down. I promise you, we shall take *extraordinarily* good care of him."

"He could be bluffing," Malcolm said, still holding up at least half the weight of Terix's unconscious form.

Maybe, Trip thought. *But you gotta know when to fold 'em.*

"You know, I've survived a whole lot of bad stuff since all this craziness got started," Trip said. "But I'm not fool enough yet to think I can roll sixes whenever I need 'em. Put him down, Malcolm."

Great, he thought. *I don't get to recover the missing data, which was the whole point of coming here in the first place. And on top of that, I've just lost the option of destroying it.*

On the other hand, he just might survive long enough to make plans to do something about all of that. Which was better, he had to admit, than nothing.

"Cover us, T'Pol," he said. "Let's get the hell out of here while that's still an option."

After engaging the launch thrusters, T'Pol checked the sensors for any evidence of either outbound *Ejhoi Ormiin* vessels or incoming Romulan patrol ships; she could find no sign of either so far, though she knew that the planet's problematic ionosphere might conceal a multitude of dangers, at least until the shuttlepod attained a high enough altitude to clear the atmosphere entirely. Even then, another ship could always hide itself by flying just beyond the limb of the planet itself.

Satisfied that the shuttlepod was now relatively safe, at least for the moment, she watched in silence as the planet's surface continued its swift retreat until it became a vast aquamarine curve far below Shuttlepod Two's ventral hull.

Several soundless, nearly concurrent explosions appeared like rapidly blooming orange flowers a few moments later, despite the dense cloud layer that covered them.

"So Sopek wasn't bluffing after all," Trip said as he stared out one of the windows on the shuttlepod's starboard side, just to the rear of the cockpit.

"Vulcans never bluff," T'Pol said. "I suppose the same might be said of other related species as well."

"It's good to see you again, Trip," Lieutenant Reed said, turning his copilot's seat to the side to face Trip. "Even if you do look like Old Scratch himself at the moment." Turning back toward T'Pol with wide eyes, he added, "No offense meant, Commander."

T'Pol shook her head. "None taken, Lieutenant." She made a mental note to do some research on Earth's religious mythologies before deciding whether or not Mister Reed had given her any reason to take offense. Of course, the fact that yet another human knew the secret of her people's genetic relationship with the Romulans was of far greater importance than her ethnic pride.

Setting those matters aside, she decided she had to agree wholeheartedly with his underlying sentiment; it was indeed good to see Trip again. And although she regarded it as an unlikely possibility, she found herself hoping for an opportunity to tell him that herself, away from Reed. She wanted to reach out to Trip, to touch him outside the surreal confines of the telepathic link that had finally drawn them back together.

"Likewise," Trip said.

"You don't sound very happy," Malcolm said. T'Pol was inclined to agree.

Out of the corner of her eye, T'Pol saw Trip shrug. "I just wish your timing had worked out a little better, that's all," he said.

T'Pol frowned at the patent illogic of that comment. She was certain that the Romulan, whom Trip had identified as Centurion Terix, would have killed Trip where he'd stood had she and Reed entered the room only a few seconds later.

Before she could press him on this point, Trip asked, "What are the chances of anything surviving those blasts?" He seemed to be addressing no one in particular as he continued studying the distant embers of the explosion, which were moving swiftly beyond the planet's eastern limb owing to the combined motion of the shuttlepod and the planet.

"I'd tend to doubt it," Reed said. "The explosives they were using must have had one hell of a yield to produce a flash intense enough to be this visible right through such a heavy cloud deck."

"But that doesn't mean they couldn't have hotfooted it out of there at the last second, just like we did," Trip said, his tone growing increasingly sour. "Between this planet's cloud layer, the weird local ionospheric effects, and the electromagnetic pulse those fireworks just put out, Sopek could have flown a small ship right past our sensors and we'd never even know it.

"And if *that's* happened, then that warp-seven drive data his people stole is still in some pretty damn untrustworthy hands."

"It might already have been too late to prevent that

from happening even before we arrived, Commander,"
T'Pol said as she laid in a course away from the planet
and began powering up the main drive. She wondered
silently whether Trip actually considered the hands of
an aggressive and expansionist Romulan military to be
significantly more trustworthy than those of the political radicals who at least nominally stood against them.
After all, the enemy of one's enemy could sometimes be
one's friend, as Surak's adversary T'Karik had pointed
out on more than one occasion.

But such considerations could be complicated enor-
mously by rogues such as Sopek—agents whose true
loyalties were anything but clear.

"Don't you think I *know* that?" Trip said, his evident
anger creating a jarring counterpoint to his outwardly
Vulcanoid appearance. "Data is the hardest thing of all to
contain once it gets out. And your kicking down Sopek's
door didn't make dealing with the thieves any easier, especially now that they've taken a Romulan centurion prisoner. They'll take their time trying to wring everything
they can out of him, just like they did with Ehrehin."

Trip turned to the side, the planet's reflected light
surrounding him in a faintly bluish aura. Although she
could see him only in profile, she noticed that his eyes
had taken on a haunted, faraway cast that she could
only wonder about. He seemed somehow disappointed,
and perhaps a little angry as well. She wondered if his
feelings stemmed from a mission that had ostensibly
failed. Or whether he was disappointed by his apparent
failure to extricate himself from a dangerous situation
unassisted.

"I wish you two hadn't come," Trip said quietly, almost as though he had read her mind. As she watched
him stare down at the slowly rotating alien world below,
she considered their mental link again, and decided that

he might indeed have picked up a cue from her on some subconscious level.

"You're welcome, Commander," Reed said sourly. "My apologies for misjudging the situation down there so badly. I should have realized you were just trying to lull this Terix fellow into a false sense of security when you let him get the drop on you."

Malcolm's mention of the Romulan's name brought a shudder to T'Pol's spine. Not because she recognized his name, but because she had recognized his face. She had seen him several days earlier, via the mind link, torturing Trip.

T'Pol watched in silence as Trip turned toward Reed, bristling. "At least *I* managed to get in there without setting off the goddamn self-destruct system."

Reed seemed to be running out of patience. "Would you prefer we set you back down on the planet so you can have another go at this?"

Trip's eyes widened as though he had suddenly become aware of just how ridiculous he sounded. Then he shook his head and chuckled. "Of course not, Malcolm." He paused, apparently gathering his thoughts. "On the other hand, Terix and I left a scoutship down on the planet only a few klicks from Sopek's base, just a short ways from the spot where you two parked the shuttlepod. If that ship is still intact, I can't risk leaving it down there. It'll be easy pickings for any *Ejhoi Ormiin* who might happen by."

Though T'Pol desperately wanted to get the shuttlepod back to the relative safety of Coalition space as quickly as possible—and with Trip aboard it—she knew that she couldn't dispute his logic.

An alarm sounded on one of the sensor consoles, persisted for perhaps two seconds, and then stopped by itself.

"What is it?" Trip said as he approached the front of the cockpit.

T'Pol studied the readout and frowned. For a moment, something that strongly resembled the profile of a large vessel had appeared. Then, just as suddenly as it had appeared, it vanished.

"Nothing, evidently," she said, shaking her head. "A sensor ghost, perhaps. Or our reflection bouncing off the planet's ionosphere."

"Looks like it's gone, whatever it was," Reed said, facing forward again in order to study his own console. "There's still no trail to follow, in any case."

"I will take us back down," T'Pol said, trying not to show how much the brief sensor apparition had rattled her. "Once the conflagration on the surface dies down somewhat."

"Thanks," Trip said, his expression grim.

Reed turned back toward Trip. "If I may say so, Commander, I don't think I've ever seen anybody look quite this unhappy after receiving such a textbook hair-breadth rescue."

Trip allowed himself the luxury of a small smile. "I suppose I made my peace with dying with my boots on months ago. Just as long as the cause is a good one. And I can't think of a better cause right now than keeping the secret of sustained high-warp travel out of Romulan hands. Valdore's *or* Sopek's."

"Too bad we weren't able to get our own hands on a complete set of that data," Reed said. "Imagine what it might do for Starfleet's warp-seven program."

T'Pol watched as Trip nodded, his eyes once again growing distant. "Captain Stillwell's wet dream," he said, puzzlingly. "But that's moot for the moment, Malcolm. Hell, it might have been better for everybody if we'd decided to just shoot it out down there."

T'Pol was having trouble believing what she was hearing. "At least one of us would almost certainly have been killed," she said, frowning.

"But not all of us," Trip said. Though his gaze was cold, his expression was otherwise as unreadable as that of a *Kolinahr*-disciplined Vulcan. "It would have taken only one of us to make sure that the stolen data never got off the planet."

"But the only way to do that," Reed said, clearly aghast, "would be to have somebody stay behind with the data until the explosives detonated."

Trip nodded. "Like I said, that idea looks a lot less scary than you'd think to somebody who's already dead."

"But you're *not* dead, Trip," T'Pol said, convinced that she was largely responsible for that simple fact.

His cold eyes began to blaze with a fire that reminded her of the savage, destructive historical epoch that preceded Surak's golden age of logic and intellectual discipline on Vulcan.

"No, T'Pol. I'm *not* dead. But I *am* all the way back to square one in terms of my overall objective, aren't I? So I hope you'll excuse me if I'm not overflowing with gratitude for your timely entrance, okay? I'm a little too busy at the moment trying to figure out what I'm going to tell Admiral Valdore about this little setback. If I'm *really* lucky, he might just assume the worst and have me summarily executed."

"Then why don't you simply come back with us?" T'Pol said almost before she realized that the words were leaving her mouth.

"Thanks for the offer," Trip said, his voice more gentle. "But I've been officially declared dead, remember? We'd have to undo that somehow, along with a whole hell of a lot of expensive Adigeon Prime plastic surgery. I'd like to have a little more to show for all of that before I decide to pull the rip cord on this warp-seven-drive business."

"Staying in Romulan space is a pretty risky proposition, Commander," Reed said.

"Leaving strikes me as even riskier, under the circumstances," Trip said, shaking his head. He turned to face T'Pol directly. "I'm sorry, T'Pol. The stakes are just too high right now for me to up and leave. I have to find a way to salvage whatever's left of my mission here." Then he turned back to stare again in silence at the cloud-streaked world below.

T'Pol felt a parsec-wide gulf open up between them. She had saved Trip's life. She might even have prevented the Romulan military or the dissidents who opposed it from capturing him and subjecting him to tortures like those she'd glimpsed through the mind link.

But Trip's sudden remoteness told her more eloquently than words that none of that really mattered to him at the moment. For the first time, she wondered if her rescue had inadvertently prevented him from executing some crucial contingency plan, thus closing some window of opportunity that might never open up again. And she discovered she felt extremely reticent about asking him whether or not this was so.

At last she began to understand the true enormity of her obsessive insistence on coming out here to Romulan space, as well as the ultimate futility of it. However anyone might attempt to excuse her actions—she could easily imagine an advocate at her upcoming court-martial citing her emotional vulnerability owing to residual trellium-D damage and the recent death of baby Elizabeth—she now understood in a deep and visceral way that she couldn't run from their possibly ruinous larger consequences.

She understood now that she had done a good deal

more than merely damage her relationship with her captain and friend, Jonathan Archer, to say nothing of having allowed Malcolm Reed to do the very same thing; she had also grievously damaged whatever might have remained of the intimate bond she'd forged with Charles Tucker—all because she had believed it necessary to save his life at all costs.

A bottomless abyss of pure, unalloyed shame opened within her. *Perhaps I actually* disrupted *Trip's mission. A mission that was the very reason he risked suffering a second, more permanent death inside the Romulan Empire in the first place.*

To her horror, she realized that her illogical, emotional actions might have compromised the safety of both of their homeworlds.

Not to mention that of the entire Coalition of Planets.

THIRTY

PHLOX MADE A STUDIOUS ATTEMPT not to count exactly how many armed Klingons had crowded into the medical treatment chamber. Though the warriors had to a man either ignored or failed to understand his polite requests that they stand outside the mobile sterile surgical field he had set up, he did his best not to appear intimidated. In fact, he was far more appalled than intimidated by the casual disregard these people seemed to have for even the most elementary surgical protocol.

Corporal Ryan, one of the two MACO troopers who had accompanied Captain Archer to the planet's surface, had called him to one of the Klingon capital's minimalist medical facilities. Because Archer's team had taken *Enterprise*'s last remaining shuttlepod, and because time was of the essence, Phlox had had no choice but to beam down to the facility, an experience he still found troubling even under the best of circumstances. And this was hardly the best of circumstances.

Regardless, he was grateful that Corporal Ryan's summons hadn't come any later than it did. Archer had suffered significant blood loss during what Phlox had been told was a duel with a Klingon admiral named Krell—whom Phlox could see had gotten the worst of the injuries—and had needed an immediate transfusion. Whether or not the hulking Klingon physician Kon'Jef, in whose infirmary Phlox was now working, could have fixed Archer's wounds was immaterial; Phlox doubted that his Klingon counterpart could provide human-compatible hemoglobin to Archer, much less the stored units of whole blood Phlox had brought with him from *Enterprise*.

Apparently finally taking notice of the crowded conditions in the surgical bay, the giant Klingon doctor barked a few terse orders, and the majority of the assembled warriors obligingly shuffled outside into the flagstone-lined corridor. Phlox heaved a quiet sigh of relief that Archer's transfusion tubes were no longer in danger of being yanked out by an accidental encounter with the tip of a *bat'leth* some broad-shouldered Klingon soldier was carrying across his back.

One of those who remained behind was a striking Klingon woman. Her teeth were sharp and her breasts were pushed up and half exposed in a revealing outfit made of fur and leather. She stood near the table upon which Krell lay, displaying as much grief as Phlox had ever seen on a Klingon face.

"Thank you for clearing the operating chamber," Phlox said, looking over to the Klingon doctor with what he hoped was a nonthreatening smile.

"It was not for *your* benefit, *DenobuluSngan*," Kon'Jef said, fairly spitting the words from underneath a long, squared-off gray beard.

Phlox nodded, tilting his head to one side. "Nevertheless, I appreciate the gesture."

He worked quickly on the shirtless and unconscious Archer, using a hand-held antimicrobial cleansing unit and a protein fuser in an attempt to repair the captain's disconcertingly deep thoracic wound.

Archer's breath changed and he stirred. He tried to rise from the flat stone bier beneath him, then winced and ceased making the effort. "Am I gonna live, Doc?" he said, his voice weak.

Phlox looked down at his captain's face for an instant, nodding, then returned to his duties. "Yes, Captain, but you *will* be rather sore for a while, once you're up and moving about. Luckily, the Klingon weapon missed your liver and several other major organs. Unfortunately, it chipped two of your ribs badly. You may experience some respiratory discomfort for the next several weeks, I would imagine."

"How about Krell?"

Phlox spared a glance over to the other table, where the Klingon doctor and an assistant purposefully went about their work, their blue surgical gowns spattered in purplish gore. The woman still stood nearby, watching the proceedings intently.

"It would appear that your opponent will indeed live. From what I could see, he has a compound fracture in one leg, a dislocated shoulder, and a rather cleanly detached arm."

Archer winced again. "That would be because I sliced it off," he said quietly. "Hope there won't be a lot of hard feelings about that."

"Well, Shran is finally on speaking terms with you again, isn't he, Captain?"

Archer chuckled, remembering how angry the former Andorian soldier had been during and after the knife duel they had been forced to fight late last year. "Compared to what happened to Krell, Shran only got a haircut, Phlox," he said. "And I doubt that Klingon limbs grow back on their own the way Andorian antennae do."

"True, Captain," Phlox said, nodding. "However, the physician attending to Krell believes that he *might* be able to reattach the severed arm. The admiral's other injuries, while painful and messy, appear eminently repairable as well."

Phlox inspected his handiwork closely, pleased at the results so far. "I've done what I can for the moment, Captain. You will still need to lie down for a while and finish your transfusion. Were this any ordinary circumstance, I would prescribe bed rest for at least a week. I understand, however, that our current circumstances may not allow you that luxury."

"No, they won't," Archer said, smiling weakly. "I'm glad you noticed. Let's hope it means we won't be on opposite sides of one of those tired old 'captain-you're-in-no-shape-to-leave-sickbay' arguments that doctors like to start."

"That depends entirely on how careful you can be over the next few days about not undoing all the work I've just done stitching you back together," Phlox said around what he hoped was a reassuring smile. "Now, with your permission I would like to offer my assistance to Doctor Kon'Jef."

"That's fine by me, Phlox," Archer said. "I'll just try to go back to a less painful place in my head."

Phlox stripped off a pair of surgical gloves and put his hands under a sanitizing sprayer mounted on one of the dull metal walls. Grasping another pair of gloves, he approached the woman and the two male Klingons who were working on Admiral Krell.

Although he hadn't known the identity of Archer's wounded opponent at first, Phlox realized that he was quite familiar with him once he'd heard the man's name. Less than a year ago the fleet admiral had been intent on destroying everyone at the Qu'Vat colony—including Phlox and Archer—in order to halt the spread of the augment-derived metagenic virus.

"I'd like to put my skills at your disposal in your

efforts to reattach the admiral's arm," Phlox said. "I have done extensive work in neurological reconstruction, and I have made a close study of the tissue-regeneration techniques of the Adigeons."

The woman spat at him, glaring. "I will not allow *you* to touch Krell. The virus *you* inflicted upon him has done *enough* damage to our House already."

The Klingon doctor growled something at the woman in their native tongue, but the words were too quick and low and guttural for Phlox's translator unit to pick up. The woman glared again, baring her fangs, then stepped up to Phlox.

He swiftly pulled his eyes up from where they were— his gaze had immediately focused on the point where her deep cleavage swelled most provocatively—and met her angry gaze.

"If you harm Krell any further," she snarled, "you will not see another sunrise, *DenobuluSngan*." She spat out the Klingon name for his race as though it were a curse.

As she moved away from him, Phlox stepped in to examine the work already being done by Kon'Jef and the other Klingon medic. The work seemed to be competent—at least so far—but Phlox feared it would leave Krell with only partial use of his hand.

"Please allow me to assure you and the admiral's . . . wife, that I will do everything in my power to help him."

Kon'Jef glared at him with hard, steel-gray eyes. "She's his *sister*. *I* am his husband. And I will make *certain* you do nothing wrong."

Being a Denobulan with three wives, each of whom had three spouses of her own, Phlox had no reason to find Krell's family arrangement in any way unusual. Nodding, he reached for a microscalpel that lay on a nearby tray. "Do you have a pair of fiber-enhancers and some brighter surgical lights?" he asked the other two medical personnel. "I'd like to make *certain* that Admiral Krell regains the full use of his arm."

Archer sat up painfully on the hard surgical slab as Chancellor M'Rek strode into the medical chamber, flanked by several warriors.

"Captain Archer," M'Rek began. "Your tenacity and stubbornness, not to mention your savagery in battle, mark you as a spirit who was probably *meant* to be a Klingon. The pink, fleshy form that spirit now resides in notwithstanding."

Archer tried to smile, and winced at the pain in his face, a lingering souvenir of Krell's attempt to rip his cheek from his skull. "I consider that a great compliment, Chancellor." He put up a hand to discourage Phlox from approaching. Phlox backed away, lowering his gaze as well as the medical scanner in his hand.

"Despite your unwillingness to kill your opponent—an outcome we truthfully thought to be impossible to begin with—you have fulfilled your part of our bargain," M'Rek said.

"So you're going to tell me the plain truth about the attacks on Draylax."

M'Rek shook his head. "No, *I* will not. *That* duty will fall to Admiral Krell." He turned to regard the Klingon whom Archer had been told was the High Council's chief physician. "Doctor Kon'Jef, can you rouse Krell long enough for him to perform his duties?"

Archer thought he saw a look of anger flicker over the doctor's face, but the man merely nodded. Archer imagined that even a chief physician would think very carefully before daring to defy the wishes of the leader of the Klingon High Council.

"He has just endured a long and intricate surgical

ordeal, Chancellor," Kon'Jef said. "It will be painful for him, but I believe I can wake him without causing him any permanent harm."

"Do it," M'Rek said. Turning back to Archer, he said, "The evidence that he shows you will *not* be allowed to leave Qo'noS."

"But how am I supposed to convince my superiors that—"

"That is *your* problem, *Tera'ngan,* not mine," M'Rek said, interrupting him. "Your government expected us to take *your* word as to its intentions. If your superiors expect us to trust *you,* then surely *they* will not mind affording *us* the same respect."

Archer nodded. *Whatever I'm about to learn must embarrass the hell out of the Klingons,* he thought. *Or else they wouldn't care so much about hard evidence leaking out.*

He could only hope that, as M'Rek had said, his own word would be enough to assuage the suspicions and fears of the decision-makers of the Coalition of Planets.

THIRTY-ONE

Taugus III

TRIP FELT A PALPABLE SENSE of relief when his own eyes finally confirmed that the explosion that had laid waste to Sopek's hideout hadn't taken the *Scoutship Drolae* with it. The blunt-shaped, eight-meter-long vessel remained parked on the same nearly level stretch of rock-strewn hillside where Trip and Terix had left it, some three klicks and change away from the still-burning remains of the dissident compound.

"Are you sure you'll be able to fly this thing solo?" Malcolm said, eyeing the gray-green hull of the alien vessel with unconcealed suspicion. Shuttlepod Two cast a long shadow behind him and T'Pol as the late-afternoon sun continued to sink ever lower in the sky behind it. The bloated orb's orange-refracted rays were painted brown and ocher by the durable but slowly diminishing column of smoke and fire that marked the ruins of Sopek's base.

"There's only one way I can think of to find out," Trip said with a grin as he slapped the hull with an open palm. "Hell, I'm not even sure I can get the hatch open without Terix's advance written permission. I just have to hope he left the computer a note."

"I take it he wasn't exactly the trusting sort," Reed said.

"We're talking about a Romulan centurion, Malcolm. Not an eagle scout." Trip placed his right hand on the recognition pad that was mounted to the immediate right of the forward hatch. The hand-plate was recessed so that it was flush with the rest of the hull when its tough duranium cover was in place.

To Trip's relieved surprise, the hatch hissed obediently open two or three heartbeats later.

"Let's hope your friend Terix didn't leave any booby traps active in there," Malcolm said, his expression grave as he nodded toward the open hatch, through which a few of the scoutship's faintly glowing instrument panels were visible.

A swarm of butterflies fluttered in Trip's gut; he could think of only one way to put *that* notion to the test as well.

T'Pol took a couple of steps closer to Trip and the open hatchway before she stopped between the two men and folded her arms before her. "Perhaps the centurion anticipated that he might have no alternative other than to trust you under certain extraordinary circumstances."

That sounded reasonable to Trip. It was also far more encouraging than Malcolm's paranoia, however justified it might be. "I guess he could have told the computer to let me drive if he was too injured to take charge himself. Even if he didn't trust me completely, he might have figured I'd expect my chances of staying in Valdore's good graces to suffer if I were to use this ship to run away—or if I came back to Romulus without my escort."

"Unfortunately, that's exactly what's happened," Malcolm said. "How do you intend to explain Terix's absence to Valdore?"

Trip stared thoughtfully into the middle distance, gazing with unfocused eyes at the pillar of combustion debris that still rose above the site of his most recent brush with death. Sopek, who had probably escaped the explosion along with some of his people, had also probably left Terix to die in the conflagration. But if Sopek had decided to take Terix along, then both men were surely already very far from here by now; Terix would be a prisoner of a group of dangerous Romulan political dissidents who had managed to spirit him off-planet without leaving any detectable radiation trail to follow.

"I have no idea, Malcolm," he said at length. "I'm afraid I'm just going to have to keep making it all up as I go. And I'm going to start by returning to Romulus to check in with Valdore. If I don't, he'll think Terix was right in suspecting me of being a spy."

"Judging by what you've told me, I think Valdore will *know* you're a spy soon enough," Reed said. "That is, if Terix really did survive and somehow finds a way to get a report to him. And that's assuming that he and Valdore don't *already* know a lot more than you think they do."

T'Pol nodded. "I agree. Valdore nearly killed both you and Lieutenant Reed once before. It would be a serious mistake to underestimate him now."

Trip nodded as he considered T'Pol's warning. But although he'd never forget how close he and Malcolm had come to dying when they had struggled with Valdore over control of an experimental remote-controlled Romulan drone ship last year, Valdore wasn't a man Trip could simply run away from.

"Besides, you don't have to keep doing this," Reed said, spreading his hands before him. "I know firsthand how this kind of clandestine work can take over your life if you let it. Maybe you've *already* accomplished enough here. Maybe it's time you thought about coming in from the cold, so to speak."

Coming in from the cold, Trip thought, mesmerized for a moment by that tantalizing thought. *Rising from the dead.* The notion had occurred to him many times since his Romulan sojourn had begun. But circumstances had always conspired to make the goal of coming home seem as unreachable as the Andromeda Galaxy.

"I must concur with Lieutenant Reed," T'Pol said, her dark eyes taking on an almost pleading cast that Trip had seen only rarely; the last time was when Doctor Phlox had worked frantically, though without success, to save the life of their dying baby.

"Others could take over for you," she continued. "I ask you again to let us . . . take you *home*." T'Pol gestured toward the crest of a nearby hill, where the trio had carefully set down Shuttlepod Two among piles of gray boulders and short stands of blue-green scrub vegetation.

Home, Trip thought, not entirely certain he fully recognized the concept anymore.

"I'm certain Captain Archer could use your help more than ever now," Reed said. "What with all the trouble between the Klingons and the Draylaxians we've been hearing about."

"Yeah, I picked up some intel about the Klingon thing just before I left Romulus," Trip said, stroking his cheek as he mulled his friends' words over. "I was hoping to find proof that the Romulans were really the ones behind *that* little problem as well. No such luck."

He paused as he realized that he had just reinforced the very argument his friends were trying to make, though they were probably as dismayed as he was that the Coalition seemed to be facing imminent war on two fronts rather than on just one.

Tucker came to a firm decision then, arriving there with a certitude that surprised him. "I appreciate what you're trying to do, both of you. But my business here isn't anywhere near finished yet. I *have* to stay. Hell, I haven't even found out for sure what happened to Terix yet."

T'Pol raised an eyebrow, clearly incredulous. "Commander, Terix is an enemy who will doubtless try to kill you again the first time he gets the chance. He would surely compromise you, which in Romulan space would effectively be the same thing as executing you."

"He's an enemy, that's true enough," Trip said, nodding. "But he's an enemy I was in the midst of serving with on a mission that was at least as important to the security of the Coalition as it was to the Romulan military. Which sort of makes Terix a comrade, as weird as I know that sounds.

"I've never been in the habit of leaving anyone behind, T'Pol. And I'm sure as hell not gonna start now."

"But even if you do manage to find Terix still alive," Reed said, raising his voice, "you'll probably have to kill him straightaway, just to maintain your cover. You say you can't leave a comrade behind, which I assume comes out of your sense of duty. But can you *kill* him when your duty demands it?"

Trip didn't want to think about that at the moment. "There's still the threat of the Romulan stardrive to consider, Malcolm."

"But the Klingons—" Malcolm said.

Trip interrupted him, determined to protect his resolve against any further assault. "The captain can handle the Klingons, if you guys are both behind him."

T'Pol and Reed exchanged silent and uncomfortable looks.

"You guys *are* both behind him, right?" Trip asked. "He must have sent you here before he knew about the Klingon-Draylax thing."

Reed paused to cough into his fist. "Not exactly.

We sort of . . . came on our own. Without telling the captain."

Jesus! Trip thought. *Why am I not surprised?*

Shaking his head, he said, "Well, you've just given me another good reason not to go back with you. I wouldn't want to be standing anywhere near ground zero when you report to him."

T'Pol raised an eyebrow. "Ground zero?"

"Wherever the captain happens to be when he sees us again," Malcolm said.

"I have to stay behind for a much better reason: I'm still the only one close enough to the Romulan stardrive problem to prevent it from becoming an even bigger threat. Whether it's the dissidents or the Romulan military who eventually get control of the stolen data and get the damned thing into production, when it happens it'll make the Klingon Empire look about as dangerous as a basket of day-old kittens in comparison."

T'Pol's mouth formed a grim slash, but she said nothing further. She evidently knew when it was illogical to keep trying to change Trip's mind, even if she didn't find his mind to be a particularly logical one.

Trip wished he could gather her up in his arms right now, reassure her that everything was going to work out just fine in the end. But there was no time for that, and he wasn't sure he believed it himself. Besides, she just might break his arm if he got physically demonstrative with her now, right in front of Malcolm.

"So you're just going to hop into this thing and fly it right back to Romulus," Malcolm said, gesturing toward the open hatchway of the *Scoutship Drolae.*

Trip nodded as he set one of his boots on the little vessel's open threshold. "Yup. If I want to maintain my cover here, it's really the only thing I *can* do."

"Even though it's probably even money that Admiral

Valdore will decide that you're actually a spy who gave his centurion watchdog the heave-ho sometime during the last mission. And then he'll kill you."

"I'll just have to hope he accepts my word that I'm a loyal Romulan. The fact that I'm going to Romulus as opposed to running will have to mean *something* to him. Anyway, it's our best hope of neutralizing that warp-seven drive. Or better yet, getting the equivalent of it to Captain Stillwell's people."

T'Pol held up her right hand, which she bifurcated into a familiar "V" gesture. Her stoic features looked as hard as the boulders that surrounded the shuttlepod behind her, though her eyes glistened with what appeared to be excess moisture.

"Live long and prosper," she said.

Standing on the threshold of the *Drolae*'s hatchway, he faced her and returned the gesture. He tried to make himself repeat the traditional words of both greeting and farewell, but found he couldn't get them through a throat that had suddenly gone as dry as Vulcan's Forge.

"Ah, *hell,*" he said, lowering his hand.

He dropped back to the rocky ground, closing the meter or so that separated him from T'Pol in less than a second. Gathering the extremely surprised Vulcan woman in his arms, he kissed her, full on the lips. Out of the corner of his eye, he thought he saw a huge grin spreading across Malcolm's face as the kiss lingered ever so slightly longer than even the laxest interpretation of Vulcan propriety might have excused.

His eyes widened in surprise when she squeezed him tight and returned the kiss with a passion that he doubted most Vulcans—and probably quite a few humans—could tolerate. The moment stretched as their very essences seemed to blend together, and he only became truly conscious again of the passage of time when he realized that she was squeezing him nearly tightly enough to crush his rib cage.

It took most of his strength to break off the kiss, and the rest to hold her at arm's length with his hands on her shoulders. He suspected that another three to five seconds might remain before she either kissed him again, or got really angry with him for stirring up such intense emotions within her.

"I'm going to, um, take a walk," Malcolm said. "Check on the shuttlepod. For, say, twenty minutes?"

"Thirty," T'Pol said.

Trip watched in mild puzzlement as Malcolm abruptly turned on his heel and walked away, quickly disappearing over a nearby rise. T'Pol joined Trip in the scoutship's open hatchway a heartbeat later, shoving him unceremoniously across the threshold and following him inside.

"Thirty minutes," Trip said as she approached him closely and the hatch hissed shut behind her. "What do you suppose we can do—"

Her eyes aflame, she grabbed his shirt and tore it open. "Do not waste the time talking."

Reed dutifully waited thirty full minutes before walking slowly back to the scoutship.

The Romulan vessel was still right where he'd left it, though neither Trip nor T'Pol were anywhere within view. The main hatch was closed.

At least the ship isn't rocking, he thought, thankful for small mercies. *But please, don't let me have to knock on the door. . . .*

As though in response to his thoughts, the scoutship's main hatch hissed open. T'Pol emerged, looking like a portrait of staid dignity, with every hair in place.

Trip followed her out of the craft a moment later. He was flushed, sweating, disheveled, and grinning like an idiot.

Reed returned the grin. This was the image of Trip he wanted to keep in his memory forever.

In case, he thought, *he never manages to come in from the cold.*

"Till next time, okay?" Trip said, gathering T'Pol into another embrace near the scoutship's open hatch. Trip felt as torn about parting from her now as he had before this whole damned spy business had begun.

T'Pol nodded, apparently at an uncharacteristic loss for words.

He released her and turned back toward the hatch. Malcolm was standing in the way, and caught him in a quick bear hug.

"Keep safe, Commander," the tactical officer said as he released Trip. "Or *I'll* murder you. Fair enough?"

"Fair enough, Malcolm." Trip grinned as he hopped back up into the open hatchway, alone this time. "And let's all hope that fortune really does favor the foolish."

Which covers all three of us, he thought as the hatch hissed closed, separating him from his friends.

Perhaps for the very last time.

THIRTY-TWO

Tuesday, July 22, 2155
Qam-Chee, the First City, Qo'noS

To ARCHER it felt as though only hours had passed since
he had last entered the Klingon High Council's main assembly chamber, though he knew he had little grasp of
time as it was reckoned on alien planets. Qo'noS, like
countless other worlds, had its own calendar based upon
the unique motions of the planet and its satellites, none
of which corresponded neatly to United Earth Standard. Combined with his time in the arena and in the
medical facility afterward, Archer wasn't at all certain
exactly what time it was when Krell began presenting
the evidence that M'Rek had promised would exculpate
the Klingon Empire over the attack on Draylax.

With his doctor husband looking annoyed nearby,
Admiral Krell moved slowly but restlessly about the
front of the otherwise nearly empty chamber, using a
crutch tucked under his good arm to support his considerable weight. Although Krell once again had two
arms—a hard cast held the reattached limb immobile
against the admiral's side—it was clear that his every
movement was causing him excruciating pain. Though
he had emerged from the duel in slightly better shape
than Krell had, Archer felt grateful for the hard bench
on which his weary weight rested at the moment; with
the wound in his side still smarting even as it was heal-
ing under Phlox's ministrations, he certainly wouldn't

want to have to stand for any length of time, despite his own restive desire to get back to work protecting Earth and the Coalition. *This guy obviously doesn't deal with enforced idleness any better than I do,* Archer thought, feeling a surge of sympathy for a kindred spirit as he watched Krell's unconscious fidgeting.

Mounted on the wall beside Krell was a giant flat screen, not unlike the central viewer that adorned the forward wall of *Enterprise*'s bridge. Standing sentry at the door were several armed Klingon warriors, all of them evidently carrying enough rank and privilege to be allowed to witness the admiral's presentation; because of the sensitive nature of Krell's briefing, Chancellor M'Rek had insisted that Archer's MACO escorts wait outside the chamber, and Archer had nearly had to fight another duel to convince the chancellor to overrule Krell's initial refusal to allow Phlox to stay.

Using his one functional hand, Krell gestured toward the screen, which had shifted to an oblique overhead starboard view of the busy bridge of a Klingon battle cruiser. "As you can see, the captain and crew of the *I.K.S. Kaj'Deel* were taken completely unawares by the total loss of instrumentation control on their bridge," the admiral said.

"Why is the system still generating an audiovisual record if all the other bridge systems have failed?" Archer asked. Beside him, Phlox moved his medical scanner over the captain's shoulder area, and Archer turned his head just enough to see the doctor frowning at the results. Though Phlox's reaction certainly piqued his curiosity, he had no time to pursue the matter at the moment.

"A secondary crew happened to be aboard the *Kaj'Deel* at the time, recording these images for instructional and training purposes," Krell said. "Their equipment was not tied in to the ship's systems."

On the screen, Klingon personnel rushed around, shouting at one another in evident anger and frustration. Several even pounded their fists ineffectually at the consoles in front of them.

Then, in a scene inset within another, the Klingon battle cruiser's bridge viewer changed images; instead of displaying a neutral star field, it now showed a dark emerald Romulan bird-of-prey. The orientation of the warship didn't permit Archer to see its ventral underbelly, which the captain knew from experience usually carried a garish, predatory bird design; nevertheless, there could be no mistaking the horseshoe-crab configuration of this vessel as anything but Romulan.

The image on the screen-within-the-screen changed again, backing off to a longer view, even as the agitation of the *Kaj'Deel*'s crew ratcheted even higher. The audio quality of the recording played havoc with the language matrix of Archer's translation device, enabling him to parse only every fourth or fifth word at best. But he was absolutely certain he understood *why* the Klingons on the screen were so excited.

The *Kaj'Deel*'s viewer showed a second Klingon vessel, this one apparently a fuel tanker, of the same class that the Klingons had used to carry deuterium fuel when *Enterprise* had aided the pirate-besieged deuterium miners of the settlement on Yeq three years ago.

"What are they saying?" Archer asked.

"They were shouting that most of the ship's systems had gone offline," Krell said. "Life support and communications were among the first to fall. The weapons systems were apparently still functioning at this point, though the weapons control interfaces were not. Therefore the *Kaj'Deel* could neither call out for help nor warn the freighter *PeD NIHwI'* that their weapons systems had targeted the vessel, all on their own."

"Was the freighter similarly affected?" Archer said, scowling. Phlox had begun scanning him again, and he waved his arm in mild annoyance to encourage the doctor to back away.

Behind him, M'Rek spoke up, apparently having grown irritated by Phlox's kibitzing as well. *"Denobu-luSngan!* Is it *necessary* for you to coddle your captain during a classified briefing?" A pair of Klingon soldiers began to advance toward Phlox, evidently taking a hint from the chancellor's stern tone and Krell's decision to pause his audiovisual presentation.

Phlox nodded toward the otherwise empty Council bench where the chancellor sat, and showed no sign of even having noticed the Klingon officers who now flanked him. "Chancellor M'Rek, despite his victory today, Captain Archer could still face grave complications because of the injuries he has sustained. I fear that his *tertiary lung* might have suffered an undetected laceration, and that he is developing a severe *penile-craniotomological distension.*"

What the hell? Archer bit his tongue slightly. Clearly Phlox was up to something, but he wasn't about to inquire into it at the moment. Turning to M'Rek, he said, "My apologies, Chancellor. I will instruct my physician to be a bit less obtrusive. But he is right to point out that humans react differently to trauma than Klingons do."

M'Rek scowled, but said nothing further, pointing instead toward the viewscreen on the wall. Archer saw the two soldiers back away from Phlox as Krell depressed a small switch on a hand-held device, allowing the images and sounds to begin playing again.

On the *Kaj'Deel*'s screen, blue-green weapons-blasts suddenly became visible, arcing forward toward the relatively defenseless fuel freighter. Moments later, the tanker exploded in a series of brilliant plasma bursts, sending an expanding cloud of metallic debris and superheated gases roiling into the void of space.

Krell paused the images again. "If it was not clear, Captain, that salvo came from the *Kaj'Deel*, not from the *RomuluSngan* ship. Those treacherous *ghargh* have found a means of turning our own weapons against us." He turned back toward the screen, allowing the images to resume.

On the Klingon warship's viewscreen, the Romulan vessel reappeared, and then all hell seemed to break loose. A loud gonging sound and random shouts rose to a frantic crescendo almost instantaneously as the picture begin to waver and shake. Archer surmised that whoever had been capturing the images was no longer entirely in control of his equipment, or of much of anything else.

Which, Archer realized, was *exactly* the case.

"As you can see, the artificial gravity of the *Kaj'Deel* was then compromised along with the rest of the basic life-support functions," Krell said. The images on the screen gradually became a bit more coherent as whoever was holding the recorder seemed to acclimate himself or herself to the null-gravity environment. "The failure of the life-support systems eventually forced the crew into a barely conscious state.

"Any external sensor scan would have revealed that most of the crew were still alive, even days later," Krell said.

"But there would be no way anyone outside could know that the crew was utterly unable to access or control any of the ship's systems," Archer said, a resigned frustration creeping into his voice. He willfully ignored Phlox, who had continued quietly scanning him from a meter or so away.

Krell nodded. "From this evidence, gleaned from the emergency log buoys of both ships and transmissions relayed directly from the recording equipment used on the *Kaj'Deel*, the Klingon Defense Force has concluded that the *RomuluSngan* ship somehow gained remote access to, and control over, not only the *Kaj'Deel*, but the *PeD NIHwI'* as well."

On the screen, Archer saw a familiar face float past the weightless camera's eye for a moment. "Freeze that," he shouted, mindful a millisecond later that shouting commands at Krell was probably poor protocol, to say the least.

After casting Archer a cold glare that could have made a snowman shiver, Krell stopped the recording. The face that Archer had recognized was still on display, nearly dead center, trapped in place like a fly in amber.

Archer turned toward M'Rek, though he gestured back toward the screen. "That is the Klingon woman we found in the wreckage at Draylax. The only survivor we came across."

"The one who died so swiftly under the tender mercies of your chief medical officer?" Krell said. Archer turned his head in time to see him cast a withering stare directly at Phlox.

"The woman was too far gone for anyone to save, Admiral," Archer said. "My doctor did everything possible for her, even if all he could do in the end was make her journey to the afterlife as smooth as possible. She fought death until the end, and died with honor, at least as far as I'm concerned."

"Her family will be pleased to hear that," M'Rek said. "She will have a place in *Sto-Vo-Kor* among the honored dead. Of course, you will return her body to us immediately so that we may *verify* the honorable nature of her death."

Archer nodded toward the chancellor. "Of course. Just as soon as I am back in touch with my ship." He turned back toward Krell. "If she was aboard the *Kaj'Deel*, that means your hijacked battle cruiser was among the ships that attacked Draylax."

Krell nodded as he allowed the images to resume, though with muted sound. "Yes. Before they died, the officers running the independent imaging equipment managed to transmit images of that attack to one of our remote outposts. The data then reached the Klingon High Command via the outpost's subspace relay station."

The images on the screen moved through a quick progression of shots of the *Kaj'Deel*'s unconscious bridge crew, views of exploding Draylaxian vessels, and *NX*-class starships taking heavy fire from Klingon battle cruisers, and finally ended just as a trio of heavily armed, undamaged Klingon battle cruisers opened fire. The final image was a flash of an apparently dead Klingon male, his hair floating around his head as he drifted upside down in the *Kaj'Deel*'s microgravity environment.

"Had we received word of it sooner," Krell said, sounding wistful at the prospect of such wasteful, honorless killing, "we might have prevented entirely what happened at Draylax."

"If it hadn't been for that camera crew, you might not have gotten there at all," Archer said. Addressing M'Rek, he said, "Chancellor, I believe it would be in *everyone's* best interests if you were to authorize me to show these images to the representatives of the Coalition of Planets. It proves that the Romulans have developed some kind of remote-control weapon capable of seizing control of the space vessels of other species. If they take what Admiral Krell has just shown me at face value, they will have to absolve the Klingon Empire of any responsibility for what happened at Draylax—"

"No, Captain," M'Rek said, standing. "That the *RomuluSngan* have made us pawns in their cowardly ambushes is bad enough, but for you to make the Klingon Empire appear so . . . *vulnerable* in the eyes of your world's leaders, and those of the Coalition of Planets . . . The shame and dishonor is simply more than can be borne."

Krell spoke up, the rising timbre of his voice showing very clearly that he was still in great pain from his exertions. "There are security considerations as well, Captain Archer. These recordings show the bridge and instrumentation of a Klingon battle cruiser with great clarity and in considerable detail. I doubt that Starfleet or any of its allies would hesitate for an instant to begin reverse engineering our command-and-control architecture and other related technologies based on what they find in these images."

Archer rose from the bench where he'd been seated, noticing only then that Phlox had finally quit scanning and was putting his medical scanner away. "Chancellor M'Rek, for the leader of a warrior society, you seem to have some fairly ridiculous fears."

M'Rek bristled, leaning forward to grasp the railing in front of his bench with both hands. "You dare?"

A still, small voice somewhere deep within Archer counseled caution, but at the moment he felt too angry to listen to it. "You're damned *right* I dare," he said, jabbing an accusing finger into the air. "You would allow your people to become embroiled in a dishonorable war against the Coalition of Planets instead of going after the *real* authors of the conflict? You'd let the Romulans get away with doing this to you, just to save yourself some *embarrassment?*"

"We act to spare the Klingon Empire from dishonor,

Tera'ngan," M'Rek said, his voice pitched in a dangerous tone that seemed to provoke his soldiers to hair-trigger readiness.

But Archer knew he couldn't afford to back down now. "Even if that aversion to dishonor could mean the difference between a war with the Coalition and a war against our common enemy?"

M'Rek sneered. "Do not presume to lecture *me* on the subject of honor, Captain. If you fear war against us, then you must find your *own* way to convince your leaders that the Klingon Empire will not take the blame for the attack upon Draylax. Persuading them will be *your* responsibility."

I'm getting awfully damned tired of playing errand boy for one side against the other, Archer thought, his fighting instincts rising even as his diplomatic side struggled to maintain control of a very bad situation.

But, unless he had badly misjudged that situation, he knew he would leave Qo'noS with far more information than the Klingons realized.

THIRTY-THREE

Tuesday, July 22, 2155
Enterprise **NX-01**

"YOU KNOW, JONATHAN, about a hundred or so years ago what you just did would have been called bootlegging," Erika Hernandez said, a grim smile on her face.

Archer nodded toward the new viewscreen that sat on his desk; Burch had assigned a crew to install a replacement terminal after Archer's "accident" with the previous computer prior to his trip to Qo'noS. The new screen, its image area split down the middle at the moment, displayed the faces of both Hernandez and Admiral Gardner. Archer had contacted them both only a few minutes earlier, eager to see their reactions to the images taken aboard the hijacked Klingon battle cruiser.

"I had no idea what Doctor Phlox was really up to at the time," Archer said. "At least until his constant 'medical scanning' started becoming obnoxious." He didn't feel any pressing need to tell them about Phlox's cover story about the disorder that had supposedly afflicted his third lung, or the doctor's good-natured phallic-based putdown.

"Well, thank God that Denobulans seem to have the same capacity for sneakiness that we humans do," Gardner said. *"Though using a medical scanner to eavesdrop on so much audiovisual material is a new one even to me."*

"So do you agree with me that this information in Phlox's 'bootleg' is vital?" Archer asked.

Gardner shook his head. *"I agree that it could be vital, Captain Archer. If the Coalition Council believes it, it would certainly be one more nail in the coffin for the Romulans. But you have to realize that some will say that the Klingons faked the whole thing just to get themselves off the hook."*

"Begging the admiral's pardon," Hernandez said, a look of concern on her face, *"but the idea that the Klingons would have gone as far as they have—destroying their own ships, killing their own people—for the sake of a propaganda video they had every reason to believe we would never see . . . that's just paranoid talk."*

"I won't take offense at your characterization, Captain Hernandez, because I know it wasn't directed at me," Gardner said. *"But that still doesn't mean that the Tellarites or any of the other races won't be suspicious of the Klingons."*

Perhaps it was the wound in his side or the way his ribs still ached whenever he breathed, but Archer found he was having a hard time keeping his temper in check. "How much more evidence is the Coalition Council going to need, Admiral? Do they need an engraved invitation to war, delivered by a skipping Romulan schoolgirl, before they'll believe the truth?"

Gardner scowled slightly. *"While Starfleet's tech people get busy building countermeasures to this new Romulan weapon, I'll have my analytical staff comb through every shred of evidence we've got—including your doctor's surreptitious recording—in order to make a presentation to the Coalition Council. But I can't make any promises as to what the politicians will finally decide to do. Especially if the Klingons aren't willing to go public with the real culprits behind the attacks on Draylax. Until that changes, it's going to be very hard for some not to go right on blaming the Klingon Empire for what happened at Draylax."*

"*Admiral, Draylax was probably just the* start *of hostilities,*" Hernandez said, worry creasing her brow. "*If the Romulans can seize control of Klingon ships, then they can disguise any of their own attacks as Klingon aggression.*"

Gardner moved one hand up to run his fingers through his close-cropped gray hair. "*As far as most people in this part of the galaxy are concerned, the Klingons are* already *aggressive and untrustworthy. So how do you propose we differentiate between normal Klingon aggression and Romulan-controlled Klingon aggression?*

"*Here's the deal,*" Gardner continued. "*In my judgment, the best use of our forces is for both of you to resume your original tandem mission patrolling the Coalition's shipping lanes.*"

He held up his hands, palms outward, as if to ward off the arguments he knew must be coming. "*I know neither of you thinks that will be helpful, but now at least you know what to watch for. Or at least you know what you* might *face. Most of the attacks so far, other than the Draylax incident, seem to have occurred in Coalition-controlled space. So while you're out preventing any further attacks that might lead to a Coalition-Klingon war, I'll be doing my damnedest to get the Council on board.*"

"*I don't know what that means yet,*" Gardner said. "*And I have serious doubts that the Klingons will be willing to ally themselves with us, even to punish the Romulans. What's your take on that, Captain Archer?*"

"I . . . yes, I don't think an alliance with us is in their plans," Archer said. "If they're going to go to war against the Romulans, their crazy sense of pride is probably going to demand that they do it on their own. But if M'Rek was making serious plans to go to war against the Romulans anytime soon, he certainly kept them hidden from me. Which is exactly what I would expect him to do."

Gardner nodded. *"Me, too. So all I have to do is convince the Council not to move against people upon whom we can't rely for help against the Romulans, even though those same Romulans can attack us any time they damn please while making it look as though the Klingons are really the ones responsible."*

Pointing toward his own screen—and presumably at both captains—Gardner continued: *"It's going to be your job to stop any further attacks, which I know is going to be extraordinarily difficult until we find an effective countermeasure to this . . . Romulan hijacking device. I know you're spoiling to go on the offensive, regardless. Unfortunately, we've been forced into a defensive posture, at least for a while."*

Archer listened as Gardner gave a few more instructions to both him and Hernandez, but his insides were tying themselves in knots, and not solely because of the residual pain of his injuries. Despite his own desire to take more precipitous and direct action, he had to admit that the admiral's words made a good deal of sense.

Still, it was hard to calm himself in the face of the overwhelming worry that he might not be able to act in time to prevent an unnecessary interstellar war—just as he had failed to reach Coridan Prime in time to take any action that might have prevented the Romulans from effectively destroying most of the planet's surface. Despite all he had done—and the combined efforts of everyone serving aboard both *Enterprise* and *Columbia*, and Trip as well—the duplicitous nature of the Romulan remote control system had all but perfectly framed the Klingons as the bad guys du jour.

And the Coalition Council, whose members all too frequently seemed only barely able to trust one another to begin with, might be swayed all too easily by such a convenient narrative. Even after adding to the equation the new evidence he had just acquired on Qo'noS, Archer could hardly fault anyone who had ever gotten on the wrong side of a Klingon captain for failing to believe the Klingon Empire to be unequivocally innocent of the Draylax incursion, much less beyond a reasonable doubt.

Still, as he said his good-byes to Gardner and Hernandez, then reached for one of the alien herbal painkillers that Phlox had prescribed for him, Archer was at least comforted by the knowledge that he would be taking the more hazardous patrol route. According to Gardner's orders, *Columbia* would be headed for safer territory, while *Enterprise* was to set a course for the Gamma Hydra sector, perilously near Romulan space. The fact that the region was under dispute by both the Romulans and the Klingons—as well as near the Coalition-proposed "Neutral Zone" intended to create a buffer separating both the Klingons and the Romulans from Coalition territory as well as from each other— meant that if another ship-to-ship engagement was in the offing, it was more likely to occur on *Enterprise*'s flight path than on *Columbia*'s.

Archer exited his ready room and entered the bridge, the determination in his stride slowly wrestling the pain from the duel with Krell into submission.

"Travis, lay in a standard commercial convoy heading for Gamma Hydra, section ten," he said. "And don't spare the horses."

THIRTY-FOUR

Interior Minister Haroun al-Rashid felt nowhere near as serene as he strived to appear. Though he kept his hands folded meditatively atop the wide, semicircular negotiation table in the Coalition Council Chamber, he waited anxiously for the hammer to fall on a pair of urgent but still-unresolved questions.

The foremost of these questions involved the rising likelihood of war with the Klingons. And the second, whose long-term implications arguably outweighed most conceivable consequences of the recent Klingon-Draylax incident, would almost certainly have a profound effect upon the outcome of the first.

The heavy oaken doors that separated the central auditorium from the small private conference rooms at the rear of the building opened with an echoing impact that made al-Rashid believe that the metaphorical hammer had fallen at last. Momentarily glancing away from the senior representatives from Andoria, Tellar, and Vulcan who were striding purposefully through the doorway at the opposite side of the chamber, he saw his own internal feelings of tense anticipation reflected on the faces of the humans who sat at the table with him: United Earth's Prime Minister Nathan Samuels and Centauri III's Ambassador Jie Cong Li.

Like al-Rashid, both of his fellow humans had opted

to have no staff members or junior functionaries accompany them to today's special closed-door meeting,
in hopes of blunting the prevalent nonhuman percep-
tion that *Homo sapiens* was attempting to dominate
Coalition business. In the same spirit, al-Rashid and
his human colleagues had all agreed not to apply undue
pressure on the nonhuman Coalition members to close
the current human-nonhuman political rifts in favor of
Earth and Alpha Centauri.

Despite the new compromise proposal that the representatives of both the United Earth and Alpha Centauri governments had signed off on yesterday—and
the looming conflicts it would no doubt engender—al-
Rashid still had no reason to think that anything had
changed since the last time the full Council debated the
issue; so far as he knew, Vulcan, Andoria, and Tellar still
vehemently opposed Earth's initiative to confer full Coalition membership upon the human-inhabited Alpha
Centauri settlements, citing as unfair the resulting "species voting bloc" that would favor humanity's interests
over the Coalition Council's nonhuman world.

*It's going to take a long time for us all to learn to really
trust each other,* al-Rashid thought as the Vulcans approached the table, followed by the Andorians, the Tellarites, and Grethe Zhor, the official diplomatic observer
from Draylax. Feeling dispirited by the nearly constant
birth agonies that the nascent alliance continued to experience, he tried to buoy his sense of hope by reflecting
on the manifold difficulties humanity had already over-
come over the past century on its painful way to resolving Earth's internal strife and numerous social evils; his
own people, for one, had both bled and shed the blood
of others for generations prior to the eventual peaceful resolution of the long-standing and bitter Israel-
Palestine conflict. If humanity could find peace among

its own, then surely it could do so again out among the stars.

I wish I could have been a fly on the wall in that closed-door meeting they just came out of, al-Rashid thought, rising to his feet along with his human colleagues to face their nonhuman counterparts as they reached the opposite side of the semicircular ranks of the council tables.

But as the assembled delegates from six worlds acknowledged one another with silent and respectful nods, al-Rashid found his eager anticipation slowly morphing into a gradually deepening sense of dread. *What if today is the day it all finally falls apart?* he thought, not relishing the prospect of Earth suddenly finding itself standing friendless and alone against the heavily armored belligerence of the Klingon Empire.

Although the somber Vulcan contingent—which consisted of Vulcan Minister Soval, flanked by Ambassadors L'Nel and Solkar, his senior aides—reached the council table first, they remained standing until each of their colleagues had taken their seats. The hirsute Ambassador Gora bim Gral of Tellar and his two all but indistinguishable aides were the first to sit, followed by Andorian Foreign Minister Anlenthoris ch'Vhendreni and his somewhat younger adjutant, Ambassador Avaranthi sh'Rothress, and finally Grethe Zhor of Draylax.

"Thank you all for agreeing to attend this special meeting today," said Nathan Samuels, addressing all the nonhuman delegations simultaneously once everyone had taken their seats. Casting a significant glance at the woman from Draylax, he added, "I know I speak for everyone here when I offer my sincere hopes for our success in maintaining interstellar peace, especially beyond the present boundaries of Coalition space."

Not to mention inside *them*, al-Rashid thought, taking comfort in a bit of gallows humor.

But no amount of humor, gallows or otherwise, could contain his mounting impatience to discover the outcome of the nonhumans' just-concluded meeting-within-a-meeting. Addressing his alien colleagues, al-Rashid said, "Have you come to a decision yet about how to deal with Draylax's, ah, Klingon problem?"

Samuels scowled, evidently not comfortable with such a blunt frontal assault, while Li seemed only mildly surprised at the forwardness of al-Rashid's question. Fortunately, none of the nonhumans present appeared offended. Gral, Thoris, and Grethe Zhor merely looked silently toward Minister Soval, almost as though they had all agreed to make the phlegmatic Vulcan their spokesman regarding the matter.

Steepling his fingers contemplatively before his pursed lips, Soval said, "Vulcan, Andoria, and Tellar have each agreed to defer their final decisions about whether to declare war on the Klingons until after Earth's military experts present us with a new intelligence briefing on the issue."

Minister al-Rashid nodded, thankful for whatever restraint the other Coalition members—particularly the Andorians—were willing to exercise.

"This decision is only a provisional one, of course," Thoris said in a cautioning manner. "As far as the Andorian government is concerned, at any rate. My people are not in the habit of allowing threats of incursion to grow unchecked, whether they arise near our homeworld or our colonies. But my government has agreed to stay the hand of the Imperial Guard for the moment— at least until we have more complete information about this . . . Klingon problem."

"Thank you," Samuels said. Coming from the notoriously touchy Andorians, this was practically a declaration of pacifism.

Let's hope their restraint lasts long enough for us to find a way to keep the whole Coalition from being dragged into a major shooting war, al-Rashid thought. *And to keep our allies at our backs in case diplomacy with the Klingons fails at the end of the day.*

"Regarding the other matter before this body," Soval said, "I believe we have come to a far more definitive decision."

"You are referring to Minister al-Rashid's compromise proposal regarding Alpha Centauri's petition for Coalition membership?" said Samuels.

The prime minister's gaze broke with Soval's long enough to communicate very clearly to al-Rashid that there would be hell to pay if the Coalition continued tearing itself asunder over this extraordinarily sensitive issue—particularly with a Klingon war apparently looming on the horizon.

"Indeed," Soval said. "We have all decided to accept the interior minister's compromise offer. Vulcan, Andoria, and Tellar will support Alpha Centauri's admission to the Coalition—if Earth and Alpha Centauri will both support the simultaneous admission of Draylax."

Li displayed a smile of gratitude that gave every appearance of utter sincerity. "Alpha Centauri will be pleased to share with the Coalition of Worlds all the mutual defense responsibilities to which we have already committed with both Draylax and Earth," she said.

Just as our nonhuman allies will no doubt be delighted to share in Alpha Centauri's shipbuilding resources via the Coalition, al-Rashid thought as he cast a grin back at Li. *It would certainly suit their individual governments' interests better than allowing humanity to keep those resources all to themselves via exclusive Earth-Centauri arrangements*—*even if they still don't much like the idea of humans getting more than one vote on the Coalition Council.*

Ambassador sh'Rothress's next utterance almost made al-Rashid wonder if the Andorian woman had somehow read his thoughts. "Andoria, likewise, will be pleased to dilute the resulting overly strong human plurality in the Council vote by adding *another* new nonhuman member to our alliance," she said, nodding toward Grethe Zhor, who stared back in silence, her vertical pupils revealing no emotion; Ambassador sh'Rothress seemed to be trying to demonstrate that her people were most definitely *not* kowtowing to Earth or any other world, in or out of the Coalition.

"I trust this new Coalition member will prove far less disagreeable than have my esteemed Andorian colleagues," said Gral, who bowed his porcine, gray-maned head toward Grethe Zhor with uncharacteristic deference. Then al-Rashid noticed that the Tellarite's gaze lingered a little too long on the Draylaxian woman's conservative gray tunic, and the three breasts it concealed. Why that particular anatomical detail seemed to fascinate Gral escaped al-Rashid completely; he thought it unlikely that Draylaxians would be considered attractive by the esthetic standards of Tellarites, who considered six nipples the norm as far as he knew.

Though she made no reply to Gral, sh'Rothress's antennae flattened slightly against her scalp, signaling her displeasure with the Tellarite's insult. But such exchanges were nothing new, al-Rashid reflected; as long as the Andorians and the Tellarites weren't reaching for knives or phase pistols, he wouldn't worry.

Maybe my plan won't go down in history alongside the Missouri Compromise, al-Rashid thought, looking down at his hands, which remained placidly folded on the tabletop. *But it should keep the Coalition from coming apart at the seams, at least for another few months.*

He heard several sets of footfalls approaching rapidly from the back of the auditorium. Looking up, he saw a small group of uniformed humans walking almost at a march directly toward the council tables. At the forefront of the group were four gray-haired men, three of whom wore formal Starfleet uniforms, complete with neckties, while a fourth was attired in MACO dress whites. All four men were distinguished from the small cluster of aides and security personnel that partially surrounded them not only by their bearing, but also by the impressive array of medals and ribbons displayed on their chests.

Right on schedule, al-Rashid thought. The time had finally arrived for the military briefing that might well prove to be the basis for a horrific war. He knew he could do little now other than pray that whatever was to come next, the coolheadedness of the Vulcans would prevail over the excitability of the Andorians and the Tellarites.

May whatever these men have to share with us today not tear open the wound of blind fear we all have worked so hard to suture, inshallah.

Admirals Gregory Black and Sam Gardner formed almost matching bookends flanking Captain Eric Stillwell of Starfleet's tactical technological branch and the commandant of United Earth's MACO forces, General George Casey. Since all four military officers were already familiar to the assembled delegates, Gardner wasted no time on introductions, opting instead to plunge straight into his much-awaited briefing about the latest news concerning the Klingon situation.

"Captain Jonathan Archer has just uncovered critical new information while he was on the Klingon homeworld of Qo'noS," Gardner said without preamble. "In short, Captain Archer has determined that the Klingons are *not* responsible for the recent acts of aggression that have occurred in the Draylax system."

"Allah be praised," al-Rashid muttered as the Andorian and Tellarite delegates erupted in a gabble of surprise and consternation.

"It would appear that Captain Archer has once again performed a great service to this alliance," Soval said, raising his voice slightly in an effort to restore decorum to the room.

"May we assume that you have hard evidence to back up this . . . extraordinary claim?" Gral asked, his piggy eyes overflowing with suspicion. The Andorian contingent seated near him appeared equally skeptical.

"We do indeed have such evidence," said General Casey, nodding. "The audiovisual records supporting Captain Archer's findings will be made available to each of you later today." He paused momentarily before adding, "I must admit up front that the quality of the images is less than optimal; as with many intelligence finds of this sort, it had to be obtained using less-than-optimal means, and under less-than-optimal circumstances."

Something in the MACO general's tone warned al-Rashid that pressing him on those "less-than-optimal" means and circumstances would be less than welcome.

After the two Starfleet admirals had finished spending the next twenty minutes furnishing the details of Archer's fateful discovery, Soval said, "Attacking the Klingons would have been a grievous error on our part." Despite his people's vaunted emotional control, the Vulcan foreign minister looked somewhat rattled by the enormity of what the Draylax affair had nearly caused.

"*We* would have been the aggressor," said Samuels,

his expression mirroring Soval's, only without the hard veneer of Vulcan composure. "The Klingons would have felt entirely justified in striking back at us, and hard."

"There will be no war with the Klingon Empire," al-Rashid said, sinking back into his chair as he allowed a tremendous sensation of relief to take wing; his words, which he had aimed at no one in particular, sounded almost like a benediction in his own ears.

A woman's voice sliced through al-Rashid's joy like a hot blade. "Why do you seem so happy about this?"

He found himself blinking his incomprehension at the official observer from Draylax, who regarded him with undisguised puzzlement from across the table.

"I'm afraid I don't understand," al-Rashid said. "The Klingons weren't behind the attack against your people. You don't *want* war with them, do you?"

Grethe Zhor shook her head, sending a cascade of golden hair tumbling around her leonine face. "Of course not, Minister. But instead of an easily conceptualized enemy to rally my people to straightforward action, we now must contend with a mystery attack by phantoms *disguised* as Klingons."

"Which is why Starfleet is already busy planning tactical countermeasures against the new Romulan weapon," Samuels said.

"Until those countermeasures become available," the Draylaxian said, "and perhaps for a goodly period afterward, we *will* be at war with phantoms, Minister, make no mistake. Against whom shall we rally the varied peoples of the Coalition in such a phantom war—a struggle in which one cannot even see the enemy's face? At whom shall we point the Coalition's guns?"

"Pfagh," Gral said. "Romulans are no more phantoms than are Klingons. And there is no more reason to fear them than the Klingons."

The silence that came from both the Andorian and Vulcan delegations spoke more eloquently than any counterargument al-Rashid could have devised.

Recalling the terrifying holovids he had seen of the charred bones and burning seas of Coridan Prime—the handiwork of phantoms—Earth's interior minister began to believe that the Draylaxian had the bleakest vision of the future of anyone in the room.

He also thought it was probably the clearest.

THIRTY-FIVE

Day Thirty-nine, Month of K'ri'Brax
The Hall of State, Dartha, Romulus

NIJIL TRIED to affect a look of cool composure as he watched Valdore rise from behind his massive shera-wood desk. The admiral remained quiet until his impressively broad form had finished unfolding to its full height.

"I have given you all the time I can spare, Nijil," Valdore said. "Praetor D'deridex and First Consul T'Leikha are both growing restless, as are the admirals of the fleet. Is the *arrenhe'hwiua* telecapture system finally ready for general deployment?"

While there was no way to know for certain whether the new offensive system would work perfectly in actual use, the tests thus far had given Nijil every confidence that the fleet would experience no significant problems with it.

Which meant that there was only one thing Nijil could afford to say. "It is ready, Admiral. The Coalition vessels we have just acquired with the system will provide all the cover we need, in addition to illustrating the need to apply the telecapture technology more generally against all our adversaries."

Nijil was aware, of course, that the enemy ships the fleet had taken most recently hewed to the same general technological principles as did the Romulan fleet. But he also had the good sense to avoid mentioning that fact to Valdore, who was obviously in a mood to hear answers that were as positive as they were unequivocal.

Valdore nodded his acknowledgment, looking well pleased. "Good, Nijil. Outstanding."

The scientist was well acquainted with Valdore's moods when he was *not* pleased. Indeed, he had encountered the man's disruptor-like glare just this morning, after another subordinate had failed to discover anything new about Centurion Terix's apparently failed mission to recover the *avaihh lli vastam* stardrive data the *Ejhoi Ormiin* assassins had stolen from the late Ehrehin's lab—radicals who had paid Nijil rather handsomely in exchange for his giving them access to the late scientist.

Nijil rejoiced at the fact that *he* wasn't among those who had to deal with the admiral's bad side. *At least, not recently.*

The admiral continued, "Our advance forces will mobilize just as soon as you finish verifying the installation and calibration of the attack fleet's telecapture units."

"My people can complete the last of the settling-in adjustments in an *eisae*," Nijil said, nodding. "Perhaps less. I only wish we were able to produce and install more than two telecapture units per squadron in the time allotted."

"Two per squadron will suffice, Nijil." A broad smile spread across Valdore's face. It was a rare sight, and a welcome one. "The fleet will move against the Isneih and Sei'chi systems, right on schedule."

Nijil nodded. From those beachheads, the Romulan fleet would face few serious impediments to its ultimate goals, provided it maintained the advantage of surprise. Even if the Coalition were to discover prematurely what was coming, they could do little to keep the point of the

Empire's spear from reaching the worlds that constituted the very beating heart of the Coalition of Planets.

The alien *lloann'mhrahel* who populated the vast regions of space that lay beyond the Avrrhinul outmarches that marked the Empire's present-day borders would no longer be safe, assuming all went well as the very near future began to unfold. Not even ancient, ruddy Thhaei—Vulcan—itself could stand for very long against Romulus's most glorious onslaught in recent memory.

"I have more news for you, Admiral," Nijil said.

The admiral raised an eyebrow.

Scarcely able to contain his excitement, Nijil began to explain the warp-speed breakthrough his theoretical people had just stumbled upon. "The technology division may very soon render Centurion Terix's mission moot. . . ."

THIRTY-SIX

Romulan *Scoutship Drolae*
Near Romulus

As THE OVERSTRAINED LITTLE SHIP obediently transitioned from nearly warp six to a relatively sluggish warp two, Trip breathed a new prayer of thanks to any deity who might be monitoring such things anywhere in the vast empty spaces between Romulus and Earth. He was grateful not only that the vessel around him had successfully endured yet another brutal bout of rapid acceleration and deceleration—not to mention the sustained hard use it had suffered in between those extremes—but also for the simple fact that, as one of Trip's automotive-engineer ancestors might have put it, Centurion Terix had apparently left his keys in the scout vessel's ignition, so to speak.

That simple, unaccountable fact also proved to be a source of nagging disquiet from the moment Trip had left the Taugus system until now, when Romulus was already becoming visible on the long-range sensors as a small but brightly shining cerulean bauble, locked in a perpetual gravitational dance with the ruddy wasteland of Remus, an ugly, blotchy orb that appeared to be perched on the blue planet's shoulder like some grimly vigilant gargoyle.

Despite his relatively trouble-free passage to Romulus thus far, Trip still continued to worry that Terix had set some sort of elaborate trap for him—one whose jaws still had yet to spring shut on him. *Talk about paranoid,* he thought. *All Terix had to do was rig the warp core to lose containment once I started accessing the helm station. He really didn't need to set any traps more complicated than that.*

But he still had his nagging doubts. For one thing, it just wasn't like Terix, a man who clearly did not give his trust easily, to be so sloppy. But not only had the *Scoutship Drolae* apparently *not* been rigged to explode in the absence of a special surreptitious abort code, the sturdy little vessel's com system had actually allowed him to maintain constant surveillance over the subspace frequencies being used by the Romulan fleet, apparently thanks to Terix's simple failure to log off of the com console just prior to disembarking for the Taugus raid.

But most fortunate of all—not to mention most suspicious of all—was the fact that this blunder had left Trip with access to many of the fleet's highest-security channels.

As he initiated his sublight approach to the steadily growing sapphire planet, rehearsing the verbal report he would make to Valdore all the way, some of the chatter he was hearing on the secure com channels began to both intrigue and frighten him. For starters, the Romulan fleet's technology division appeared to have just made an unspecified but apparently significant breakthrough in following up on the late Doctor Ehrehin's warp-seven stardrive research.

Trip wasn't at all sure what that meant—let alone how they had managed it without Ehrehin—if the news turned out to be anything other than a hopeful rumor. *Well, it was bound to happen sooner or later,* he thought. *After all, somebody else would have built the first airplane back in the early twentieth century if Orville and Wilbur had decided to throw in the towel early.*

The other messages he intercepted soon afterward began to chill him to the depths of his soul. Disciplined-sounding voices familiar to anyone with military training, regardless of language, had begun speaking in clipped, determined phrases of fleet movements. *Large* fleet movements, which were being discussed only on what Trip had identified as the highest-security channels to which he had access. All of the fleet movements were apparently covert.

And all of them were headed away from Romulan space, proceeding in the general direction of the core Coalition worlds.

Two specific destinations, which he assumed were Romulan place names for Coalition locations, had already recurred frequently enough to draw Trip's attention. *Isneih, Sei'chi.* He hadn't heard either name before, so he couldn't translate them readily into their English equivalents. But he imagined those places wouldn't be hard to locate using the data files on the *Drolae*'s nav computer. After activating the autopilot, he immediately set about doing just that.

Isneih. A supermassive white star located about nineteen light-years from another marker, which Trip had already designated as Earth's solar system.

Trip's heart raced as he compared his own mental star map to the one displayed on the nav console. *The Calder system*, he thought, his spine chilled as though suddenly exposed to a total vacuum. *That's getting a little too close to Andoria and Vulcan for comfort.*

With Calder pinned down on the map, it took only another few moments to locate the Romulan fleet's other frequently mentioned objective: Sei'chi.

His stomach abruptly went into freefall. *Alpha Centauri. Only a bit more than four light-years from Earth.*

A proximity alarm interrupted Trip's grim musings,

forcing his attention back up to the forward windows. The space in front of them was quickly growing very crowded, and not merely because the *Drolae* was fast approaching Romulus.

A flat, horseshoe-crab-shaped Romulan bird-of-prey had just dropped out of warp directly between him and the looming planet. The rapidly approaching vessel was oriented so that the glare of Eisn, the bright yellow sun around which Romulus and Remus orbited, provided garish illumination to its ventral hull, which displayed the bright red plumage of a predatory bird.

Without warning, a disruptor beam lashed out from the warbird, scoring a direct hit that rocked the little scoutship and rang her hull like a colossal clapper striking an outsize cathedral bell. Fortunately, Trip's flight harness kept him from being flung from the pilot's seat.

He engaged the throttle, and wasn't a bit surprised when the warp drive failed to engage.

Swell. Terix, you sadistic bastard. You really did plan this all along, didn't you? Trip felt physically pinned down, as though he'd just been literally caught in the steel jaws of a bear trap.

But he knew that even a trapped animal was anything but helpless. Few creatures were more dangerous than a wounded bear, after all, and Trip understood that he wasn't entirely out of options, trapped or not. He began entering commands into his partially disabled engineering console, beginning by punching up the fuel-containment subsystem.

His com console light flashed, signaling an incoming hail. A harsh male voice came over the speaker. *"Scout vessel* Drolae. *You will heave to and deactivate your weapons. Prepare to be boarded, or vaporized."*

Trip shut off the speaker, then extended his left arm toward the forward window in order to make a decidedly un-Romulan hand gesture. Though he seriously doubted that anyone aboard the other vessel could see it, it still felt damned good. *Let's see how many of you I can vaporize right along with me,* he thought as he returned his attention to the console before him and entered a new string of commands.

A moment later, a small screen before him began displaying the Romulan numerals that denoted the beginning of a final, brief countdown to oblivion.

Next, he began frantically working the com console, trying to open a channel to somebody, *anybody,* in either Starfleet or the United Earth government. He estimated he had only a few seconds at best before he was blown out of the sky, and he was determined to put his last moments to the best possible use.

Your plan all along was to let me almost *get away with this, wasn't it, Terix? You* wanted *me to see what Valdore was about to do to the Coalition planets. Just as long as I couldn't actually do a damned thing about it.*

Nothing. No subspace connections. And nothing evidently wrong with the *Drolae*'s transmitter. The receiver, on the other hand, was suddenly awash in an oceanic wave of pure static.

He looked up at the approaching ship. *He's jamming me,* he thought, despair at last beginning to zero in on him with all the force of a plummeting asteroid. *Looks like I'm not getting any warnings out to anybody.*

It occurred to him then that he had parted company with his friends back on Taugus without disabusing them of the idea that the Klingon Empire now constituted the gravest threat to peace in the galactic neighborhood. *Now* he knew better. The most serious danger the Coalition now faced emanated from Romulus, rather than the Klingon homeworld. And he was the only one who knew this—and the location of the

Romulans' targets—to a bedrock certainty, other than the Romulans themselves. And the forward weapons tubes of the approaching bird-of-prey argued eloquently that the Romulan Empire would soon have the exclusive franchise on that knowledge, no matter what might happen to Charles Anthony Tucker III in the next few moments.

At least, Trip thought, *until after it's way too late for anybody in the Coalition to do anything about it.*

THIRTY-SEVEN

Tuesday, July 22, 2155
Columbia **NX-02, near Alpha Centauri**

ADMIRAL GARDNER'S NEW ORDERS had arrived only about six hours after *Columbia*'s repairs were completed; alone in her ready room, Captain Erika Hernandez received them with a heavy sense of fatigue. She knew she wasn't the only one who was feeling worn out at the moment, either. Like all of *Columbia*'s alpha-shift bridge personnel, Lieutenant Russell Hexter and his beta-watch crew and Lieutenant Charles Zeilfelder and his gamma-shifters had been working far past their standard shifts for the duration of the repair operations. The double-teaming had put quite a strain on just about everyone.

Prior to returning to her command chair on the bridge, Hernandez had put in an order with the galley to prep some caffeinated drinks for the alpha-shift bridge crew. Before Ensign Valerian, the com officer, had managed to take her first sip, however, she received a partially garbled distress call from a line of cargo vessels reporting that they had come under attack in the Alpha Centauri system. Coffee and tea were put aside, forgotten and cold, as *Columbia*'s bridge crew shifted immediately into rescue mode.

"Any ID yet on the attackers, Sidra?" Hernandez said, turning her command chair toward the communications console. She hoped that another batch of Romulan-commandeered Klingon vessels wouldn't prove to be the culprits here; that might push a touchy Coalition Council right over the brink of launching a misbegotten war against the Klingon Empire. *Give me plain vanilla, garden-variety pirates anyday,* she thought.

"Still no luck on that, Captain," said Ensign Valerian. "And all I'm getting right now is static. Maybe the attackers are jamming the cargo ships at the source."

If they haven't destroyed them outright already, Hernandez thought, immediately kicking herself for her pessimism.

Facing front and leaning forward toward the helm, she said, "What's our ETA at Alpha Centauri?" She knew she probably sounded like a child asking "Are we there yet?" But given her current lack of sleep, as well as her preoccupation with Jonathan Archer's long-shot attempt to avert a seemingly inevitable war with the Klingons and/or the Romulans, she regarded it as a minor miracle that she sounded even halfway coherent.

Lieutenant Akagi turned from her station, a slight smile on her lips. "Just a hair under twenty minutes, Captain. Five minutes less than the last time you asked. Would you like me to put a counter on the screen, sir?" she teased, her almond-shaped eyes crinkling at the edges.

Hernandez gave her a mock scolding look. "No, that won't be necessary. I'll try to restrain my enthusiasm until we get there." She looked over to the front left of the bridge, where Valerian's hands were a blur at her communications console, while her face showed unhappy concentration.

"Any luck restoring communications with the convoy, Sidra?" Hernandez asked.

Valerian shook her head. "No, Captain. I'm picking up snatches and pieces of subspace messages, but nothing I can lock onto for any length of time. The signals are all tremendously fragmented. It's as if the main ship trans-ceivers are either jammed or destroyed, and the message fragments I'm receiving are being transmitted by private, low-power communication devices carried by shipboard personnel. Most of them appear to be personal mes-sages. . . . They're trying to say their good-byes."

The thought made Hernandez shiver. *If their commu-nications are being jammed, could this be another Rom-ulan stunt?* She imagined the cargo vessel crews all trying to defend their ships, even as they used whatever small com devices were on hand to send farewell messages to their loved ones. *If that's the case, then we may already be too late to help anybody.*

She toggled the communicator on her command chair's arm. "Karl, see if you can pump a bit more power into the engines. Even shaving off a minute or two of travel time might make all the difference."

"I'll see what I can do, Captain, but we're gonna bust our new stitches if you push my little Liebchens very much harder," Lieutenant Graylock replied, clearly con-cerned about undoing the just-completed repairs to *Co-lumbia*'s nacelles and the other recent war wounds she had sustained.

"All I ask is that you *try,* Karl," Hernandez said before signing off.

"Coming up on fifteen minutes," Akagi said from her station half an eternity later.

"Do we have long-range visuals yet?" Hernandez asked.

At the tactical station, Lieutenant Kiona Thayer shook her head, her long braided hair undulating across her back with the movement. "Not yet, Captain. Even if we did, whatever we saw would already be old news because of the relativistic light-lag. On the bright side, our sensors aren't currently picking up any subspace signatures consistent with weapons fire. Which could be a good thing."

"Or it could mean that the battle's already been lost," Hernandez said, feeling glum.

"Well, aren't *you* a bag of oranges and morning sunshine?" Commander Veronica Fletcher said in her lilting New Zealand accent as she exited the turbolift and strode purposefully to her traditional spot at the engineering console to Hernandez's right.

"Only if they're fully pulped oranges," Hernandez said tartly in response. Her answer made her think of poor Jonathan Archer, who really *looked* like a bag of pulped fruit after his fight on Qo'noS. She was glad she hadn't been on *Enterprise* when Archer had returned, or she would have had to battle the temptation to take care of him. *He always* has *had that effect on me,* she thought, even though she never doubted for a moment that her instinct to protect *Columbia* and her crew would have overruled the impulse. Of course, she couldn't deny that she'd found the current hotheaded, secretive version of Jon Archer far less attractive than the man she once might have married. So much about the man had changed over the past few years. Particularly since the death of Trip Tucker.

Hernandez got a status update from Chief Engineer Graylock on several belowdecks repairs and retrofits that had just been completed, including some system redundancies that could act as extra computer firewalls that had been put into place after Archer's warning about the new weapon the Romulans were using.

A hand signal from Akagi told Hernandez that only a few minutes remained before *Columbia* was due to drop out of warp in the outer Alpha Centauri system.

"All right, everyone, we're on tactical alert," Hernandez said. Once the bridge illumination had dimmed to combat levels, she continued: "We already know that the cargo fleet is under attack, so I want us coming in locked and loaded for bear. I know you've all been briefed already, but let me remind you that the hostile we are about to encounter may be *either* Klingon or Romulan ships. Either way, we're going to target their weapons and propulsion wherever possible. I want to capture one of these bastards, if the opportunity arises. If it doesn't, we'll do whatever we have to do." She looked toward Fletcher, nodding slightly at her executive officer.

"If we end up facing Klingon battle cruisers, keep in mind that their crews may not be in control of their own helms and weapons," Fletcher said, effortlessly picking up where Hernandez had left off. "And if they aren't really the ones running their own control panels, then it's likely that they won't return our hails. If the hostile vessels really are being controlled remotely, then their tactical maneuvers might be a bit more sluggish than you might expect. But don't bet the farm on that in the absence of hard information. Until we actually engage the aggressors, I want every sensor focused on telling us whether or not the hostile vessels' crews are actively piloting their ships, or if they might just be along for the ride, so to speak."

"Two minutes, Captain," Akagi said.

"Arm phase cannons. Load and arm torpedoes," Hernandez said, settling back firmly into her chair. "The moment we exit warp, charge the hull plating. Ensign Valerian, open a broad-band hailing channel as soon as we go sublight."

"Major Foyle reports that his full MACO complement is standing by if we need them," Fletcher said. "They're also deployed near all emergency containment areas, and ready with pressure suits, just in case."

"Thank you," Hernandez said. "Helm, take us out of warp as close as you can to the line of scrimmage. We want the element of surprise on our side."

The deck plates shuddered beneath Hernandez's boots, and *Columbia*'s entire spaceframe groaned in a familiar yet still disconcerting manner. The main viewscreen at the front of the bridge showed the distorted streaks of the stars aligned with the ship's flightline compressing to almost dimensionless pinpoints as *Columbia* abruptly decelerated to subluminal speeds.

Squaring her shoulders and setting her jaw, Hernandez looked directly toward the screen's center, knowing the viewer would pick her image up in the same manner as any other audio/visual hail. "This is Captain Erika Hernandez of the United Earth *Starship Columbia*. We are responding to acts of aggression against cargo vessels under the protection of the Coalition of Planets. All aggressor vessels must stand down and submit to boarding. Any resistance will be considered an act of aggression, and will be met with deadly force. Hostile vessels, this is the *only* warning you will receive."

Out of the corner of her eye, Hernandez saw Lieutenant Commander el-Rashad turn toward her from his science station, a gobsmacked expression on his chiseled, mocha-colored features.

The reason for his reaction appeared on the main viewscreen a moment later. The visual sensors displayed what lay in *Columbia*'s path. The aggressor vessels and the cargo fleet they menaced came into sharp focus, and it was immediately clear that the attackers were of neither Klingon nor Romulan design. Nor was their identity a mystery; the attackers' long, blunt-nosed central hulls, with each of their aft sections surrounded by a single wide, ring-shaped warp-propulsion module, were all too familiar to everyone present.

"*Vulcans?* Why would—" Hernandez said under her breath, scarcely able to contain her incredulity.

"Captain, sensors confirm the presence of two *D'Kyr*-type Vulcan combat cruisers," Thayer said from her tactical station. "Particle-beam residue readings show that they *are* the aggressors here. Should I hold fire?"

Hernandez stood, raising her hand to signal restraint. "Yes. Hold fire. What the *hell* are they doing?" Her mind galloped to find an explanation, but the longer she stared at the image, the more insane it seemed.

"They're not responding to hails, Captain," Valerian said.

Hernandez continued staring at the vista on the screen, trying to drink in every detail. The beleaguered convoy consisted of five cargo vessels, many of them already severely damaged. One seemed completely beyond salvaging, as plasma fires burned on what little remained of its outer hull, apparently fed by atmosphere that continued to escape from interior compartments. The cargo vessels almost seemed to cower in the presence of the Vulcan ships that appeared to have instigated the entire situation.

"One of the ships is charging up its weapons again!" Thayer shouted. On the viewer, Hernandez watched as the forward particle-beam tube on the ship nearest to *Columbia* began to emit a baleful emerald glow.

"Charge hull plating to full!" Hernandez shouted.

"Their weapons lock isn't focused on *us*, Captain," Fletcher said.

A moment later, a brilliant green beam shot forth from the underbelly of the Vulcan cruiser, lancing into the hull of one of the more heavily damaged cargo ships. Almost immediately, the wounded vessel exploded, sending an expanding cloud of metal debris and ignited gases into space. The effect reminded Hernandez of a

Fourth of July fireworks display she'd seen as a child, though her mood at the moment was anything but celebratory.

"Have they responded to our hails yet?"

"No, sir," Valerian said.

"Try to disable the lead vessel," Hernandez ordered, hoping that she hadn't just made the mistake of her career.

"The second ship is charging weapons and targeting *us*," Thayer shouted before she'd managed to fire her first shot.

"Evasive maneuvers!" Hernandez returned to her chair, strapping herself in place as her crew got to work.

As *Columbia* lurched and vibrated in response to Hernandez's demands, the captain studied the viewscreen, which showed several of Thayer's phase cannon blasts making contact with one of the *D'Kyr*-type cruisers. The concentrated energy bursts seemed to warm the greenish hull up a bit, while a photonic torpedo exploded against the cruiser's underbelly without doing any apparent harm.

"Incoming!"

Hernandez felt her ship shudder for a moment as one of the Vulcan vessels returned fire, and the lights on the bridge—already crimson-hued from the moment *Columbia* had gone to full tactical alert—flickered and dimmed significantly.

"Status?" she yelled.

"Hull plating is down to eighty percent," Thayer said.

"Fire at will, Lieutenant," Hernandez shouted to the tactical officer. She tapped the com unit on her chair. "Karl, we need that hull plating at full."

"I'm working on it," Graylock said, sounding testy.

"Firing!" Thayer said, and the viewscreen showed that *Columbia* was swooping over what appeared to be the dorsal surface of one of the combat cruisers. This time, a full spread of *Columbia*'s photonic torpedoes struck the warp ring of the ship, resulting in a blazing arc of bluish energy that crackled around the surface of the ring.

"Bring us about for another salvo," Hernandez said.

"They're targeting another one of the cargo ships," Fletcher said.

"Get us *between* the Vulcans and the cargo fleet," Hernandez said. "Our hull plating can take the pounding better than theirs can." She didn't add the words "I hope" out loud, though she felt certain she wasn't the only one on the bridge thinking them.

"*Both* Vulcan ships are opening fire!" Thayer said.

"I need every last amp of power you can send to the hull plating, Karl," Hernandez shouted into her com unit.

Perhaps a second later, *Columbia* shuddered and jumped as though she'd been struck by the fist of some angry god. The sharp impact threw Hernandez from her chair. Above her head, the hull rang like a gong, and the bridge abruptly plunged into darkness. She heard several screams and thumps from across the bridge, and saw showers of sparks as various duty stations overloaded.

The continued illumination from the console fires showed that most of her bridge crew had either been thrown from their posts or had barely managed to hang on to them. Luckily, no one seemed to have been seriously hurt.

Fletcher and el-Rashad were the first to break out the emergency hand beacons and fire extinguishers, which they immediately brought to bear against the worst of the electrical fires. The emergency lighting finally kicked on as the crew attempted to access *Columbia*'s almost uniformly downed systems. The drinks, which had remained mostly untouched after their arrival, had become airborne momentarily, and the emptied cups now rolled in the liquids that had pooled across part of the deck's port side, where cups and contents alike now lay forgotten.

"Systems are down shipwide," Akagi said, an apprehensive tremor in her voice.

That fact alone didn't tell Hernandez very much of value. "I need to know how badly we've been damag—"

"Internal communications coming back online now, Captain," Valerian said, interrupting.

The com system crackled, and the chief engineer's Teutonic-accented voice issued from it. *"Captain? Whatever they hit us with really fubared us. The warp core is* kaput, *at least temporarily. It'll take us several hours to fix it, even if the rest of the systems were working fine. Which they aren't."*

So much for the repairs we just completed, Hernandez thought ruefully. She stared at the main viewscreen, which had yet to return to life. "Are they targeting us again?" Hernandez asked, hoping the bridge's interval of blindness would be a brief one.

"Sensors are coming back up," Akagi said, coughing at the acrid by-products of the damped-down electrical fires that still lingered in the air.

The ship's ventilation system must be down, too, Hernandez thought, cursing inwardly. But she knew *Columbia* had to deal with issues even more urgent than life support.

To Hernandez's relief, the viewscreen lit up and displayed a three-dimensional tactical image of what lay above *Columbia*'s dorsal hull. The two Vulcan ships seemed to be doing nothing, though Hernandez was pleased to see that the warp-propulsion ring encircling the one they had fired upon appeared to be damaged and offline.

"Transmit our bridge flight recorder files to Starfleet Command now," Hernandez shouted to Valerian. "They need to know what the Vulcans are up to, in case they don't give us time to send a report."

"I'm trying, Captain," Valerian said. "Subspace communications seem to be working only intermittently."

"I don't understand any of this," Fletcher said as she wiped the sweat away from beneath her blond bangs. "Why would the Vulcans fire on other Coalition ships?"

"Maybe they had intel that told them something about the cargo they were carrying?" Hernandez wondered aloud.

"Maybe. But that wouldn't explain why they fired on *us* as well," Fletcher said.

Hernandez's mind reeled as she realized she had no answers. All she knew for certain was that this situation was *not*, in the words of members of a certain pointy-eared race, *logical*. Unless . . .

"Unless the Vulcans aren't the ones piloting those ships," she said, her voice low enough that only her XO would hear. "What if the *Romulans* have learned to commandeer Vulcan tech, like they did with the Klingon battle cruisers at Draylax?"

"Captain, sensors are picking up three more incoming ships!" Thayer shouted.

Hernandez stared, slack-jawed, as the image on the viewscreen changed yet again.

Dropping out of warp were two more *D'Kyr*-type combat cruisers, and one of the larger, better-armed *Sh'Raan*-class ships, which looked like a spear jammed through a hoop. The weaponry the newcomers carried between them would be more than enough to blow both *Columbia* and the remnants of the cargo fleet to little more than drifting trails of vapor in a few seconds, polarized hull plating notwithstanding.

"Some days you just can't win," Hernandez said as she slumped back into her chair. Turning toward her XO, she said, "Better prepare to launch the log buoy, Veronica. While we still can."

THIRTY-EIGHT

Tuesday, July 22, 2155
Enterprise **NX-01, near the Gamma Hydra sector**

"Shuttlepod Two is making its final docking approach now, Captain," Hoshi said.

Archer nodded, rising from his command chair. "I'm going down to the launch bay to meet them," he said. "You have the bridge, Hoshi."

The bridge was running with a skeleton crew at the moment; the most overworked of *Enterprise*'s personnel, including O'Neill and McCall, were taking well-deserved breaks during the outbound voyage, at least until the time came to bring the ship about deep in the Gamma Hydra sector, retracing the original patrol route back toward Earth.

As he traveled down to E deck in the turbolift, Archer was glad that relatively few people would be around to witness the return of the stolen shuttlepod. No one had questioned him about it directly over the last few days, but by now scuttlebutt had placed T'Pol and Malcolm on any number of secret missions. He felt fairly certain that none of the crew's guesses had come even remotely close to the reality, whatever that might actually turn out to be. He was eager to learn the truth himself.

For the past several days, whenever he hadn't been preoccupied with some emergency or other—his life-or-death duel on Qo'noS sprang instantly, not to mention painfully, to mind—Archer had mentally rehearsed what he planned to say to T'Pol and Malcolm once they returned. The chance that they might *not* make it back had been a variable he hadn't allowed himself to consider; he couldn't bear to dwell on the possibility that he might have lost two more of his most valuable officers and friends so soon after Trip's "death."

But now, as his reunion with the two errant officers neared, he felt his anger being pushed into the recesses of his mind by a rising sense of relief; his momentary pleasure at that unexpected feeling calmed his soul. Whether the root cause was mere fatigue or an emotional ricochet off the ceaseless frustrations all the recent political uncertainty within both Starfleet and the Coalition Council had caused him, by the time he reached the entrance to Launch Bay Two he had settled into an almost Vulcan state of serenity.

The hatch slid open in front of him, and Archer saw that Ensign Bougie was scuttling about outside the newly docked shuttlepod, making post-flight checks of the little ship's outer hull and external propulsion components. The launch bay's magnetic docking arm stood just above the shuttlepod's roof, and the launch bay air seemed charged with expectation, along with the traditional chill it usually carried immediately after the bay had been repressurized.

"Ensign, I'd like a bit of privacy to welcome my officers back aboard," Archer said.

Bougie looked up, apparently surprised and caught in mid-thought, his mouth twisted to one side. "Yes, sir," he said finally, gathering his materials up quickly. Archer noted that he still used old-style writing implements and clipboards, checking off the items on his duty list manually rather than relying on computers and datapads.

A few moments later Archer had positioned himself

directly outside the shuttlepod, standing beside its stabilizer wing as he waited for the dorsal hatch to open. T'Pol exited first, followed by Reed. Both wore dark, tight-fitting but otherwise nondescript clothing, which was partially covered by loose Vulcan-style travelers' robes.

"Welcome back aboard *Enterprise*," Archer said, inflating his words with an air of laconic drollness. In spite of himself, he was enjoying the look of discomfiture he saw on both their faces, especially Malcolm's.

"Captain, we can explain," Reed said in a guilt-ridden tone, before T'Pol had even had a chance to open her mouth.

Archer released a long exhalation through pursed lips. He wanted to ask after Trip Tucker, whose absence now seemed as conspicuous as a corpse at a funeral. At the moment, however, he was in no mood to hear what could well prove to be very bad news. Instead of saying anything, he opted instead merely to smile as he held both arms out before him, making the universal gesture for "give me a hug."

"You can save your explanations for later," he said. "First, are both of you all right?"

Reed stepped awkwardly into the hug, half embracing Archer while patting him on the back lightly, though just hard enough to force him to suppress a wince. T'Pol merely stood in place, looking nearly as awkward as Reed did.

"We managed to make it back in one piece, with no scratches or dents, as has the shuttlepod," Reed said in overemphatic tones as he pulled back just enough to make a close study of Archer's bruised face. "Which is apparently more than we can say about you, Captain."

"Cracked ribs," Archer said. "I had a mean encounter with a Klingon admiral, but I think he ended up looking even worse than I do. Long story, short ending.

"Like I said, we'll have a long talk later about what the hell you two were doing when you took that shuttlepod," Archer said, trying to color his words with the same stern, scolding authority he remembered from the occasional childhood reprimands he had received from his father. "All I'm going to say on the subject right now is that I'm getting a bit tired of my most trusted officers deciding that the rules don't apply to *them*. Finding a detour off the main road doesn't automatically make it the route to take. And *if* my most trusted officers want to *continue* being my most trusted officers, they'd better have an explicit understanding that there *will not* be any more detours."

T'Pol raised an eyebrow. "Captain, you have my sincere apologies. Our actions *were* inappropriate and badly timed. I hope that you will allow me and Lieutenant Reed to make amends."

Archer turned and strode in the direction of the hatchway that led out of the launch bay and deeper into E deck's interior, T'Pol and Reed following in his wake. "As far as anyone on this ship other than myself is concerned, you won't *need* to make amends. Phlox is the only person other than the three of us who knows that what you did wasn't authorized. Everybody else thinks you were on some kind of secret spy mission for Starfleet."

"Which is true, except for the Starfleet part," Reed said, grinning sheepishly.

Archer turned—a bit too sharply for his ribs—and growled, "Nobody else needs to know that. My log will show that T'Pol needed a *lot* of therapeutic meditation, and that you, Malcolm, were in your quarters recovering from the worst case of the Altairian quick-step in the history of human space exploration."

Reed made a face, but said nothing in response.

"Captain, the ship that helped ferry us in and out of Romulan space was a Vulcan intelligence vessel," T'Pol said.

"I was wondering how you were going to manage to pull off that part of your plan," Archer said. "You *were* flying a short-range Starfleet shuttlepod, after all."

"Apparently, a craft as small as a shuttlepod *can* escape detection even deep inside Romulan space so long as it calls no undue attention to itself," T'Pol said. "Unfortunately, the only way we could discover that fact was to proceed with our plan."

"Gaining access to a Vulcan spy's rather detailed Romulan star charts didn't hurt either," Reed added.

Archer stared at him as the hatch that led to E deck's corridors opened in front of them. "You've got *maps*?" The official Coalition maps of the Romulan Empire were astonishingly incomplete, cobbled together mainly by means of long-range scans. Archer didn't know what good Reed's maps would do anyone at the moment, but he suspected that they might become extremely valuable in the days ahead.

Reed nodded, grinning an "aw-shucks" grin that he had developed after four years of close association with Trip. "I certainly hope those maps will buy us back some of the goodwill we've lost."

"I'll consider it a down payment," Archer said. "As long as it stays in trustworthy hands, and away from certain shady characters I could name." The idea of having a resource that the mysterious black-garbed Agent Harris and his secretive Starfleet intelligence organization might lack appealed to him greatly.

Reed swiped his index finger across his chest, miming the letter X. "Cross my heart, sir. This little adventure of ours had *nothing* to do with the bureau."

As they approached the central turboshaft, T'Pol

spoke again. "Captain, while we docked with the Vulcan vessel, we also discovered some intelligence related to *you*."

"Me?" Archer said as he came to a stop just outside the turbolift door, which slid obediently open for him.

She nodded. "We know, for instance, about the evidence you presented to the Coalition Council concerning the Romulans and this new ability of theirs to remotely commandeer Klingon vessels."

As the trio stepped into the turbolift, Archer said, "Good. That ought to make it easier to persuade the Council not to get caught up in the wrong war against the wrong enemy." The doors hissed closed and Archer directed the turbolift to A deck, and the bridge.

"Our understanding, at least from those aboard the Vulcan ship," T'Pol said, "was that the Vulcan government may be far more inclined to accept your interpretation of the danger posed by the Romulans than are the other Coalition members."

"I wonder how much of that agreement stems from the relationship we know exists between the Vulcans and the Romulans?" Archer said. He knew that Reed *had* to know about that relationship by now; he couldn't have undertaken an extended mission into Romulan space without gaining some exposure to the startling physiological similarities between the two races.

"I am not sure, Captain," T'Pol said with evident sincerity; Archer knew that this was an extremely sensitive topic for her.

Noting they were about to reach the bridge, Archer pressed the stop button on the control pad. "Before we go any further, I want to cover the one topic we've all been avoiding since you two came aboard." He wasn't certain he wanted to hear the answer, but he had to know the truth. "How is Trip? Did you find him?"

Reed nodded and displayed a sober expression. "We found him, and arrived just in the nick of time, too. Whatever these psychic flashes or connections that T'Pol has been having with our 'late' chief engineer, she was right; his life *was* in danger. After we helped get him out of the jam he'd gotten himself into, we offered to bring him back, but he refused. He felt he still had a mission to complete."

"Something about the Romulan warp-seven project?" Archer asked.

"That is at least *one* of the objectives he appears to be pursuing," T'Pol said, her voice dropping lower. "He had also gathered other information, which he passed on to us. It concerned the Klingon attack on Draylax."

"He found more evidence that the Romulans were behind what happened at Draylax?"

T'Pol shook her head, looking almost wistful. "No, Captain. His Romulan intelligence contacts had led him to believe that the Klingons were indeed the aggressors at Draylax."

Archer was puzzled. "But we already know that can't be true. How could he discover something that isn't true, unless . . ."

The answer to his question dawned on him before he could finish his sentence, and the idea chilled him to the core.

"Unless he was *purposely* being misled," T'Pol said. "Meaning that his identity as a spy may well have been compromised."

Archer shuddered, trying desperately to force his mind not to wander down the path it was already navigating. If Trip was indeed compromised, any information he was finding was likely to be tainted. And if he failed to pass along what was almost certainly disinformation concocted by the Romulan Star Empire's intelligence services—or if he managed to discover that Romulus's own spymasters were using him as a pawn in their game—then he was likely to end up in the crosshairs of some Romulan assassin.

Archer knew that in the shadowy world of espionage, compromised spies frequently ended up very dead.

THIRTY-NINE

Tuesday, July 22, 2155
S.S. *Kobayashi Maru*, Gamma Hydra sector

KOJIRO VANCE TRACED the swell of the woman's dusky-hued hip as she slumbered, his fingertip traveling over the exquisite area he had so recently ravished. She had tasted like plums, although he granted, in retrospect, that it might have been the liqueur they had consumed before they'd had passionate sex against nearly every flat surface in his opulently appointed quarters.

Orana Shubé clearly wanted to go places on the ship, but Vance wasn't certain that there was any place for her to go. After all, she wasn't particularly intelligent, and her mechanical aptitude was laughable. He suspected that she would best serve him exactly where she was, in the captain's bed. Or, perhaps, in the galley, preparing food for the crew and passengers. And, of course, the . . . temporary guests.

Yawning, he clambered over his plaything and padded naked toward the shower, absentmindedly scratching his groin as he walked. Stepping into the shower, he mourned the days on Earth when he'd been able to enjoy real showers, with unlimited supplies of hot water. But on a fuel carrier like the *Maru*, carrying the huge quantities of water needed for such a personal extravagance was not something he could justify, either to his financial backers in the Tau Ceti system, or to the crew that would expect to share this amenity. *And since the* Maru *is a retrofitted Klingon fuel carrier,* he thought, *having any luxury at all is, well, a luxury itself.*

He heard a chime at his door, and poked his head out of the shower stall. "Enter!"

Jacqueline Searles, the chief engineer of the *Kobayashi Maru*, stepped into the cabin, first noticing the nude woman on Vance's bed, then turning her head just enough to ascertain that her captain was in the shower.

"What is it, Jackie?" Vance asked, reaching for a towel.

She made a face. "Whatever is in that cargo we picked up for the *Horizon* seems to be slowing us down."

"How is that possible?" Vance asked, spreading his hands wide and shrugging. The towel fluttered to the deck.

Searles made another face and put a hand out as if to block her view of his nakedness as she turned away. He noticed that she seemed to object a great deal less to viewing Orana's plump behind. "Would you mind terribly putting some clothes on, Captain?" Searles said. "I don't need to talk to . . . *all* of you."

Shrugging again, Vance walked naked to his large wardrobe, which he opened so he could consider which of his many fanciful outfits he was going to wear. After all, if he was to be dealing with his . . . temporary guests again, he wanted to make the best of impressions, regardless of their present demeanor.

They'd picked up the nearly two dozen new passengers nine days ago, along with their cargo, at Altair VI. The Earth Cargo Service freighter *Horizon* was supposed to have been the ship to ferry them, along with their equipment, from the *Maru*'s destination of the Sataghni II fuel depot in the near side of the Gamma Hydra sector all the way to the outskirts of the Tezel-Oroko system, deep in section ten. But the *Horizon* hadn't been heard from in about a week, and Vance had agreed to perform the *Horizon*'s run—surreptitiously, of course—for triple his regular fee. Finding out a little bit about the sensitive nature of the mission had also been part of the bargain Vance had struck with his clandestine passengers.

He'd kept the full facts about the mission, at least as he knew them, from his first mate, Arturo Stiles, a man whose pragmatism was matched only by his excitability. So far as Stiles knew, they were making an unscheduled but highly paid delivery, and that was all he needed to know for now. The unexpected windfall ought to have made the economics-minded Stiles very happy indeed.

But if Stiles were to learn that the Vulcans aboard the *Kobayashi Maru* were headed for a stable cometary body in the Tezel-Oroko system's Kuiper belt, where they intended to fortify and expand a small, covert listening post whose electronic ears and eyes were aimed at both the Romulans and the Klingons, he would probably go ballistic. Vance didn't much care about the galactic politics involved, though he knew he would prefer that the stodgy Vulcans have the upper hand over either the Klingons or the Romulans; from what little he'd seen, both empires were far too capriciously aggressive to suit a free spirit like Captain Kojiro Vance.

But Vance felt confident that his crew would forget whatever the Vulcans were up to here within a few short days, once the *Maru* was engaged in another cargo run to some other, less perilously located world. Even Stiles would no doubt forgive all, should he ever discover the truth, once he received his share of the handsome profit the current Gamma Hydra run had already generated.

Vance selected a slimming, dark purple set of breeches

and a full-sleeved maroon shirt. He held them up against himself and noted with pleasure how nicely they complemented his straight black hair and olive-gold skin.

"Are you even paying *attention* to what I'm saying, Vance?" Searles asked.

Vance turned, suddenly remembering the presence of the engineer in his room, and regarded her with a smile he hoped she would consider charming. "Of *course*, Jackie. You were chattering on again, something about not liking the technology we're carrying for the Vulcans."

Searles balled her hands up into clawed fists and growled, clearly exasperated. "Essentially, yes, that is what I was saying. The Vulcans keep quote helping unquote my engineering staff with quote multiple system upgrades unquote, but it seems to me that all they're doing is further screwing up our already overtaxed systems. Yes, we're heading toward our destination *faster*, but the warp core is running *wicked* hot, Vance. And we're having a lot of system glitches as well. Plus, the stuff in the Vulcans' shipping crates may be the source of the strange, low-level radiation my people have been picking up on the internal scanners. It's making everyone very uncomfortable."

Vance frowned as he pulled the stitching at the waist of his pirate breeches tight, making sure not to catch anything important in the loops as he cinched them tighter. "Why would this radiation you're picking up necessarily have anything to do with the Vulcans or their matériel? I love her like I love myself, but the *Maru* is *always* springing a leak in some system or other. I mean no offense to your skills, Jackie, but the old girl is perpetually in need of *some* repair or other." He paused, then added with a flourish, "Unlike *myself*."

"I just want . . ." Searles frowned, seemingly searching very hard for the right words. "Can you just keep the Vulcans *out* of my engine room, please?"

"All right," Vance said, pulling the shirt on over his head. The satin felt smooth against his skin, luxurious. "I'll ask them to stay away. As long as *you* keep things running smoothly and make sure we get there in record time."

He crossed back to the bed, where he laid a hand on the sleeping Orana's rump. "I notice that you seemed to favor *this* sight more than my own impressive Davidesque nakedness. Would you like a quick taste, my dear, to make the more prosaic chores of the rest of your day more bearable? I must say, it's done wonders for *me*."

Searles extended her right hand toward him, middle finger defiantly raised, even as she turned and slammed her other hand into the wall-mounted hatch-control mechanism.

As the door slid open and she stalked out of the room, Vance chuckled quietly. *What a waste of a perfectly good offer,* he thought. *It would have been fun to watch, if nothing else.*

After all, one of the benefits of being master and commander of the *Kobayashi Maru* was that the position afforded him the means of enjoying life to its fullest—so long as nothing interrupted the incoming revenue stream, and naysayers like Stiles and Searles didn't keep the *Maru* in dry dock rather than out among the stars, earning more of the stuff that made life worth living. And enjoying life was something Kojiro Vance intended to go right on doing.

No matter *who* came out on top in the Vulcans' clandestine struggle against the Romulans and the Klingons for the reins of galactic power.

FORTY

Romulan *Scoutship Drolae*

EFFECTIVELY OUT OF OPTIONS, Trip could think of little to do other than to continue staring out the forward window at the angry glow of the approaching bird-of-prey's main disruptor tube. Only occasionally did he allow his gaze to flick momentarily down to his engineering displays.

The relentless downward progression of Romulan numeric pictographs on the console put him in mind of an hourglass whose sands had all but run out. Whether incoming Romulan disruptor fire killed him, or the sudden, explosive release of the mutually annihilative particles that powered the crippled scout vessel, he knew he would soon be very dead.

Dead for real this time, with no fakery involved.

Good thing T'Pol and I got to say good-bye properly instead of just doing that hand-jive the Vulcans do, he thought.

A disruptor pistol lay in his lap, against the remote possibility that the Romulans might somehow detect and undo his attempt to scuttle the *Drolae* prior to boarding her. He wished he'd taken a phase pistol from Shuttlepod Two—he far preferred a weapon with a stun setting—but he couldn't risk allowing an Earth weapon to fall into Romulan hands, which was almost certain to happen once the *Drolae* was boarded. But so far, he'd seen no evidence that the warship out there was attempting either to transmit helm override signals or to send over a boarding team.

Just as the countdown entered its final minute, Trip suddenly noticed a tingling sensation that made him imagine thousands of overly caffeinated ants running frantically all over his skin. In the same instant, a shimmering curtain of light revealed the cause of the weird sensation.

Transporter beam. Damn it!

The cockpit of the *Drolae* swiftly vanished around him, to be replaced a few heartbeats later by the cold greenish metal walls of a narrow, utilitarian chamber. Trip fell with a hard thump to the unyielding surface beneath him, the contoured pilot's chair that had been supporting his weight evidently having remained aboard the scoutship. As he scrambled to reach the disruptor that had transported with him, a pair of grim-faced Romulan *uhlans*, both brandishing gleaming disruptor pistols of their own, stepped quickly up onto the small circular stage upon which Trip had just materialized.

"I suppose you're gonna take me to your leader now," Trip said as the guards flanked him, kicked his weapon out of reach, and hauled him roughly to his feet. The only response the unsmiling pair made was to hold his arms behind his back as they shoved him toward an open hatchway.

Trip worried he might suffer a dislocated shoulder as they frog-marched him along the narrow curve of a conduit-lined accessway. A seeming eternity later, they pushed him into another chamber not much wider than the room in which Trip had materialized.

Trip immediately sized up the cramped but roughly circular place as the bridge. The chamber was built around a central pillar that served as an anchor for a compact array of consoles and viewers that faced outward to a ring of similar equipment that lined the curved walls. A handful of purposeful-looking Romulan military officers were distributed around various control stations, occupied with the familiar moment-to-moment business of keeping a starship flying.

Trip looked toward the back of the command chair that was positioned just forward of the room's central pillar. A male Romulan officer sat there, as still as a marble sculpture, perhaps transfixed by the large forward viewer before him. The screen displayed an image of the *Drolae*, adrift and broken. *Rode hard and put away wet*, Trip thought, grateful that the battered little ship hadn't given up the ghost at an earlier, less opportune time.

"The scout vessel's warp-core pressure is still heading toward critical, Commander," said a young woman who was posted at one of the portside consoles.

The captain, who still faced away from Trip, nodded. "Retreat to a safe distance, Decurion."

I know that voice, Trip thought, startled.

A moment later the image of the *Drolae* vanished, replaced first by a brilliant if short-lived bloom of orange molecular fire, which quickly gave way to a rapidly expanding sphere of sun-dappled metal shards. Within a few seconds, the debris cloud grew nearly as diffuse as the vacuum surrounding it. The *Drolae* disappeared, as though it had never existed in the first place.

"Put us back on our original course," the captain said, still staring straight ahead.

"Yes, Commander," said the young male officer who was posted at what Trip assumed to be the helm panel. The star field displayed on the viewer smeared into multicolored streaks as the warp drive engaged. The subaural vibrations transmitted into Trip's boots via the deck plates increased sharply in frequency, marking the vessel's quick transition from station-keeping velocity to warp five or thereabouts. And the brief sensation of lateral acceleration Trip felt before the inertial dampers fully engaged told him that they were headed *away* from Romulus.

Trip could barely contain his astonishment. *They're not going to take me the rest of the way to Romulus? This is definitely not going according to Hoyle.*

When the man seated at the room's center turned his chair toward the bridge's aft section, Trip finally had an inkling as to why.

He also had about a thousand new questions.

"Take the prisoner to my office," the captain said, apparently in anticipation of those very questions.

"Sopek!" Trip said after the guards had finally left him alone with the man in charge.

"I prefer Ch'uihv, if you please, Commander Tucker," said the erstwhile Vulcan captain. "At least while I'm operating in Romulan space."

Trip sat heavily in the chair that his captor had offered, gently flexing his sore, badly manhandled shoulders. "This galaxy is getting *way* too small," he said, his mind still reeling.

"You are no doubt referring to the apparent element of coincidence underlying our present meeting," the other man said, steepling his fingers before him and planting his elbows atop the small transparent desk behind which he had seated himself. "But people in our profession are frequently drawn together by common circumstances, Commander. Particularly when their mission objectives overlap as much as ours do."

Trip knew that even if he lived to be a hundred, he would never rid himself of a few truly ghastly memories. One such indelible recollection was the swath of indiscriminate devastation that an experimental Xindi

particle weapon had wrought upon his Florida hometown, where his little sister Lizzie had died a little over
two years ago.

Another equally ineradicable mark on his psyche was
the image of Sopek, or Ch'uihv, murdering Trip's original bureau partner, Tinh Hoc Phuong, in cold blood.
With a single disruptor blast, Sopek had reduced a
brave but helpless-human being into a smoldering pile
of ash and gristle.

"What the hell makes you think you and I have *anything* in common?" Trip said, glowering.

Either unaware of or unconcerned by Trip's hostility,
the other man said, "I know that you are conducting espionage on behalf of the Coalition of Planets. I am conducting similar operations under the auspices of the principal
intelligence agency of one of the founding members of
that body: Vulcan."

Trip frowned, incredulous. "*You* work for the Vulcan
Security Directorate?"

"I have been a V'Shar agent for many years," the older
man said, nodding. "Among my numerous ongoing di-
rectives is the task of continuously monitoring the evo-
lution of the Romulan Star Empire's military posture in
order to accurately assess its threat potential to Vulcan.
To perform these duties successfully, I must keep certain key individuals within the Empire convinced that
I am, in fact, a loyal Romulan. Simultaneously, others
must believe that I am leading an insurgency of sorts
against the Romulan military."

Trip involuntarily displayed his teeth. "So which of
those audiences were you playing to when you murdered Tinh Phuong?"

The man on the other side of the desk released a sigh,
an almost haunted expression momentarily displacing
his usually dour demeanor.

"Suppose I were to tell you that the V'Shar had obtained proof that Mister Phuong had become a grave threat to Vulcan security?" he said at length. "His death may well have saved a hundred other lives, both on Vulcan and elsewhere in the Coalition."

"That's a damned convenient charge for you to make," Trip said, "especially now that Phuong's not around anymore to defend himself. I suppose I should expect you to pass that same sort of judgment on *me* now that I know way more about you than you ever wanted me to. Unless Valdore catches up to this ship in the meantime and serves up a little fire and brimstone to the both of us, that is."

"I assure you, Commander, that I have taken great care to remain several steps ahead of Admiral Valdore," Sopek/Ch'uihv said. "Particularly after the . . . *unpleasantness* you and I experienced on Rator II."

Anger and astonishment wrestled one another to a standstill within Trip's chest; whatever "unpleasantness" the dissident leader had endured while fleeing from Valdore's assault force, what Phuong had suffered was infinitely worse.

Easy, Charles, he told himself. *Calm down. Try to make it look like you were* born *with these ears, even if this guy really knows better.*

"How do I know you're not secretly working for Valdore?" he said aloud. Making a broad gesture that encompassed the entire small office chamber, he added, "After all, it can't be easy to pinch a bird-of-prey right out from under the admiral's nose."

"No, it isn't," Sopek/Ch'uihv said. "It was extraordinarily difficult, in fact. But we had an advantage of which Valdore is unaware."

"And that is?"

Sopek/Ch'uihv leaned forward, the fingers of both

hands interlaced atop his desk. "Some of my *Ejhoi Ormiin* compatriots recently learned about a secret Romulan military weapon capable of usurping the command and control computers of Vulcan vessels. This weapon may also be able to usurp the technology of other Coalition worlds as well, which is why I have decided to share this knowledge with you."

Huh, Trip thought. *So he's not gonna kill me. I think.*

The other man continued: "My people applied what knowledge we could gain of the principles behind this new weapon to the task of liberating *this* vessel"—he paused to gesture broadly at the walls that surrounded them—"from a repair dock located in the Taugus sector."

This ship would have come in really handy when he needed to make his quick vanishing act from Taugus III, Trip thought. *And it also probably explains those sensor ghosts T'Pol and I saw when we were on the shuttlepod.*

It occurred to Trip then that one very prominent loose end remained from that incident. "What did you do with Terix?" he asked.

"The centurion who accompanied you to Taugus III," the other man said, his expression emotionless even by Trip's notions of Vulcan standards.

Trip did what he could to restrain his impatience. "Yeah. Him."

"Unfortunately, Centurion Terix . . . succumbed during debriefing."

Debriefing, Trip thought, parsing the gentle euphemism for its real, less benign meaning. *Interrogation.* Terix might have been an adversary, but he didn't deserve to die screaming on the rack.

"So when are you going to bring the thumbscrews out for *me*?" Trip said.

Sopek/Ch'uihv favored him with a blank, bewildered stare. "Excuse me, Commander?"

"Whether you're working for Valdore or the *Ejhoi Ormiin* or the Vulcan Spook Bureau—or all three at once—I can't see you just letting me go without first trying to pick *my* brain the way you picked Terix's."

A look of dawning understanding crossed the enigmatic man's face. "Ah. You were expecting a thorough and coercive interrogation. Under normal circumstances, I would not hesitate to do just that to anyone who has been such a close associate of the late Doctor Ehrehin. However, I have agreed to forgo that—and to do what I can to keep you from falling into Valdore's hands."

Trip ran a hand over his frown-crumpled brow, and nearly recoiled from the highly corrugated texture of his artificial forehead ridge. *Jeez. My great-granddaddy could have scrubbed his overalls on this thing.*

"Why?" he said aloud.

"It is a personal favor to an associate of mine on Vulcan."

That didn't tell Trip nearly enough. "Who are you talking about?"

"Someone with whom *you* share a close mutual friend, Commander," Sopek/Ch'uihv said.

Someone in the spy trade on Vulcan is saving my bacon? Trip thought, astonished. Although he had no idea for whom the other man was doing favors, he felt certain he knew the identity of the "close mutual friend" he had in common with this unnamed individual.

T'Pol.

That woman's determined to go right on trying to rescue me, one way or another, Trip thought, his feelings of helplessness and frustration threatening to boil over. *Whether I've asked for her help or not.*

"You are an extremely fortunate individual, Commander Tucker," said the Vulcan double agent. "You have cheated death more times than any other man I have ever encountered."

Trip shrugged, feeling worse rather than better despite the compliment. After all, it wasn't as if he'd had a lot of control over his destiny over the past few weeks; he was getting damned tired of being able to do little more than merely react to events as they happened.

"If everything you've just told me is true, then my luck wasn't good for much more than pure survival," he said. "After all, it didn't let me get wind of Valdore's . . . remote hijacking system until after *you* did. And if this thing actually works, it could be at least as dangerous as anything else I've uncovered in Romulan space so far."

Sopek/Ch'uihv nodded. "Indeed."

"On the plus side," Trip said, "I suppose I can assume that you've already told the V'Shar all about this remote-hijacking thing."

"Of course. And it is more properly referred to as the *arrenhe'hwiua* telecapture system."

That's easy for you *to say,* Trip thought as he tried to imagine wrapping his Alabama-Florida accent around that particular verbal mouthful.

Aloud, he said, "I really should get in touch with my superiors about this, too. Just to make absolutely sure that the *rest* of the Coalition sees this threat coming."

The other man shook his head. "I'm afraid we need to maintain communications silence at present. At least until after I am reasonably certain that Valdore's forces can neither listen in on us nor pursue."

That's pretty damned convenient, too, Trip thought. He studied the other man's face, but found it as inscrutable as that of any Vulcan he'd ever met. *Well, I'll know which side he's really on after the first big Romulan mili-*

tary engagement with this new weapon goes down. If Co-alition ships really do see this thing coming in advance, then I might be able to afford to trust this guy. But if the good guys end up getting caught with their britches down again, the way it happened at Coridan . . .

He suppressed a shudder.

Of course, it wasn't as though he had a lot of alternatives at the moment to taking his captor's words at face value. After all, challenging this man too much could get him just as dead as Phuong, any number of favors to friends of mutual friends notwithstanding.

"I suppose you'll have to put a lot of light-years between this ship and Romulus pretty quickly if you want to stay ahead of Valdore," he said, eager to change the subject to something a little less volatile. "What's your heading?"

The other spy gazed contemplatively at a bulkhead as he considered how much to reveal on the subject. Evidently deciding that Trip was harmless to him now—or perhaps having concocted another convenient lie—he said, "We are presently making best speed for the Tezel-Oroko star system."

Trip had no trouble maintaining a blank expression; though he thought he might have heard that system's name before, he assumed it was distant enough to lie beyond the "Here There Be Dragons" point on his mental star charts.

"What's at Tezel-Oroko?" he asked.

"The intelligence services of both Vulcan and Earth are jointly constructing a covert listening post near the system's edge," the other man said. "Its purpose is to monitor military activity inside the boundaries of both Romulan and Klingon space."

"All right," Trip said. "So why is *this* ship going there?" *There I go, challenging this trigger-happy thug again. I've really got to watch that.*

Sopek/Ch'uihv did not appear offended in the least at the question. "A freighter that had been expected to bring some of the last technical components and other matériel needed to bring the listening post online is overdue. We are going to do whatever we can to assist the listening post's crew in dealing with any related supply-line deficits or security problems."

Trip nodded in silence, a strange calm suddenly descending over him, displacing most of his earlier frustration and despair. He found the feeling remarkable, especially given that there was still a very good chance that he was soon to die among enemies—digested in the proverbial belly of the beast, no less—no matter what he tried to do to alter his circumstances.

But damned if it doesn't feel good to be charging off to do something, he thought. *Actually performing a rescue instead of just waiting around for the cavalry to arrive.*

Unless, of course, Sopek had just handed him the Vulcan equivalent of what Trip could imagine his father calling a line of pure horse puckey.

FORTY-ONE

Tuesday, July 22, 2155
Gamma Hydra sector

JACQUELINE SEARLES DIDN'T KNOW PRECISELY what she expected the end of the world to sound like; but the continuous shuddering groan the *Kobayashi Maru*'s warp core sent through the fuel carrier's entire structure sounded enough like a doomsday knell to convince her that the end had grown uncomfortably near.

"Vance!" The rising din of the overstrained engines forced Searles to shout to be heard across the narrow expanse of the fuel carrier's bridge. "The dilithium chamber's getting too hot! I have to shut the whole propulsion system down!"

"We have a *schedule* to keep, Jackie," said Kojiro Vance, who seemed far too calm and collected to have a firm grasp of the current situation.

Executive Officer Arturo Stiles, who stood beside the *Kobayashi Maru*'s eccentric master and commander, displayed a far better understanding of reality—as well as a good deal less equanimity. "What's the point of keeping to the schedule if we don't get where we're going in one piece?" he said.

The captain merely sat contemplatively in his worn leather-upholstered chair, stroking his chin as he weighed the dire warnings of his two most senior officers. For all Searles could tell, Vance might have been gazing into his closet and ruminating over which one of those damned pirate shirts he was going to wear next. She hated to think she might have no choice but to take command just to keep everyone aboard the *Maru* alive; there would be repercussions afterward, and the last thing she needed right now was to lose this job.

Correction, she thought. *The last thing I need is to get vaporized because my boss is obsessed with delivering the mail on time.*

Fortunately, Vance himself took that fateful decision out of her hands a moment later. "All right," the captain said, his shoulders sagging despite the broadening effect of the epaulet-like decorations that adorned his blousy tunic. He fixed her with an almost pleading gaze. "Take us out of warp, Jackie. At least until you can sort out what's going wrong back there."

Vance's order had scarcely left his lips before the exec hopped over the railing that separated him from one of the boxy forward duty stations, where he assisted a junior male crewman in entering the appropriate commands into the console. The young crewman, an engineer's mate named Simonson, looked as relieved as Searles felt; she wondered if he'd been about to stage a mutiny of his own.

This wasn't the first time Searles had justifiably feared that the alien contraptions she had reluctantly allowed into her engine room might do them all in. *Secret Vulcan gadgetry doesn't seem to come with a straightforward user's manual,* she thought, wishing Vance had never approached her with the stuff.

"We'll let her cool down for an hour or so before we try to bring the warp-power mains back online," Vance said, addressing nobody in particular as he made the first verbal footprints in the bridge's new-fallen blanket of silence.

Searles noticed then that Stiles was staring at her, an

urgent question burning in his dark eyes. The only answer she could offer him was a helpless shrug.

"I'd like a chance to pick up the pieces back in the engine room first," Searles said, casting her gaze back upon Vance. "*Then* we ought to decide how much downtime the main propulsion system is going to need."

Vance looked intensely uncomfortable with that, though he uttered nothing other than a muttered, half-intelligible curse. *Why do ship captains seem to think we engineers can get them special waivers for the laws of physics?* she thought.

"Captain, I think you and I need to have a word in private," said Stiles, his eyes hurling thunderbolts in Vance's direction.

"You'd better set the table for three, Captain," Searles said. *Looks like the jig is finally up,* she thought, feeling a sense of relief at the prospect of no longer having to protect an awkward secret on Vance's behalf. *Vance should have let his first mate in on this thing at the beginning.*

Vance sighed and chewed his lip as he stared off into the middle distance. Then he looked up, first at Stiles, then at Searles.

"All right. I owe the both of you at least that much." He rose from his chair and made a grand "after you" gesture toward one of the two doors located in the bridge's aft section. "In my cabin, if you please."

Arturo Stiles couldn't quite bring himself to accept the chair Vance had offered; until he'd had a chance to process the startling admission the captain had just made, he preferred to stand.

"So we've really come all this way to help the Vulcans set up a military listening post?" Stiles asked, gesticulating as though his hands were semaphore flags as he stood between the two places where the captain and the chief engineer were sitting. "Just when were you two planning on letting *me* in on this? I'm only the goddamn *first mate*, after all."

Vance met Stiles's roar with remarkable composure. "To be absolutely candid with you, Arturo, I *wasn't* planning on letting you in on this. I would have been content to quietly drop off a few of the personnel we've been carrying as passengers, along with a number of sealed crates, once we finished the voyage to the outskirts of Tezel-Oroko. Then we would have quietly returned to our original itinerary, with nobody the wiser."

Stiles still couldn't quite get his head around any of this. "But why keep it from *me*?"

Vance flashed that damned insouciant smile of his, the one that said, *Honey-this-isn't-what-it-looks-like-even-though-you've-caught-me-red-handed-canoodling-with-an-Orion-animal-woman.* "For your own protection, of course," the captain said.

"I don't get it, Vance. You're acting like a common smuggler. Have you gotten us involved in something illegal?" Stiles knew it wouldn't be the first time his skipper had played fast and loose either with interstellar law or the UESPA regs.

"*Illegal* and *clandestine* aren't necessarily synonymous things, Arturo," Vance said.

"You just told me that the *Maru* is secretly transporting both people and matériel on behalf of the Vulcans," Stiles said as he finally allowed his weight to land on the proffered chair. "Why would a race that can't even tell lies need to use an old Klingon rattletrap like the *Maru* as a secret courier?"

"Don't be so naïve, Arturo," said the chief engineer, crossing her legs on the low, lumpy couch near the desk behind which Vance reclined. "Vulcans lie like rugs, and you know it. They do it all the time; they just never got quite as good at it as we did."

Vance grinned. "And that fact may explain why humans and Vulcans seem to be so much stronger together than apart. It's a perfect partnership of brains and guile."

Stiles could barely suppress a volcanic surge of anger as he hiked a thumb toward Searles. "You didn't seem to have a problem letting our chief engineer in on the truth before now. And how did this Vulcan problem land in the *Maru*'s lap anyway?"

Vance spread his hands helplessly. "The Vulcans probably didn't think their own military or merchant vessels could maintain as low a profile as an Earth Cargo Service vessel could, what with the Klingons and the Romulans both so touchy lately about Coalition naval movements. So after the *Horizon* failed to make its cargo-pickup rendezvous with the *Maru*, it fell upon *us* to deliver what the *Horizon* would have carried to its final destination."

"And that meant we needed to make up for a considerable amount of lost time very quickly," Searles said.

"Right," Vance said. "Unfortunately, this vessel's maximum warp capability was simply not equal to the task."

That explains our sudden change to a hell-for-leather course all the way out to Tezel-Oroko, Stiles thought. He couldn't help but wonder whether any humans had ever before ventured out so far.

Or so fast.

"So the captain felt he had no one to turn to except me," Searles said. "If this, um, mission for the Vulcans was to stay on a completely need-to-know basis, that is."

Stiles thought he was beginning to understand the captain's need for secrecy, though he still felt insulted and deceived—and perhaps even a bit betrayed.

The exec cast a hard glare at Searles. "So how did you get this much giddy-up into an old bucket of stem bolts like the *Maru*, Jackie? Did the Vulcans help with that, too?"

She nodded. "Vance's contacts on Vulcan supplied the parts. I just turned the wrenches, with a little help from a couple of the experts bound for Tezel-Oroko."

The captain paused to clear his throat before he continued with the explanation-cum-briefing. "I had to resort to using certain . . . engine components that the Vulcan government had entrusted to me against an eventuality such as this one."

"What *kind* of components?" Stiles asked, his curiosity thoroughly piqued. He knew that the *Maru* would be able to make it the rest of the way to Tezel-Oroko in just a matter of a few hours, once her warp drive was back up and running; he'd never seen a human-piloted ship make that kind of time before, including Starfleet's fancy *NX*-class jobs.

Apparently responding to the blank look on the captain's face, Searles glanced up at the ceiling as she began reciting her mental list of the ad hoc modifications her warp drive had undergone. "A new antimatter flow regulator. A dilithium matrix wave-guide like nothing I've ever seen before. Something called a flux capacitor. And a couple of other things I wouldn't have recognized without a little help from one of our expert passengers."

Vance nodded. "One of the experts with pointed ears, that is. At any rate, I needed Jackie's cooperation to get all the new drive pieces properly installed, along with the systems designed to monitor them."

Those propulsion widgets must have still been in their packing crates when those Starfleet engineers were crawling through the Maru's *guts*, Stiles thought. He wondered how long Vance could have maintained his present cool demeanor had Captain Archer been the one challenging him with ticklish questions about secrecy, legality, and lies, Vulcan or otherwise.

Then it occurred to him that Starfleet would probably pay handsomely for access to those secret Vulcan engine parts. Arrogant, condescending bastards that they were, the Vulcans had always done their damnedest to curtail such wholesale transfers of technology from their world to Earth. Stiles wondered if their nearly century-old de facto technical embargo against humanity was finally about to end.

"No wonder those rabbit-eared elitists swore you to secrecy, Vance," Stiles said. "I never met a Vulcan who didn't at least drop a few broad hints that we Earth folk are still a little too wet behind the ears to venture out of our own solar system."

Vance made a noise of agreement. "If it had been up to the Vulcans, there'd be nothing in the Alpha Centauri system right now but ancient ruins and tumbleweeds. And the idea of humans flying a fuel carrier like the *Maru* under the flag of a settlement on Altair VI would be just another one of Doctor Cochrane's pipe dreams."

Searles put a hand to her chin as her forehead crumpled into an elaborate frown. "Kind of makes you wonder why the Vulcans would lend us this stuff, even with their own experts aboard the *Maru* to babysit us."

"Something out here must worry the Vulcans a little bit more than the prospect of warp-six-capable humans does," Vance said. "It would certainly explain why they'd want to set up a secret listening post to keep close tabs on it."

Stiles's thoughts drifted toward his own half-formed nightmare images of the mysterious Romulans, shadowy mental pictures derived from countless stories and rumors of fearsome warships whose bellies were painted to resemble the blood-red plumage of predatory birds. The Romulans would be the nearest likely subject of any Coalition listening post placed in this sector. Regardless, the Vulcans' decision to allow a human freighter crew to play with their supercharged high-warp goodies continued to puzzle him.

His spine shuddered with the cold of the grave as the simplest possible explanation of the Vulcans' largesse occurred to him: *Maybe they really don't expect us to survive any encounter with whatever might be lurking out here.*

A moment later, the *Kobayashi Maru* shook as though the Hephaestus of Earth's ancient mythology had just slammed his hammer right into the ship's vitals. Searles cried out as Vance's office fell under a blanket of darkness. Stiles immediately experienced the stomach-churning freefall sensation that signaled the abrupt failure of the gravity plating. And he could hear Vance speaking in the darkness, his voice as understated as she had ever heard it.

"Uh-oh," the captain said.

FORTY-TWO

SEATED AT THE DESK in his ready room, Jonathan Archer listened to the joint report from T'Pol and Reed in almost meditative silence. T'Pol wrapped up the brief presentation with a solemn dignity that Archer usually associated with eulogies.

"By now," she said, "Trip has already reached Romulus."

Where he's probably already had to face whatever rough justice Admiral Valdore had in store for him, Archer thought. Though he respected Trip's abilities both as an engineer and as a highly survival-adept Starfleet officer, he hadn't been an intel operative all that long, and Archer knew that Valdore was no fool either.

He despaired of seeing his friend ever again.

"Unfortunately, our encounter with Trip didn't change the Coalition's current tactical situation in any way that really matters," Reed said, looking nearly as mournful as Archer felt. "He still has to get his hands on workable warp-seven engine plans, though this may be simply because the Romulans themselves have yet to come up with a completely workable design. And his Romulan intelligence sources had him convinced that the *Klingons* were the ones behind the attacks against Draylax and our shipping lanes, rather than any Romulan culprits."

Archer nodded, becoming all but resigned to the bleak prospect of a hot war with the Klingons; it was beginning to look inevitable, despite the evidence Archer had found exculpating the Klingon Empire, which had no present hostile intentions toward any member of the Coalition of Worlds.

But we just might kick over the anthill anyway, he thought. *And touch off a conflict that will cripple most of two quadrants for decades, and probably kill millions of innocents on both sides. The Klingons will consider us shoot-on-sight enemies then, sure as gravity. And the Romulans will sit back and laugh through the entire bloodbath, waiting until both sides are too weak to stop them from swooping in to pick up the pieces. . . .*

The intercom on Archer's desk whistled, presenting a welcome interruption to the captain's gloomy ruminations. Toggling the channel open, he said, "Archer here. Go ahead."

"We're receiving a priority communication from Starfleet, Captain," said Hoshi, a note of urgency audible in her voice. *"It's Admiral Gardner."*

"Thanks, Hoshi. Pipe it straight to my ready room, please."

Archer wasted no time activating the blank monitor atop his desk, which quickly shifted to the weary but hyperalert visage of Sam Gardner. T'Pol and Reed immediately began moving toward the ready room door to give Archer some privacy, but stopped after he motioned them to stay and positioned his monitor so that its visual sensor pickups showed the admiral everyone present in the room. The motion forced him to suppress a wince of pain, a reminder of his ordeal on Qo'noS.

The silver-haired admiral noted the presence of Archer's subordinates with a nod, and then focused solely on the captain. *"Archer, you* still *look like hell,"* Gardner said with a sympathetic nod before abruptly switching into his "all-business" mode. *"Captain, the Coalition Security Council has been busy evaluating the evidence you brought back from Qo'noS. From where I'm sitting, it appears to have changed everything."*

Archer forced himself to absorb this apparent good news with at least some degree of caution. "I hope that's a change for the better, Admiral," he said.

Gardner nodded again. *"It is. Because the Klingons have made no aggressive moves against us since you delivered their ultimatum, the Coalition Security Council has tabled all plans to adopt an aggressive defensive posture against the Klingon Empire. Even the hotheads on Andoria have agreed to hold their horses a while longer—unless they believe the Klingons to be acting in direct defiance of the ultimatum."* A small, relieved smile somehow slipped out onto the admiral's otherwise granite-hard countenance, reminding Archer that few people are more reticent about wars than the hardened warriors charged with fighting them. *"Well done, Captain."*

"Thank you, sir," Archer said. "Let's hope we can keep the proverbial dogs on their leashes this time."

Gardner's smile abruptly vanished. *"We still may not have that luxury. Starfleet Command has just received word that Centauri III and the Calder II science outpost have come under attack."*

"Do you believe the Klingons to be responsible for either of those attacks, Admiral?" T'Pol asked.

Training his suddenly narrowed eyes squarely upon T'Pol, the admiral said, *"Not as far as we can determine, Commander."*

Thank God, Archer thought, though he remained uneasy. So long as the Coalition Council remained balanced on the razor's edge of a declaration of war against the Klingon Empire, whose ships had already been proven to be vulnerable to hijacking by a hostile third party, he was certain he was going to continue feeling that way. He could only hope that the evidence that he and Phlox had found on Qo'noS would prevent the Council's more hawkish members from going off half-cocked should the Klingons appear to have defied the Coalition's ultimatum.

"The Romulans must be responsible, sir," Malcolm said. "It's got to be the Romulans."

Breaking eye contact with T'Pol, Gardner shook his head. *"We've found no definitive evidence of that either, Lieutenant."*

"Then who *is* responsible?" Archer wanted to know.

"Brief transmissions from Columbia *and from personnel at Calder II have tentatively identified the aggressors in both attacks as* Vulcan *military vessels. The hostiles appear to have jammed outgoing communications in both locations before we could learn any additional details. Starfleet Command is trying to keep this information under wraps, of course, for obvious reasons.*

"But Command had to inform the United Earth Council."

"And they jumped to the conclusion that this was true?" Archer asked. "They've seen the Klingon recordings. How could they consider blaming Vulcan?"

"Captain, I don't need to remind you that many people have problems with the Vulcans. They have never understood why they held humanity back, insisting that humans were not ready to move into deep space."

Archer was having trouble accepting any of this. "The problems I've had with the Vulcans over the years have never been a secret, Admiral. But I can't believe that Vulcan would ever—"

"No, neither do I. But I answer to Earth's government, as do you, Captain. However, it has been suggested that Commander T'Pol be relieved and confined."

T'Pol's only response was to lift a single eyebrow in an evident gesture of defiance. Reed looked on in openly astonished silence.

"With all due respect, sir, I'll be damned if I'm throwing my exec into the brig. . . ."

Gardner held up a hand to forestall any further argument. *"I said it was 'suggested.' While the Council believes their eyes, Starfleet believes there is a more devious force behind this. You're not the only one fostering a new alliance; Starfleet shared all of this data with the Vulcans."*

"Romulans," Archer offered. Finally someone at Command was listening. "The Romulans may have just found a way to defeat us without firing a shot. All they need to do is drive wedges of suspicion *between* members of the Coalition. And the best way to start is to convince one Coalition world that another member has turned against it.

"Admiral. Please don't tell me that Starfleet has gone so far as to place Soval and his aides under arrest."

"Captain," Gardner said in scolding tones. *"Starfleet Command and the United Earth government don't want this Coalition to come apart any more than you do. But Starfleet will have to enforce Earth's decisions once they're made"*

"Fair enough, Admiral."

"Let's both hope that Earth understands that whatever's happening at Alpha Centauri and Calder is probably analogous to what those rogue Klingon ships did at Draylax."

Archer nodded. *"Enterprise* is a lot closer to the Calder system than Alpha Centauri. At maximum warp we can reach Calder II in—"

Gardner interrupted him again. *"No. The Calder II outpost is small and almost entirely defenseless. There probably won't be anything left of it by the time you arrive."*

Archer glanced at Reed, whose rueful nod tacitly endorsed the admiral's coldly factual tactical assessment.

"Understood," Archer said, facing his terminal again. "We'll head straight to Alpha Centauri then, and do whatever we can to reinforce Centauri III's defenses."

"*Negative,*" said the admiral. "*Columbia is on her way, since she's already in the Alpha Centauri sector.*"

Archer couldn't believe Gardner wanted *Columbia* to face the threat alone. "Captain Hernandez deserves to have *Enterprise* at her back," he said. "Even if we have to get to the party a little bit late."

Looking a little regretful, the admiral shook his head again. "*No. I'm afraid another problem has come up. A . . . backchannel joint operation that Command has been involved with. And* Enterprise *is the only vessel currently in position to deal with it in time.*"

Archer closed his eyes for a moment and stroked his forehead, behind which a knot of intense pain—an agony utterly unrelated to the aftermath of his combat on Qo'noS—had begun to form. "Admiral, what could be a higher priority for *Enterprise* than what's happening right now at Alpha Centauri and Calder?"

Archer was glad he was already sitting down when he heard the admiral's answer: "*A fuel carrier called the* Kobayashi Maru."

FORTY-THREE

JACQUELINE SEARLES TRIED not to think about how much
freefall always made her want to puke.

The *Maru*'s bridge was as dark as a proverbial tomb
until the dim, red emergency lighting reluctantly flared
to life. Searles breathed a silent prayer of thanks that
the fuel carrier's perpetually expense-averse skipper had
finally heeded her repeated requests that he bankroll
the upgraded backup redundancies she'd installed late
last year.

*Too bad he was willing to settle for the cheapo brand-X
artificial gravity plating, though,* she thought as her stomach lurched. Her gorge rose to a higher orbit as Simonson drifted into view; the young pilot's neck was bent
into an unnatural shape that vaguely resembled a question mark. She didn't want to think about how many
others aboard the *Maru* might have shared Simonson's
fate. Moving with cautious deliberation, she secured the
dead man to one of the chairs at an unoccupied duty
station and somehow resisted the urge to become violently ill.

I must be in shock. Moving on autopilot.

"What the hell did we hit?" Vance said as he launched
his weightless form from console to console with surprising grace.

Employing considerably less grace, Stiles clung to

one of the ops consoles as though his very life depended on it. He pounded on its side, bringing it back to a blinking, flickering semblance of normalcy using a technique he liked to call "percussive maintenance."

"Dunno just yet," the exec said. "But it's for damned sure we didn't run over a cat. Thank God you managed to get through to Earth on the compic, Vance."

A fat lot of good that's going to do us right now, Searles thought. She wondered idly how many weeks it would take for a ship from Earth to reach this remote part of the Gamma Hydra sector.

Orienting herself so that she faced one of the forward stations, Searles pushed off against a section of wall near the bridge's ceiling. Her inner ear had convinced her body that she was plunging downward at breakneck speed, despite the evidence of her eyes, which confirmed that she was moving fairly slowly relative to the console.

She drifted across the three meters or so of space that still separated her from the console, into which she slammed with a surprisingly hard and loud thump. Scrambling to avoid caroming off in some random direction, a slave both to microgravity and to her own inertia, she grabbed one of the console's gravity-failure handholds—designed for this very sort of mishap—and began checking the internal com grid. The ship's intercom network was pretty thoroughly jammed up, with upwards of three hundred people trying to call the bridge simultaneously to find out what was going on. Rebooting the console allowed at least a few individual voices to separate themselves from the background gabble of the rest of the multitude.

"What's going on in the rest of the ship?" Vance called out, cutting through the cacophony.

"We have a lot of dead and injured in the passenger

and crew areas," she said, disabling the speakers to keep the horrific noise from drowning out all conversation on the bridge. A horrible bleakness shrouded her soul as she paused to speculate on whether the dead might be the lucky ones, with rescue such an unlikely option this far from Earth.

"Those cloak-and-dagger Vulcan passengers of yours must be responsible for this somehow, Vance," Stiles said, all but accusing the captain of blowing up the ship himself.

"We've got massive hull breaches, Captain," Searles said, interpreting the multiple alarms she saw on her console.

"Drive status?" Vance asked with a note of hope that Searles wished she could share.

Searles punched a button on the com console, nearly launching herself willy-nilly into the microgravity environment in the process. "Searles to engine room," she said into the voice interface. "Engine room, come in."

Nothing. Just like the first attempt she'd made back in Vance's office.

Searles noticed then that the *Maru*'s exec was frantically entering commands into one of the adjacent bridge consoles. "Arturo, I've got to get back to the engine room. Find out if my people—"

"It's going to have to wait, Jackie," Stiles said. "The hull breaches made the emergency bulkheads slam shut."

"Do we have any idea yet why this is happening?" Searles asked.

He shook his head. "I'm still not sure about that. At least I don't think we were fired upon."

"Why not?" Searles said, her brow crinkling.

"Because if somebody had wanted to blow us to kingdom come with, say, a torpedo of some kind, then they probably already would have launched a second one by now, and finished us off already." Stiles paused, frowning at his console. "Hey, why am I picking up such heavy graviton counts in here?"

Searles shrugged. "Beats me. With the gravity plating offline, the graviton levels ought to be way *below* normal."

"Then the gravitons must be leaking in from *outside* the *Maru*," said Stiles.

Vance launched himself quickly into the space between Searles and Stiles, using one of the emergency handholds to bring himself to a stop.

"The Romulans and the Klingons have gone to war a number of times over control of this sector," he said. "And the Romulans have been known to use gravitic mines to defend their territorial claims."

"Gravitic mines?" Stiles said, an eyebrow raised.

"I've heard of them," Searles said, nodding. "They're compact, high-yield graviton generators designed to focus the equivalent of huge tidal energies on a vessel's hull, or on its spaceframe."

"What?" Stiles said, his eyes glazing visibly in response to her explanation.

"Fancy bomb," Searles clarified. "Make part of the ship go *boom*. Sometimes more than one part, and not always all at once."

"Oh. So we still might take even *more* damage from the same damned weapon. Crap."

"Could be worse," Searles said. "If that mine had clipped one of our neutronic fuel tanks, we wouldn't be having this conversation."

The exec turned toward his captain. "Vance, you're a gambling man. If you were handicapping our chances of getting rescued out here, how would you estimate the odds?"

The orange "incoming" light on the com panel near Searles began flashing insistently at that precise moment. A calm, reassuringly competent-sounding female voice emerged from the hash of static that issued from the speakers.

"Kobayashi Maru, *this is* Enterprise. *We are on our way to your present position.*"

Searles watched as a broad grin spread across Vance's face. "I'd say our odds just got a hell of a lot better, Arturo."

Searles allowed herself the luxury of hope, if only for a moment.

Then she heard and felt the low rumble, which immediately preceded a great roar and a gale-force wind that slammed her backward into one of the battered monitors.

FORTY-FOUR

Tuesday, July 22, 2155
***Enterprise* NX-01, Gamma Hydra sector**

AFTER ARCHER SIGNED off with Gardner and returned to the bridge, the Starfleet Academy cadets' code for imponderable mysteries kept swirling through his mind.

Whiskey. Tango. Foxtrot.

Mentally translating those time-honored military placeholders into less polite nonmilitary parlance, he thought, *What. The. Fuck.*

"The *Kobayashi Maru*?" Reed asked from his position at the bridge's tactical station. "I find it hard to believe that Starfleet considers that rattletrap a priority."

Seated in the big chair in the bridge's center, Archer spread his hands. "That's our mission, Malcolm. We are to guarantee that vessel's safety, at all costs."

According to Gardner, Starfleet regarded the beleaguered fuel carrier's mission as critically important to both of its covert sponsors, Starfleet and the Vulcan High Command—even if Earth now harbored doubts about its partnership with Vulcan. Recognizing how vital a secret listening post in the Gamma Hydra sector could be to Coalition security vis-à-vis both the Klingons and the Romulans—after all, both empires still occasionally fought each other for control of the region—Archer could find no reason to question the admiral's orders, however unorthodox they might seem on the surface.

He only wished he could help *Columbia*. Her captain and crew now had to face peril alone.

What *Enterprise* needed was more speed, but Archer already knew there was no way to open the throttle any wider—not without transforming the starship into a light-year-long plume of ionized debris. The vibrations in the deck beneath his boots confirmed that Mike Burch down in engineering had already pushed *Enterprise*'s mighty warp-five propulsion system as far as he could.

Archer glanced toward the portside communications station, where Ensign Sato continued her tireless efforts to raise the stricken freighter. "*Kobayashi Maru*, repeat your message, please. This is *Enterprise*. Repeat, we are on our way to your present position. Please confirm your status."

Archer leaned forward anxiously. "Travis, how soon will we reach the coordinates Admiral Gardner sent us?"

Travis gave his chair a half turn away from his helm console and toward the captain. "We're leaving Gamma Hydra, section fifteen, Captain. Entering section fourteen at coordinates twenty-two by eighty-seven by four. That still puts us nearly twenty minutes away from the *Kobayashi Maru*, sir."

Archer nodded to Travis, then glanced at Hoshi, who continued frantically working her console.

"Anything yet, Hoshi?"

"I'm relying on the computer to enhance the carrier signal, sir." The youthful com officer's usually smooth-as-porcelain forehead wrinkled slightly as she concentrated. She adjusted her earpiece and tried again to distinguish the cry of a single voice from the background roar of a cosmic ocean.

She shook her head sadly a moment later. "I thought

I had them for a moment, but the signal keeps degrading. Their com system might have sustained some damage, and I'm picking up a lot of interference on the other end—"

A burst of fragmented voice commingled with a shrill squall of static interrupted her, the rush of noise pouring from the bridge speakers in a torrent. "—*imperative! This is the* Kobayashi Maru, *nineteen periods out of Altair VI. We have struck a gravitic mine and have lost all power! Our hull is penetrated and we have sustained many casualties*—"

Despite the layers of distortion imposed by both distance and disaster, Archer immediately recognized the English-accented voice on the other end of the channel as that of Kojiro Vance, the flamboyant master of the S.S. *Kobayashi Maru.*

"*Kobayashi Maru,* this is *Enterprise,*" Hoshi said, her fingers entering commands at a brisk pace as she tried to isolate and enhance the tenuous subspace lifeline she had just reestablished. "Please confirm your position."

"Enterprise, *our position is Gamma Hydra, section ten. Hull penetrated. Life-support systems failing. Can you assist us,* Enterprise? *Can you assist us?*"

"Hoshi, tell Captain Vance he won't have to hang on for more than another twenty minutes, tops," Archer said. "*Enterprise* isn't going to let the *Kobayashi Maru* sink."

Hoshi nodded. As she busied herself relaying his reassurances, Archer hoped he hadn't just promised Vance the impossible.

FORTY-FIVE

Tuesday, July 22, 2155
Columbia **NX-02, near the Alpha Centauri system**

"The new arrivals are not answering our hails either, Captain," said Ensign Sidra Valerian.

Now why doesn't that surprise me? Hernandez thought as she leaned forward in her command chair. She barely succeeded in holding back a cough precipitated by the ozone-tinged air with which neither the bridge ventilation fans nor the fire-suppression system seemed quite able to cope.

Though many of the bridge consoles and monitors had been rendered inoperable during the last exchange of fire with the Vulcans, there was nothing wrong with the central viewer, which gave her a crystal-clear view of several of the ring-and-spear-shaped vessels of Earth's former friends as they came about to begin what they no doubt intended to be their final concerted attack. Since the Vulcan reinforcements had arrived on the scene, Hernandez had lost count of just how many guns must be trained on *Columbia*'s vitals at the moment.

Talk about overkill, she thought. *Leave it to the Vulcans to leave absolutely nothing to chance. These guys must be the original belt-and-suspenders personality types.*

Hernandez turned toward Veronica Fletcher, who stood beside the command chair, her body as taut as a bowstring. "Recommendation, Commander?"

"I recommend we run like hell," *Columbia*'s laconic first officer said.

"With all the battle damage she's taken today, Commander, *Columbia* can barely *limp*, much less *run*," said Lieutenant Commander el-Rashad, the Syrian science officer. "Even if we were five-by-five right now, I doubt we could outrun their slowest ship."

Hernandez smacked the intercom on her chair with the side of her hand, opening a channel. "Hernandez to engineering."

"Graylock here," came the chief engineer's Austrian-accented response. *"I already know why you're calling, Captain, so I must apologize in advance."*

Hernandez closed her eyes. "Go ahead and give me the bad news, Karl."

"The warp core is still down, and the relays and energizers are completely fertiggemacht. *I'm going to need several days, at least, to pick up the pieces."*

Hernandez thought she knew Graylock well enough not to have to question the man's Teutonic pragmatism. Though she had seen him work miracles, Hernandez knew she couldn't expect him to do the flat-out impossible.

"Do what you can, Karl. Hernandez out." *Probably for the very last time.*

"I hope this sort of thing isn't happening anywhere *else* in Coalition space right now," Fletcher said, her voice pitched in that low "for-the-captain's-ears-only" tone that she used when she didn't want to exacerbate the anxieties of the rest of the bridge crew.

Amen to that, Hernandez thought.

"The new arrivals are powering up their weapons," said Lieutenant Thayer, the young woman running the starboard weapons console. Though the console was still functioning, using it now struck Hernandez as hardly any less futile than trying to run any of the burned and melted instrument panels nearby.

"I'm detecting active weapons locks, Captain," el-Rashad said, his voice rising to a pitch half an octave above its normal register. Up on the screen, the weapons tubes of each of the newly arrived Vulcan vessels exuded an extremely noticeable, menacing glow.

Hernandez swallowed. "Polarize the hull plating, Kiona," she said to Thayer. "And launch the log buoy."

Thayer scowled down at her console and shook her head. "Hull charging system is down, Captain. As is the buoy-jettison system."

"Thanks for the epitaph, Kiona," Hernandez said. She rose, turning so that she faced her officers en masse before adding, "It's been an honor serving with you all."

To their credit, every member of the bridge crew continued to maintain focus on his or her particular job, even as noises of enthusiastic agreement went around the room, punctuated by brief but obviously heartfelt, respectful glances cast at Hernandez.

No tears, she told herself firmly. *No time for tears. No time for* anything.

"The reinforcement vessels are opening fire," el-Rashad said with a calm that befitted the man's conviction that death was merely an anteroom to a far better place than the material world.

Wish I could bring myself to believe things like that, Hernandez thought as she turned back toward the screen and took her seat.

She was glad she'd somehow managed to resist the all but overwhelming urge to close her eyes before the end came.

The weapons tubes on each of the recently arrived Vulcan ships emitted brilliant globular flares that would have been blinding had the luminosity filters on *Columbia*'s external visual sensors not intervened to dim them. A pair of the Vulcan ships that had damaged *Columbia* earlier suddenly went ablaze, large areas of their hulls engulfed almost instantly by short-lived molecular fires, conflagrations fed both by the weapons of their attackers and the wounded vessels' own escaping atmospheres.

Relief warred with an overwhelming sense of déjà vu as Hernandez realized what she was witnessing: *The Vulcans are opening fire on their own ships!*

"Didn't we just see this exact same holovid last week at Draylax?" Fletcher said as she blew several thick strands of blond hair away from her eyes, perhaps in an effort to cover a loud, irrepressible sigh of relief.

"One time is an anomaly," Hernandez said, nodding. She watched as the silent yet fiery pageant of ship-to-ship carnage continued before her stunned, horrified, fascinated eyes. "But twice . . ."

"But *twice*," said Fletcher, finishing the captain's thought out of long-honed practice, "is a conspiracy."

And we'd damned well better flush out the Romulan snakes who are really behind *the conspiracy,* Hernandez thought, her backbone chilled as though it had somehow just become exposed to the hard vacuum that lay beyond the protective confines of *Columbia*'s outer hull. *Or else we're liable to see a hell of a lot more scenes just like this one all across Coalition space.*

"Lifesign readings, Kalil?" she asked, turning toward el-Rashad's station.

He shook his head. "None that I can pick up, Captain. But that *can't* be right. The sensor array must be damaged."

Hernandez turned back toward the helm. "Reiko, do we have maneuvering thrusters?"

"Barely," said Lieutenant Reiko Akagi, the senior helm officer.

"What do you have in mind, Captain?" Fletcher said.

"I want to get a closer look at one of those crippled ships, Veronica. Jonathan Archer convinced me that the Romulans must have been behind the attack on Coridan, as well as most of the other weirdness that's happened since then."

The exec frowned as she mulled the matter over. "What's in all this for the Romulans?"

"If they can convince Alpha Centauri and Earth that the Vulcan High Command can't be trusted, they could split the Coalition right along its natural fault lines," Hernandez said. A development like that would surely spread terror throughout several adjacent sectors, blunting any attempt to mount a serious organized resistance to a Romulan conquest.

The bastards could overwhelm Earth, and have their flag flying over Starfleet Headquarters, Hernandez thought. *That is, if they even* use *flags.*

Not for the first time, she wondered what a real live Romulan actually looked like.

Fletcher nodded. "I suppose that would give an aggressive empire one less big, organized rival to worry about."

"I want to get to the bottom of it," Hernandez said. "One way or another."

"I'm not sure we'll get the chance," el-Rashad said as he leaned over the hooded scanner unit built into his console. "I'm getting extremely erratic energy readings from some of those damaged vessels."

"Warp-core overloads," said Fletcher. "They must be doing it deliberately."

Damn! Hernandez thought. She focused her gaze on the panoply of gutted and still-burning ships that now drifted across the central viewer. Several were still sustaining grievous, scorching phase-cannon hits, courtesy of the most recently arrived Vulcan vessels.

A few moments later, the fusillades ceased; the reinforcement vessels turned, their impulse engines flaring a brilliant Doppler red as they left their victims behind.

"I'm reading runaway reactor cores on *all* the damaged ships now," el-Rashad said. "They're going to start going off like a string of firecrackers in two, three minutes, tops."

"Of course," Hernandez said. *The Romulans who must actually be piloting those ships need to cover their tracks, whatever it takes. They can't afford to risk letting us discover anything that might vindicate the Vulcans.*

"Back us away, Reiko," Hernandez said, facing the helmsman. "Take us to a safe distance, best speed at impulse." Turning toward the aft com console, she added, "Sidra, keep hailing the, ah, newcomers. Let them know we could use some assistance."

The word "newcomers" felt increasingly awkward in Hernandez's mouth, inasmuch as those ships had already put thousands of kilometers between their sterns and the flotilla to which they'd laid waste.

"Aye, Captain," the communications officer said. "I've been repeating our hail ever since they arrived, but they're still not responding. On top of that, our subspace transmitter is kind of . . . balky at the moment. Maybe the Vulcans just aren't receiving us."

"They're going to warp," Akagi said. A moment later, the retreating Vulcan vessels—which Hernandez assumed to be the only truly genuine articles *Columbia* had encountered today—vanished in a rapidly collapsing nimbus of light.

How very Vulcan of them, Hernandez thought. *They'll*

go to the trouble of saving your life, but they won't stick around to ask if you need any help fixing your flat tires.

"I guess we can't blame the Vulcans for not wanting to stay around to chat," Fletcher said. "After all, it's got to be embarrassing as hell when your ships go rogue and start attacking your allies."

Hernandez nodded. *The Vulcans must be at least as embarrassed about this as the Klingons were when the same thing happened to them at Draylax.*

Sitting pensively in her command chair, she watched the viewer, upon which each of the hostile vessels exploded like distant eruptions of ball lightning, each blast separated from the next by only a few seconds.

And hoped with all her heart that the detonations didn't symbolize the gradual self-immolation of the Coalition of Planets.

Valerian cried out from the com station. "Captain! I'm receiving something from Starfleet."

Hernandez spun her chair hard in Valerian's direction. "You've got the com system up and working again. Good work."

"Reception is still iffy, Captain, and transmitting anything is out of the question until I can get the entire com system pulled out for an overhaul," Valerian said, sounding apologetic.

"One thing at a time, Sidra," Hernandez said. "What does Starfleet have to say?"

The com officer adjusted her earpiece, staring straight ahead as she concentrated, no doubt trying to focus past a great deal of static to make sense of what she was hearing. "There's another attack just like this one in progress elsewhere in Coalition space, Captain. The target is the Earth outpost at Calder II."

Unlike Alpha Centauri, which had sizable human populations and at least *some* defenses, Calder II was home only to a small, all but unprotected science station.

"Whose ships?"

"Vulcan ships again, Captain."

Piloted by more Romulans, no doubt, Hernandez thought. *Romulans who probably took over the very ships the Vulcan High Command assigned to discourage piracy in the Calder sector.* Horror jolted her almost like an electrical shock as she projected what the attackers were almost certain to do next with their purloined fleet.

"I don't get it," Thayer said from the tactical console. "Why attack a small target like Calder II?"

"Isn't it obvious, Lieutenant?" said Fletcher, her ashen face telling Hernandez that her exec was thinking along exactly the same lines as her captain. "It won't take the Romulans long to wipe out a couple hundred scientists and their families. Then they'll have the whole planet to use as a beachhead for attacking Vulcan, Alpha Centauri—"

Hernandez interrupted. "And Earth."

Shi'Kahr, Vulcan

"I have just received word that the hijacked vessels attacking Alpha Centauri have all been neutralized, Minister," said Minister Kuvak, desert sunlight streaming in from behind him through the partially open office door.

T'Pau, first minister of the recently reconstituted global civilian government now known as the Confederacy of Vulcan, nodded a silent acknowledgment to her silver-haired aide. She could sense from the tension in his posture that Kuvak had not yet finished delivering the latest news—and that what he had yet to report would prove even less pleasant than the tidings from Alpha Centauri.

"And what of the assault against Calder II?" T'Pau asked as she rose from behind her simple yet gracefully curved desk. Although Calder II's scientific outpost was primarily populated, staffed, and administered by humans, the Vulcan government had taken a strong interest in the settlement for decades.

As the lower-ranking government minister took a moment to assemble his thoughts, T'Pau studiously avoided commenting upon his all-too-evident lack of composure.

"Starfleet's forces may have arrived too late, First Minister," the middle-aged Vulcan said a moment later. "As have ours, apparently. Early reports are sporadic, of course. But the hostiles may have already succeeded in establishing a military toehold at Calder."

Hostiles, T'Pau thought. *It is a fine euphemism.*

T'Pau stood stock-still in the center of her office. The sparsely appointed stone-veneer walls, bare but for a single minimalist meditation tapestry, now seemed somehow too busy, too stimulating to look upon as she struggled to master her own rising fear and agitation.

"Summon all the senior *enriov* of the High Command," she said. "And alert the entire High Assembly, as well as the Coalition Security Council."

"I shall do so at once," Kuvak said just before he disappeared through the same doorway he'd used to enter the office.

T'Pau continued to stand alone in the room's center, feeling a bereft sense of desolation she hadn't experienced since Syrran had died protecting Surak's *katra* from the predations of Administrator V'Las, T'Pau's ousted predecessor.

Surak had always believed that the logic of peace transcended all other considerations. T'Pau, however, was becoming bitterly aware that such logic often broke down when one was beset by uncompromising, rapacious hostiles such as those who had just attacked Alpha Centauri and Calder.

Especially when those hostiles were Romulans, misguided cousins of Surak's children, bent on destroying everything that Vulcan and her allies had worked so hard to create.

FORTY-SIX

Gamma Hydra sector

THE MORE TIME HE SPENT on the busy bridge of Sopek's bird-of-prey, the warier Trip felt.

Why hasn't the bastard just tossed me into a cell? Trip thought as he ran a hand slowly over the bridge console to which the Vulcan-Romulan double agent had posted him. Since the console was out of order—its lone functioning monitor displayed a blood-green pictogram proclaiming that it had been closed down temporarily for diagnostics and repair—Trip assumed that Sopek didn't expect him to be able to do much harm here, right out in plain sight, no less.

But why is he letting me anywhere near any of this stuff, whether it's working or not? It can't be because he's decided he trusts *me all of a sudden.*

Glancing toward the hulking armed *uhlan* who stood watching him from beside the nearest turbolift entrance, Trip realized that Sopek might have allowed him onto the bridge for reasons altogether unrelated to trust. The situation brought to mind a twentieth-century flatvid film, an organized-crime drama that he had seen with T'Pol on a long-ago Movie Night back aboard *Enterprise,* years ago and parsecs away. According to one of the gangsters portrayed in the film, it was best not only to keep one's friends close, but also to keep one's enemies *closer.*

Maybe Sopek even thinks there's a chance I'll volunteer

to sign up with his own warp-seven engineering team if he holds me captive long enough.

The exclamation of a junior com officer interrupted Trip's ruminations. "Commander Ch'uihv! I am picking up a subspace transmission from the vicinity of Tezel-Oroko."

"Put it on audio, Sublieutenant," said the bird-of-prey's commander, whom Trip still had trouble thinking of by any name other than his Vulcan nom de guerre, Sopek.

A crackling rush of static heralded the panicked utterance of a deeply terrified-sounding human male. *"—imperative! This is the* Kobayashi Maru, *nineteen periods out of Altair VI. We have struck a gravitic mine and have lost all power! Our hull is penetrated and we have sustained many casualties—"*

Extremely conscious of the disruptor-carrying *uhlan* who continued to eye him from the rear of the bridge, Trip moved away from his dead console and cautiously approached the central command chair upon which Ch'uihv/Sopek sat.

"Is this the freighter you mentioned?" Trip asked, trying to pitch his voice so that only the captain could hear him clearly. "The one that's carrying the spy gear you said you wanted to help Earth and Vulcan set up at Tezel-Oroko?"

The other man only nodded before looking down at a small display screen built into the arm of his chair; whatever it showed lay just outside Trip's immediate line of sight.

"Well, aren't we going to rescue her?" Trip asked, scarcely able to contain his mounting impatience.

"Something tells me we might not have to, Commander," Sopek said, still staring down at his hidden display.

A moment later, another human voice rose above the background hum of the bridge's instruments. "Kobayashi Maru, *this is* Enterprise. *Please confirm your position.*"

Hoshi! Trip experienced the first real surge of hope he'd allowed himself to feel since he'd encountered T'Pol and Malcolm at Taugus III.

"Enterprise, *our position is Gamma Hydra, section ten,*" said the frightened man aboard the freighter. "*Hull penetrated. Life-support systems failing. Can you assist us,* Enterprise? *Can you assist us?*"

"Kobayashi Maru," Hoshi said. "*We're on our way to you now. Please stand by. We'll reach your coordinates in approximately twenty minutes.*"

Trip craned his neck in an attempt to gauge the freighter's position relative to Sopek's vessel, making a few quick mental conversions and translations in the process.

He turned back toward Sopek quickly enough to prompt the *uhlan* to reach for his weapon. "We could reach the *Kobayashi Maru* and start a rescue operation nearly *twice* as quickly as *Enterprise* can."

"We could indeed, Commander," Sopek said, apparently unfazed by Trip's accusatory tone.

Understanding was settling uncomfortably onto Trip's consciousness, like a heavy, smothering blanket. "But that's not what you're planning to do, is it?" At the moment he didn't care what the rest of the crew heard, and it seemed clear that neither did Sopek.

The other man shook his head. "Regrettably, no. We cannot afford to be too close to the freighter when Valdore's people engage their *arrenhe'hwiua* telecapture system against it. It's going to happen very soon." .

Trip scowled. "How the hell could *you* know so much about Valdore's plans?"

Before Sopek could say so much as a word, the answer to Trip's own question now seemed blindingly obvious to him: The only plausible way for this man to know as much as he did about sensitive military matters like the new Romulan starship-telecapture system—while apparently running a dissident group with impunity—would be if he had been secretly working for Valdore all along, allowing the admiral to use him to test the loyalty of underlings like Ehrehin and Terix.

This man could stand astride the twilight espionage worlds of both Vulcan and Romulus, posing as an enemy of the latter while discreetly pushing buttons on Admiral Valdore's behalf.

An even simpler but far more chilling explanation for Sopek's behavior toward him occurred to Trip then: *What if this cruel son of a bitch is only keeping me alive to make me watch the bloodbath he's really planning?*

The only answer the other man offered to Trip's question-cum-accusation was an enigmatic half-smile. The mannerism prompted Trip to wonder, not for the first time, whether this man had been born Vulcan or Romulan.

"Have a seat now, Commander," Sopek said, his smile hardening into something akin to sharpened steel. "I don't want you getting underfoot after the crew and I become preoccupied dealing with the *arrenhe'hwiua* system's target."

Trip nodded. Hyperconscious of the armed *uhlan*'s watchful eye, he slowly moved toward a nearby unattended console, one that lay even closer to Sopek than the dead panel to which he had been posted earlier. *He wants to "deal with" the Romulan weapon's target,* Trip thought. *He's not here to help the* Kobayashi Maru *establish an Earth-Vulcan listening post. He's here to stamp it out.*

He wondered ruefully whether his suspicions were well founded, or if he had merely—finally—started to *think* like a Romulan.

"We are venting atmosphere rapidly, Enterprise!*"* said the increasingly frantic voice from the wounded freighter.

If Sopek really is secretly Valdore's guy, Trip thought, *then he might be the one who's really running the telecapture gadget he seems to know so damned much about. And he would probably have to do it all from* this *ship.*

"Enterprise!" the man on the *Kobayashi Maru* cried, barely outshouting the background deluge of static. *"We have very little time left to us!"*

The repetition of the name of the ship that had been his home for four years brought another horrifying realization in for a hard landing right on top of Trip's soul: With the *Kobayashi Maru* so badly damaged, it made no sense to bring the Romulan Empire's new starship-hijacking device to bear against her.

Enterprise, however, was quite another matter.

Trip sat on the chair beside the new console, staying directly in Sopek's line of sight so as not to rouse any undue suspicion. *Captain Archer wouldn't let a whole field of gravitic mines keep him from trying to pull off a rescue operation,* he thought. *Especially if he knows about the* Kobayashi Maru*'s secret mission.*

Trip didn't want to do anything that might abort the rescue op Archer was sure to attempt. But he also knew that Earth could afford the loss of the *Kobayashi Maru*—including everyone and everything aboard her— far better than it could afford to allow one of her *NX*-class starships to fall into Romulan hands.

Gotta get a warning to Enterprise, he told himself as he discreetly activated the console's main actuator.

"Don't bother trying what I *think* you're trying,

Commander," Sopek said from behind him. "That station is only a backup environmental-systems monitor. I put you at that particular station only to keep a somewhat closer eye on you—and so you wouldn't succumb to the temptation to try to patch into our subspace transmitter."

Trip allowed himself a few moments to read enough of the pictographs on the console displays to confirm what Sopek had just told him. Then he allowed his hands to fall limply to his sides.

Shit!

But there had to be *some* way to use the console to get a message out to his former captain. As bad as things had frequently gotten at times during his long sojourn in Romulan space, he had yet to find himself facing the truly insurmountable odds of a no-win situation.

Several agonizingly long minutes passed, like ice boulders slowly rolling down a hill in reluctant deference to Triton's skimpy gravity. Once he realized that neither Sopek nor any of his increasingly busy crew seemed able or willing to invest much attention in him, he resumed his quiet exploration of the console before him. He made no attempt to move furtively, since that would probably attract more of the unwelcome attentions of the disruptor-toting guard whose eyes he could already feel drilling into the back of his head like laser-powered asteroid borers.

But he *did* try to hide his triumphant smile from view after the answer finally came to him.

FORTY-SEVEN

"LEAVING SECTION ELEVEN, CAPTAIN," Mayweather said. "Entering section ten. Contact with the *Kobayashi Maru* on long-range navigational sensors."

"Very good, Travis," Archer said, wincing slightly as he leaned forward on his chair. Despite the lingering pain in his side, he found the movement hard to resist, as though by gaining a few additional centimeters of proximity to the main bridge viewer, he might make any lurking hull-breach hazards more apparent and avoidable. "Steady as she goes. And keep scanning for gravitic mines or anything else that might sink us."

"The sensors are already tuned to maximum resolution enhancement, Captain," said T'Pol, most of her attention apparently riveted to the hooded scanner on her science station.

"Tactical systems are also running everything through a pretty fine sieve, Captain," said Reed, who stood at the aft tactical array, entering commands and studying representations of power curves and marching columns of figures. "Phase cannons and photonic torpedoes are ready as well. I'll be damned if I let anything bigger than a Ping-Pong ball get within ten thousand klicks of us."

Despite his lingering mixed feelings about the unauthorized actions T'Pol and Reed had recently taken, Archer was nevertheless grateful for the restoration of the core of his alpha-watch crew. The entire bridge crew seemed keenly aware, as he was, that this far away from any human-inhabited world, rescue was a commodity that was strictly BYO—Bring Your Own. All Starfleet personnel, from midshipmen up through the admiralty, recognized this sobering fact.

But in the case of the vessel toward which *Enterprise* now hurtled, rescue was indeed on the way. *The master and commander of the* S.S. Kobayashi Maru *has got to be the luckiest freighter captain in the history of maritime disasters,* Archer thought.

Despite the remoteness of this region of space, Archer was already somewhat familiar with the portion of it that *Enterprise* had just entered; it lay well inside the boundaries of a not-yet-ratified "neutral zone" that Vulcan and Andoria had recently jointly proposed as a buffer zone between Coalition space and the vast unknown regions controlled by the mysterious Romulan Star Empire. None of the other Coalition member worlds, including Earth, had raised any serious objections to the idea.

Archer, however, harbored serious doubts that the Romulans would pay even the slightest attention to any such resolution. He was certain that they would go right on scrapping with the Klingons over the many resource-rich systems scattered across this swatch of what the stellar cartographers had dubbed the Milky Way's Beta Quadrant. And that was to say nothing of their current plan to foment dissension and possibly even warfare between the Coalition's member planets.

"The *Kobayashi Maru* should be coming within extreme visual range now, Captain," T'Pol said.

"Graviton counts at the vessel's coordinates are going through the roof," said Reed.

"That would be consistent with the detonation of a gravitic mine," T'Pol said crisply, in full Vulcan mode.

"Let's have a look at her, T'Pol. Maximum magnification."

The star-flecked darkness that lay ahead of *Enterprise* swiftly gave way to the grainy image of a badly battered freighter; the tapering shape was silhouetted only faintly in the dim reflected glow of one of the countless irregularly shaped ice bodies that made up the frigid halo of cometary debris that surrounded the dim and distant star Tezel and its co-orbital partner, the even dimmer gasgiant-protostar Oroko. Though the vessel's long, narrow lines gave it only a superficial resemblance to a Klingon battle cruiser, Archer's central nervous system found the similarity close enough to make his hackles rise.

"What's our ETA, Travis?" Archer asked, finally succumbing to the urge to rise from his chair and begin pacing across the middle of the bridge.

"We'll come within transporter range in about four minutes, Captain," the helmsman said as he checked a nav display and entered a small course correction.

"The MACO and Starfleet emergency boarding teams are assembled and ready, Captain," said T'Pol. "They've prepped the shuttlepods in both launch bays, and are standing by at the transporter pad."

"Sickbay reports ready as well, Captain," Hoshi said from her com station.

"Captain, I'm reading another vessel in orbit around one of this system's Kuiper bodies," Malcolm said, sounding alarmed.

Archer's hackles stiffened even further. "What kind of vessel?"

"Her profile is consistent with that of a Romulan warship, Captain," Reed said, sounding almost eager to get a closer look.

Romulans. Great. Swell. On the other hand, this could be an opportunity to gather whatever additional proof of Romulan aggression even the most skeptical Coalition representative might require. "Location?"

"About two million kilometers on the other side of the *Kobayashi Maru*."

Well, they can't do very much damage to either of us at that range, Archer thought. "Keep tabs on it, Malcolm. Let me know immediately if she starts moving."

"Aye, sir." Reed immediately set about entering a new series of commands into his tactical station.

"Hoshi, raise the *Kobayashi Maru's* captain," Archer said.

Hoshi's fingers moved nimbly across her com console. "Opening a channel, Captain."

"Captain Vance, this is *Enterprise*," Archer said, raising his voice slightly for the benefit of the com system's audio pickups. "We can begin transporting your survivors in two minutes."

"*—Archer, I never thought I'd be so glad to hear your voice again,*" Vance said, all but shouting over a sibilant background wash of static. "*Seems unlikely, doesn't it?*"

Archer let a small smile crease his lips, since he was certain that he knew a good deal more about the *Kobayashi Maru's* mission than Vance would have preferred. "Probably about as likely as your ship sailing so far off the edge of the map, Captain."

"*Believe me, Captain Archer, the* Maru *would be navigating far safer waters right now had the* Horizon *showed up for our rendezvous when she was supposed to.*"

Mayweather turned his chair so that he faced Archer, his eyes wide with concern.

Picking up on his helmsman's obvious distress, Archer continued addressing Vance. "The *Horizon*? Are you referring to Paul Mayweather's Earth Cargo Service freighter, Captain Vance?"

Another blast of static preceded Vance's scratchy

reply. *"The same. We were supposed to transfer our, ah, cargo to her at Psi Octantis, which is a whole lot closer to the Coalition side of this sector. She never turned up there, so we're making the delivery she was supposed—"*

The tide of static rose abruptly, drowning out whatever Vance might have had to say next.

"Hoshi, can you clean that up?" Archer said, frowning.

Scowling down at her console, the youthful communications expert shook her head. "Sorry, Captain. There's just too much external interference. It's almost as though—"

"Almost as though somebody a little closer to her than we are is jamming her signals," Archer said, interrupting. "That damned Romulan ship."

"What could have happened to the *Horizon*?" Mayweather said, looking up from his helm seat; he was obviously rattled emotionally, though he seemed to be working hard to conceal that fact. "The booby trap that the *Kobayashi Maru* hit can't have been the only one the Romulans or the Klingons left lying around in this sector. Maybe—"

"Let's not get ahead of ourselves, Travis," Archer said. He stepped toward the pilot and laid a hand gently on his shoulder. "I promise you we'll get to the bottom of this, just as quickly as we can."

Mayweather nodded, his dark eyes gleaming with both appreciation and worry. "Thank you, sir."

Turning back toward Hoshi's station, Archer said, "Why the hell would even the Romulans try to jam distress calls from a human freighter way out here in the boondocks?"

"It's actually a modified *Klingon* freighter, Captain," Malcolm said. "The Romulans might be taking over her systems with their new weapon, as part of another one of their territorial skirmishes against the Klingons."

Or maybe they know full well that the Kobayashi Maru *is filled with defenseless humans and they're doing this just for the sheer sadistic hell of it,* Archer thought. He knew he'd never forget how they'd tried to annihilate the civilization on Coridan Prime, even if he never succeeded in proving their involvement definitively. *Maybe they're trying to force us to fire some of the first shots in the new war we all know is coming.*

"We're receiving another incoming signal, Captain," Hoshi said as she examined the frequency and modulation graphs on her displays.

"From the *Kobayashi Maru*?" Archer said.

"No, sir. The point-source vector doesn't match at all, and the signal seems to have bypassed the worst of the jamming effect."

Archer's eyebrows rose involuntarily as he approached her console to get a better look at the incoming message scrolling on her displays. "Starfleet Command?"

"No, sir. It's in the wrong frequency range. And it's in the lowest portions of the subspace bands, so low it's hard to sort out from the cosmic subspace background noise."

"Enhance that signal and pinpoint its source," Archer said.

Hoshi swiftly tapped new instructions into her board, and her brow crumpled in puzzlement as she studied the new data that resulted. "Looks like it's coming from the *Romulan* ship, Captain."

"Audio?" Archer asked.

She shook her head. "No, only modulation pulses. It's almost as though somebody on that ship is 'tapping' against the ship's own signal-jamming protocols, using some other on-board system to create the 'taps.'"

"The way you might bang out a Morse code message by rapping a monkey wrench against a pipe," said Archer.

"Exactly."

"Any idea who the sender is?" Archer said, although he already had a pretty good idea of the identity of whoever was wielding the "subspace monkey wrench" on the Romulan ship.

"Just the name 'Lazarus,' Captain—just like the message we received back in February. The name keeps repeating throughout the message." He saw her eyes widen in evident recognition of the name, which he knew she had encountered once before not so very long ago.

"Pipe it to my ready room, Hoshi," Archer said, then turned so that he faced both the main science console and the tactical station.

"Malcolm, you have the bridge. T'Pol, you're with me."

Then he was practically in a footrace with his first officer to discover whether or not "Lazarus" had returned from the dead yet again.

FORTY-EIGHT

The Depths of Tezel-Oroko's Kuiper Belt

Powerless to take any direct action to stop the proceedings that were unfolding before him on the bird-of-prey's bustling bridge, Trip sat with his back to the console where his captors had parked him. He watched in silence as Sopek finally gave the order that confirmed nearly all of Trip's worst suspicions.

"The lead vessel has activated the *arrenhe'hwiua* tele-capture system, Sublieutenant," the turncoat captain said to the youthful male officer seated at the forward helm console. "*Enterprise* will come within the system's operational range when she closes with the freighter to commence rescue operations. The attack force will reveal itself then, while bringing the device fully to bear against the Earth vessel."

Trip watched. But he wasn't watching helplessly.

Despite the slight shaking of his hands, no doubt caused by the close presence of both Sopek and his crew—not to mention the disruptor-packing two-legged watchdog posted near the turbolift doors—Trip hadn't found it all that difficult to take surreptitious control of a couple of the ship's more innocuous-looking systems.

The backup coolant valves that governed the dispersal of the life-support system's waste heat had taken only a few short minutes to figure out. Using those bursts to create a corresponding pulsation within the adjacent tertiary subspace communications backup system—a little-noticed system that engaged automatically during signal-jamming operations—had taken even less time.

The trickiest part of the gambit had been trying to look casual while digging a finger deeply into his right ear in order to gently extract the small universal translation unit that the Adigeon plastic surgeons had concealed there.

Hate to lose either one of these things, Trip thought, remembering how difficult it had been to fix this one after it had temporarily failed a few weeks back. *But I can get by with just the left one if I really need to.*

Right now, what he *really* needed was to tap out a message on his improvised equivalent of a subspace telegraph. But any telegraph operator required the use of a telegraph key, of course, and Trip suspected that his ear-implant device would fit the bill nicely, given the right combination of skill and luck.

Pretending to stretch, he palmed the tiny, raisin-sized control mechanism, then allowed it to roll to a stop between his right thumb and forefinger. Relying both on his sense of touch and his memory of the repairs he'd already once been forced to make on the unit, he found the tiny actuator switch that controlled the receipt of inputs from the jaw-implanted bone conduction microphone that allowed him to "converse" with the device on a silent, subvocal level.

Too bad I can't just use the subvocal interface directly over a voice-channel link, he thought as the little unit began automatically running up and down the local wireless interface frequencies, seeking a match with the console-accessible systems Trip had just seized. *But I suppose you can't have everything.*

He could only hope that what he now had would prove to be enough—and that someone aboard *Enterprise* would notice that somebody *here* was sending them a signal, albeit an unorthodox one. Reasoning that his best chance to get Captain Archer's attention quickly was to start with a familiar, easily recognizable message, Trip started by repeatedly sending the equivalent of the name "Lazarus," the code name he had used months ago, while trying to send *Enterprise* advance word of the attack on Coridan. Memories of the Coridan disaster, which had claimed more than a billion lives despite his last-minute warnings, filled Trip with foreboding.

As did the realization that whether or not Captain Archer received and understood his transmissions in time to act on them, at least one ship and crew was all but certain to come to a terrible end today.

Unobtrusively squeezing the ear implant in his hand in a rhythmic but silent tattoo of dots and dashes, Trip began tapping out a message.

ARCHER, YOU ARE HEADED INTO A TRAP. ROMULAN SNEAK ATTACK COMING, BY REMOTE CONTROL. FREIGHTER NOT SAVABLE. TURN ENTERPRISE *ABOUT IMMEDIATELY, MAX WARP.*

As he finished the third iteration of his message, Trip made direct eye contact with Sopek. He wondered for an instant whether the turncoat captain suspected anything, or if he was merely trying to extract some perverse enjoyment out of Trip's reactions to the coming disaster.

"Commander, what's that in your hand?" Sopek said, confirming the former while not ruling out the latter. Turning his head, the captain nodded toward the hulking armed *uhlan*, who reacted by displaying the self-satisfied expression of a man who had finally been issued a license to do something very nasty—something he'd been forced very reluctantly to refrain from doing for far too long.

Oh, crap.

Before the *uhlan* managed to close half the distance that separated them, Trip jumped over the chest-high railing that stood between him and the sublieutenant whose hand guided the rudder. Taking advantage of the split second of surprise the maneuver had bought him, he shoved the helmsman out of his chair, sending the young man sprawling across the deck's hard duranium gridwork. Then he grabbed the momentarily untended throttle and opened it up all the way.

As he slammed the portside lateral thrusters open, sending the bird-of-prey into a hard starboard turn, he grabbed the helm console with his free hand to prevent the heaving, cockeyed deck from throwing him off his feet. Trip turned his head to the left just in time to observe that Sopek had been neither fortunate nor skilled enough to do the same.

Focusing his attention on the central viewer at the front of the bridge, Trip watched as one of the dirty-gray ice bodies of Tezel-Oroko's Kuiper belt drew inexorably closer, its shape visible mainly as a dim, distorted crescent of reflected stellar light.

Too bad Sopek's damned telecapture doohickey isn't on this ship, he thought. *I'd mind dying a whole lot less if I knew I was taking that thing with me.*

Then something blunt and heavy struck Trip very hard across the back of the head, casting him abruptly into darkness.

FORTY-NINE

ARCHER WAS AFRAID he knew what Hoshi was going to say before she said it. *"Sorry, Captain,"* said the communications officer via the intercom unit on Archer's ready-room desk. *"The subspace modulations carrying that signal have just . . . stopped."*

"Thanks, Hoshi. Keep scanning for any follow-up transmissions." He closed the channel before pushing the chair beneath him away from his compact desk. Looking up at T'Pol, he said, "Trip's message stopped right in the middle of that last repetition." A tight fist of worry clutched at his guts.

T'Pol stood tensely in the center of the small chamber, hands clasped behind her back.

"Did you understand the message, Captain?"

"I did," Archer said, nodding. "I'll admit I'm a bit rusty at Morse code, but evidently not much more rusty than whoever sent that message."

Her head tilted slightly in evident curiosity. "Morse code?"

"An Earth communications code that's even older than EM-based luminal-speed radio." He took a moment to confirm the brief message's exact verbatim contents with Hoshi via the intercom, and shared the information with T'Pol in the process. "What the hell do ' you suppose happened during that last repetition?" he said as his XO considered the message in silence.

The Vulcan woman raised an eyebrow, making Archer think that she might be wondering if his question had been purely rhetorical. "It would appear that Trip is no longer transmitting."

"If it really *was* Trip transmitting," Archer said.

Her reply was as devoid of doubt as the rocks outside the New Berlin lunar settlement were free of water. "It was. What do you intend to do about his warning?"

"I wish I knew," Archer said. "I need a little bit more to go on to justify leaving a whole ship and crew out here to die—starting with why the transmission was cut off. Did the Romulans find out what he was doing? Or did he have to stop transmitting in order to *keep* from being discovered?"

T'Pol shook her head, responding again with bedrock certainty. "He *has* been discovered, Captain. Trip is in extreme danger again."

Archer allowed himself a puckish smile, despite the pain in his face and the distinct lack of humor in this situation. "Another Vulcan hunch, T'Pol?"

"An objective fact," she said, an almost mournful expression lengthening her olive-toned face.

The shrill whistle of the intercom interrupted his search for a reply that might both encourage and convince her. *"Captain, the Romulan vessel is on the move,"* Reed said, sounding alarmed.

Archer hopped out of his chair and leaned on the reply button on his desk. "On my way."

Leading the way through the hatchway that connected the ready room to the bridge, Archer wasted no time taking a seat in his command chair. The main viewer displayed a computer-enhanced image of the blast-damaged, almost completely unilluminated *Kobayashi Maru* as it continued its slow, unpowered tumble through the stygian void.

"I've dropped us out of warp, Captain," Mayweather said. "Decelerating at impulse to match velocity with the *Kobayashi Maru*, at a current distance of just over eleven kilometers."

"Sensors read approximately two hundred life signs, Captain," said Hoshi. "Some of them very faint."

Two hundred people, Archer thought. He couldn't abide the idea of just leaving them out here to die, Romulan sneak-attack warnings or fire-breathing dragons notwithstanding. But if Trip's message was to be believed, the *Maru*'s problem was an insoluble one, no matter what he tried to do about it.

"Position of the Romulan bird-of-prey?" Archer said.

"That's strange," said Malcolm, speaking from behind the captain's chair at the aft tactical station. "The Romulan vessel seems to have moved directly into the path of one of the cometary bodies. There's been a collision, but the ship appears to be intact."

Archer looked away from T'Pol. *I hope to hell she was wrong about Trip being aboard that ship*, he thought, even though he knew that she had a singular habit of being right about such things.

"So the Romulan ship might still be able to direct an attack against us remotely," Archer said.

"That's possible," Reed said. "It's also possible that the Romulans have installed their remote-hijacking device aboard one or more of their captured Klingon vessels by now."

"At least the communications jamming has stopped," Hoshi said. "It coincided exactly with the moment that Romulan ship hit the iceberg. Whether or not it's directing other ships, the bird-of-prey must have been the source of all the com interference."

Nodding an acknowledgment to the com officer, Archer said, "Commence rescue operations on the *Kobayashi Maru*." Though he was addressing the entire bridge crew, his gaze settled on T'Pol, who had begun working at her science console. "Once that job is done, we'll investigate the crash of the Romulan ship."

He approached T'Pol closely, and spoke in a volume intended for her ears alone. "Maybe the sneak-attack plans we were warned about crashed along with that Romulan ship."

Looking more stricken than reassured, T'Pol merely glanced down at her console and said, "Both shuttle-pods have launched, Captain. Lieutenant O'Neill is running the transporter."

Archer nodded. Opening an intercom channel on the console adjacent to T'Pol's, he said, "Archer to O'Neill. Report."

"The system's having some trouble establishing a positive lock on any of the survivors, Captain," said D.O.; her tone suggested that she might soon give the finicky transporter's control console a swift kick in the annular confinement circuits.

"What's the problem, D.O.?"

"When isn't this damned thing having problems, sir? My best guess is that the residual hull graviton flux from the mine the freighter hit is interfering with the transporter lock. We might need to find a way to disperse the remaining particles,"

"A low-yield photonic torpedo tuned to radiate anti-gravitons might do the trick," Reed said.

Archer nodded. "Get on that with Mike, Malcolm. We're going to need to get the transporter up and running ASAP. The shuttlepods might not be enough to rescue all the survivors before whatever's left of their life-support system decides to give up the ghost."

"Aye, sir," Reed said just before his attention became riveted to one of his tactical displays. "Captain! I'm reading two incoming warp signatures. No, make that three. They're dropping out of warp, and just about right on top of us."

T'Pol hunkered over the hooded scanner built into her science console. "Configuration is Klingon," she said, immediately switching from what Archer recognized as the depths of Vulcan grieving back to no-nonsense officer mode. "All three are *D5*-type battle cruisers."

And if those ships really have Klingons behind the wheel, then I'm Dorothy Gale from Kansas, Archer thought, recalling both the evidence he'd gathered on Qo'noS and the mysterious warning about an imminent Romulan sneak attack.

Aloud, he said, "Tactical alert! Recall those shuttle-pods." A heartbeat later, the bridge lights dimmed.

"Polarizing the hull plating," Reed said. "All weapon systems armed and tactical crews summoned to battle stations. Lieutenant Burch is preparing a photonic torpedo to disperse the graviton flux around the freighter."

"Shuttlepods returning to launch bays," Hoshi said.

"Give me a tactical display on the Klingon ships, Malcolm," Archer said, returning to his seat.

The image of the mortally wounded fuel carrier vanished from the viewer, replaced by a computer-generated grid depicting the local region and all five ships that now maneuvered within it. The two white computer-generated icons that represented, respectively, *Enterprise* and the *Kobayashi Maru* were so close they almost touched at the viewscreen's center, while the three outlying long-necked gray deltas that stood in for the approaching Klingon warships wasted no time deploying themselves in a loose triangle that encompassed most of the screen.

"They're trying to surround us," Archer said.

"And there's a good chance we'll never get away from them if they do," Reed said in strictly matter-of-fact tones. "Their weapons tubes all read as hot. The nearest vessel is at ten thousand klicks and closing rapidly."

"Are the shuttlepods docked yet?" Archer asked, scowling.

"Shuttlepod Two reports successful docking capture," Hoshi said. "Shuttlepod One is making its final approach."

"The nearest Klingon vessel is opening fire with its main disruptor," said Mayweather.

The bridge rocked, but not nearly as hard as it might have had the gunner attacking them really meant business.

Archer turned toward Reed, who displayed a puzzled frown. "They should have hit us a hell of a lot harder than that."

Archer shook his head. "They *would* have—if it really *was* the Klingons pushing the buttons on those ships."

"And if they're really Romulans, Captain?" T'Pol asked.

"If they're Romulans, then they'll want to capture more of their enemies' ships," Archer said. "The bastards will try every trick in the book to take *Enterprise* intact."

"At least at first," Reed said with a gallows grin. "Once they realize they *can't* have her intact, they'd probably be inclined to make sure that nobody else can have her either. Present company included, of course."

Archer nodded. "We'll have to gamble on whether their patience will run out before time is up for the *Kobayashi Maru*'s survivors."

"And on whether or not we can pull off a rescue and

get out of here in one piece before *both* deadlines expire," Reed said. "I recommend we don't press our luck here, Captain. They might only be lobbing snowballs at us now, but we're still outgunned and outnumbered three to one."

"We should stay long enough to rescue as many of the survivors as possible, Captain," said T'Pol. "That first shot bought us some time. The Romulans just showed us that destroying *Enterprise* is not their top priority."

"Commander," Reed said, his voice raised slightly, "if we start taking serious hits, even with our hull plating polarization activated, the warp drive could go down. And if that happens—"

"If that happens, Malcolm," Archer interrupted, "then we'll all have a whole lot less paperwork waiting for us after the mission."

Reed nodded. "I suppose there's always an upside to everything, sir."

Archer grinned. "That's the spirit, Malcolm. Let's get those residual gravitons cleared out and beam as many of the survivors as we can off that ship."

As Reed busied himself at his console, Hoshi said, "Shuttlepod One has just docked, Captain. Do you want to redeploy?"

Archer shook his head. "No. Let's hedge our bets and leave 'em both docked, since we still might have to make a quick exit. There's no way to know exactly when—"

The bridge was suddenly plunged into inky darkness, startling Archer into silence and prompting exclamations of alarm all around the bridge.

The surreal red glow of the emergency lights suffused the bridge a few frantic heartbeats later, turning the room into a colossal Hieronymus Bosch painting.

"What happened?" Archer asked as the main viewer

rebooted, dropping the tactical display in favor of an image of the wounded *Kobayashi Maru*.

Reed consulted one of his now dimly glowing displays before answering. Owl-eyed, he said, "*Enterprise*'s life-support system has just failed. Complete shutdown."

Hoshi's translation of a mortally injured Klingon woman's dying words whispered anew in Archer's ear: "*The first thing they did was . . . to use some remote means of seizing and deactivating each of our systems, one by one. They started with life-support . . .*"

Over the fading echoes of that grim recollection, Archer recalled the warning message he'd received more recently: "*ROMULAN SNEAK ATTACK COMING, BY REMOTE CONTROL.*"

"Captain, the Klingon vessels nearly have us surrounded," Reed said. "But we still have full warp capability."

Archer heard the unspoken "for now" at the end of Malcolm's sentence loud and clear.

"Can't let 'em have *Enterprise*," he murmured.

He noticed then that Mayweather was looking up at him expectantly from the helm station. "Sir?"

Looking around the faintly illuminated bridge, Archer saw similar looks of expectation on the faces of everyone there. The ruddy glow of the emergency lights cast harsh, bizarre shadows across the features of T'Pol, Reed, Hoshi, and Mayweather, greatly accentuating every anxiety they must have felt, as well as his own.

ARCHER, YOU ARE HEADED INTO A TRAP. ROMULAN SNEAK ATTACK COMING, BY REMOTE CONTROL.

But I can't just leave all those people here to die, he thought, anguished.

FREIGHTER NOT SAVABLE.

He slammed the side of his hand onto the intercom

unit on the arm of his chair. "Archer to O'Neill. Any luck transporting those survivors yet?"

"There's still too much graviton particle flux on the hull, Captain," O'Neill said. *"I'm sorry. I wish I had better news for you, sir."*

Damn.

FREIGHTER NOT SAVABLE.

I can't accept that!

"Captain!" Reed cried. "The hull polarization system has gone down, just like life support did. I can't determine exactly why yet."

But I *can,* Archer thought, recalling the dying Klingon woman. *Defensive and tactical systems were the next dominoes to fall after life support.*

TURN ENTERPRISE *ABOUT IMMEDIATELY, MAX WARP.*

Forgive me.

But Archer seriously doubted he would ever develop a large enough capacity for self-forgiveness to accept absolution for what he knew he had to do.

"Travis, get us out of here," Archer said. "Pedal to the metal."

Mayweather regarded him silently for a moment, his eyes widening into pools in which disappointment and relief commingled, as did both repugnance and understanding.

"Aye, Captain," the helmsman said, turning toward his console and bringing the ship into motion. The whine of the engines and the vibration in the deck plates signaled *Enterprise*'s quick transition from subluminal velocity to high warp speed.

Archer stared straight ahead at the viewer. The dying *Kobayashi Maru* immediately fell away astern, dropping into the infinite, just another piece of flotsam on the cosmic ocean. Not wishing to see what he had already seen once in Travis's eyes and in the gazes of the rest of his crew, he continued staring straight ahead long seconds after the fuel carrier had completely vanished from sight.

"The lead vessel is pursuing," Reed said. "But she's slowly losing ground to us. The other vessels seem to be converging on the *Kobayashi Maru* and powering up their weapons."

Without tearing his eyes from the star field ahead of him, Archer opened an intercom channel. "Archer to engineering."

"Burch here, Captain."

"We need to get life support back up, Lieutenant."

"My people are already on it, Captain. We should have everything five-by-five before it even starts getting stuffy around here, sir."

"Captain Vance is hailing us again, Captain," Hoshi said quietly. After a long, pregnant pause she added, "What should I tell him?"

He slowly turned to face her, and allowed his gaze to sweep the rest of the bridge. The eyes of everyone looked like small mirrors of shock and accusation.

He wondered if he could stand to see the same look in Admiral Gardner's eyes, whether or not Starfleet Command ultimately vindicated the decision he'd just made.

"The Klingons have opened fire on the *Kobayashi Maru*," Reed said, an audible quaver in his voice.

"One of the vessel's neutronic fuel tanks appears to have exploded, causing a chain reaction," T'Pol reported a moment later from her science console. Then she drew away from her scanner and turned to face Archer directly. "Captain, the *Kobayashi Maru* has been destroyed."

Archer closed his eyes tightly.

God forgive me.

FIFTY

Wednesday, July 23, 2155
San Francisco, Earth

PRIME MINISTER NATHAN SAMUELS WOULD have preferred to have a pleasantly dull and utterly uneventful morning, but he realized now that not only was it shaping up to be a most decidedly unpleasant day, it was likely only a sample of many weeks, or perhaps months, of similarly eventful days to come.

The Coalition Security Council had called yet another one of its now-ubiquitous emergency sessions, and the decisions he expected today's meeting to yield had an even heavier air of gravitas than any action the body had taken during the previous several weeks. It was one thing to threaten war, but quite another to follow through and actually declare it. Regardless, the latest images Starfleet had relayed to the ministries of the United Earth government clearly showed that the nascent alliance had an extremely limited number of options.

All of the Coalition delegates—including those representing the most recently inducted members, Draylax and Alpha Centauri—were seated at their customary spots at the semicircular array of conference tables. Mounted on the wall at one end of the room was a wide, flat video monitor, which played and replayed an endless, grainy loop of the previous day's debacle in the Gamma Hydra sector. Starfleet Admirals Sam Gardner and Gregory Black, MACO commandant General

George Casey, and several other members of Starfleet's top brass were seated near the giant viewscreen, their expressions uniformly grave and somber.

"I still believe that the Klingons *must* be involved in this," Gora bim Gral of Tellar said in his customary testy manner. "Note that only *their* ships have allegedly succumbed to this so-called Romulan superweapon. Therefore I think they must be acting in collusion with the Romulans."

Samuels saw Vulcan Foreign Minister Soval glance toward Ambassadors L'Nel and Solkar, one eyebrow raised. But none of the three Vulcans made any audible response to Gral's assertion, leaving the minister to wonder what they might be thinking.

"We concur," said Grethe Zhor, one of the two newest delegates to the Council. "Draylax has already been a target of one of these deadly attacks. Regardless of the so-called evidence Captain Archer has gathered for this council, the fact remains that it was Klingon vessels that fired the volleys that killed so many of our people, and destroyed the Tau Cetan freighter *Kobayashi Maru*."

Anlenthoris ch'Vhendreni rose to his feet, the Andorian foreign minister's cerulean antennae bent almost parallel to the white-maned slope of his skull. "The images *clearly* show the presence of a Romulan ship, as well as the Klingon vessels that destroyed the *Kobayashi Maru*. Are any of you really naïve enough to believe this to be a coincidence? That the Romulans just *happened* to be at the site of an apparent Klingon attack?" He glared around the assemblage, reinforcing his point with his icy gaze before sitting down again.

Gral snorted. "Has no one considered that if the Klingons *are* responsible, that they may be using a Romulan ship in order to misdirect our retaliation? This is only the second piece of evidence we have seen that the

Romulans might be involved in anti-Coalition aggression, however peripherally, and yet we have seen *many* examples of Klingon barbarism!"

"Two other attacks occurred just last night, including one in *my* system," Centauri III's Ambassador Jie Cong Li said. "Why has Starfleet not yet made even a preliminary report about either of them?"

Interior Minister Haroun al-Rashid cleared his throat, then spoke. "Two other attacks did indeed occur last night. One was directed at the science outpost on Calder II, and the second incident happened near Alpha Centauri. Starfleet dispatched Earth's second *NX*-class vessel, *Columbia*, to assist in Alpha Centauri's defense."

"And what happened after that?" Gral asked, wrinkling his porcine nose.

Samuels knew that al-Rashid must have been squirming inside, although his exterior looked enviably cool and calm. Both men had been present at Admiral Gardner's secret briefing, and therefore knew the potentially explosive secret that both Earth and Starfleet had deemed it prudent to conceal, at least temporarily, from their Coalition peers: the fact that both *Columbia* and a source on Calder II had confirmed that Vulcan military ships had initiated last night's attacks.

Vulcan ships that Starfleet now firmly believed had acted under Romulan control, like the Klingon vessels that had attacked Draylax.

Samuels watched as al-Rashid glanced toward the Starfleet brass before spreading his hands and addressing the other Coalition delegations. "We don't yet know *exactly* what happened last night," he said, dissembling only as much as absolutely necessary. "And we haven't heard much from *Columbia* since just before her engagement with the hostiles near Alpha Centauri."

"And how long ago was that?" Thoris—the name that

Anlenthoris ch'Vhendreni used most commonly among his diplomatic peers—looked surprised, his antennae cued almost bolt upright.

"It's been approximately ten hours," al-Rashid said. "*Columbia*'s silence may be due simply to transmitter damage, but Starfleet won't be able to confirm her status until another vessel can reach her and get a report on what's happened out there."

"What about Centauri III's defenses? Have you no fleet to protect your own?" Gral asked.

Before an annoyed-looking Ambassador Li could respond, Minister Soval stood, holding one hand out to preempt the discussion. "My government dispatched several Vulcan Defense Force vessels to Alpha Centauri III yesterday to reinforce the system's defenses. Like Starfleet, we have heard nothing conclusive from our vessels, as yet, regarding the outcome of the engagement." He sat back down, tucking his hands into his robe sleeves.

So much for Vulcans not being able to lie, Samuels thought, suppressing a sly smile. *Even if Soval believes what he's saying, that only means that somebody higher up on Vulcan must have lied to* him.

Samuels saw Gardner and Black exchange inscrutable looks in response to Soval's words. He also noted that at least one of their subordinates had surreptitiously pulled out a datapad and was quickly entering something into it with his stylus. He sincerely hoped that the aide was merely researching the veracity of Soval's claim, rather than leaking something to the press; he'd seen enough *"Worlds at War?"* headlines during the past week to last several lifetimes.

"So we have missing or incommunicado Vulcan *and* Starfleet ships at Alpha Centauri, and we already know what happened with *Enterprise* near Tezel-Oroko," Thoris said. "What has become of the Calder II outpost?"

Minister al-Rashid shook his head again. "We have not heard all the details as yet, but the final, fragmentary transmissions Starfleet received hint that the entire outpost was probably destroyed."

"By whom?" Gral demanded. "Or what?"

"The scientists at the outposts apparently couldn't transmit any clear visuals of their attackers before the hostiles jammed their central transmitter," al-Rashid said.

Grethe Zhor rose to her feet, scowling in evident anger as she crossed her arms beneath her triple bust. "I realize that I am one of the two newest inductees to this council, but I find I must question whether all the effort Draylax has expended in order to join this group can be justified. During the past week, there have been nearly a dozen smaller attacks that can be attributed to this same unfolding pattern of aggression, whether on the part of the Klingons, the Romulans, or perhaps even some never-before-seen alliance of the two. Almost *all* Coalition worlds and their colonies have been affected in some manner by these assaults.

"Yesterday, *three* such attacks occurred in or near Coalition space," she said, continuing with rising passion. "Starfleet was unable to stop any of them—*Znoc,* Captain Archer fled with *Enterprise* like a frightened child— and the Vulcan fleet may have just proven equally useless at Alpha Centauri. We need to decide beyond all doubt and debate *who* the aggressor is, and then go after that aggressor. All of our endless equivocating and discussion will only result in more death. More destruction."

Samuels watched the Draylaxian in silence, a few of her words sticking in his craw as she paused to pound her hand on the conference table in an effort to emphasize her point. "In case some of you have not been paying close attention, we are *already* at war. An enemy has attacked us, and continues to do so even as we argue. It is already long past time for us to begin fighting back."

Sensing that the tension in the room was about to erupt, Samuels pounded his gavel loudly against the central lectern, breaking through the rising mixed gabble of assenting and dissenting murmurs.

"Ambassador Grethe Zhor is right about many things," he said. "However, I must object strongly to her characterization of Captain Archer's actions. If the Romulans were indeed attempting to capture one of our most advanced starships, then he had no choice other than to withdraw as he did. Of course, given the admittedly ambiguous circumstances near Alpha Centauri, it may already be too late to get that particular horse back into its stable. For all we know, our mutual enemy may already have gained control of Starfleet, Vulcan, *and* Klingon technologies."

Samuels watched Soval flinch ever so slightly in response to his conjecture; he wondered if the idea truly hadn't yet occurred to the stoic Vulcan foreign minister, or if the Vulcans were simply hiding their knowledge that the worst had already occurred. *As usual.*

Samuels clenched his jaw tightly for a moment, grinding his back teeth slightly before he resumed speaking. He hated having to say what he was about to say, and had felt the words coiled in the pit of his stomach, like poisonous snakes preparing to strike.

"Circumstances force me to suggest that this Security Council may not be the most effective venue for many of the decisions that will have to be made in the very near future. I move that *each* of our worlds prepare to convene a council of war immediately, with full input from each of our militaries."

Even as he said the words, the Council members all

began getting to their feet, gesturing and shouting—mostly in agreement—and Samuels wondered if this moment, rather than the signing of the Coalition Compact, might turn out to be the one for which history remembered him best.

God help us all, he prayed silently, closing his eyes in the forlorn hope of shutting out the tumult that had erupted in the Coalition Council Chamber, if only for an instant.

It was one thing to threaten war, to give speeches and to debate the merits and pitfalls of interstellar conflict. But even given history's inescapable lessons about the all-too-frequent necessity of going to war against aggressors, Samuels knew that *he* did not want to lead humanity—so recently unified and at peace with itself—into a brand-new age of conflict out there.

Just as he knew from those around him—those allies whose worlds and governments and societies and cultures and families were threatened with annihilation—that before the week was out, they *would* be at war.

As always, none of the Vulcan diplomats spoke at all before they reached their heavily guarded consulate, and the interior chambers that they kept shielded from both listening devices and sensor scans.

Once inside, however, it was Solkar who spoke first. "How soon should we inform the Coalition Council about what became of our ships at Alpha Centauri?" he asked.

Soval crossed to his desk, near the central wall of the pentagonal chamber. He decanted a vessel of T'Rukh spiced tea there, and poured some of the glowing orange liquid into a glass. "We are still investigating precisely what happened, and how it happened. The optimal time to inform the others, of course, would be sometime prior to *their* discovery of the same truths."

L'Nel paced, agitation clearly showing on her smooth, unlined face. "Which depends on the status of *Columbia*, which our fleet reports as having been relatively undamaged at the time of their withdrawal from Alpha Centauri."

"Calm yourself, L'Nel," Soval said, calling upon his well-honed Syrannite disciplines to filter all emotion from his being as he spoke. "The commanders of those vessels were under strict orders to destroy evidence of any Vulcan involvement in the Alpha Centauri attacks, and to attempt to deploy countermeasures designed to prevent the Romulans from gaining any further access to our technology. They were *not* charged with safeguarding Starfleet vessels after the Romulan threat had been neutralized."

"And what will happen if *Columbia* has fallen into Romulan hands in spite of the efforts of our fleet?" L'Nel said, clearly still struggling to calm herself. "They have already shown themselves quite adept at seizing control of both Vulcan and Klingon technology, our countermeasures notwithstanding."

Soval stared into his glass, then took a sip of the spiced liquid, feeling it burn his tongue as he swallowed. Finally, he answered.

"I feel confident that Vulcan will take part in the offensive against the Romulans that is to come. And if Starfleet's technology *has* become compromised, we will introduce new countermeasures to make certain that Vulcan remains, as always, insulated and protected."

Despite their relative youth, L'Nel's and Solkar's facial expressions told Soval that they understood what he was saying. Vulcan had played a larger role than humanity would ever know in moderating the breakneck pace of Earth's development into an interstellar species. As with the secret listening post near Tezel-

Oroko—a facility that still needed to be staffed, resupplied, and completed—Vulcan was good at keeping secrets.

Thursday, July 24, 2155

Keisha Naquase stared at the message that had come into her datapad seconds ago. She was tremendously protective of the device—it was actually locked to her wrist with a tether—but now, in the crush of other reporters outside Starfleet Headquarters, she gripped it even more tightly as she backed away from the other assembled members of the press corps.

They all knew *something* was up. During the last thirty-six hours, a significant number of new military personnel had arrived, representing every member of the Coalition: Vulcan, Andor, Tellar, Draylax, Alpha Centauri, and even members of several species that she and the other human media had only recently been able to identify as potential Coalition allies.

But security and secrecy had been tight, and Starfleet was taking every step to make certain that no leaks occurred.

Except that she *had* one. He hadn't been in contact for several days, but he *was* on the inside.

And she had just gotten a message from him.

"Come on, Nash, pick up," she said to herself, hearing the chimes in her earpiece. She stole a quick glance in the direction of Gannet Brooks, who stood with several of the others; Brooks always seemed to scoop just about everybody when it came to Starfleet-related news, but so far today she had been mum. And Keisha had been working her own contact for weeks now, setting him in place. It was amazing the kind of loyalty that good sex could inspire—and the sob story she'd given him about having a relative serving aboard the still-missing *Columbia* hadn't hurt either.

Finally, just as she was about to try another editor at the sub-net, Nash McEvoy picked up his comlink.

"What is it, Naquase?" he asked breathlessly, as though he'd just entered his office at a flat-out run.

She toggled the headpiece vidcam she wore, activating it even as she turned her back to face the rest of the press gaggle. She didn't want them to see the "on" light on the headset.

"I *promised* you I'd scoop your girl," she said, subvocalizing into her throat mic. "And I recorded your promises. So don't even *think* about trying to back away from our deal."

"This had better be big, or else you just torched your bridge while you were still standing on it," McEvoy said, hiding none of his testiness.

"Oh, it's *big*, all right," Keisha said, holding the datapad up to where the camera's eye—and Nash—could see it.

Thursday, July 24, 2155
Grangeburg, Alabama

Albert Tucker balanced the four plates of waffles in both hands as he exited the kitchen. He had picked the strawberries in their patch of the communal garden at sunrise, then sliced them thinly in order to add them to the multigrain batter. He knew how much his dad loved strawberry waffles, and he and Mom visited so rarely these days that Bert wanted to make certain they both had a good time.

"All right, Dad, here's your favorite," he said, entering the dining room.

Seated at the table were his father, Charles, and his

mother, Elaine, while Bert's husband, Miguel, stood nearby. They all looked stunned and grief-stricken.

What now? Bert thought. They had already lost Bert's sister in a Xindi attack on Earth, and his brother, Trip, had been killed on the *Starship Enterprise* only a few months back. Today everyone in the room bore the same signature of tragedy he'd seen on both of those other terrible occasions.

"What is it, Mike?" he asked, holding the shifting stack of plates like an inexpert juggler.

Miguel pointed to the nearby wall-mounted flatscreen, which he often left turned on as a soundless visual wallpaper. Though the sound was muted as usual, he could see the silent news anchor mouthing words, the screen split between him and a stern-looking uniformed Starfleet official.

Bert watched as his father took his mother's hand. "Say goodnight, Gracie," said Dad, incorporating his nickname for Mom into what was doubtless some sort of obscure, centuries-old pop-culture reference calculated to cheer her up.

It didn't seem to be working, however; Mom's misting eyes remained riveted to the image on the screen, which Bert finally began looking at closely.

Crawling across the screen's bottom, in large white capital letters superimposed onto a red stripe, was a single ill-omened phrase.

The stack of plates left Bert's nerveless fingers in time-dilated slow motion, smashing on the floor with the same silence as the screen's three endlessly marching words:

COALITION DECLARES WAR!

FIFTY-ONE

Friday, July 25, 2155
Enterprise **NX-01, Gamma Hydra sector,**
near Sataghni

EVERY TIME CAPTAIN ARCHER and Commander T'Pol were off the bridge, Travis Mayweather's mind took him to the worst places imaginable. It wasn't significantly better for him when they were *on* the bridge—*Enterprise* had been mostly stopped dead in space, undergoing a number of in-place emergency repairs and systems diagnostics ever since the Tezel-Oroko confrontation and the *Kobayashi Maru* disaster—but at least having command staff in place on the bridge meant that they weren't sequestered away exchanging secret messages with Starfleet Command.

Malcolm Reed and Hoshi Sato had both tried to reassure him that even if Starfleet was calling with news, it wasn't necessarily related to the disappearance of the *Horizon*. That hadn't helped. He already *knew* that; the specter of impending war had been haunting the ship like all of Charles Dickens's Christmas spirits wrapped into one.

He knew that things were bad everywhere. *Columbia* hadn't been heard from in days either, ever since she had gone to Alpha Centauri. And rumors were floating around that the Romulans had managed to get control of other kinds of ships besides those of the Klingons. But if those rumors were true, nobody had confirmed them yet.

But *Columbia* wasn't the *Horizon*. Mayweather's family wasn't on *Columbia*. *Paul, Mom, where are you?* he thought for perhaps the three-thousandth time in the last few hours, his slightly shaking fingers manipulating the controls as he checked and double-checked sensor readings to the limits of *Enterprise*'s resolution.

Mayweather knew from his conversation with the *Kobayashi Maru*'s first mate—the man whom he had trusted to deliver his letters to his family and friends aboard the *Horizon*—that the Mayweather family's freighter was supposed to have met the *Maru* in the Coalition side of the Gamma Hydra sector. But the *Horizon* hadn't made her scheduled rendezvous, according to every port of call he had managed to contact. Nobody had heard from the *Horizon* for over ten days; it was as if she just dropped off the edge of the star maps.

He couldn't believe that his family and their crew would allow themselves to fall prey to some stupid deep-space accident, which meant that *somebody* had to be responsible for their disappearance. They were too tough and clever to become the victims of garden-variety space pirates. And given the recent wave of remote-control attacks that had caused so much grief across Coalition space lately, the Romulans seemed to be the best suspects.

Mayweather scowled down at his controls for several minutes, trying not to allow himself to return to the depths of his personal darkness. He hadn't been able to sleep for days, and could barely eat. But he knew he needed to keep his focus strong. He needed to concentrate on his duties, to lose himself in them, now more than ever before. *Come on, Travis, keep it together and concentrate.* He could almost hear his mother alternately admonishing and encouraging him, just as she had all through his life. He would have given anything to hear her speak to him again, even if it was only to scold him for leaving his quarters looking like an explosive decompression accident.

He heard the door to Captain Archer's ready room slide open, and turned his head to see Commander T'Pol exiting the room, with Captain Archer a few paces behind her. The Vulcan woman appeared even more dour than usual, but she didn't look in Mayweather's direction, perhaps deliberately so. Whatever was going on at the moment, Mayweather thought it likely that it had nothing to do with either him or the fate of the *Horizon*.

Captain Archer, however, glanced his way as he stepped onto the bridge, then looked away again a moment later, seeming to survey the bridge. Mayweather was glad his back had been turned to the captain over most of the last three days; he hadn't agreed with Archer's decision to leave the *Kobayashi Maru* defenseless when he'd ordered *Enterprise* to withdraw.

I would have found a way, he thought. *There's always a solution, and turning and running isn't it. Leaving helpless people behind to die* can't *be the solution.*

It didn't help that the *Kobayashi Maru* was a freighter, like the *Horizon,* or that Mayweather had made casual friends with the *Maru*'s first mate, Arturo Stiles, when *Enterprise*'s crew had helped the fuel hauler with her repairs last week near Altair VI.

Captain Archer just left them to die.

As he sat at the helm of Archer's ship, Mayweather's mind wandered, not for the first time, back to the question that bothered him the most: Would Archer have abandoned the *Horizon* as callously as he had the *Kobayashi Maru*?

And with that gnawing question remaining unanswered, he wondered whether he could ever again really have faith in his captain's decisions.

Archer looked out across his bridge as he exited his ready room behind T'Pol. The first crew member's eyes he caught were those of Travis Mayweather. The helmsman had seemed distraught for days, understandably concerned about what had become of his family after their vessel had seemingly disappeared. Archer had tried to learn anything he could about the freighter's whereabouts, but had run into dead ends everywhere he'd looked. He had even reached out to the shadowy Agent Harris to see if the man in black knew anything, aware that even by asking him, he was taking on a debt that would have to be repaid someday, probably in blood. Unfortunately, the spymaster had failed to furnish any hard information, or even conjectures that Archer hadn't already considered.

Archer's gaze moved across the rest of the bridge, taking in each of his officers. D.O. was there, once again pulling a double shift, and Hoshi Sato looked over from her station, a look of expectation on her face; since she was in charge of monitoring the subspace bands, she would know when something very big was happening, usually before even he did. Ensigns Malvoy and Prince turned from their posts, and even the MACO guards he had assigned to bridge watch swiveled their heads to look toward him. Malcolm Reed was the last to lift his gaze from his console's displays, where he appeared to have been running computations or battle simulations.

If Reed was as clued in to what was about to happen as Hoshi appeared to be, Archer was confident he was already creating some entirely new battle tactics.

All across the bridge, the air seemed charged with tension and anticipation. The entire crew had been on pins and needles over the last thirty-six hours, ever since the incident at Tezel-Oroko and the destruction of the *Kobayashi Maru*. The reports now circulating through the interstellar media and Earth's newsnets, combined with Starfleet memos and general scuttlebutt, had ratcheted up shipboard anxiety levels to an almost unbearable peak.

The turbolift doors opened, and Doctor Phlox exited onto the bridge, his wide-eyed expression of surprise undimmed. Archer had asked him to come up, so that Archer could address his senior staff all at once. Their simultaneous presence called attention to the gaping hole he still felt inside because of the absence of Trip.

Archer continued surveying his bridge, and seeing the expectancy of those who had looked up to him for so long, he wondered how they really felt about him now. He knew that some of them must have resented the decision he had made regarding the *Kobayashi Maru*; though it did little to expiate the guilt he felt when he considered what had become of the *Maru*, he still drew comfort from the knowledge that his crew and his ship had remained intact solely because of what he had done that day. He clung to that, particularly when he thought he glimpsed an accusatory glare, or overheard a snippet of conversation that would suddenly break off as he entered the galley or stepped out of his ready room or his quarters.

If ever a crew needed an inspiring speech from its captain, now was the time. But Jonathan Archer found that he could muster neither the words nor the thoughts necessary to rally his people to face the challenges that lay ahead. There were no trumpets to sound, no cry of

"Charge" to yell, no steed to ride up and down the ranks of his troops, no saber to thrust into the air as he tried to brace them for what was coming.

Now the heading for *Enterprise,* for Starfleet, for the Coalition, and for mankind itself, was about to change drastically.

Archer spread his hands wide and hesitated for a moment, catching his breath and steadying his voice.

"It's begun."

EPILOGUE ONE

TUCKER AWOKE GRADUALLY, feeling something hot on his cheek. A swipe of his hand brought some relief, but also sent pain coursing through his system. As soon as the burning stopped in one area, however, he felt two other inflammations ignite the nerves of his skin.

Opening his eyes warily, he saw the reason why. His body was crumpled on the floor, underneath a console on the deck of Sopek's Romulan bird-of-prey. The console itself was throwing an intermittent shower of electrical sparks in various directions; some of them had landed on his face, causing his minute but painful burns.

His hearing began to return along with his equilibrium as he sat up gingerly, wondering when he would be rendered unconscious again. His last memory was of pushing the Romulan ship's throttle hard to starboard, directing the helm right toward one of the nearest icy cometary bodies of Tezel-Oroko's Kuiper belt, and he'd felt the blow to his skull. He could recall nothing more.

Looks like I missed all the fun, Trip thought, wincing as he made a halting attempt to stand. *The ship must have collided with one of those icebergs.* He thought for a moment of holovids he'd seen re-creating the seagoing *Titanic* disaster of the early twentieth century, and developed a ludicrous mental picture of a dinner jacket–clad Romulan string sextet playing below decks.

All around him on the dimly lit bridge were the unconscious—or perhaps deceased—bodies of Sopek's crew. Sopek himself was crumpled against a far wall, a splash of green above his head that was smeared down to the spot toward which his face was turned.

Trip limped over to one of the instrument panels that still seemed to be in working order and attempted to read the gauges he saw there. The main ship's systems appeared to be completely down, so he knew that sensors were useless, but the artificial gravity and life-support systems were still functional, if only at one-third efficiency.

If he hadn't been in such pain, Trip supposed he might have chuckled at the irony of the situation; the *arrenhe'hwiua* telecapture system he'd learned about that the Romulans were using to hijack ships apparently left the imprisoned crews similarly barely alive, though not in control of their vessels. Unfortunately, that system apparently hadn't been installed on Sopek's ship, so he had no chance to destroy it now. But Trip realized with a start that he could at least stop *this* ship from causing any further trouble.

From what he knew of the layout of the upper decks of this particular type of Romulan vessel, the second level had two escape pods. He prayed that at least one of them would be operational before he began to enter commands manually into the redundant auxiliary system.

He heard a sound behind him and saw one of the female bridge crew members sitting up, a disruptor pistol clutched in one shaky hand.

"Get away from those controls," the young Romulan said, her words slurred slightly as she appeared to have bitten partially through her lip during the impact.

Trip's eyes flicked to the side, and he saw another

disruptor lying on the deck near where he had gotten up. *Why didn't I pick that up before?* he asked himself silently. As he dove for the weapon, he heard the sizzle of an energy blast go past his falling body, connecting with part of the metal framework of the bridge. His attacker didn't seem overly concerned about hitting the sparking control systems; Trip reasoned that either she'd expected the equipment to be able to take it, or else she was just in shock and not thinking clearly.

Hitting the deck hard, he snatched up the disruptor and aimed it quickly in the general direction of his attacker, squeezing off two quick blasts. By the time he blinked, he saw the Romulan woman sliding downward against the wall, a gaping hole burnt through the right half of her head. Trip turned away quickly; the blast may have cauterized the wounds, but that hadn't stopped some of the remnants of the insides of the woman's skull from dislodging with a wet *plop*. He closed his eyes for a moment, concentrating on keeping his suddenly buoyant gorge from rising any higher.

Holding the disruptor protectively in one hand now, Trip continued entering the string of commands the woman had interrupted. As he finished, he heard another member of the bridge crew coming to, noting that this man's back was to Trip.

I don't want to do this, Trip thought, though he knew the situation was inescapable. What made killing the crew with a disruptor any worse than rigging their ship to explode after he escaped? *They* had planned to kill not only everyone who'd been aboard the freighter he had seen earlier, but also the crew of *Enterprise,* and God only knew who else to boot. *Besides, if I don't kill them, then they'll chase and kill me, not to mention a whole pile of others.*

He pulled the trigger, shooting the Romulan down

before he could finish getting up. His unarmed foe slumped facedown on the deck, dead. Despite his repeated efforts to convince himself that this was necessary, Trip felt ill.

Time to go, he thought as his fingers entered the final commands into the override system. Stepping over the bodies on the deck, he neared the hatchway and ladder that led to the secondary level—the turbolift, or its Romulan equivalent, was down—and opened it.

Before he made his descent, he moved quickly over to Sopek's body, kneeling beside it to feel for a pulse. The man's respiration was shallow, but Trip could tell that he was still alive, if only barely. *Of all the people on this ship,* he *might be useful to keep around,* Trip thought, though he knew what he was doing was dangerous in the extreme.

Grabbing Sopek's collar, he dragged the man's limp body over to the hatch, then clambered down the ladder to the secondary deck below. Reaching up, he pulled the Romulan down the hatch, awkwardly catching the heavy man against his upper torso as the body toppled onto him like an extremely heavy rag doll.

Panting from his exertions, Trip suddenly heard noises coming from somewhere. *The bridge deck, or* this *deck?* he wondered as an adrenaline rush of fight-or-flight intensity sharpened his senses until he felt certain he was really alone in the narrow companionway—and quickly oriented himself. Noting that the escape pods were located near the back of the corridor, he began dragging Sopek toward one of them.

"Halt!"

The order came from a Romulan man who had appeared around a corner from the other direction in the corridor. Trip couldn't tell whether or not the man was armed.

"Go to hell," Trip said, firing his disruptor at the man. The bolt hit the bulkhead near his would-be assailant, and as the Romulan ducked out of the way, Trip let loose three more disruptor blasts as quickly as he could.

Working quickly, Trip yanked Sopek the rest of the way in a few steps, pulling him into one of the cramped escape pods with him. He smiled as he noted that the pod's launch controls worked independently of the main ship's systems, which stood to reason for something that was used only during times of shipboard emergency. Slamming his hand down on a control, he sealed the pod's hatch, as well as the pod bay hatch beyond the escape pod's hull. As the hatches closed, he thought he saw the Romulan man approaching from the end of the corridor. Trip didn't even flinch, knowing that the man was too late to stop them now.

Working quickly, Trip entered the commands he thought would activate the pod's ejection system, and saw, to his relief, that his assumptions—bolstered by the knowledge he'd gained about Romulan spaceship technology over the last few months—had proved to be correct.

All the onboard systems lit up as Trip felt the thrusters firing, the sudden acceleration shoving him against the wall of the pod as the little escape vehicle moved quickly away from the crippled bird-of-prey. Trip considered his options now. *One pistol, one hostage, minimal impulse thrusters, and no powered hull-plating.* He knew it was a meager list of assets, but it was better than what lay behind him.

Almost a minute passed before Trip felt a concussive wave bash into the hull of the pod, and the reinforced transparent aluminum viewport filled with a light so brilliant that he had to shield his eyes with his arm. The bird-of-prey had just self-destructed, right on schedule, instantly consigning everyone he'd left aboard her to the Romulan equivalent of hell.

Trip turned and rummaged around in a small supply box until he found some cables, which he used to bind Sopek. Using a trick Malcolm had taught him, he bound the man's hands to his neck rather than behind his back; if Sopek woke up, any attempt he might make to untie himself would be entirely conspicuous. He also bound the man's feet together at the ankles and knees, attaching one end of the cord to a nearby box of small tools. *Let Sopek try to surprise me now*, he thought, satisfied at his preparations.

Finally allowing himself a moment to relax, Trip looked down at the man, trying to ascertain which part, if any, of Sopek's story might be true. Was he a Romulan who had infiltrated the Vulcan military structure? Or a Vulcan who led a Romulan paramilitary insurgency group? Or was he a free agent who was playing both ends against the middle for some other not-yet-revealed purpose?

Of course, the fact that Trip had brought Sopek along with him didn't guarantee that he'd receive any forthright answers from the man. And he had more immediate problems, such as not knowing enough about what was happening in fairly close proximity to the escape pod's thin skin. For all he knew, the Klingon ships Sopek had known were coming were still embroiled in a pitched battle against *Enterprise*. Or, *Enterprise* had won. *Or*, he thought, a wave of dread slowly cresting within him, *she might have* lost. He had never gained any degree of control over the psychic link that sometimes seemed to enable him to communicate with T'Pol, but he knew he couldn't feel her now.

Don't you go thinking that way, Charles Anthony

Tucker the Third, he thought. After all, "Gracie" Tucker hadn't raised him to be a defeatist. Or a nihilist. *But she also didn't raise you to shoot unarmed Romulans in the back,* something deep in his mind said, something that felt like guilt. He pushed the thought aside, but something else his mother had told him as a child took its place.

She had read to him regularly at night before bedtime, often from books of fairy tales and fables. One particular fable came to him now, about a frog that carried a scorpion across a river. When they'd gotten halfway across, the scorpion stung the frog, poisoning him. As they slipped beneath the water, the frog asked the scorpion why he had stung him, knowing that they would both drown.

"Because it's my nature," the scorpion said. "You knew I was a scorpion when you picked me up."

Was Sopek the scorpion and he the frog?

He cursed whatever had possessed him to agree to come to Romulus in the first place, the pride that had let him believe that he could stop these people. The Romulans were scorpions and vipers, and living beside them, hiding among them, he was becoming like them. He had not died from the poisonous sting—at least not yet—but knew that he had been poisoned all the same.

But instead of experiencing death, he had undergone a metamorphosis. And whatever he was developing into was not something he thought his mother would recognize, even if the master surgeons of Adigeon Prime were to bob his pointy ears and restore his original human appearance in every detail.

A light on the escape pod's small, simple instrument panel began flashing green, the Romulan color of danger, and this was followed instantly by a shrill beeping. Trip turned away from Sopek and read the instruments, then peered out the narrow viewport to try to get a better sense of what was causing the proximity alarms to go off.

Dead ahead, far too close now for the maneuvering thrusters to miss, was a dark shape illuminated only by the escape pod's external running lights. Despite the device's slow tumble relative to the pod, and the fact that it was visible only as a silhouette, Trip recognized it immediately from his studies of Ehrehin's files.

It was one of the many gravitic mines that the Romulan military had deployed throughout this region over the past several decades in their never-ending effort to discourage the Klingons.

And the escape pod was about to smack straight into the damned thing.

How do I keep getting myself into these situations? Trip asked himself, perhaps for the final time.

Then he closed his eyes and thought about T'Pol.

EPILOGUE TWO

Day Forty, Month of K'ri'Brax
The Hall of State, Dartha, Romulus

THE DECURION FINISHED his report, snapping to attention the moment he finished speaking.

Valdore so loved when his subordinates did that, as if they were puppets who could speak only when *he* chose to permit it. *"Khnai'ru rhissiuy,"* he said, thanking the young man for his report. He dismissed the soldier by returning his salute, then leaned back in his chair, turning his head to favor Nijil with a broad smile.

"It's all going according to my plan," Valdore said. "The *arrenhe'hwiua* telecapture system is working flawlessly." The assault on Isneih had been a brilliant success. The small settlement there had fallen quickly to the Vulcan vessels Valdore's forces now controlled—ships that the Vulcan Defense Force had deployed in the system to protect Vulcan's interests in the planet's scientific outpost—and even now his soldiers were setting up a beachhead in the system, from which Valdore's forces would mount their next wave of attacks against the so-called Coalition of Planets. The pangs of conscience he had felt in the wake of the deaths of so many on Coridan had faded, tucked away behind a barrier made of stuff as stern as the walls that the Vulcans built up around their emotions.

From a recess below the surface of his sherawood desk, he pulled out the bottle of *carallun* wine again.

Luxuriating in the moment, he poured himself and Nijil two glasses of the amber liquor. Passing one to the scientist, he said simply, "Drink."

Of late, something in Nijil's manner had made Valdore feel ill at ease. He wasn't certain what it was precisely, and he had been unable to find any evidence that the brilliant scientist was anything but a loyal supporter who would rather cut his own throat with the green *ehrie'urhillh* glass from the *carallun* bottle than betray his master. But *something* still tickled the hairs at the back of the admiral's neck.

Soon, he would create a level of comfort with Nijil in sharing a celebratory toast to Valdore's successes. *And one day, when I deem it most appropriate and necessary, you will drink, my ally, and I will not,* Valdore thought. *And then we shall see what secrets you are hiding.*

"My only disappointment," Valdore said, moving a sip of the sour liquor around in his mouth as he spoke, "is that we never succeeded in capturing control of either one of Starfleet's *NX*-class starships."

Nijil nodded gravely. "We still do not know precisely what happened to *Columbia*. She may well still be intact. If so, we will have other opportunities to determine whether she is more vulnerable to the *arrenhe'hwiua* than *Enterprise* proved to be."

"When the fleet strikes in full against Sei'chi, we may yet learn *Columbia*'s fate," Valdore said, smiling. He stood and walked over to the rounded window, outside of which the turrets and spires of the city speared the sapphire sky and framed the Apnex Sea beyond. "And we will no doubt soon make another run at *Enterprise*."

The war he had just begun would be a glorious one for the Romulan Star Empire and for Praetor D'deridex. But he had been setting up his own plans as well as he moved the Praetor's agenda forward, with no small amount of aid from one very well-placed and trustworthy agent in the Tal Shiar. An agent he felt he could trust as much as he trusted anyone other than himself, or perhaps Nijil, or even the late, lamented Centurion Terix.

When the time was right, and the Empire's victory had become all but inevitable, he would finally make his move. T'Leikha, the First Consul who had once had him cast into one of the Praetor's stinking dungeons, would pay for her crimes, as would the Senate that had ratified her decision.

And even D'deridex himself will tremble. . . .

ACKNOWLEDGMENTS

WITH THEIR THIRD *STAR Trek: Enterprise* literary outing, the authors would again like to recognize the contributions of the many who enriched the contents of these pages: Rick Berman and Brannon Braga, who created *Star Trek: Enterprise*; *uber*-editor Margaret Clark, whose patience and enthusiasm kept us on track; Paula Block in CBS's licensing department, for her keen eye and perspicacious observations; Mike's wife, Jenny, and their sons, James and William, and Andy's partner, Don, for both long-suffering patience and inspiration; the kind and indulgent folks at the Daily Market and Café, where much of Mike's portions of this novel were written.

Harve Bennett, Jack B. Sowards, and Nicholas Meyer, who conceived and executed the Starfleet Academy *Kobayashi Maru* training test whose prehistory we have revealed in these pages; illustrator David Neilsen, whose 1983 conjectural designs and blueprints of the *S.S. Kobayashi Maru* inspired the descriptions of this novel's eponymous neutronic fuel carrier; Ronald D. Moore, who christened two important warships, one Klingon (the *Ya'Vang* from *DS9* "You Are Cordially Invited") and one Romulan (the *Terix* from *TNG* "The Pegasus"), thereby supplying the names (and namesakes) of two characters who appear in these pages, and who also supplied the name (Qam-Chee) of the Klingon homeworld's First City (*DS9* "Looking for *par'Mach* in All the Wrong Places").

David R. George III, whose 2003 novel *Serpents Among the Ruins* introduced one of the beverages in Admiral Valdore's wine cellar on Romulus; David Mack, who unwittingly furnished us with an obscure Vulcan diplomat

(Ambassador L'Nel), whom we stole from his 2005 *Star Trek: Vanguard* novel *Harbinger*; Dayton Ward and Kevin Dilmore, for originating a Romulan unit of distance (the *mat'drih*, roughly analogous to the kilometer), which we stole from their 2006 *Star Trek: Vanguard* novel *Summon the Thunder*; Judith and Garfield Reeves-Stevens, for creating the Vulcan V'Shar (*ENT* "The Forge"), supplying the original old Romulan name for the capital city of Romulus (in William Shatner's Kirk novels), and (along with Manny Cotto) for shaping the canonical story arc that immediately precedes the time frame of *Star Trek: Enterprise*—*The Good That Men Do* and this book (*ENT* "Terra Prime" and "Demons"); Eric A. Stillwell, whose name became attached to a fictional Starfleet captain in the *Enterprise* series finale, a tradition that we have continued; Mike Burch of Expert Auto Repair, whose mechanical skills keep Andy's own sturdy transport running and who graciously lent his name to *Enterprise*'s current chief engineer; actors Peter Miller and Frankie Darro, whose exploits in the Altair system in *Forbidden Planet* (1956) inspired the naming of Altair VI's Darro-Miller settlement; S. D. Perry, whose novel *Star Trek Section 31: Cloak* anticipated Judith and Garfield Reeves-Stevens' canonical revelations about Section 31's distant past; Keith R. A. DeCandido and Susan Shwartz and Josepha Sherman, whose novels *Articles of the Federation* and *Vulcan's Heart* enabled us to hide a historical Easter egg or three within these pages (as well as in *The Good That Men Do*); Keith DeCandido (again), for inspiring the name of a Klingon supernumerary (Qrad), as well as for insight into the Klingon calendar, both here and in *Forged in Fire*; Dr. Marc Okrand, whose seminal xenolinguistic work *The Klingon Dictionary* (1992 edition) was an invaluable reference; the collected Romulan-related novels of Diane Duane (collected in 2006's *Rihannsu:*

The Bloodwing Voyages), for guidance on Romulan culture, language, and naming customs; the online linguistic scholars who assembled the vast Rihannsu language database found at http://atrek.org/Dhivael/rihan/engto rihan.html, for furnishing various Romulan time and distance units, numerals, and word roots that helped us create several Romulan proper names. Wikipedia, Memory Alpha, and Memory Beta contributors everywhere, including the online codifiers of speculative Vulcan (and by extension Romulan) calendrical minutiae at Starbase 10; Franz Joseph, whose *Star Fleet Technical Manual* (1975) lent us the Vulcan outpost planet Trilan; Doug Drexler and Michael Okuda's *Ships of the Line* hardcover (2006), which inspired certain events aboard *Columbia*, foreshadowed here and realized in detail in David Mack's forthcoming *Star Trek: Destiny* trilogy; David Mack, for the extensive work he did on the aforementioned trilogy in creating the *Columbia* crew members, which allowed us to debut them in these pages, and for establishing the location of the *Kobayashi Maru*'s demise in his 2004 TNG novel, *A Time to Heal*; Geoffrey Mandel, for his *Star Trek: Star Charts* (2002), which kept us from getting lost in the galactic hinterlands many times; Michael and Denise Okuda, whose *Star Trek Encyclopedia: A Reference Guide to the Future* remains indispensable; Connor Trinneer and Jolene Blaylock, for breathing life into Charles Anthony "Trip" Tucker III and T'Pol in front of the cameras; the legions of Trip and T'Pol fans out there eager to see what the fates (and the authors) have in store for *Star Trek*'s most star-crossed couple; Scott Bakula for leaping into not one, but two, of science fiction's most compelling and conflicted heroic roles, and thus providing his excellent characterization of Captain Archer; and Gene Roddenberry (1920–1991), for having created the entire universe in which we now play in the first place.

ABOUT THE AUTHORS

MICHAEL A. MARTIN's solo short fiction has appeared in *The Magazine of Fantasy & Science Fiction*. He has also coauthored (with Andy Mangels) several *Star Trek* comics for Marvel and Wildstorm and numerous *Star Trek* novels and e-books, including *Star Trek: Excelsior—Forged in Fire*; *Star Trek: Enterprise—The Good That Men Do*; the *USA Today* bestseller *Star Trek: Titan—Taking Wing*; *Star Trek: Titan—The Red King*; the Sy Fy Genre Award–winning *Worlds of Deep Space 9 Volume Two: Trill—Unjoined*; *Star Trek: Enterprise—Last Full Measure*; *The Lost Era 2298: The Sundered*; *Deep Space 9 Mission: Gamma Book Three—Cathedral*; *Star Trek: The Next Generation—Section 31—Rogue*; *Starfleet Corps of Engineers* #30 and #31 ("Ishtar Rising" Books 1 and 2, reprinted in *Aftermath*, the eighth volume of the *S.C.E.* paperback series); stories in the *Prophecy and Change*, *Tales of the Dominion War*, and *Tales from the Captain's Table* anthologies; and three novels based on the *Roswell* television series. His work has also been published by Atlas Editions (in their *Star Trek Universe* subscription card series), *Star Trek Monthly*, Moonstone Books, Visible Ink Press, Grolier Books, *The Oregonian*, and Gareth Stevens, Inc., for whom he has penned several *World Almanac Library of the States* nonfiction books for young readers. He lives with his wife, Jenny, and their sons James and William in Portland, Oregon.

ANDY MANGELS is the *USA Today* bestselling author and coauthor of over a dozen novels—including *Star Trek* and *Roswell* books, and a story for Moonstone Books'

Tales of Zorro anthology—all cowritten with Michael A. Martin. Flying solo, he is the bestselling author of numerous nonfiction books, including *Iron Man: Beneath the Armor*, *Star Wars: The Essential Guide to Characters*, and *Animation on DVD: The Ultimate Guide*, as well as a significant number of entries for *The Superhero Book: The Ultimate Encyclopedia of Comic-Book Icons and Hollywood Heroes* and its companion volume, *The Supervillain Book: The Evil Side of Comics and Hollywood*. His forthcoming books include *Lou Scheimer: Creating the Filmation Generation* and *The Wonder Woman Companion*.

In addition to his publishing work, Andy has produced, directed, and scripted documentaries and provided award-winning Special Features for over forty fan-favorite DVD box set releases, ranging from such live-action favorites as *Ark II*, *Space Academy*, and *The Secrets of Isis* to animated fare such as *He-Man and the Masters of the Universe*, *The Archies*, *Flash Gordon*, and *Dungeons & Dragons*.

A member of the International Association of Media Tie-In Writers, Andy has written licensed material based on properties from numerous film studios and Microsoft. Over the past two decades, his comic-book work has been published by DC Comics, Marvel Comics, Dark Horse, Image, Innovation, and many others. He was the editor of the award-winning *Gay Comics* anthology for eight years. Andy has also written hundreds of articles for entertainment and lifestyle magazines and newspapers in the United States, England, and Italy. Writing as "Dru Sullivan," Andy penned the exploits of "Miss Adventure, the Gayest American Hero," for the late, lamented *Weekly World News*.

Andy is a national award-winning activist in the Gay community, and has raised thousands of dollars for charities over the years, including over $43,000 raised for Domestic Violence shelters during his October "Wonder Woman Day" events. He lives in Portland, Oregon, with his long-term partner, Don Hood, and their dog, Bela. Visit Andy's website at www.andymangels.com.